# BEHIND CLOSED DOORS

D1322010

# CAROL WYER

THOMAS & MERCER

Text copyright © 2022 by Carol Wyer

Published by Thomas & Mercer, Seattle

www.apub.com

Amazon, the Amazon logo, and Thomas & Mercer are trademarks of Amazon.com, Inc., or its affiliates.

ISBN-13: 9781662506116
ISBN-10: 1662506112

Cover design by kid-ethic

Printed in the United States of America

# BEHIND CLOSED DOORS

# JULY 1992

'Please . . . Please . . . Please.' Each terrified plea sucked the scratchy material of the bag into her open mouth and nostrils, yet she couldn't cease her mantra. Through the sack fibres she could see light and made out the by now familiar sound as he flicked his nails together in unison in a steady *click-click-click*.

He cleared his throat: an angry grunt. Movement. The shuffling of feet and vague shapes skimming her eyeline. Her heart began pounding. He was going to kill her. She yelped in fear at the sharp yank on the chains that bound her hands above her head.

This time he didn't hit her. The agonising throbbing in her shoulders and forearms eased as he lowered her arms. Relief flooded her veins when no further punishment was forthcoming. He was going to release her. Dad had paid the ransom. It was over.

The hood, however, remained in place. He engulfed her right hand with his own, guiding it onto a surface. Miniscule needles scoured her palm, reminding her of the surface of a log. She couldn't work out what was happening. His hand pressed hers down firmly, ensuring she couldn't move it. Maybe her abductor was going to undo the chains that rubbed against her wrists, chafing them raw. Her sudden desire to return home overtook the terror she'd been living with for the last, how long had it been? Two days? Four? Since her arrival, time had become muddled.

When he had first removed the hood, as he did from time to time, she had thought her captor was a bald, old man, with an almost comically wrinkled brow. It had taken a while to realise she was staring at a rubber mask.

There'd been no indicator of time passing. It was almost always dark under the hood and when she sensed light, she couldn't tell if it came from lightbulbs or the sun. She'd been given water, cold porridge and two cheese sandwiches. Maybe only a day had passed.

The large, soft-fleshed hand pressed against hers, forcing it against the rough surface, bringing her back to her senses. Why was he forcing her palm against the log? Why hadn't he removed the hood? There was a sharp crack, the sound of a twig snapping, before fear froze her blood. Her brain registered sticky, wet fingers, then she began to scream, the cloth choking her.

'Shh! You'll be fine. It's only a finger.'

She struggled to escape his vice-like grip, wriggling for all she was worth, only to feel the metal cuffs pull tightly against her wrists again.

'Keep still. I need to fix you up or you'll bleed to death. Now, calm down. If you do, I'll give you something for the pain. If you don't, I'll chop off every finger.'

She obeyed at once. He would follow through with his threats if she didn't. Her teeth chattered uncontrollably as the man bandaged the wound. Something had gone wrong. Something had prevented her father from paying the ransom. What would happen if he didn't pay at all? Feeling light-headed, she began to drift. The man tutted and undid the bandage again.

'There's too much blood. Hold still.'

His voice floated away. Her mind began to shut down, dragging her to the edge of consciousness.

'Why did you cut off my finger?' she mumbled.

'To send to that mean son of a bitch who won't pay up. He needs to be reminded I mean business.'

The severe throbbing in her hand was nothing compared to the wound in her chest. Dad wasn't going to save her, and she knew, no matter what he said, this monster was going to kill her.

# DAY ONE

## APRIL 2022

## WEDNESDAY – 4 P.M.

Stacey O'Hara checked the temperature of the oven, ensuring it was sufficiently low to slide in the takeaway box. She shut the door, then raised a glass to her reflection in the darkened kitchen window. The tip-off she'd been given had resulted in a first-hand account of a recent, huge drug-busting investigation and an exclusive interview with the DCI behind Operation Touchdown.

She tucked a stray hair behind her ear, fingers grazing the rough, scarred surface. Its deformation didn't bother her any more than the lack of a pinkie finger on her right hand. Yes, now and again, she'd catch strangers, new colleagues or interviewees, trying hard not to stare at the misshapen ear, or at her right hand. Doubtless, they were wondering how she lost both. Nobody really knew what happened to sixteen-year-old Stacey O'Hara. Even she didn't know. Suffering profoundly from dissociative amnesia, the event had been wiped from her memory.

Following her rescue, a swift move from Staffordshire to a new life in Lancashire had helped to obliterate that period of her life. A psychiatrist had explained that her brain had chosen to protect her, leaving her with nothing but dreamlike recollections, easily mistaken for nightmares or fabrications of the mind. As far as Stacey was concerned, everything about her abduction could reside in the past forever.

She sipped the chilled wine, allowing fruity flavours to burst over her tongue. She'd splashed out more than she ordinarily would on this bottle, the most expensive in the local shop. Today was a day worth celebrating. Her story had made the front page and, once again, she had been approached by one of the major publications with an offer to jump ship and write for them. Even though she appreciated being invited, she'd declined the offer. She belonged at the *Lancaster Echo*, where she was a very big fish in a small pond – the senior reporter. She was content, living in her terraced cottage in the peaceful village of Hornby. She enjoyed the nine-mile commute to the newspaper offices, which allowed her to take in views of the meandering River Lune and settlements along the picturesque Lune Valley. She felt safe.

She was, she decided, satisfied with her lot. Even though the dreaded five-oh birthday was four years off, she was comfortable in her skin.

An urgent knock on her front door disturbed her musings. She opened the door, her mood changing in a flash.

She hadn't seen Jack Corrigan in almost a year, the last time during a chance meeting at the courthouse in Lancaster. While her hair had begun to turn grey and she'd gained a few pounds during the three years they'd been apart, her ex-husband still appeared trim and sandy-haired, and his handsome face showed no signs of premature ageing. His eyes, a shade of blue bordering on violet, emitted an intensity she'd only seen when he was worked up. She didn't want Jack to sour the moment. She'd allowed him to trample over her in the past, put down her efforts, convince her she was worthless. She'd fought back since she left him. She had made something of herself. She tried to shut the door. He blocked it with his foot.

'Stace. I need to talk to you.'

'I don't think we have anything to discuss,' she replied. Jack could be the sweetest man on the planet. He could also be controlling and cruel, whichever approach got him what he wanted. 'Now, move your foot.'

He stretched out his hand, clung to the doorframe so she couldn't exert enough force to close it. 'It's Lyra.'

His words weakened her resolve. Lyra was Jack's thirteen-year-old daughter by his first marriage: a girl who'd inherited her father's physique and her mother's Scandinavian looks. Over the four years Stacey had been with Jack, she'd developed a deep fondness for the girl. Leaving Jack hadn't been as hard as leaving Lyra because, despite the girl's rare visits, usually confined to school holidays, Stacey and Lyra had formed a bond. One that had continued even after her split from Jack.

Although their contact was mostly confined to WhatsApp, they communicated regularly, with Lyra updating Stacey on her life at boarding school and at home in Oxfordshire, where she lived outside of term time. When Lyra stayed over with her dad in the seaside town of Morecambe, she'd often meet Stacey for a catch-up, although their last physical meeting had been in December 2021, a quick, pre-Christmas get-together at a café, sharing presents before she departed with a warm hug and promises to meet up again during her next visit. A vision of the girl as she rode her bike along the promenade, back towards Jack's house, swam in front of her eyes.

'What about Lyra?'

'It's serious, Stace. Please let me come inside and explain.'

She took in his earnest look. She'd been fooled before by his acts, too many times. Jack knew how to press her buttons, manipulate her, then grind her down. This time though, it was different. His eyes were red-rimmed and full of anguish, signs of true emotion, causing her to reflect that, in spite of everything, he'd never previously involved Lyra in his manipulations.

'Please.'

She stood back. 'Okay.'

'Thank you.'

She showed him into the kitchen, where he stood, hands on the back of a chair. His shoulders were rigid with tension.

'Go on. What's all this about Lyra?'

His face contorted. 'I don't know how to . . . what to . . . do . . . I'm . . .'

The choked, inarticulate response was out of character. Jack was never at a loss for words. This wasn't the same egotistical person she'd walked out on. The man in front of her was deflated, lost.

He shook his head slowly. 'I'm frightened, Stace.'

This was no act. Jack was afraid of nothing. His distress was genuine as well as disturbing. Jack thought the world of Lyra. She was his little girl, his princess. Whatever was going on with her had shaken Jack to the core.

'Jack, no matter what it is, it's bad enough for you to come and seek me out. Has she got into trouble? She hasn't contacted me about anything.' She wondered why Lyra wouldn't have rung or at least messaged her if she was having difficulties. She knew Stacey wouldn't be judgemental, no matter what she got up to.

'I hoped you'd be able to . . . Well, what I mean is . . . you'd at least have an idea of what is happening in her life . . . Something . . . Anything to help me . . . to understand what's going on.'

His eyes rested on hers and in their depths, she saw fear.

'Okay. Sit down. Let's talk.'

He shook his head, reached for his mobile and unlocked it before passing it to her. 'Play it.'

The video was shot in a dingy room, a dim yellow glow from a single bulb revealing a girl tied to a chair. Lyra.

The camera panned to a note, composed of a selection of newspaper cuttings. The message was clear.

**£500,000**

**YOU WILL BE CONTACTED AT 6 PM**

**NO POLICE**

**OR I WILL CHOP HER INTO PIECES**

The sound of panicked screaming punctuated the silence. All the while, the camera focused on the note for what felt like forever. She glanced at Jack; he winced at each high-pitched 'No! Stop!'

Eventually the video ended.

A stone filled Stacey's throat.

'I have no idea what to do,' said Jack. 'I came to you because—'

There was no need for him to finish the sentence. Jack thought she might understand his predicament, even be able to offer advice.

Her immediate reaction was to report this, get professionals onto it as quickly as possible. At the same time, a younger version of herself seemed to whisper warnings against taking that course of action, reminding Stacey that Lyra could be killed if the kidnapper didn't receive the ransom. Her father had been advised not to pay hers. The anti-kidnap team had convinced him they would save her. They had not. Had an officer, completely unconnected to her kidnapping investigation, not appeared at the eleventh hour by chance, Stacey wouldn't be here today.

Jack wiped a hand across his chin, left it there for a moment and sighed. 'Shit, Stacey. I haven't the foggiest of what to do. It's all . . . surreal. I don't have that sort of money. Nowhere near that amount. At a push, I can probably raise fifty grand, only a fraction of what they're demanding. I'm shit scared I'll fuck this up. What should I do?'

Jack was a lawyer, one who in 2016 had taken over a small practice in Lancaster. To her knowledge, his salary was substantial, and certainly greater than her own.

'Have you no other savings at all?'

He gave a quiet snort. 'Savings? Come on, Stacey. I'm not a bloody millionaire. My salary gets eaten into by bloody high-rate tax, house renovation costs and heaven knows what else. I've never really got back on my feet since I bought the practice. I was stupid to have taken it on. Half of the clients on the books have passed away. I should have stuck it out at Bowles, Fisher & Hancock.' Jack had hoped to make partner at the large practice in Manchester, yet when he was overlooked for promotion for the second time, he'd been so put out, he'd piled every penny he had into buying the smaller law firm, then called Babcock LLP. Roland Babcock took retirement very soon afterwards, leaving Jack to run the place.

He rolled his eyes. 'Commercial property has suffered massively during the pandemic, and we've only taken on a few new clients who need my expertise.'

Jack had always been dissatisfied with his choice of career. He'd bounced from one law firm to another throughout his working life, placing blame for his lack of advancement on others rather than himself. It had always been a sensitive topic that, when broached, had resulted in a sour expression, often followed by harsh words.

Stacey changed the subject. 'What about your car? What do you drive nowadays?'

Jack loved sports cars, treating himself to a new model every year. 'I've taken the Porsche into account, but it was purchased on finance, so even if I sold it, I wouldn't get much back. I've got a couple of decent watches I could sell and a small amount of emergency cash.'

Another thought struck her. 'What about Freya? How's she taking this?'

'I haven't told her.'

'You must! She has a right to know and a say in what to do about it.'

'No! Absolutely not. She'll want to involve the police. Freya's in hospital, undergoing surgery – a hysterectomy. That's why Lyra's in Morecambe.'

Stacey was surprised Lyra hadn't mentioned it. Even though Freya and Stacey had never been friends, this was news Lyra maybe should have shared.

As if reading her mind, Jack said, 'Freya didn't want anyone other than family to know about it. She's upset enough about having to undergo the surgery without finding out about this. It's a major operation. She'll need plenty of rest afterwards and this . . . is too much on top of everything else. I need . . . help though. I'm terrified if I make this official and the police don't act in time, something terrible could happen to Lyra. Like it did to you.'

He took her hands in his, gently caressed the right one with its missing finger. His voice was honeyed. 'I know that the kidnap team didn't reach you before . . . before you were . . . *harmed.* I don't want the same thing to happen to Lyra. Please don't ask me to report it.'

His words, or maybe the shock of seeing the video, or both, had an effect on Stacey. A hazy vision floated from the recesses of her mind. She saw herself as a terrified teenager, tied to a chair, a hood over her head. Her heartbeat increased. She didn't want to remember.

*Can't breathe. Pitch-black.* She shut her eyes, willing the thoughts to vanish, back to whatever locked chamber of the brain they'd escaped from. They faded, to be replaced by a sickening dread that Lyra might be enduring something similar. This was an impossible situation. All the same, she felt compelled to assist, but how? She was no detective, merely a reporter. Jack clearly didn't see it the same way.

'I thought with your investigative talent and . . . personal experience, you could offer . . . some solution.' He squeezed her hands gently before releasing them. 'I'm worried, Stace. Worried that the police won't reach her in time, just like they didn't save you before . . . I understand you don't want to drag up the past—'

Her heart flipped at his words. History could well repeat itself. 'It's not that I don't want to, Jack. You know I can't. I can't recall anything about my kidnapping.'

'What about the therapy you underwent at the time? What was it called again?'

'Guided visualisation.'

'Yes, that. Didn't that give you some of your memory back?'

Jack had made it sound like a magic act when it was anything but. Unlike other patients, Stacey had struggled with the sessions, where she'd been encouraged to place herself back in time by imagining walking into a golden tunnel or travelling a path to a beautifully calm place. It had taken months before her therapist had found a way to access her memories, tapping into an experience Stacey closely associated with her mother – being in a specialist movie theatre with the feel of bygone days, showing mostly black and white films, favourites such as *Casablanca*, *It's a Wonderful Life*, *Some Like it Hot* and *Brief Encounter*. It had become Stacey and her mother's treat, their special 'us' time. It was also a tradition Stacey had continued with Lyra, although the cinema they frequented had none of the quirkiness of her mother's cinema.

It had been because of this routine that the psychotherapist had chosen to take Stacey down the path of image therapy, inviting her to imagine watching a black and white film in which she had the starring role. Whether it was because she associated the fictitious

11

auditorium so strongly with her deceased mother, or because the images shown on the imaginary screen were far too frightening for her to watch, the result only made matters worse. The very thought of entering the imagined cinema, pulling down the folded plush seat, then sitting while the projector behind spluttered into life, only served to send Stacey into a wild panic, until, after numerous sessions, the therapist, worried for the long-term effects this would have on Stacey, had given up. Her mind had refused the assistance it needed, mixing up reality with fiction until she was sick with confusion.

Stacey shook herself free from the past. Jack was looking at her intently.

'I have a few vague memories. I'm not sure if they're real or not. They make no sense.'

'Surely you remember where you were when you were taken? Or even just a little of what happened?'

She shook her head. 'Nothing that would be of use to us in finding Lyra. The therapist told me it was the worst case of severe dissociative amnesia she'd come across.'

He tutted sympathetically. 'All the time we were together, I assumed you simply didn't want to talk about it. Especially as it caused a rift between you and your dad.'

That much she had divulged to her ex-husband. She had long harboured misgivings about how her father and the police had handled the kidnapping. After she'd been released from hospital, Henry tried to make things up to her, showering gifts on her, presents she never really wanted. A weekend away with her father would have counted for far more than the CDs, clothes, books that he'd leave on her bed for her to find while he was at work. She'd never wanted things, only his time and a little affection. Presents didn't hug her, or tell her she meant the world to him. Material goods could never make up for the fact that, for whatever reason, he hadn't paid the ransom to secure her release. Moreover, as time passed, nothing he bought made amends for being let down by the man who should have ensured her safe return. He had never explained himself, only blaming the kidnap unit he'd trusted for making poor decisions. Stacey lost more than her little finger and the top of her ear when she was abducted – she also lost belief and trust in her father.

Jack's voice brought her back to the present. 'Jeez, Stacey. I shouldn't put this on you. You went through the most horrendous ordeal. I don't know what I was thinking, asking you to drag up the past to help rescue Lyra. This must be even worse for you than it is for me.'

She felt the weight of his anxiety. Had he really come to her, believing she could help? Did he think she truly had insight, or was there still something he wasn't saying? A glance at the mobile in his hand reignited her fear for the girl and quashed the doubt. He wasn't hiding anything. He was clutching at straws. All she had to offer were muddled black and white visions that seemed to be triggered at whim, or activated by a smell, a sight or even certain words. The image of Lyra tied up like that sent her brain scrabbling for similar images until she could see herself on an identical chair, staring into a camera lens. Yet had she? Had she ever been tied up, made to face a camera and plead to her father? It felt like she had. Her mind persuaded her she'd faced the exact same scenario, yet she reasoned she was only imagining it because of the video. In reality, she couldn't be of much help to Jack or Lyra. He had wasted his time seeking her out. His clear eyes were trained on her, his features a mixture of sorrow and compassion.

'I ought to go.'

The anguish in his voice speared her. Once upon a time, they'd been happy together. She'd loved him wholeheartedly. Whatever had transpired to break them apart ought not to affect this situation. Stacey had to step up, try and access some memories, use her skills to assist in any way she could. Stacey understood and shared his reservations about the police, which meant they had little choice other than to handle this themselves. After all, Lyra meant so much to them both; the idea she might be harmed or killed was unbearable. 'No. It's okay. We'll figure this out somehow.'

She felt compelled to offer words of consolation or even some physical contact to help eradicate his fear and hurt, until the smell of burning cardboard sent her rushing to the oven. The takeaway box was blackened. Regardless of the state of the contents, she was no longer interested in them. Time was of the essence.

'Let's start with the message. When did you receive it?'

'Eight o'clock this morning.'

With the kidnapper due to contact him in an hour, Jack had left almost no time for action. There was even less time to work with than she imagined.

His shoulders sagged. 'I know. We don't have much time to come up with a plan. At first, I thought it was a hoax. I was numb for . . . ages. Then . . . I panicked. I went through the options, hesitated about ringing the police, paced up and down. I checked my finances to see if I could raise any cash at all. Then . . . I came to you.' His eyes became glassy. 'I didn't know which way to turn,' he whispered.

This time, she reached for his hands. 'It's okay. Let's take this one step at a time. Run through exactly what happened. When did you first realise Lyra was missing?'

He swallowed hard, pulled away, raked fingers through his hair. 'Shit, Stacey. I screwed up. The fact is, I didn't realise she wasn't at home. I didn't have a clue until my phone pinged and the video arrived. As you probably know, Lyra was at Kelly's house last night.'

Stacey blinked away prickling tears. The last couple of weeks, Lyra hadn't been in touch. Knowing her to be coming to Morecambe, Stacey had messaged a few times, inviting her for a day out. When she'd had only vague, non-committal messages back, she'd assumed the girl was behaving like any other teenager with a full social calendar and little time for her ex-stepmother and let it slide, assuming there'd be time this week to catch up. She'd been too wrapped up with work to pursue it. Now she wished she had rung Lyra. She'd no idea about Kelly or any of Lyra's plans this trip.

Jack continued, 'I . . . I went out with mates. She rang me at eight fifteen last night to say she was about to leave for home, and I was . . . having a good time, so I told her I'd be back later. She was cool with that. There was some programme she wanted to watch on television. I stayed at the pub longer than I intended. By the time I got in, around midnight, there was no sign of her downstairs. I didn't check on her in case I woke her up. You know that she's totally reliable. If she says she's coming home at such-and-such a time, she does. I had no reason to suspect she wasn't in.' His voice caught on a sob. Stacey hadn't the heart to read him any riot act.

'And you've rung her today, haven't you?'

'It goes straight to voicemail. I tried. Several times.'

'Don't you have a Find Me app to track her phone?'

'I didn't want her to think I was spying on her or spoil the trust we share. As it is, I hardly ever see her. I didn't want to be the parent who was always on her back. She gets a hard enough time from Freya.'

Stacey bit back the urge to remind him that parenting wasn't a popularity contest. Ensuring the safety of an offspring was not spying, but rather behaving responsibly. She understood his desire to be a cool dad, whose daughter looked up to him. Nevertheless, his laissez-faire approach had led to this. She held her tongue. One look at his face showed he was already being eaten away by guilt.

'I am such a fuck-up. When she comes back home, I am never, ever again, going to let her out of my sight. We will get her back, won't we?'

She wanted to reassure him, promise everything would be fine, yet she couldn't.

'What should we do, Stace?'

Her brain unfroze. This was on her. She needed to use her skills, resources and contacts to track down the girl. As an investigative reporter she was used to working out how to surmount seemingly impossible difficulties or situations. She'd broken many a story that others had been unable to. She'd probed, cajoled and wheedled information when other journalists had simply given up. Stacey racked her brains for any investigation that might be of use in finding Lyra, landing on a story about a missing boy whose disappearance she'd covered. She'd spoken to friends, neighbours and classmates, discovered from his best friend he'd been abused by a relative. She'd handed over the information to the team dealing with the case and he'd soon been located, locked in a bedroom at an uncle's house. This situation didn't afford her the luxury of interviewing those people who might know Lyra. What would a missing person's team do? They'd probably attempt to track down the person via their mobile device; however, with messages going directly to the answerphone, the kidnapper had most likely turned off Lyra's mobile or even ditched it. She scratched about for more ideas.

'The video also came from an unknown number?'

'Yes.'

She tapped her forefinger lightly against the kitchen top, her heart pounding. 'Right. We need to work out who sent the text. We could involve a specialist technical team. They're best placed for this. They can examine the video, look for clues about where it was shot. The kidnapper need know nothing about it.'

'No! No police means no tech teams or surveillance, or anybody else connected with law enforcement. It's you and me or . . . it's me alone. Besides, the kidnapper will ring me on my phone. If there's a delay before I pick up or, worse still, I don't pick up, they may kill her.'

'Jack, you might have to side with me on this. Be logical. You can't pay the demand. I'm a journalist, with no training in how to handle kidnap situations. We require professional, experienced help to get her back!'

He lowered his gaze and shook his head. 'Stacey, we can't. Remember what you told me? About how you believed the police could have done more to find you? Do you think things have changed that much?'

It was true. She'd always thought they'd handled her situation badly. Had it not been for chance, she would have died. She'd shared these thoughts with Jack on several occasions.

'What makes you think they'd do a better job this time around?' he asked.

'I . . . I don't know. I just feel it's too big for us.'

'Are you willing to risk the same thing happening to Lyra? You still harbour resentment towards those officers for not finding you, for giving your father poor advice and for almost abandoning you. That's how you described it to me, didn't you? You felt abandoned?'

She sighed. 'Yes. Yes, I did. And I still do. However, like it or not, we're going to require outside help.'

'I don't see why. You have great intuition. I . . . I need some-body who is calm, who can see the bigger picture. Someone who can investigate, probe, get to the truth of the matter.'

'I follow leads. I get tip-offs. I hunt down stories, then write about them. I'm not a trained police officer.'

'You have investigative skills. You were promoted to senior reporter because you stood out from the others. I believe in you. Somewhere, inside that clever mind of yours, lies a solution, a way we can get Lyra released, without involving the police. Stace? What do you say? Do you really want to entrust her life to them?'

She took in his earnest regard. He was pinning all his hopes on her.

She gathered her thoughts. They needed assistance from somebody unconnected to the police who could help her track the kidnapper's number. The answer came to her. 'I don't possess any superpowers. And no matter what you think, we can't do this without some help. I know somebody who isn't on the force. A freelance hacker who works for all sorts of government institutions and companies. Let me speak to them. Trust me. The kidnapper will never have heard of them or get wind of what I'm doing.'

He opened his mouth, seemingly to object, then paused and gave a soft, 'Okay. Only if you're sure.'

'I'm positive.' She scrolled through her contact lists, stopping at a name: Ox. Jack walked to the other side of the kitchen and stared out of the window.

'Hi, Ox, it's Stacey O'Hara.'

'Hello, O'Hara. What can I do for you?' The voice was melodic, semi-sultry.

'Do you remember that favour you owe me?'

'Uh-huh.'

'I'd like to call it in.'

'Okay.'

'This is nothing to do with work. It's personal.'

'How intriguing. Go on, I'm all ears.'

'I need you to track and locate an unknown number.' She kept an eye on Jack, who didn't move. 'The caller is going to ring at six tonight.'

'Your number?'

'Not mine.' She reeled off Jack's number along with the name of his phone provider.

'Have you heard from this person before?'

'Only once. A text message that came in this morning at eight.'

'Is that the exact time?'

'Let me check.' She relayed the request to Jack, who pulled up the details and gave her the precise time. She passed them on to Ox.

'I'll need at least ninety seconds to trace the number once they ring. It would be ideal if you could keep them on the phone for two minutes.'

'Ox, there's something else. Another number.'

'Is that a second favour, O'Hara?'

'It's tied in with the first.'

Ox's chuckle was low and soft. 'Go on.'

'There's another number I need checking out. I'd like to know who, if anyone, called it last night.' She gave out Lyra's number.

'I'm on it.'

'Thanks, Ox.'

'A pleasure. It means we're square now.'

'We're square.'

Jack was still by the sink. 'You rate this person?'

'If anybody can locate a phone, Ox can. It's what we do with that information once we get it that will count. We can't go charging after the kidnapper alone. We're assuming there's only one abductor, but there could be more. I'm out of my depth here, Jack.'

'You aren't. I have faith in you. I can't go the police route. Damn it! If only I could find a way to pay the ransom. That would be the best solution. She'd be set free then.'

Even though the impulse to walk away was strong, her mind returned her to the place she'd visited during therapy sessions in her youth, to the cinema in her head. Blinking couldn't dispel the strong image that blocked out reality, and with a dawning realisation that old habits had kicked in for reasons she did not comprehend, she stared at the large screen, where a black and white vision of what she assumed to be a memory began to play . . .

*Water drips onto the floor, a steady plop-plop-plop. She tries to shift position, but her hands are once more cuffed above her head and her shoulders ache badly, so badly. The hood is suffocatingly warm and each breath she makes is small and hesitant to prevent inhaling the fibres. Dad will be out of his mind with worry by now. He'll surely have been to the bank and got the money he needs to save her. It will be at the pickup point.*

*She whispers a plea to him, as if somehow he will hear her.*

*'Dad, I promise. I'll be the best daughter ever. I'll never do anything wrong again.'*

*A creaking above her head interrupts her monologue.*

*He's back.*

*Urgent, heavy thudding crosses over her head.*

*He slams the door.*

*He thunders down the stairs, each footstep speaking volumes – he hasn't got the money.*

Where had this come from and was it even real? It had to have been triggered by Lyra's terrible situation.

'Stacey?'

The mental picture receded at the sound of Jack's voice, leaving her confused momentarily.

'Stace?'

She snapped out of her reverie. 'Listen, if Ox comes up with a lead, let me alert the right authorities. Please?'

'No. Things can go wrong very quickly. One sniff of a police presence and—'

He pressed his lips together, head shaking from side to side, unable to continue.

Although she was worried that they hadn't alerted the police, she understood. Much depended on Ox. If the phone couldn't be traced, they needed another avenue to pursue. How would the professionals deal with this?

*Think, Stacey. Think.*

'Have you spoken to Lyra's friend, Kelly?'

'I wanted to, but I didn't know what to say without making her suspicious or, worse still, so worked up she told her parents or the police. Shit! She's probably already wondering why Lyra hasn't been in touch today. I mean, aren't teenagers always on social media?'

'Certainly Lyra is, although she's usually messaging her boarding school friends. She misses them during the holidays. Kelly's not the same. Lyra told me her parents are outdoors types and disapprove of her wasting time online.'

Stacey hadn't seen the girl in a long while, but could picture athletic Kelly Richards, head and shoulders taller than Lyra, even though they were the same age. She was into surfing and sailing and spent summers camping or fell walking with her parents. Lyra had met Kelly at Morecambe sailing club, where they'd both been learning to windsurf. A friendship had arisen. Because she visited the seaside town infrequently, Lyra had made few friends in this area. Kelly was her 'go-to', somebody other than Stacey or her father she could hang out with.

Stacey said, 'I don't know. I'm no expert on such matters but there's every chance she's already wondering why Lyra isn't responding to texts and calls. She knows Lyra's here. They might even have made arrangements to meet up today.'

Whiskers rasped as he dragged a hand over his chin once more. 'You could be right. What on earth do I tell her?'

'That Lyra has lost, or broken her phone and is out of contact.'

He stared at the mobile screen. 'I can't. I'll screw it up. She'll be able to tell there's something amiss. You know I'm lousy at hiding or disguising my emotions.'

*Icy looks that broke her resolve. Contempt oozing from his pores.*

'Okay. Let me do it.'

It had been a long while since she'd spoken to Kelly, who, when she and Jack were married, had been a near-constant presence whenever Lyra was with her father.

'Kelly, hi. It's Stacey. Lyra's stepmum.' It felt strange using the title again, and she still felt unworthy of it.

'Oh, hey. How's it going?'

'Good, thanks. I just wanted to give you the heads-up on Lyra. She busted her phone and will be out of contact for a while until it's repaired.'

'Oh, okay. Cool. I hope they fix it. She took some photos of Teddy and said she'd send them to me.'

'Oh, is that your new puppy? Lyra told me all about him. He sounds gorgeous.'

'Yeah, he is. She videoed him going mental on the beach, racing about with the other dogs. He was hilarious.'

The dog-friendly beach was popular with the locals. If it was busy, somebody following the girls could easily blend in.

Kelly was still talking. 'I thought she'd forgotten to message it to me. She promised she would before I went away.'

'When are you going?'

'First thing tomorrow. We're off to Scotland to visit my nan for a week. Will you remind her to send the video and photos?'

'Sure. I won't let her forget.' She paused before asking, 'Kelly, was Lyra okay last night?'

'What do you mean?'

'Was she a bit quiet or off her game at all?'

'I don't think so.' There was a pause and when she next spoke, there was a hint of concern. 'Maybe. Why? What do you think is up with her?'

Stacey couldn't fail to detect the note of suspicion in the girl's voice. She had to backpedal quickly. 'I don't really know. I didn't want to pry and ask her outright. I wondered if it was to do with a boy. Maybe she was seeing somebody. Was she afraid to tell us about him?'

That was clumsy. She should have put it a different way. Now she really would have aroused Kelly's suspicions.

'Are you asking me if Lyra's been seeing somebody in secret?'

'I suppose I am. I'm worried about her, Kelly. That's all. I want to be there for her and recently, she's been pushing me away.'

There was another silent wait, during which Stacey worried she'd overstepped the mark. She held her breath until Kelly spoke again.

'If she's seeing anyone, she hasn't told me about it.'

'So, if it isn't a boy, something else must be troubling her. I guess she'll tell us both in her own good time.'

'I guess so.'

Stacey cast a look at Jack. This wasn't going well. Maybe she ought to have asked the girl outright if Lyra had intended meeting anybody or stopping off anywhere on her way home last evening.

Kelly spoke again. 'Maybe . . .'

'Maybe, what?'

'Maybe she's worried about her mum's operation.'

'Oh, she told you about that.'

'Yeah. If it was my mum and she was in hospital, miles away, I'd be worried.'

'You're probably right. I'm probably overreacting. You know how much I care about Lyra. I like to know she's okay.'

She left a gap in case Kelly had anything to add, but there was no comeback.

'Right then. I'll try to stop worrying and get back to work.'

'It would be that worrying her, wouldn't it? Her mum's operation, I mean?'

'She hasn't mentioned anything else, has she?'

'No, but maybe she just didn't want to tell me.'

'I'm sure she'd have confided in you, Kelly. You've known each other a long time. You know you can tell me if she said something. I won't say anything to Lyra.'

'No, she hasn't.'

'Well, if there was anything bothering her, you'd be the first person she'd tell.'

'Yeah, probably.'

'Don't worry about this. I've more than likely read too much into the situation. You know what it's like sometimes with parents. They don't understand when you're having an off day.'

Her comment elicited a small laugh, followed by, 'Yeah.'

'Listen, have a good trip. Say hi to your folks for me. I'll ask Lyra to send those photos as soon as she can.'

She ended the call and glanced at Jack, who was watching her keenly. 'They took Kelly's dog to the beach, which means they could have been spotted or followed by any number of people. It's what, a fifteen-minute walk from Kelly's house?'

Jack nodded. 'Yes. Stacey, do you think this might not have been a planned abduction? That Lyra was snatched only because she was in the wrong place at the wrong time?'

'Kidnappers don't take people without knowing their loved ones have the finances to rescue them. They might have planned on taking Kelly and grabbed Lyra instead, but that's a big leap to make.'

He shuffled from one foot to the other, head lowered again.

Stacey said, 'Let's try to make sense of what we already know. At some point, on her journey home, she was abducted. Was she on foot?'

'She took her bike. After the video arrived, I checked the shed. It wasn't there.'

'Are there any signs she returned home after leaving Kelly's? Anything to suggest she came back, then went out again?'

'No.'

'Then we must assume she was taken somewhere between Kelly's house and yours. We should search around that area.'

'I already did. I went looking for her bicycle, or anything to indicate where she might have been grabbed. I drove every possible route between the two houses and came up with nothing. Either they took her bike as well as her, or somebody else has found and kept it.'

Stacey weighed up both options. The kidnapper would require a vehicle capable of stowing her bicycle, although it wouldn't have to be very large. If there'd been sufficient time and for whatever reason Lyra hadn't put up a fight, the kidnapper would have had time to drop the back seats in any vehicle to make space for a bike, or even strap it to a bicycle carrier. What she couldn't decide was whether the person would be willing to add to the risk of being spotted by taking the bike as well.

There hadn't been a great deal of opportunity to take the girl. The two houses were only about two and a half miles apart. Lyra would have taken the most direct route, along the main road, which meant there'd been a strong chance of somebody witnessing the abduction. Had the kidnapper seized an opportunity, even knowing they could have been spotted? A proper unit would now be appealing for witnesses, yet she and Jack couldn't canvas door to door or put out an urgent appeal.

They could try one thing though.

'Here's what we'll do. I'm going to put in a request to the CCTV control room in town and ask the staff there to hunt for the girls on recordings taken from the cameras. I'll say it's for an article I'm writing. Have you got a decent, up-to-date photo of Lyra? The last one I have is from last year, when she was wearing a Christmas jumper and reindeer headband. I want to send a clearer one to them.' There were thirteen cameras covering the town.

and the promenade, along with another five in the West End that recorded 24/7. If necessary, she'd try to access other surveillance cameras; however, for the time being, these would suffice.

Jack sorted through his phone, looking up from the photo gallery. 'Isn't the CCTV run by the police?'

'No. Town council operators monitor all the cameras. They have a direct link to Lancashire Constabulary and, obviously, if they spot any suspicious activity, they alert the local force at Poulton Square.'

'Right. So, the police won't know about this?'

She shook her head. Jack's determination to not involve the police was beginning to bother her. While she understood his reluctance in light of her own experience, this constant unwillingness to involve anyone else suggested he might be holding something back. 'Why are you being so insistent about the police?'

'I wasn't aware that I was.'

'You seem really concerned that the police will get wind of this.'

'Only because I'm dead scared for Lyra. My head's all over the place. You can't blame me for being super-cautious, especially knowing your situation.'

There it was again. The reminder of what had happened years ago, bringing with it a whirlwind of doubts and fears. Maybe that was the sole reason he was so worked up about involving the police. All the same, they would never find Lyra by themselves. 'We have to do this, Jack. There could be footage of the kidnapper's car.'

'I . . . No. You're right. I want her home. I want her safe. I trust you.'

Her phone pinged at the arrival of the image. The girl looked deliriously happy, hugging a cute cockapoo puppy. The photograph was flattering. It showed a girl on the cusp of becoming a young woman. She had high cheekbones like Freya, and her silken, ash blonde hair, which normally hung loose to her waist, was lifted in a ponytail, revealing an unblemished forehead and a flawless complexion. Sadness sliced through Stacey's chest. They had to save her.

'Kelly's puppy?'

'Yes. And the reason Lyra wanted to visit Kelly rather than invite her to ours. She's been pestering me for a dog. Day in. Day out. It's all she's talked about since she got here. I was even thinking of giving in. She really wants one. I'll buy her one. When she—' His voice snagged again.

Prior to coming to Morecambe, Lyra had mentioned the puppy several times in her messages, even confiding that she was going to work on her father to buy her one. Stacey had doubted he would give in, especially as Lyra rarely visited him and he'd get saddled with the animal when she wasn't there. The sight of the girl made her heavy-hearted. This wasn't a stranger's daughter whose life was at stake. This was Lyra. The thought was accompanied by a tsunami of memories and emotion. Lyra was still *her* stepdaughter.

'What was she wearing when you last saw her?'

'Blue hoodie, jeans and pale-lemon, high-top sneakers.'

'Coat?'

'No.'

'Bag?'

'A backpack, black with a 3D picture of sunflowers.'

She knew the bag. Lyra had picked it out from a shop window display in Lancaster during the summer holidays the year before, and Stacey had bought it for her. She made the call to the CCTV control room, spoke to an operator manning the cameras and explained she was following up some important information for an article about missing youngsters and was searching for two girls. After ending the call, she emailed the operative Lyra's photograph.

'Okay, that's done. Now we need to work out who might harbour a grudge against you or Freya.'

'Don't you think I've already racked my brain? I wasted two hours trying to fathom out who could be responsible and how many ways I'd make them pay for this.' Anxiety seeped from his pores, glistening his brow.

'Anyone who might harbour any feelings of resentment or animosity towards you or your family? Business rivals? Disgruntled clients?'

He shook his head with effort, then let out another lengthy sigh. 'Nobody who'd want to do this. If I could get my hands on the full amount, I'd hand it over in a heartbeat. Now, I don't care who's responsible. I only want Lyra back.'

His words sent her mind on another track. If they could get more money together, maybe it would satisfy the kidnappers or at least buy them more time. She could ask her father for help. A small voice told her not to. He was a sick man. This revelation could trigger all sorts of memories and guilt that might cause a second stroke. He was still recovering from the first. 'Listen. I have savings I've been setting aside for my retirement since I was in my thirties. I could get my hands on it, but it would take time to withdraw it all.'

'You'd give it to me?'

'To get Lyra home, yes.' Another memory, a projection flickered in her mind and a hushed voice spoke . . .

*'He's the youngest judge in the country. I bet he's pulling in a decent wage. Half a mil is nothing to somebody like him. We really should ask for more, shouldn't we, Stacey?'*

*The hood pulls against her skin as invisible hands tear it from her head.*

*She blinks. The pitch-black is replaced by gloom. An eerie orange light illuminates a corner of the room, casting a giant shadow of her captor against the wall.*

*A voice.*

*'It's time to send your father a message, Stacey.'*

*A face suddenly looms in front of her. An old man grinning toothlessly at her. She squeals in terror and he laughs.*

*'Now you see me!' he booms.*

*She shrieks, making him chuckle even louder. When the laughter subsides, his voice drips venom.*

*'We're going to give your old man a good reason to pay up.'*

*He moves closer and she spies the kitchen scissors in his hands.*

*'Scream for the camera, Stacey!'*

*Light glints off the blades as he snips them together and steps closer. The screech begins somewhere in her chest and rises to fill the room.*

The imagined reel broke at the sound of Jack's voice. 'I'll repay every penny. When I get back on my feet.'

'We can talk about that when the time comes.' She pressed lightly between her eyebrows, eased the tension building there, and thought hard. Offering a fraction of the ransom money might afford them some time to uncover whoever was behind this, yet she wasn't sure. She again worried that she couldn't pull it off without help from the police. She voiced her concerns.

'We've already been through this. Absolutely not. There's no way I'm endangering her life. The more people you bring into this, the greater the risk to Lyra. If I don't abide by their rules, they'll kill her, Stacey!' He shook his head. 'I shouldn't have involved you. It's my problem and I'll handle it.'

Her heart beat furiously. The memory, if indeed that's what it was, had given her a jolt.

Was she transposing what she imagined had happened to her onto Lyra? Her stomach cramped. Fear won out. She couldn't allow the same thing to happen to Lyra.

Jack was halfway to the front door when she called out to him. 'Stop! We'll do it your way.'

He turned. 'You sure?'

'What choice do I have?'

'I didn't mean to put you under pr—'

She put up her hand to silence him. 'I care about Lyra too. I'll not walk away from this.'

'Okay, but we really can't involve anyone else. What do you suggest?'

She chewed at her lip for a while. Jack had brought it up yet again: his insistence that there should be no outside involvement. With so few options available to them, she shouldn't dwell on that. He was probably muddled and fearful. 'If you could persuade them to take fifty thousand pounds as a sweetener until you raise the rest of the ransom, we might be able to put a tracker on the money.'

She floundered for a moment. This sounded more like fantasy rather than protocol. Jack, on the other hand, appeared to be processing her words, thumb pressed against his lower lip.

With the kidnappers due to contact Jack very soon, there was insufficient time to come up with a better plan. She mentally crossed her fingers that the CCTV footage would turn up something enabling them to identify the abductor, before this all blew up in their faces.

'You can get your hands on a tracking device?'

A name had come to mind. 'Not me. A guy I know. He's a private investigator.'

'Do I know him?'

'No, although I might have mentioned him in passing. He was an undercover police officer on that murder case I covered in 2018. You remember the one? Ashraf Khan.' Her heart missed a couple of beats as she spoke his name.

His eyebrows knitted in concentration. 'Yeah, I remember. You met him at court, didn't you?'

'That's right. He'd left the force by the time it came to court, set up a private investigation business with another ex-police officer.'

'I've repeatedly said that nobody else can be involved.'

'Why? Why not somebody like him? He isn't going to blab to the police! I get that you don't want the police to stuff up on this. I understand you're worried sick, but we can trust this man. Unless there's another reason you're not telling me why you want to go it alone? Well, is there?'

He shook his head. 'No. Of course not.'

'We need that tracker. There's no time for us to hunt one down ourselves. If we don't try this, then I'm not sure what else we can do.'

'What makes you sure this private investigator will be free to help? If he's any good at his job, he'll have other clients and cases to resolve.'

'He'll find time.'

'You seem sure about a guy you haven't seen since 2018.'

She couldn't explain why she knew Ashraf would drop everything for her. It would enrage him to know Ashraf had made her promise if ever she needed his help, she was to ring – no strings attached. 'You're being obstructive, and we're wasting time. He's somebody else who owes me a favour.'

Stacey counted ten heartbeats before he finally agreed.

'Okay,' she said. 'We'll give this our best shot. If the kidnapper agrees to taking your fifty grand, I'll ensure the money gets tracked.'

'And if they refuse?'

'We'll have to think of something else . . . sharpish.'

She glanced at her watch. The leaden weight in her stomach was testament to how little she trusted this flimsy, cobbled-together plan. The fact that Lyra's fate rested in her hands terrified her more than she cared to admit.

'If anyone can work out how to reach her, you can,' said Jack.

He offered her a ghost of a smile. It wasn't enough to fill her with confidence, yet it went some way to healing the emotional chasm that had opened between them. Jack needed her. Lyra needed her. She wouldn't let either of them down.

# DAY ONE

## WEDNESDAY – ALMOST 6 P.M.

With Jack slumped in the chair opposite hers, chewing on his thumbnail, she excused herself for a while. She needed time alone to assess the situation. She headed upstairs to the bedroom and shut the door.

Jack had forwarded the video to her mobile. She played it again, volume on the lowest setting. She zoomed into the grainy footage to better see the girl's face, pausing it, all the while hoping beyond hope this wasn't Lyra, even though in her heart she knew it was.

Another picture flitted into her mind, one that quickened her pulse, of another girl tied to a chair. She tried to stabilise the vision by closing her eyes, imagining herself pushing the heavy door to the auditorium, hunting in the gloom for a row, sidling past seats, the smell of warm popcorn in her nostrils, until she found a suitable spot to sit down. Eventually, the frames ceased flickering and began to roll . . .

*Pitch-dark.*

*She's having difficulty breathing. The hood or sack or whatever it is itches against her skin. She keeps sucking in the fibres. Each breath causes her to cough, and once she starts she can't stop, until her chest feels bruised and her lungs wrung out. Her misery is compounded by the continuous chafing of her wrists, so sore she dare not move them. A dull throb drums a steady beat through every nerve in her shoulders. She's been chained upright for what feels like forever. She can't stand this any longer. She's so exhausted she can't even cry. To detract from the constant throbbing pain, she goes back over what has happened, trying to convince herself that this ordeal will shortly come to an end.*

*She can guess why the man in the mask cut off her hair. It's so her father will believe the kidnappers have her. She must remain patient. And hopeful. Her dad will send the money. He's rich. He will give this man whatever he asks.*

*A door slams and her heart jackhammers in her chest. Urgent steps thump across the floor and she hears angry snorts. He clears his throat, with a rapid, gunfire-like* huh-huh-huh.

*'Henry's not listening, Stacey.'*

*She holds her breath, trying not to cough, terrified of what is to come next.*

*The hood is ripped off so quickly she yelps.*

*The mask is directly in front of her. Framed by a feeble light, it is even more terrifying than the first time she saw it. His smell washes over her, cloying, peppery with sour undertones.*

*'Now you see me!'*

*This time the mantra is spoken angrily, the words forced out as if they've been clogging his throat. The wrinkled rubber face remains impassive, but the man's large fists curl and uncurl as he speaks.*

*'He's going to need more convincing, Stacey. How do you think we should do that?'*

Stacey's stomach flipped. Had she been imagining what Lyra might be facing, or was she genuinely remembering what had happened all those years ago? These were memories she hadn't experienced before, yet in the past she'd experienced other flashbacks that transpired to be false, simply visions created by current events. She searched her mind for clues: the soft glow in the room on the video was uncannily reminiscent of the one in the vision; the fibres scratching the back of her throat had felt real. All the same, her memory was not to be trusted. This could all be a fabrication, brought about by the trauma of Lyra's disappearance. It unnerved her, made her question her sanity in even agreeing to assist Jack. She wasn't stable enough to make judgements that might save Lyra.

She paced the floor. It was a mistake to get involved. She'd not thought about her own kidnapping for decades. All of a sudden, she was getting flashbacks or what felt like them. She wrapped her arms around herself. She didn't want to remember what had happened. She owed Jack nothing. Their marriage had degenerated quickly from a love story. What she'd understood to be his love turned out to be nothing more than a narcissist's fierce possessiveness. Cracks appeared from the off. Jack had wanted her to relinquish her job, be a housewife. He'd objected to her working in a male-dominated environment. Once the honeymoon period was over, and only a few months into their marriage, he first began laying down rules, then, when she disobeyed, mentally abused her. She hadn't recognised it for what it was – gaslighting. She'd believed she was invariably at fault, that when things went wrong it was because of something she had or hadn't done. Each sharp word, every argument was deserved and Stacey – clever, confident Stacey – believed she was the one who needed to change, not him. Until finally, she'd been working on an article about forms of abuse and the scales had fallen from her eyes. That same day, she packed her bags, waited for him to return from work and explained why she was leaving him. Despite his assurances he would change, and pleas for her to stay, she'd stuck to her guns and walked out.

Here he was again. As if the past and his lousy treatment of her hadn't happened. He was toxic. Yet however much she tried to convince herself to walk away from this situation and from him, she couldn't. Even now, he still possessed a magnetism, an invisible hold over her. Worse still, it was one she seemed powerless to resist. It troubled her that she still felt drawn to him, even cared about him. Enough to help him get back his daughter – her stepdaughter.

'Stacey?'

Jack was peering around the door, his face long, eyes pleading again. 'It's almost six.'

'I needed a moment, that's all.'

'Of course. I've put a huge amount on your shoulders. How are you coping?'

'I should ask you the same question. I'm terrified, Jack. Absolutely terrified.'

He walked towards her, his hands outstretched. He reached for hers with a sincere 'Thank you. Thank you for being here with me, helping me through this.'

She pulled away, with a half-hearted smile. She didn't want him touching her or getting any ideas that this was about anything other than saving Lyra. The girl was counting on them – on Stacey – and she was determined she wouldn't make the same mistakes that her father had all those years ago. She would do whatever was necessary to ensure the girl was released unscathed.

Returning to the kitchen, she slid onto a chair to study the rough plan she'd pencilled on a notepad.

'Are you clear on what you're going to say to them?' she asked.

'That although I can't get all the money immediately, I'll give them fifty thousand pounds to buy me more time until I can get together the full amount.' Jack paused, eyebrows pulling together in a sharp V. 'What happens when I can't pay the rest of the ransom?'

'We'll cross that bridge when we reach it. Maybe Freya's parents—'

'No chance. They don't have a bean. What about—?'

Her mobile buzzed. Stacey answered, then mumbled thanks before updating Jack.

'That was Ox. Nobody rang Lyra's number after she contacted you last night at quarter past eight. Her phone was switched off eight minutes later. The last ping places it in the Wakefield Avenue area, around the time she rang you. Ox reminded us to keep the kidnapper on the line for at least ninety seconds and he is going to run a trace on the phone as soon as you answer.'

The sound of Jack's ringtone broke the brief silence that fell between them. He reached for it, *Number Withheld* flashing on the screen. 'It's them.'

'Answer it.' She moved closer to him, her arm brushing against his, as he lifted the phone between both their ears. She started a stopwatch app on her phone, placing the screen in Jack's eyeline. He nodded.

'Hello.'

The voice was synthesized. 'You have twenty-four hours to raise the money. I'll ring the same time tomorrow with instructions on where to deposit it.'

'No, wait! There's no way I can raise that in twenty-four hours,' Jack began. 'I'll give you everything I have. Just not the full amount yet. I need to sell assets, which takes time. Let me hand over what I have, and in return you give me more time to find the rest.'

'How much money have you got?'

'Fifty thousand pounds.'

The robotic voice was silent. Jack spoke again. 'Are you still there?'

'You don't love your daughter.'

The stopwatch was only showing twenty-nine seconds had passed. She mouthed, 'Keep talking.'

He returned a sharp nod. 'I do. I do love her. You chose the wrong person. I'm not wealthy. I don't have half a million pounds to hand. I'll find it though, I promise. I simply need more time.'

'Lies. Such lies. Lawyers like you earn at least 150K a year, plus what about those *extras* from some of the clients you represent.'

'I don't earn that amount! I don't get any extras. I beg you. I'll pay you. I promise. Take my offer as a goodwill gesture, a down payment, whatever you want to call it, and in return keep Lyra safe. Please. I implore you. I *will* pay you.'

'Maybe.'

Stacey tapped the phone screen to show him he needed to keep talking. He nodded again. 'Where shall I leave the money?'

He repeated the question, hand now rubbing the top of his head frantically as he tried to keep the kidnapper on the phone. 'Let me speak to her? Please. Hello? Hello!'

The phone went dead. Jack's shoulders slumped.

The knot in Stacey's stomach uncoiled a fraction. She held up the stopwatch. Jack had only kept them on the phone a little over one minute. 'Okay, we've probably bought some time to find Lyra.'

'You reckon?'

'They didn't say no to your offer.'

He lifted his face. 'They didn't say yes, either.'

She called Ox, hanging up with a sigh. 'As we suspected. There wasn't enough time to trace where the signal was coming from.'

He groaned loudly. 'Why Lyra?'

Stacey thought about how the person who had abducted Lyra had accused Jack of earning undisclosed income. 'Are you being honest with me about the state of your finances?'

'Why would I lie about such a thing?'

'What about the extras they mentioned?'

'I don't know what the hell they were on about. I earn a salary, nothing like the amount they suggested. I'm not a crooked lawyer, taking bribes, if that's what you're implying. Lyra's life is at stake!' His face reddened with indignation, and he turned away, back rigid.

'Okay, sorry. I had to ask. They seemed to think you were lying about not having sufficient funds. This might be somebody you know. Somebody you work with or represented.'

'No! This is some frigging nutcase who has targeted me because I live in a nice house and drive a fancy car. They know *nothing* about my firm or me! They've made assumptions – inaccurate ones. How can you possibly believe I would lie about something so serious? If I had the money, I would hand it over in a heartbeat, not put Lyra or myself through all of this.' He dragged both hands over the top of his head and faced her again. 'For crying out loud, Stacey, you know me better than that.'

She gave a sharp nod, even though she couldn't shake off a nagging feeling that the kidnapper knew more about Jack than he believed. She let it go. It was imperative they made plans to locate Lyra rather than bicker about Jack's finances.

'Only somebody who knows you could have known Lyra would be staying with you this week. Was her visit a last-minute decision?'

'No, it's been planned for a couple of months. Ever since Freya was given the date for her operation.'

Stacey stared into space, fingers dragging backwards and forwards over her jaw. 'I really think it's somebody you or Freya know.'

'Shit, Stacey. We know lots of people.'

'Are you sure you can't think of anyone who might wish you ill?'

'I've pissed off quite a few people in my time, but not enough for someone to do this.'

'What about Lyra? Has she mentioned any problems at school or with somebody in Oxfordshire to you? Maybe this is the work of someone who wants to give her a nasty scare,' she said.

'I doubt it. You'd know about it if that were the case. She tells you everything.' His voice hardened for a moment. He tried to recover it by changing tone, a tactic she knew he'd employed in the past, when trying to convince her she was in the wrong. On this occasion he was too slow to cover his slip-up, leaving Stacey to consider the possibility Jack was jealous of her relationship with his daughter. She'd witnessed his possessiveness first-hand. It seemed he might have extended it to Lyra.

'You know what she's like,' he said, softly. 'She's easy-going. She hasn't mentioned any difficulties. She loves school. Misses being there during the holidays. Sometimes I think she'd rather be there than be with me.' His voice faltered, and a flicker of sympathy for him eclipsed Stacey's immediate worries. Regardless of the copious amounts he lavished on her whenever she visited, Lyra had never spent more time with him than necessary. She preferred her life away from Morecambe, with her mother. She'd once told Stacey that it wasn't that she didn't love him, rather that she didn't have the same connection with him as she did her mum. He was always smothering her, not giving her enough space and bossing her about.

She changed tack. 'Do you know any of her social media passwords? If we could get into her accounts, we might work out if there was anything going on in her personal life.' Jack shook his head. Panic constricted her throat. They were thrashing about in the dark. She focused on the handwritten plan. The money. It was their only hope.

'I should speak to Ashraf and make arrangements for tracking the money. Why don't you head home and try and rest up? If you receive any contact from the kidnapper, let me know immediately.'

He pocketed his phone. She accompanied him into the hall. When he reached the front door, he paused. 'I'll do anything to get her home safe and sound.'

'I know you will.'

The aromas of blackcurrant, bergamot, patchouli and musk lingered in the kitchen well after he'd left. The familiar fragrance of his favourite cologne drew her back in time, to the beginning of their relationship, when she'd been crazy about him. She inhaled, reminding herself again that it had not always been bad between them. Before the cruel words and worse. She shivered, tried to refocus on Lyra, only to find herself questioning Jack. The kidnapper had been certain Jack could afford the ransom. Could Jack be holding out on her about the state of his finances? He'd always played his cards close to his chest. When they were together, they'd had separate bank accounts, shared the bills and never discussed income. She logged onto Companies House's website and pulled up information about Corrigan & Babcock LLP. The most recent accounts were late for submission and hadn't yet been audited. If she wanted to ascertain the true state of his finances she'd have to speak to his accountant. To do so would create questions and concerns. It would also get back to Jack. For now, she'd have to trust he was telling the truth.

She searched for the number she'd not used in four years, hesitating briefly before pressing the dial button. She thought back to the lengthy trial with the ex-undercover detective who'd sat next to her in court every day. Although the magnetic pull between them had been evident from the start, what became a good friendship only turned into a physical relationship after she and Jack split up. Their relationship had been the tonic she'd needed to help her get over Jack and regain some self-esteem.

The past was the past. Ashraf might have moved on. Nevertheless, she held her breath, her heart beating a little faster than usual until he picked up.

'Ashraf Khan.'

'Ashraf. It's Stacey.'

There was a pause, during which she pictured him, head back, face lifted towards the ceiling as he pondered how to deal with the voice from his past.

'Stacey. How are you?'

'Good. Thanks. You?'

'Very good.'

'I won't beat about the bush. I need your help on a sensitive matter.'

Ashraf released a small hiss. Stacey wasn't sure if it was anger or dismay. His voice suggested the latter.

'I'm not sure this is a good idea. We . . . Us . . . It was a long time ago and I'm in a new relationship—'

A small firecracker of disappointment went off in her chest. Part of her had been glad of the excuse to talk to him again, yet unlike her he had moved on. She kept her voice level, her words slightly harsher, tone cooler than intended. 'It's purely business. We can keep it to phone calls and emails if you prefer. When you've provided the info, I'll be out of your hair. I'll pay the going rates. I'm interested in your expertise. Nothing more, Ashraf.'

She waited. Listened for clues, wondered if he, like her, had been catapulted back to a moment they knew couldn't last.

'Professional?'

'Yes. And I expect you to keep this conversation to yourself. Don't discuss this with your partner. This is highly sensitive.'

Ashraf always enjoyed a challenge. She was banking on him not having changed that much over time.

'Alright.'

'I need you to look into a law firm for me.'

'Uh-huh.'

'Corrigan & Babcock LLP.'

'Isn't that—?'

'Jack's firm. Yes. I need you to dig about, find out if it's struggling. Make sure they're legit. No shady dealings. Whatever else you can. Maybe look into his personal finances too.'

'What's going on, Stacey?'

'I can't tell you what's happening. I need that information quickly though. Can you get it?'

She heard a voice in the background, a tiny 'Dada?' There was a muffled reply. Ashraf had placed his hand over the mouthpiece so she couldn't overhear. He returned after a moment.

'The law firm shouldn't present too much of a problem. Getting hold of personal financial information is a lot harder. There's so much security and red tape these days. I'll give it a go, but there are no guarantees. What's your email address?'

She gave it to him.

'Is it okay to text or ring you on this number?' she asked.

'Sure, but if I say "Hi, Jane", you'll know I can't speak.'

'Jane?' She gave a small laugh. 'Are you afraid to call me by my real name?'

'No. I'd just rather I didn't rock any boats here, that's all.'

There was no need to press him on the matter. She didn't want to be the cause of any rift or problems between him and his new partner. Her relationship with Ashraf was in the past and best left buried there, especially now he had a child. She ignored the sinking feeling of disappointment that, had she been more mentally stable at the time, things might have taken a different turn for them both.

'I'll get onto it straight away. Computers never sleep,' he said.

'Don't go yet. I have another request.'

'Which is?'

'A tracking device. The smallest available. Something like a TracPac.'

A TracPac was a cash-tracking system that could be hidden between currency notes.

'Uhm. I don't think so. You need sophisticated equipment to pick up their receivers. There are mini-GPS spy trackers on the market though. You can use free apps to follow them on your mobile device. I'll send you a link to a few.'

'I need it urgently.'

'How quickly?'

'By morning.'

'I'll get one for you.'

'I appreciate that. Thanks.'

He let out a sigh. 'We'll have to meet so I can give it to you.'

'Sunday café?'

'Eight on the dot.'

'Right.'

'See you there.'

She put the phone down and pressed her forefingers into her temples. The child's voice in the background had caught her off guard. Ashraf hadn't been a family man. His love was primarily for his work, driven by a desire to right wrongs and put away the bad guys. Part of her was disappointed that he was now settled. There'd been an opportunity for a fresh start with him, but Stacey had still been raw from an abusive marriage, and had backed off. Jack's treatment closed her off to any future possibilities with other men. Her trust in men had completely evaporated and Ashraf had been the casualty of it.

Stacey never wanted children of her own. Her childhood tainted the very idea: a mother who had taken her own life, a father who put work ahead of his daughter's needs and who had left her to suffer at the hands of a kidnapper. She lacked a maternal streak, or so she thought, until she'd met Lyra. Then she'd felt a kinship with the girl she hadn't expected and that had become enough for Stacey. She'd chosen her daughter, and Lyra gave her everything she needed.

But now Stacey had to step forward.

Finding Lyra and bringing her home safely would be her responsibility.

# DAY ONE

## WEDNESDAY – 9 P.M.

It was coming up for nine o'clock when Stacey looked up from her handiwork. The black polyester sports bag contained a main compartment with a zipper inner pocket, an elastic mesh side pocket and a Velcro pad connector for the two handles. Other than the white crane logo, it was a plain, ordinary sports bag. She tried hiding the pretend GPS in various places – all of them easily found. Anyone collecting the bag of money would, at the very least, feel for a tracker.

It had taken a while to work out where best to secrete it. Using strong adhesive, she stuck one side of a piece of Velcro to her mock GPS and attached the other to the pad holding the handles together. The kidnapper would be sure to check inside the bag and pay scant attention to the actual fastener. If she glued the device in exactly the right position, it would pass muster.

She peeled off her clothes and was about to hit the shower when her phone rang. Reluctantly, she picked it up and heard Jack's panicked voice.

'I got a call from the kidnapper, telling me to expect a delivery. I'm going out of my skull. You couldn't come over, could you? Please, Stace-love?'

He was the only person to use an abbreviated version of her name, lending it an air of special importance with the loving add-on. When they were first together, she'd believed the endearment was his way of showing affection. Gradually, she came to learn it was nothing more than a way of manipulating her. Hearing it again, knowing he was trying to wheedle something from her, left her cold.

'It's probably best if I don't. If someone's watching your house and spots me turning up—'

'You were my wife. They must know that I'd turn to you.'

'Jack, it's too risky.'

'I don't have anyone else I can trust with this. This delivery. What if it's . . . you know? Lyra.' His voice pleaded. Words tumbling over themselves. 'You have to come. You can do it without being seen. Park on the main road . . . Or another side street, nearby. Walk towards the old black and white pub. The one on the street behind mine. Do you know where I mean?'

'Yes.' She recalled the building that had been closed for a few years. She and Jack had been there a couple of times during their marriage, preferring it to the busier, tourist-filled places.

'There's a patch of overgrown wasteland between it and the building with a large mural.'

Stacey knew where he meant. The end wall of a row of terraced houses where Jack lived depicted colourful seaside scenes.

'A tiny, overgrown alleyway runs the length of the properties and leads to my back gate. You'd have no idea it was there if you didn't know about it. It's hidden behind some undergrowth. Text me when you are at the entrance to it and I'll come meet you, guide you to my house. You'll easily spot anybody lurking in the vicinity. Besides, they're more likely to watch the front of the house where my car is parked, aren't they?'

'If there's more than one of them—'

The beeeching intensified. 'I *can't* do this alone, Stace. I'm scared shitless. If that delivery is . . . her body, I don't know what I'll do. They might have killed her . . . All because I only offered to pay 50K!'

Doubts wrapped themselves around her heart, squeezing it, causing needle-sharp pains to radiate through her chest. She inhaled deeply, telling herself that panic, not a heart attack, was responsible for them. She'd pinned everything on the abductor being prepared to wait for the full ransom. She might have got it all wrong. Jack's fear was contagious. If he was right and Lyra's body was being dumped . . .

'Okay. I'll come round.'

She tossed the phone onto the duvet and snatched up her clothes. She couldn't think clearly for the noise of her blood pumping in her ears. She'd been sure of her decision, yet now . . . She dragged her sweatshirt over her sticky body and hunted for the car keys. 'Please, let her be safe,' she said aloud as she sprinted downstairs.

Stacey had always held a soft spot for Morecambe Bay, a short drive from Lancaster, where she and Jack had lived during their marriage. It was only after they split up that Jack moved to the coast, purchasing a rundown guest house that enjoyed fantastic views across the bay.

The tide was out, leaving a huge expanse of sand, like a wide, deep-brown desert. It wasn't the rich history of Morecambe Bay that appealed to her, or the family-friendly beaches. It was the power of nature, of tides that left huge crevasses in quicksand, the variety of birdlife, shining rocks that acted as defences against high waves on wild weather days and the ever-changing views of the

Lake District, one day shrouded in cloud, the next so clear she could make out the houses on the far side.

She parked the Kia between two other cars in a side street, a short walk from the pub. She waited until there was nobody in sight before emerging from the vehicle to hasten along the dimly lit street towards the alleyway Jack had mentioned. At first, she couldn't spot the entrance. As Jack had assured her, the undergrowth, along with a lack of lighting, hid it from view. There wasn't a soul in sight so, lurking in the shadows, she sent a text to Jack.

Within a minute, she spotted a narrow beam of light picking out small patches of tufted grass. She moved towards it.

'Follow me,' hissed Jack.

He led the way through the musty, narrow space. Cold emanated from the damp brick walls. Her feet slid over slimy weeds. Other than the torchlight it was black. Her teeth began to chatter, as was often the case when she was in claustrophobic, unlit places. She ground them together, focussing her attention on the torch beam, watching it bounce along the path until it came to rest by a gate, left ajar.

'Go ahead,' he whispered. 'I'll lock the gate.'

She squeezed past him, along a narrow pathway, towards wooden steps that led to light coming from a glass circle cut into the upper half of the door. She rushed into the kitchen, eager to dispel the anxiety inside her that was at bursting point.

Jack was behind her. 'You okay?'

'I'm fine. Anything yet?' she asked.

'No.' The word was little more than a puff of air.

She took control. 'Come on. Let's sit down. I'll make some tea, although you'll have to tell me where everything is kept.'

He pointed towards a pale blue cupboard to the left. 'Coffee, tea and sugar are in there. Milk is in the fridge behind you.' She'd already noticed the silver American fridge-freezer with an ice-making unit. It was twice the size of hers.

He plodded towards an area off the main room. It was what estate agents would call a snug: a square space filled with a pair of matching two-seater settees in grey, and a wide television screen above a fireplace. A games console lay on a thick patterned grey and blue rug, two controllers by its side. He lifted a glass from the floor, drained the dregs of whisky and wandered across to the sink to rinse it. Stacey opened the first cupboard door, her gaze immediately drawn to a box of strawberry granola, Lyra's favourite. She reached for the teabags and swallowed the lump in her throat. Emotion wouldn't help her focus.

'Mugs?' she asked.

He stacked the glass on the draining board and took the teabags from her. 'You shouldn't have to look after me. Take a seat. I'll make the drinks. I need to do something other than think about this . . . hell.'

Stacey pulled out a pastel blue stool from under an oak breakfast bar and perched on it. The place was quite unlike their old home: grander, elegant, furnished tastefully with little touches, like the colourful print of small fish and tomatoes on a plate, which she was sure Jack wouldn't have chosen.

He rested his palms against the double sink and stared ahead.

'I wish they'd put me out of this misery. What if they've already killed her?' He choked back a sob.

Rather than acknowledge such a terrifying possibility, she turned her attention to reassuring him. As much for her sake as his.

'They won't have. You've offered them a part of the ransom and assured them you'll raise the rest. They want that money. Lyra is a means to it. She's too valuable to hurt.'

'Part of the ransom. Only part of it. It probably isn't enough. I ought to have got my hands on more, if on—'

There was a clatter and they both froze.

'What was that?' she asked.

'Letterbox. Stay here.' He locked eyes with her. She saw dread.

She cursed herself for mishandling this. She ought to have stayed outside, not joined Jack in the kitchen. They'd missed an opportunity to see whoever was responsible for taking Lyra. What was wrong with her? She wasn't thinking clearly at all.

He returned. 'There's nothing.'

'Did you check outside?'

'Uh-huh. Nobody. Must have been a gust of wind. It sometimes lifts the letterbox flap. Guess we're both jumpy.'

'I'm going to find a place outside, somewhere I can keep surveillance on the house.'

'And if they spot you? What then?'

'They won't.'

'You can't guarantee that. I'm not willing to risk it.' He paced the kitchen floor.

The kettle switched itself off. He snatched it from its stand and slopped water over the two teabags.

'Okay. How about I watch from one of the upstairs windows?' she said.

He shook his head. 'Same thing. They might spy you.'

'Not if I stand out of sight, using the camera app on my phone to zoom in on the pavement below, then watch the screen.' She was on her feet instantly. 'I've done that before. Jack?'

'Yeah. Okay.' He abandoned the tea-making, talking as he led the way. 'You asked me whether I could think of anybody who might bear me a grudge. I've been racking my brains: friends, enemies, old colleagues. You know, the only person I can think of who might want to hurt me is actually Freya.'

'Freya!'

51

They reached the top of the stairs and paused by an open door. Street lamps bathed the room in light that fell across a double bed with a floral duvet, on which sat a large soft toy. Stacey recognised Fred instantly. The plush dog was a little worn through hugging and its fur had changed from white to cream, but it still had the same happy face and floppy ears. It had been Lyra's favourite companion for years. Seeing it on her bed sent a spear through Stacey's heart.

'Her room probably has the best view of the street.'

'Leave the lights off,' she said as he reached automatically for the switch. 'If anyone's watching, there's less chance they'll see us.'

He dropped onto the bed, hands on his knees. Stacey angled her phone to spot anybody outside the house or walking up the path. If nothing else, she would be able to snap a picture of their face or vehicle. Although she might appear outwardly calm, her heart told a different story. She was afraid of what was to come.

Jack was talking again, his voice soft, hesitant. 'Freya and I went through a bitter divorce. Nothing like ours. It was nasty. Messed up.' Stacey knew Freya kept all communication with Jack and her to a minimum. Initially, she'd believed this was down to jealousy. It was only after Jack began to change, becoming more controlling and colder, that she was able to acknowledge that his first wife had experienced similar behaviour, and was deliberately keeping her distance. Freya was wary of Jack, probably disliked him, maybe even hated him a little for his treatment of her, but the idea the woman would orchestrate a kidnapping of her own beloved daughter was nothing short of ludicrous. Jack was grasping at straws. She kept her focus on the screen. A car drove past without slowing or stopping. Jack's voice was low, almost like background noise.

'There was more to it all than I divulged. After I walked out, she wouldn't let me see Lyra. She wanted to deny me any access to my own daughter. I threatened her with legal action, swore I'd ensure she'd come off so badly I'd get sole custody.'

Stacey didn't speak. She'd guessed the divorce had been acrimonious. Whenever they were in the same room, the tension between Freya and Jack had always been palpable. When Freya had warned Stacey that Jack wasn't the Prince Charming she imagined him to be, and could be calculating and cruel, Stacey had paid no heed. She'd found his ex-wife to be skittish, nervous and unfriendly. Freya had made little effort with Stacey, not even for Lyra's sake, and never once set foot inside Stacey and Jack's house. Consequently, Stacey had willingly believed Jack when he'd explained Freya had been a nightmare to live with, and still suffered with her mental health. This, however, was fresh information.

Jack cleared his throat. 'I held a trump card. You see, after Lyra's birth, Freya suffered severe post-natal depression. She didn't want anything to do with our baby. She was . . . withdrawn . . . apathetic. The medication didn't help. She refused to feed Lyra, bathe her, change her, or even cuddle her. The doctors assured me she'd recover, that it was only temporary, but she didn't. Not for a long while. I did what I could but, in the end, I was forced to employ a nanny to look after Lyra, while Freya spent most of the day in bed. This went on for several months. It took a great deal of help, hours of counselling before she fully recovered, and afterwards she deeply regretted what had happened. I threatened to use that information in court, paint her as an unfit mother. One who was still on antidepressants and who had insisted on sending Lyra to boarding school because she hated being a full-time mother. I was prepared to be a complete shit about it. Moreover, she knew I would win.'

It beggared belief that Jack would stoop so low. Stacey knew he was capable of mental bullying, yet, even by his standards, this seemed a step too far. In the past, he had massaged the truth to get his own way and manipulate her. She wondered if he was doing so again, although sense dictated that he had nothing to gain by casting suspicion on Freya. However, what she was hearing now was very different to what he'd told her when they were married.

'You claimed Freya never wanted Lyra to attend boarding school. You both made the decision only because she was being bullied at her local school and was desperately unhappy.'

'Which was actually the truth. It wasn't because Freya hated being a mother. Stacey, you understand how much I love Lyra. What I've just confessed to you must surely prove the lengths to which I was prepared to go to in order to hang onto my little girl. And if it had come to it, I'd have used everything I could to convince a judge to hand over Lyra to me. Freya was scared. Of me. Of what I was capable of. She backed down.' His voice became gentler. 'I didn't want to hurt her. But there was no way she was going to prevent me from seeing my daughter. I'd have carried out my threats if need be. I'm not proud of my actions or how I treated her . . . and you. I shouldn't have—'

She shook her head. She had no desire to rake over the embers of their failed marriage.

'I understand this is hard to believe, but I've changed, Stacey. Honestly, I have. It took losing you to understand I had to do something drastic to control the irrational thoughts, the . . . bouts of anger. I saw a psychotherapist, had months of counselling to become a better person. I swear that I'm no longer that man.' He broke eye contact with a nod. 'I've managed to patch up things to an extent with Freya. We've been communicating much better of late. Even so, I can't shake the possibility she could be responsible.'

There was movement outside. Stacey held her breath as a couple halted close by. Only when a white terrier appeared from the beach, racing to draw level with them, did she exhale. They clipped a lead onto the dog's collar and continued their journey along the promenade.

Jack carried on with his theory. 'As I said, Freya and I have been getting along. About six months ago, she asked me for financial help. I flatly refused. She was . . . annoyed about it.'

'You hardly spoke for years. Why did she come to you for money?'

'Only because I was her last resort. She needed seed money for a new venture, an eco-friendly clothing company aimed at young people. She'd been planning the project for a while and had the chance to take on a large warehouse and import clothing. The bank wouldn't grant her a loan, so she thought I might help, in exchange for a share of the business. I didn't think it was a good idea and I wasn't prepared to invest at all in it, let alone give her the hundred thousand pounds she asked me for.'

'A hundred grand?'

'I know. It was a crazy idea.'

'You can't seriously think Freya would do something as extreme as this to extract money from you? Threaten her own daughter? No!'

'She's always been volatile.'

'No. I don't buy that. She wouldn't plan something as warped as this.'

'Like I said, she's always been unstable.'

Stacey bit back a retort. For all her apparent faults, Freya had done a decent job raising Lyra. Besides, who was Jack to judge her state of mind?

'Instead of accepting my decision to not invest, she kept on wheedling, insisting it was a golden opportunity for me. I'm afraid I didn't mince my words. I explained her business idea was a non-starter, that nobody in their right mind would invest that sort of capital in it. To say she was put out about it would be an under-statement. She raged at me, told me I should think of Lyra and how she would benefit from having her mother run a successful business, and that's when I told her to get out of my office. She was fuming when she left. She wanted that money, Stacey. She has motive and means. If she hired somebody to snatch Lyra while she was in hospital, she'd even have a perfect alibi.'

On the occasions they'd met, Freya had been aloof, cold even, but no parent would put their child through such trauma, would they? It was crazy for Jack to even consider the idea. All the same, there was an outside chance Freya might have arranged for this to happen, purely to force Jack into paying up. Maybe she felt Jack owed her it after the way he'd treated her in the past.

'If she is behind this, she surely wouldn't allow anything to happen to Lyra,' she said.

'I hope you're right. I've no idea what Freya is capable of, although this whole thing could be simply about scaring me into paying the ransom, so she gets the money she wants and then some.' He put his head in his hands. 'Shit! That's mad talk, isn't it? I'm not thinking straight.'

It had seemed far-fetched to Stacey's ears, yet now she considered the possibility that in desperate times people resorted to desperate measures.

'Is there anyone in Freya's life, a new partner, who might have egged her on to go to these lengths or even taken Lyra themselves without her knowing about it?'

'I honestly don't know. Lyra hasn't mentioned anything to me about Freya having a boyfriend. Has she said anything to you?'

Stacey shook her head.

'On the other hand, maybe that's not news Freya would want to share with either of us,' he said. 'Much like she didn't want people to know about her operation. If there is a boyfriend—'

'Are you seeing anybody, Jack?'

He raised his head and trapped her in his eyes for the longest moment. 'There's been no one since you.'

A bike whizzed by outside. She checked the time. It had been a whole hour since Jack had rung her.

'I never finished making that tea. I'll get us a fresh cup.' He slipped from the room.

She'd been holding her mobile so tightly that tension was beginning to cause her hand to shake. She flexed her fingers, changed hands and eased into a more comfortable position, with her elbow resting on a set of drawers for support. The pathway remained empty. She let her mind drift to Jack briefly. The way he'd held her gaze when he'd said there'd been nobody in his life since her had unsettled her. He surely couldn't think she still held feelings for him. She searched her heart, found only cold embers. She had no intention of raking them over in search of a lost spark. She'd made strides since leaving him. She'd regained her confidence and was content. Even if he had transformed, she would never feel fully comfortable in a relationship with him. She'd always be waiting for him to revert to the old Jack. No, the only good to come from their destroyed marriage was Stacey's continued relationship with Lyra.

Pounding up the stairs made her turn her head.

'Stacey, there's an envelope stuck on the back door. It looks like they broke off the padlock on the gate. Probably used some sort of bolt cutters. There's no sign of anyone in the alleyway.'

'What!'

While they had been watching the front of the house, somebody had gained access to the rear.

She tore downstairs after Jack. The padded white envelope was visible against the glass.

'Wait. There might be DNA or even fingerprints on it. We might need it for evidence. Do you have any rubber gloves?' she asked.

'Under the sink.'

She knelt to hunt among the bottles of cleaning fluid and cloths, where she lighted on a pair of blue gloves. Easing them over clammy fingers, she picked away the piece of Sellotape used to adhere the envelope to the glass.

Her stomach turned somersaults at what it might contain. Taking it to the table, she sat down to examine it. Jack took the seat next to her. Easing it open with care, she removed the contents. Jack's gasp didn't register with her. The strands of hair she held were ash blonde and long. Her mouth went dry.

'It's Lyra's, isn't it?' His voice punctuated the maelstrom in her head.

'I . . . I think so.'

Jack's mouth flapped open. 'Why? Why cut off her hair?'

Her blood chilled. It was a sign the kidnapper meant business.

'They're trying to keep you scared to make sure you pay the whole amount.'

'Is there a note?'

She moved aside the hair that filled the envelope and spied a folded sheet. Unfolding it on top of the kitchen counter, they read what was typed inside:

## 50K TOMORROW
### OR SHE DIES

For the time being, it appeared Lyra was safe. Nevertheless, Stacey couldn't shake the ominous feeling shrouding her. *The hair. The dingy room. The scissors.* This had to be an echo of her past. She offset this notion by telling herself she was reading too much into the situation. She needed to concentrate on facts.

That the kidnapper had attached the envelope while nobody was in the kitchen indicated they'd been watching the house. This might suggest they knew Stacey was there. Jack was clearly having similar thoughts.

'Do you think they'll change their minds because they saw us together?' he asked.

'If they saw me, they weren't put off. They still left the envelope and instructions. You haven't had a text or a call to say otherwise. My guess is they're less concerned about my presence and more interested in getting their hands on your money.'

'You have no idea how much I want that to be true. I've made such a mess of my life. My relationship with Lyra is the only one I've not screwed up. I can't lose her. She is my universe.'

'Even though Lyra isn't my biological daughter, I want her home as badly as you do. Listen, if we need to pay the full ransom, I suppose . . . No.' She shook her head.

'Go on,' he urged. 'Any idea is worth flagging.'

'No. I shouldn't even have considered it.' She caught the confused look on his face. 'I was going to suggest talking to my father.'

'Henry? Does he even have that sort of money?'

'I'm sure he does. Sorry, I shouldn't have said anything. He's too befuddled at times to comprehend what is going on, let alone arrange to give us the ransom money. He hasn't got long left to live.'

'I'm truly sorry to hear that.'

'It's inevitable. The dementia was becoming worse, but since his stroke he's been on a rapid downhill path. There are days when I get no sense out of him. I want to ask him, but it will be pointless. I know it will.'

He placed his hand on top of hers, gave it a gentle squeeze. 'I know you and he had your difficulties, but for what it's worth I always liked him.'

She appreciated the kind gesture. Her relationship with her father had been strained for a very long time. After the kidnapping, Stacey never felt the same way about him. She had been the dutiful rather than loving daughter, a role made easier because Henry was driven by his career and almost always too busy to spare time for her.

Jack's hand was still on top of hers. 'He probably wouldn't be in a fit enough state to understand what you were asking of him.'

'True. Even if he did understand and offered to help, it would be tricky to get the money. He'd have to run it past his financial advisors to release the funds.'

'Advisors?'

'Yes. They control his assets and finances.'

'Not you?'

She shook her head.

'Oh. That's . . . No, it's none of my business.'

She guessed what he was about to say: that it was odd for Henry to have advisors in charge of his finances. She had no heart to discuss it. If she'd had power of attorney, she could have laid her hands on the amount they needed without any trouble. 'If this whole tracking idea doesn't work out, I'll go to the bank and take out what savings I have. We'll get her back, Jack,' she said.

'I—' His phone rang, making him start.

He didn't need to put it on speakerphone. Stacey could hear the scream from where she sat. It screeched through her head like a thousand seagulls. Jack almost dropped the device, his eyes wide with panic.

After what felt an eternity, it stopped, to be replaced by the robotic voice. 'You will receive instructions tomorrow. Get it wrong and the next time you hear her scream will be the last.'

The phone went dead.

Stacey's heart missed several beats.

Jack dropped his head into his arms and began sobbing.

# DAY TWO

## THURSDAY – 7 A.M.

A quiet cough woke Stacey, and she fought her way to consciousness. A white cup hovered in front of her. She blinked several times, until Jack's face also swam into view. His eyes were lost in bruised hollows. It slowly dawned on her she was in his guest bedroom.

'What time is it?' she mumbled, her tongue thick and heavy. Fatigue dragged her eyelids shut again. She fought it.

'Seven.' The cup tinkled against the saucer as he lowered it onto the bedside locker. She'd only had two hours of sleep.

'Did you sleep at all?' she asked.

'No. I couldn't. Instead, I went online and found Freya's Facebook page. It looks like she's seeing a bloke called Mark Small. He lives in Bicester. This is him.'

She shuffled her way up the bed, dragged the voluminous pillow from behind her head and propped it so she could lean against it. The man in the photo was bull-necked and squat, with a shaved head and a determined expression. The sort who could handle himself in a fight and would even relish any altercation. He was the polar opposite of Jack. 'You aren't friends with Freya on Facebook, are you?'

'No, but Lyra is. I worked out the password to her account.'

'Really!'

'Yes. It's Sharlene13theWarriorQueen!'

Stacey rubbed sticky sleep dust from the corner of her eye. 'How did you manage to come up with that?'

'It's her gaming name and age. I tried all sorts of combinations before landing on it.' He lifted a book with a red cover from nowhere and opened it at the first page to reveal the name in large letters and adorned with squiggles.

'Is that a diary?'

'More of a notebook or journal. I hoped there'd be some clue in it, but nothing leapt out.' He sat on the bed beside her, making the mattress dip with his weight. She held out her hand for the book before flicking through its pages.

'Can I hang onto this for a while?'

'Of course. I'll let you drink your coffee. Want any toast?'

'I'm fine, thanks. Jack, can you send a photo of this man, Mark, to my mobile?'

'Sure. I'll do it while you're getting ready.'

'And find out any other information you can about him.'

'Yep. Are you still a five-cup-espresso-before-you-get-going person?'

'I'm afraid so.'

'Then I'd better get some more coffee on the go and see you downstairs.'

The mugs from the night before were still beside the sink. Jack was staring out of the window onto his back yard. In the daylight, it looked different. High, grey wooden panels marked out his territory and afforded the decked area, outdoor seating and a Jacuzzi privacy.

'You get much use of it?' she asked. 'The hot tub?'

'Not as much as I thought. Lyra likes it though. She had a hot tub party late last summer. We strung fairy lights outside and had a soft drinks bar. I set up a barbecue for them before buzzing off to leave them to it. Lyra didn't think I should be there with scantily clad teenagers around the place. She's thirteen going on forty at times!' He turned away from the window.

Stacey couldn't help but smile. Lyra had moments where she was still the excited child, choosing her favourite flavoured ice cream or sitting in wonder while she and Stacey watched some goofy, animated film at the cinema, and other times would talk passionately about veganism, deforestation or the destruction of the planet. She had strong views and wanted to make a difference to the world. Stacey believed she would.

'What else do you know about Mark Small?'

'I did an internet search. There's a Mark Small in Bicester registered to Companies House. He's had three businesses, clothing companies, all in liquidation. Apart from that, nothing else.'

'It's a start. I'll see what else I can establish. You're sure about Freya? You really think she could be behind this?'

He opened his palms. 'I can't come up with anyone else. I thought about visiting her in hospital and asking her face to face.'

'Not a wise move. If she isn't responsible, she'll go frantic with worry and undoubtedly call the police. And if she is, I doubt she'd confess. You'll have to sit tight and wait for the next call from the kidnapper.'

'Can't I come with you?'

'You ought to stay here. Go through your accounts again. See how much more money you can put your hands on. You must be able to raise collateral against the house. We need to establish how much we can amass between us.'

He turned away again. 'Okay.'

'Forget the coffee. I'd better get off. I'll stay in touch.'

'Right. Thanks. Good luck, Stace.'

Outside, she was met by a brisk wind that ruffled her hair. She strode to her vehicle, nodding a greeting to the early morning joggers making their way along the promenade. The air was fresh, and she inhaled the scent of sea, salt and something she couldn't identify, a tangy, fishy smell she always associated with the seaside. Waves coated the rocky defences with a cappuccino-like froth, leaving them slick and charcoal black, while seagulls hung in the sky like a baby's musical mobile before catching air currents and swooping over the aquamarine waters streaked with the colour of caramel toffee.

She slid into the Kia and joined the morning traffic to Lancaster, her mind jangled. Freya's potential involvement upset her more than she cared to acknowledge. A parent using a child in such a way was abhorrent. While she was unable to accept the idea that Freya could be so calculating, she wondered if the woman might have been encouraged or even pressured into it. The more she considered it, the more she was certain that Freya wouldn't come up with such a scheme alone. The idea that Freya and Mark had set this up to extract money from Jack sat more comfortably with Stacey than other options. The thought eased her concern about Lyra slightly, because Lyra might not actually be in any danger if this was the case.

As she waited for traffic to move through lights, Stacey rubbed her plume ring – a talisman she always wore – and silently prayed she was right.

The Sunday Café overlooked the River Lune and although within walking distance of the Millennium Bridge, it was set some distance away from the main drag and the more popular coffee houses. It was ideal for quiet meetings, or personal assignations, away from colleagues who would recognise her or the man she was meeting – Ashraf.

Even though it had been their go-to haunt during their time together, she hadn't visited the place since she'd broken up with him; she couldn't stop her heart from thumping a little faster as she pushed open the door.

Only one table was occupied. The man sitting at it was of average build but muscular, his T-shirt tight across a well-defined chest, thighs straining against the material of his jeans. His head was lowered and his thick, jet-black hair glossy. When he lifted his face, a smile crinkled his eyes, the colour of late autumn leaves, shades of brown, gold and orange. Ashraf hadn't changed one bit.

She ordered a latte with a triple shot and sat down opposite him.

'Still aiming for that heart attack then?' he said.

She returned his smile. Closer to him she now spotted traces of lines on his brow and a tinge of grey at his temples. There was something else in him, a gentleness when he spoke and smiled. The tough edge to his personality had been smoothed, the raw anger he possessed had gone and she could guess why.

'Always the caffeineaholic. It'll see you off one day if you don't cut down,' he said.

'Not sure caffeineaholic is a real word.'

'It's in the Urban Dictionary so that's good enough for me.'

'Urban Dictionary? Still trying to get down with the kids?'

'I gave up after my ten-year-old niece told me it was very uncool to use the word "cool" and even worse if I used words like "dope" and "lit". Apparently, I'm too much of a dinosaur to use modern language.'

She smiled. 'Nice to see you again, Ashraf.'

'You too. Not sure about the circumstances though. You want to sound me out?'

'I can't. Sorry.' The coffee arrived and she took it with thanks, removing the lid to allow it to cool.

'I have what you require.' He pushed an envelope across the table. 'There's also a note about the app you'll need for the device.'

'I'm very grateful.'

'And I'm very curious. Why no police involvement?'

'It's personal stuff.'

'Involving Jack?'

She nodded. 'You find out about his firm?'

'I did and it's a strange situation. As far as I can ascertain, the returns were completed and about to be submitted to Companies House and were immediately revoked. It appears Jack emailed his accountants and requested they held off. As to why he stopped them submitting . . .' He lifted his hands and shrugged.

'That's odd. Would he do it if he were in financial difficulties?'

'I can't see any reason why he wouldn't submit, regardless of whether he has losses or profits to declare. He has a legal obligation to do so and can only hold off for so long before he is penalised.'

She was as baffled as him. It made little sense for Jack to recall his accounts. Unless it was something to do with the 'extras' the kidnapper had mentioned. What had they meant? Ashraf interrupted her train of thought.

'As for his personal finances, I've hit a brick wall. I could enlist the help of somebody who might be able to delve into it for you. No promises though.'

'Would you ask them? And can you do something else for me?'

'Go on.'

'Find out what you can about a bloke called Mark Small. He's going out with Freya, Jack's ex. I think he's owned three clothing companies that have gone under.'

'You got anything else on him? I expect there are a lot of people with the same name out there.'

'He lives in Bicester. This is all I have.' She pulled up the picture and Bluetoothed it to Ashraf's phone.

'How long have I got?'

'It's a rush job.'

'Then I'd better get onto it immediately.'

She blew on her coffee, took a sip. 'Thanks. I owe you.'

'Don't worry. You'll get a hefty bill for my services. Are you sure you're okay?'

'You know me. I'm always fine.'

'Yeah. Tough as old boots but not as leathery.'

She chuckled. 'So, come on, before you dash off, show me a photo.'

'What do you mean?'

'Your little one, boy or girl?'

A smile washed over his features. 'You heard her, when you were on the phone?'

'Uh-huh. Let me see the little munchkin.'

He unlocked his phone and passed it over. The toddler was heart-wrenchingly lovely, a cheerful spitting image of her father. The picture of the two of them consolidated her suspicions that Ashraf was a changed man. She returned it to him.

'She's utterly adorable. What's her name?'

'Zara.' The gold in his irises seemed to illuminate as he spoke.

'I'm pleased for you. You deserve to be happy.'

'Yeah. I've been lucky. Who'd have thought it, eh? Me, a father.' He took a last look at the photo, got to his feet and slipped the phone back into his pocket. 'I'll be in touch as soon as possible.'

She jammed the lid back onto the disposable cup and rose too. She had to show her face at the office, even if it was only for a short while. She still had a job she couldn't neglect, and she needed to clear her decks in order to concentrate on finding Lyra. The picture of Ashraf and his daughter had stirred something inside – a longing, not for a baby, rather the loving bond that joined parent and child. The closest she'd experienced to this was her relationship with Lyra, which now cemented the desire to do everything in her power to get the girl home safe and sound.

After attending the morning meeting, and then delegating specific tasks to the more junior reporters, Stacey was able to leave work after only an hour. When she first joined the *Lancaster Echo*, she could never have imagined becoming senior reporter. She'd been a shy individual, in awe of the seasoned hacks who occupied the other desks. Her articles, along with hard work, had earned her respect among her colleagues, and even garnered her awards. She now had her own office together with responsibility for the junior staff. Even though she'd been offered the chance to write for two national newspapers, she preferred to stay anchored in Lancashire. That wasn't to say she was without ambition. She still had the drive and determination to advance her career, just not as a reporter. It wasn't yet common knowledge among her colleagues, but in a few months she was taking over as the paper's editor when the current editor, Francis Sullivan, took retirement. Stacey was ready for the transition.

She'd always been hungry for success. It was crazy really, especially given there was nobody to praise her or be proud of her achievements. Her mother had died when Stacey was a teenager. Her father had never been one to gush over any of her successes.

She'd left a trail of failed relationships in her wake and as for friends, well, they'd given up on the work-driven Stacey a long time ago. She was fully aware of her faults, imperious at times, socially inadequate and a lousy cook. However, nobody was perfect, and she could play a mean game of bridge, could change a tyre and was an excellent journalist. That was enough for her. For now.

Ashraf had been true to his word. No sooner had she buckled up than he rang.

'Mark is either Mr Unlucky or a lousy entrepreneur. You were right about his companies. They all went to the wall within a year of starting up. He's borrowed heavily and has a hefty overdraft and outstanding debts, totalling twelve thousand pounds, on credit cards and payday loans. He's currently working part time as a delivery driver. He's been married twice and has three children by his first marriage. He has outstanding child maintenance debts. Currently resides on a narrowboat called *Tranquillity Plus*, moored on the Oxford Canal at Upper Heyford. Need anything further?'

Even though Freya was in hospital, Stacey still had to talk to her about Mark. The problem would be how to achieve this without alerting Freya to the fact that her daughter had been kidnapped.

While Stacey puzzled over how best to deal with this problem, she knew she could still have Ashraf investigate Mark further.

'Could you find out his whereabouts for Tuesday evening?'

'I should be able to do that.'

'I'll leave it with you.'

She pulled away from the car park, pondering the idea that Mark had decided to kidnap Lyra. He certainly needed financial help or a large pot of money to help get him out of the mire. It was possible he'd encouraged Freya to back another scheme and when she'd failed to get any money from Jack, had become desperate. He would know about Freya's hospitalisation as well as the fact that

Lyra was staying with her father in Morecambe. In brief, he could well have abducted her.

Given Upper Heyford was a three-hour drive away, Stacey didn't have the luxury of time to check out if Mark was there or not, nor did she have time to visit Freya in hospital. She still had Freya's number in her contact list. She could try ringing her. Using the hands-free, she spoke the woman's name, and then waited for the call to connect.

She'd start by saying that she'd only just heard about her operation and wanted to see how she was faring, then she'd ask if Mark had visited her, pretend Lyra had told her about him. She was still unsure of exactly how she'd handle the conversation, when the answering service kicked in. She disconnected without leaving a message. She didn't even know which hospital Freya was in.

Unable to contact Freya for now, she had to stick to the plan. Attach the tracking device, then wait for the kidnapper to ring.

Only 34 mm long, 40 mm high and almost flat at 10 mm wide, with a real-time GPS tracker that updated every five seconds, the device promised to work in any location, worldwide. It was fiddly to fix to the Velcro bag handles but once in place it was imperceptible to even Stacey's keen eye.

She tested it thoroughly, pulled the bag handles apart, examined them again. If the kidnappers were savvy, they'd check for trackers. The chance of finding this one was minimal, unless they owned a special device to locate it. If so, it meant she was dealing with a more complicated situation than a greedy boyfriend.

Thoughts of Mark were put on the back burner while she hastened down to her car and threw the bag onto the passenger seat. She rang the CCTV control room from her hands-free.

'Hi. This is Stacey O'Hara. I called about footage of two girls on the promenade on Tuesday evening. I sent a photograph of one of them to help you identify her – a girl in a blue hoodie, jeans and lemon sneakers.'

'Yes, you spoke to one of my colleagues. They've gone off shift, but I've taken over the task. We think we've found her.'

'Was she with another girl, taller than her, long dark hair?'

'It might be best if you came over and looked for yourself. It's really not easy to identify her from what we have.'

'I'm on my way.'

The plain, nondescript building – one of many in Morecambe that had succumbed to age and time – was in the centre of town. Its greyed façade was impregnated with decades of sooty particles escaped from exhaust pipes and as weather-beaten as an over-zealous sun worshipper. Stacey wondered if it had been intentionally left to blend in with other neglected buildings along the street to secrete what was housed within its walls. Few members of the public were aware of its existence, with most of the local inhabitants supposing the surveillance cameras in town would be monitored by police officers at either the station in Morecambe or Lancaster.

Small cobbles belching moss and weeds from the cracks between them paved the way to the entrance, a door with various public notices stuck to the glass, preventing any visitors from seeing inside. She rang the bell and waited for a voice over the intercom to speak. She gave her name and was buzzed inside.

A young woman in a loose-fitting blouse and leggings emerged from a door marked *Private* and with a flash of white teeth accompanied Stacey upstairs with barely a word until they reached the landing, where she pointed out a cream door.

'Just knock and go in. Rick is on this morning.'

She was gone in a flash, bounding back downstairs like a graceful gazelle.

Stacey tapped on the door, heard 'Come in' and entered. The set-up here was similar to other control rooms she'd visited, with desks in front of several screens, all showing real-time movements on the streets of Morecambe. She was drawn to the middle screen, Marine Road Central, where cyclists circumnavigated pedestrians who strolled along the promenade, all unaware they were being observed. They weren't great in numbers. Even though it was Easter week, it was still fairly quiet in the seaside town. She scoured the dog-friendly beach beyond, as if she might miraculously spot Lyra and Kelly chasing after a puppy.

The operator, Rick, spoke. 'Ms O'Hara? I asked if you'd like me to run the footage for you?'

She'd been so lost in thoughts of Lyra she clearly hadn't heard him the first time. 'Oh yes, please. Sorry. I was miles away.'

'Not a problem. It's a knack – watching all the screens simultaneously. You get used to it. I was like you when I first got here. Couldn't tear my eyes away from one screen, let alone look at all of them. I soon worked it out.' He fiddled with his keyboard. The screen she'd been looking at changed, showing the tide closer to the shore. The timeclock showed it was Tuesday evening at 8 p.m. Although it was the same scene the cyclists had vanished, to be replaced by a couple with a large dog. Behind them a family with a child who was riding a scooter. She hunted for signs of the girls until Rick abruptly froze the frame.

'There. I think this is them.'

She squinted to see what he was pointing at, then spotted a puppy mid-run on the sand. A person was in the frame, only partly visible. Rick zoomed in on the picture, until Stacey could make out a jean-clad leg and a lemon-coloured, high-rise sneaker. Rick unfroze the screen. Instead of seeing the person fully appear, the puppy turned around and ran back, both it and the person disappearing from view.

'Have you got anything else?' she asked.

'Only this.'

He fast-forwarded the footage ten minutes. This time Kelly appeared, the same pup on the lead, and came to a halt. Her lips seemed to be moving, as if she was holding a conversation on a hands-free telephone or speaking to someone out of shot. It had to be Lyra. Looking at the timestamp, it would have been around the time they were making their way back to Kelly's house.

'Can you leave the footage running for a while?' she asked.

'Sure.'

They sat in silence as a jogger raced along the promenade. There was no further sighting of Lyra, Kelly or the dog.

'Would you please rewind it to before the moment we see the puppy running on the beach?'

He did as she requested.

'Stop.' She squinted at the capture. 'Is there any chance you could zoom in on that person?'

The man had been leaning against the railings, thumbing his phone, while the girls presumably chased around the sand after the puppy. He'd moved away almost immediately after they disappeared the second time.

'His head's down. I can't get a clear image,' said Rick.

'Give me what you can.'

The image broke up, then re-pixelated. He tried zooming in again and again. Each time, the clarity suffered. The man's features could not be sharpened. All they had was a squat man with a shaved head, wearing a padded jacket.

'Could you send me this capture?' She gave him her email address and almost immediately it pinged into her inbox. 'We think the girls might have walked to Wakefield Avenue. Do you have any surveillance in that area?'

'Sorry. You might get lucky with local businesses or premises. Some have surveillance equipment, but we stick to the main routes.'

It was as she feared, little chance of working out exactly when or where Lyra was snatched. 'Thank you for your help. If you spot either girl again anywhere else on that night, would you let me know? The girl with blonde hair might have come back this way on a turquoise bike soon afterwards.'

He pulled a face. 'I ran through footage right up until nine o'clock. I'm sure I didn't see her, walking or riding a bike. Why are you looking for these girls? Have they committed a crime?'

'I can't really divulge what it's about at this stage. Trust me, it's important. Really important. And I'm grateful for your help.' She gave what she hoped was a winning smile. It worked.

'I'll check it again. Turquoise bike, you say?'

'Yes. Thank you. I appreciate it.'

Back outside, she sat on a low wall beside the building and debated what her next move should be. A dustcart was making its slow journey along the street, accompanied by operatives in high-vis jackets who pulled effortlessly at wheelie bins and manoeuvred them onto the platform at the rear of the cart. The whirring of the mechanism as each bin was hoisted seemed unnecessarily loud to her ears. The clatter as emptied bins were returned to their original positions set her teeth on edge. With the noise though came a sudden thought. The video that the kidnapper had sent. Had there been any background noises that might help them locate where Lyra was being held? As the lorry approached, she headed for the sanctuary of the Kia. Inside, the disturbance was muted.

She drew up Mark's Facebook photograph and flicked between it and the capture from the CCTV camera. There was enough of a similarity to make her pulse quicken. Next, she opened the video of Lyra, wincing as it played. There was insufficient light to get a clear focus on the girl or her surroundings. There appeared to be a table nearby, the sight so fleeting she couldn't be sure. When she paused the video, the picture became too distorted to make out a great deal of detail, other than Lyra, who appeared to be dressed in jeans and what looked like a hoodie.

She ran it again, this time with eyelids shut, concentrating on any sound she might identify, yet there was no traffic noise or a distant train or any running water, nothing to help her. She set aside the phone. *Think!* The trouble was her mind had frozen. Even if they could track down whoever had taken Lyra, were they capable of rescuing the girl without help from law enforcement?

The only way would be to pay the ransom. *Money.* Once again, she toyed with the idea of tackling her father about assisting, before deciding it really would be impossible to convince him to sign paperwork to release such a large amount in the time available. There would be awkward questions when his financial advisors stepped in. If only he'd granted her power of attorney. A stubborn Henry had flatly refused to recognise how ill he was becoming, had continued to live independently and kept his finances secret. It had hurt that he'd not trusted her enough to look after him or his money. Although he might have seen it differently, she felt it was another example of how little he cared about her. She pulled herself together. As had been the case for many years, she would have to rely on herself. She would head into Lancaster and see if there was any way she could release her own savings quickly.

The kidnappers weren't making this easy. Times had changed. Money transactions were invariably made over the internet or via an app. People used plastic, not actual notes and coins. Surely the abductors understood it would be nigh on impossible to obtain such a vast amount of cash . . . Unless they knew Jack had a way of getting his hands on it.

Her suspicions about Jack grew. He had already admitted he could raise fifty thousand. She stopped the thought process before it took her too far down a rabbit hole. Lyra should be her focus, yet if Jack was involved in some nefarious activity he was keeping from her, he might also be inadvertently protecting the very person who'd taken his daughter. However, it would explain his reluctance to involve the police. He was keeping something from her, that was for sure. He might even have done something that would explain who the kidnappers were, something illegal. She smacked the steering wheel with the flat of her hands. None of these sombre thoughts were helping the situation. For Lyra's sake, she had to stick to her plan.

# DAY TWO

## THURSDAY – 1 P.M.

Stacey was in Lancaster at the bank when the text message came through.

> They just rang.

> Drop off details coming in an hour.

> Please come back.

She glanced about the half-empty room. She was still fourth in the queue for a personal advisor, and had already been waiting twenty minutes. She had no idea how much longer it would take before she'd be seen or indeed, how long the paperwork would take. She couldn't risk it. The bag for the drop was in her car. She had to return.

Ashraf rang her as she stomped back to her car. The news wasn't good.

'Mark Small's phone hasn't moved from his boat since yesterday. Looks like he hasn't travelled anywhere during the last forty-eight hours.'

'Unless he deliberately left his phone behind while he made the trip to Morecambe and is now using a burner.'

'That thought had crossed my mind. I tell you what I'll do. I'll find out what vehicle he drives.'

'If he's savvy enough to leave behind his phone to prevent it from being tracked, he might well have hired or borrowed another vehicle.'

'There'll be a paper trail if he's hired one, Stacey.'

'Then I hope he chooses to do that rather than borrow a car. I really appreciate you doing all this, but what about your other clients?'

'They can wait. I'm working for you now. There's a condition though.'

'Which is?'

'You tell me what this is about once you've resolved it.'

The urge to tell him there and then was strong. During the dark days of her marriage, he had seen through her false cheerfulness. He'd coaxed the truth from her. When she'd finally opened up about Jack, he'd told her she had to be strong and leave. He'd warned her that Jack was a narcissist, a man who would never change and who would only continue to mentally abuse her. He gave her names of hostels she could go to, of support groups, and had been there for her when she'd plucked up the courage to walk out on Jack. Ashraf had understood her better than anyone she'd ever met.

In that moment, she wanted to tell him everything about the kidnapping. He deserved her honesty, yet his contempt for Jack might affect his willingness to continue helping them. She couldn't risk that.

'Deal.'

'And you pay my going rate.'

'Goes without saying.'

'Good. Speak later.'

In Morecambe she found a parking space on the road, close to Jack's car, about a hundred metres from the house. She opened the car door for what felt like the hundredth time that day and, sensing it being tugged by the wind, held fast onto the handle. An errant, red and white foil food packet rose from the promenade to swirl and twist in the sunlight like a firework, before settling on the sand, only to be lifted almost immediately, high in the sky to perform its wild dance again. She leant into the invisible force, forcing her body against the resistance. Gusts tugged at each strand of her hair, pulling incessantly until she turned onto Jack's pathway, where the tall building afforded some protection. She rang the bell.

Jack opened the door almost immediately. 'Thanks for coming back. I was panicking. You had the bag—'

'It's fine. I understand. Where's the money?'

'In there.'

She followed him to the kitchen. Thick brown packets were lined up in neat rows on the kitchen table. 'There's ten grand in each one.' He placed his hands on top of his head, fingers entwined, and sighed. A light sheen of perspiration covered his forehead. 'This ploy had better work. This is all I can lay my hands on.'

She dropped the bag onto a chair by the table. A question that had been troubling her since she left the bank needed asking. 'I had to queue for an advisor in order to withdraw my savings. I left before I got a chance to speak to them, but I'm certain they wouldn't have handed over cash without asking a whole bunch of questions. So, tell me, Jack, where did your money come from?'

'It doesn't matter.'

'Of course it matters. I don't need to spell it out, do I? If you obtained it illegally—'

'No! I've been keeping it in my office safe. It was . . . for emergencies.'

'Don't try and pull the wool over my eyes. That's hardly petty cash.'

He blew his cheeks out. 'Okay. The kidnapper was sort of right about the *extras*. I've been offering advice to individuals for cash. It's no big deal. I don't do anything illegal. I work as a sole lawyer outside of the firm.'

'You lied to me! You bloody well lied to my face about those extras.' She stomped across the kitchen and back again, getting into his face as she spoke. 'Why do you take cash as payment?'

'There are some clients who prefer to pay in cash.' He shrugged carelessly.

'And what about your company? Shouldn't you put the earnings through your books?'

'Like I said. I operate outside the company for this sort of work.'

His jaw jutted. Even if he wasn't doing anything illegal, fifty thousand pounds was a lot of money to earn.

She looked him in the eye. 'What sort of clients, Jack?'

His silence was all the answer she needed. 'You prick! You've been holding out on me all this time and making a freaking awful situation even worse! While you've been lying your way through this, Lyra, your daughter, is in distress! Look what happened to me when my father didn't pay up on time. Go on. Look!' She held out her hand, pulled at her ear, making him flinch. 'You want this to happen to her? Or something worse?' Her eyes burned as she glowered at him. 'Didn't it cross your greedy mind one of these *clients* might be responsible for taking Lyra? After all, the kidnapper knows you take on extra work.'

'No! They wouldn't. None of them have any reason to. I've helped them, for goodness' sake. Holding Lyra hostage would be a dumb move. You don't bite the hand that feeds you.'

She couldn't suppress the groan. 'We don't know that for sure, do we? They might think you haven't done enough for them or took her for *insurance*. To stop you from dobbing them in to HMRC.'

'No. You're completely wrong. I haven't been doling out advice to gangsters. I work with businesspeople looking to exploit loopholes in the tax system.'

She shook her head. 'That's tax law. You specialise in property.'

'That doesn't mean I'm not qualified to assist in other matters.'

'You bloody idiot.' She shook her head at him and marched to the far end of the kitchen again. No matter how hard he protested, he couldn't deny that what he was doing was underhand. The frustration and anger became overshadowed by a faint smell of popcorn, and the flickering sound of a projector motor. The room began to swim. Something about a safe.

'Stace?'

Jack's concerned tone pulled her away from the cinema. His face came back into focus.

'Who knows about the money in the safe?' she asked.

'No one.'

'Your clients must have an idea. After all, they pay you in cash.'

'These guys have serious wealth. I mean serious. Not just a couple of million. That's the whole point of me helping them to find places to shelter it from the tax man. Half a million pounds isn't a big deal to these people.'

She released a lengthy sigh. She supposed he was speaking some sense.

His arms fell to his sides, and he hung his head.

'If I'd thought for one second that one of my clients had snatched Lyra, I'd have come clean. Stace, I *can't* mess this up. You know that. Ask me anything at all and I'll give you a straightforward, honest answer.'

'How much more money do you have in the safe?'

'I'm cleaned out. This was the entire stash.'

She wasn't quite done with him. 'For crying out loud! You might have given me the complete picture sooner, instead of me having to prise it from you. Do I have to spell it out for you? We haven't any time to waste. Every minute she's in . . . that place, she's suffering.'

'I know. I know, Stace. I'm sorry. I was worried if you found out, you'd walk away from this . . . from Lyra. I wasn't thinking straight. I'm so fucked up at the moment.'

The look he gave her was so contrite that the pumped-up anger inside her dissipated. Jack was clearly scared stiff for his daughter's safety. How he got together the fifty thousand was irrelevant to him. He was obviously thinking of Lyra.

'Okay. Drop the subject. It's more important we're prepared for when the kidnapper rings again. We need to get on with this.'

He unzipped the bag and began shoving the packages into it.

'I thought I'd follow you in my car,' she said.

'Is that wise? What if you get spotted?'

'You want to rely solely on the tracker? What if it fails? I might be able to observe the drop zone and see who collects the money.'

His face became even more serious. 'The tracker was your suggestion. You didn't say anything about tailing me or waiting to see who collects the money. I know you're only trying to help, but you're not a detective, Stacey. You're a reporter. Don't you think they'll be watching for someone following me? They'll assume you're a police officer and that will be that!' His voice shook.

'Okay, okay. Forget it.' She raised both palms. Like him, she was so concerned she wasn't thinking straight.

He wiped his forehead. 'I shouldn't have snapped. I apologise.'

'I understand. I ought to have run it past you before.'

He lifted another package. 'Have you found out anything more about Freya and her boyfriend?'

She couldn't bring herself to mention that she'd already talked to Ashraf. There was no need for Jack to know about it at this stage. He would only object. 'Not yet. I'm still working on it.'

'Then we really are dependent on this plan working.' He shoved in the last of the brown packages.

'You never said which hospital Freya was in.'

'I'm not too sure. Why do you want to know?'

'I thought I should speak to her about Mark. Her phone goes to the answering service.'

'Is that a good idea to talk to her?'

'If he's taken Lyra, then yes. We need all the information we can get.'

'And if she's in on it?'

'I really can't see that being the case.'

He looked away. 'But if she is?'

'Do you, hand on heart, believe her capable of pulling a stunt like this?'

He shrugged loosely. 'It's been a long time since I was married to her. I don't know her mind these days. Do we know what goes on in anybody's head? All I'll say is, she might be involved and if we alert her in any way she'll pass that information on. Then what will happen to Lyra?'

Stacey chewed her bottom lip as she weighed up his words, accepting there was sufficient doubt.

He sighed. 'If you really want to risk it, I think she might be in the John Radcliffe.'

She'd ring the hospital and see if she could be put through to the ward at the first opportunity. For the moment, they had to deal with the plan. 'What exactly did the kidnapper say when they phoned you?'

The zip fastener purred shut. 'Word for word: "I accept your offer. I'll ring in one hour with instructions."'

'Nothing else?'

'No.'

'Same synthesized voice?'

He nodded. 'Where did you put the tracker? I couldn't spot it when I looked earlier.'

'Then I've done a good job of hiding it.' She took the bag from him and Velcroed the handles together. 'It's hidden in the handles.'

'It's invisible.'

'That was the idea.'

She brought up the tracking app on her phone. A red dot flashed, indicating the bag's location. She was pinning everything on this leading them to the kidnapper's lair and Lyra. Was it a crazy idea? Jack obviously didn't think so.

'You did a good job. They'll never spot it. What do we do now?' he asked.

'We wait.'

'This is torture.'

'We can't do anything until they ring back.'

Stacey pulled out a stool and sat on it. Jack gave the bag a lengthy look before tucking his hands under his armpits. He seemed lost in thought. The kitchen downlights darkened his facial hair. She'd never seen him so unshaven. Jack always had baby-smooth skin and perfectly neat hair and nails.

'You could use the time to make a list of your clients, especially those you see outside hours, just to give us something to go on,' she said. She doubted she'd glean much from such an exercise. It was more to keep Jack occupied, rather than have him brooding over what might happen. He accepted her suggestion without protest. No sooner had she opened Lyra's journal than he'd set his laptop up beside her. The book contained as many doodles as notes, with sketches of female figures brandishing swords, lightning flashes emanating from their blades. Several pages were taken up with favourite lists: songs, food, television dramas, films and quotes from books or films. She came across bucket-list destinations, interspersed with brief passages of creative writing about the teenager's day-to-day life. While Stacey was aware of most of the topics in the diary – they'd talked about music, film stars and ideal holidays – she was unaware of the dreams Lyra had written about in almost uncanny detail. Dreams in which she was running away from someone she couldn't see, or falling from a great height.

It soon became clear from her scribbled musings that Lyra was a confused, unhappy girl. Stacey already knew as much. Maybe that was why she'd tried to remain a constant in the girl's life, an aunt or older-sister figure rather than a mother to her. Her many conversations with Lyra, since she and Jack had split up, had given her an insight that Jack didn't possess. Lyra had confided in her, revealed her boarding school wasn't the haven she let her parents believe it was, merely somewhere she found herself, when really she would have preferred a proper family life, with two parents under the same roof.

Now that he'd read the journal, Jack would also know how she felt.

Stacey cast a glance in his direction. His head was lowered as he transcribed information onto paper for her. A pang of sadness like a weak firework popped in her chest. What she took for possessiveness, and Lyra took for control, was simply paternal love. However, no matter what he believed or hoped, she knew, even after the girl was rescued, it wouldn't be many more years before she struck out on her own. Jack would eventually lose his little girl.

Lost again in the pages, she wasn't aware Jack had stood up, not until she felt the warmth of his hands as they traced her forearms and his breath as he leant forward and planted a gentle kiss on the top of her head.

'I don't deserve your time, your help or your kindness. Certainly not after the way I behaved towards you. I was so wound up about work, so bloody frustrated all the time, like a freaking huge bomb about to explode, that I stopped thinking clearly.' Stacey didn't move. This was the first time he'd spoken about what he had done or apologised for it in any way. Jack never said sorry.

Whenever he'd come home from work in a foul temper, alcohol on his breath, and criticised her for wearing a top that was too revealing, or too much make-up, he had always blamed her for his actions. It was her fault he was cross, irritated by her inability to behave correctly, as befitted a lawyer's wife. If he was very drunk, absurd accusations of flirting or infidelity would fly from his lips, and when she denied them, he'd treat her with disdain, ignoring her, being icy cold towards her for days, until she pleaded to be forgiven.

He sighed dramatically. 'That phrase . . . hindsight is 20/20 . . . is very apt. I'd give anything to erase the person I was back then.'

His lips were against her hair again, warming her scalp as he spoke. Her insides turned liquid through fear. She didn't want any affection from him or apology. It was all water under the bridge. She'd moved on and didn't want to be hauled back, under his control, ever again. The sorry-man act wasn't washing with her. In fact, it repulsed her. She wasn't helping him out of love for him. She was helping because of her love for Lyra.

'Stacey, I've missed you so much—'

Although it was expected, the shrill ringtone caused her to jump and him to step back. Jack snatched the phone from the table. The machine-like voice was audible from where Stacey was sitting.

'The town hall car park. You have seven minutes. Come alone or she dies.'

It would take Jack at least that amount of time to reach the building situated at the far end of the promenade. The kidnapper hadn't allowed for him to get to his car, or the volume of traffic on the main road. It would be tight. Terror dragged his features into a frozen mask.

'Go!' she urged, lifting the bag and thrusting it into his arms.

He unstuck with a jerk and, grabbing his car keys, hurtled towards the door. She stood away from the front window, out of sight, Jack in view. The car sidelights flashed on and off with a noisy bleep then he threw the bag and himself into the vehicle. The Porsche growled away. No one in pursuit.

The promenade was empty, strong winds dissuading visitors from their usual walks or visits. A mobility scooter puttered into view, the driver hidden behind a plastic canopy that seemed to suck in and out, as if breathing. There was little Stacey could do now other than track the bag on the app. The red dot blinked its way along Marine Road West, drawing level with the Alhambra Theatre. Volunteers had worked tirelessly to bring the magnificent Victorian building back to its former glory and make it once again a music, arts and cultural centre, but Stacey had yet to visit it. Comedy nights or music venues weren't her thing.

The dot continued along the promenade. Four minutes had passed. It came to a halt by a roundabout adjacent to the Midland Hotel and the old railway station. She could envisage Jack's frustration at being held up in traffic, mirrored by her own. It remained stationary for almost a full minute before accelerating further along the road. Jack was undoubtedly breaking the speed limit to reach his destination in time. She followed its progress, one eye on the time. One minute remained. Nearing the location, it appeared to increase in speed again before turning into the road that led to the car park. She exhaled slowly. Jack had made it with ten seconds to spare.

Within half a minute there was further movement. Had the kidnapper taken it already? She jumped at her ringtone, almost dropping her mobile. Jack's voice was loud and panicky.

'I've four minutes to get to Happy Mount Park.'

The call ended. The kidnapper was messing Jack about. A deliberate attempt to increase his anxiety. Whoever it was had it in for her ex-husband. The flashing spot travelled the length of Marine Road East and halted at the park entrance. Within seconds she received another call.

'Eric Morecambe statue. On foot this time. Twelve minutes.'

There was approximately one-and-a-half miles between the park and the statue. It was a tall ask to cover the distance in such a short amount of time. He would have to race if he was to reach the destination in time. The son of a bitch was really confounding Jack.

With the sympathy came an idea. There was something she could do to assist. She rang the CCTV control room and spoke to Rick, the operative who had helped her look for the girls. She explained she needed his help again. 'Have you got vision on Marine Road East?'

'I have.'

'There should be a man with a carryall, running along it.'

'I can see him.'

'He's headed towards the Eric Morecambe statue. Keep an eye on him and see if anyone is following him.'

'I can't see anyone.'

'Could you keep watching? I'll ring again after he's reached the statue.'

She didn't give him a chance to ask why she required his assistance. Nor could she stay on the line. She needed to be available should Jack ring her again. More importantly, she had to track the moving bag. Jack seemed to be making good progress. She willed him to maintain the steady pace. He'd been a runner when she first met him, a member of a club. According to Lyra, her dad no longer maintained his rigorous training, but still ran the length of the promenade two to three times a week. Another fact the kidnapper could well have known. It would have been impossible for an unfit person to cover the distance in such a time.

Eleven minutes and twenty seconds later, the dot stopped by the statue. Jack didn't call her. The bag continued, at a more sedate pace, past the statue back towards the house. She texted him but received no reply. She spoke again to Rick.

'Yes, he stopped at the statue, took a phone call before walking towards Promenade West. I've lost sight of him. However, there doesn't appear to be anyone following him. I'll keep an eye out for him and ring you if I pick him up again. We don't have CCTV coverage for the remainder of the promenade. This is as far as it extends.'

She could only follow the red dot's progress as it headed in her direction until finally it stopped and didn't move again. A full two minutes later, a breathless Jack rang.

'Coming back . . . Didn't dare ring . . . They . . . watching me. Left it . . . bushes beside . . . table, opposite old church.'

Stacey knew where he meant. When Lyra was nine, she had chosen the church as part of a school project about Morecambe's history, proudly bombarding both her and Jack with every fact she uncovered about the Trinity Methodist Church. She hadn't been so much interested in its rich history as a place of worship, more that it had featured in *The Entertainer*, a 1960s film Lyra had insisted on watching with Stacey. Even as a young child she had exhibited a talent for sketching, her project accompanied by neat drawings of the buildings she'd written about. The church was her best, with attention to every detail, including the boarded-up windows and central doorway and the four-stage tower with lancet bell openings, flanked by octagonal corner turrets with lead spirelets. Reminded briefly of the sketches in the girl's journal, there was little doubt she'd retained her flair for art.

She spotted Jack, face red with exertion, hair stuck flat to his head, and opened the front door for him. He stumbled into the hall, where he leant over, clutching his sides in an attempt to catch each ragged breath. She led him into the kitchen, one hand under his arm for support. The effort had extracted every ounce of energy from him. He collapsed onto a stool and rested his head on outstretched forearms against the breakfast bar. She poured him a glass of water. He rasped thanks, took it with shaking hands and gulped it down.

'Asswipe . . . pissed . . . me about . . . something chronic.'

'I know. They're jerking your strings. Maybe even punishing you for something.'

'I can't think what. Where's the money?'

'Still in place. I thought I might head to the drop-off, wait to see who collects it.'

'Don't. They'll be expecting that, won't they? That's what happens in these situations. At least it does on telly. They'll have somebody watching the bag already, waiting for the cops to appear.'

Once more, his words, along with her own heightened anxiety, unleashed vague images. The mists of time swirled in her head and parted to reveal a cinema screen. On it flickered an image of a darkened room, the place where she'd been held captive. When she'd attended therapy sessions, she'd had to follow a procedure to encourage the images. These were tumbling into her head apparently at whim, unless it had been the mention of the drop-off point or the memory of watching *The Entertainer* with Lyra that had stirred the pictures in her head. She resisted, unwilling to revisit the past, until she was overpowered by memories that forced their way to the forefront . . .

*Her teeth are chattering under the hood. The man in the mask has released her arms and is checking her injured hand. She's rigid with fear. At first, she thinks he might cut off another finger, then she realises he's dabbing at the wound with disinfectant. Although it stings like crazy, she doesn't dare cry out. Heaven knows what he might do to her, if she angers him. The thought of losing her finger makes her want to throw up, so she tries to think of something else or she'll choke on her own vomit. She must remain calm. She concentrates instead on the sunny days she'll spend on the beach with her best friend, Bella, laughing at each other's jokes, playing volleyball, chasing each other into the cold sea, squealing at how icy it is and then splashing each other and laughing, all the time . . . laughing.*

*The man has finished. He hasn't chained her hands back up above her head. Instead, they are handcuffed together on her lap. It is a welcome change, and she feels a wave of gratitude to her captor for allowing her this small freedom. A thought pops into her head. Could it be that her father has paid the ransom? Is the man getting her ready for release?*

*He doesn't speak or click his nails angrily or make weird grunting cough sounds as usual. The door closes. A flame of hope rises in her chest, settling there. He hasn't chained her back up. This is a positive sign that this ordeal is almost over. She will soon be home, able to rejoin her school friends and her life. Then this will become a blur, a nightmare. She'll forget about it in time. People will be glad to have her back.*

*A small tear escapes her eye. It is suffocating in the hood. She must still bide her time until a drop-off is arranged. She loses herself in thoughts of surfing with her friends, the waves lifting them like leaves on a breeze, before carrying them to the shore. Bella's aunt, who has a caravan in Devon, has agreed to let them stay there unsupervised for the last two weeks of the summer holiday. They're going to have such fun.*

*A clearing of a throat, an* uh-huh-huh *sound interrupts her daydreaming. The man is back. This time his voice drips venom.*

*'Henry betrayed us. The police were waiting at the drop-off point. He will have to be taught a lesson.'*

*He advances and even though she tries to stay focused on Bella, the seaside and sunshine, she can't stop the hammering in her chest.*

'Stacey?' said Jack, hand on her shoulder.

'Sorry. I was . . . thinking.' She couldn't speak about the flashback. Maybe it wasn't any such thing. Merely fantasy brought to light because of the situation they found themselves in.

'The bag. You can't place it under surveillance.'

'No. You're absolutely right. They might spot me.'

The dot remained stationary. It bothered her that the kidnapper hadn't collected the money immediately. They risked it being found by someone else. She checked the time. Half past two. It had been ten minutes since Jack dropped off the bag.

Catching her looking at her watch, he remarked, 'It's been a while. I wonder why they haven't collected it.'

'I was wondering the same thing.'

He headed for the sink and ran another cold glass of water, which he drank greedily, wiping his mouth with the back of his hand. She stared at her screen.

'Is the tracker broken?'

'I don't see how.' A sickening thought struck her. 'They might have removed it. They might have had some device for identifying trackers.'

'Oh, shit, shit, shit! No! This was our only chance to be led to Lyra.' He rested palms on the sink bowl, head bowed over it before slamming both hands down hard. 'No! We need to find out what the fuck is going on. I'm going back to see if the bag's gone.'

'You just said we shouldn't—'

'That was before you suggested the bloody tracker might be found.'

He marched out of the kitchen, Stacey following in his foot-steps. Before he reached the door, his phone rang. He came to a sharp halt, spinning around to face Stacey.

'I'm sending you an incentive for the rest of the money. It's outside your door,' said the robotic voice.

The line went dead.

Stacey pushed past Jack, yanked on the door handle. On the doorstep stood one high-rise lemon sneaker. The sight caused her mind to somersault . . .

*'What should we send Daddy? Another finger? An eye, maybe?'*

*She is paralysed with fear.*

*'He needs reminding we mean business.'*

*There's tugging at her left foot. 'No!' she screams and tries to kick away his hands.*

*'Calm down. I'm not going to cut off your foot. Not yet anyway.' He pulls at the pink laces on her Reebok high-top trainers, purchased only a month ago. Dad had given them a gimlet eye when she'd first worn them but kept his opinion of them to himself. Bella had encouraged her to buy them with her leftover birthday money. She had an identical pair that she loved. Stacey wasn't sure how she'd afforded them or if indeed she hadn't stolen them. Warmth evaporated from her foot as the boot was dragged off.*

*'This will do . . . for now.'*

*She couldn't ignore the menace behind his words. Part of her was surprised he hadn't chopped off another appendage or caused her further injury. The shoe seemed a mild option, especially as he'd already hurt her.*

'Stacey, are you okay? You've gone white as a sheet.'

She held out the shoe to him, hands quivering. The flashback had felt genuine, yet still she questioned its validity. She'd been told long ago that she'd lost a shoe. Was this vision a fabrication or were the floodgates to her mind being opened, the sight of the trainer acting like a key to something she'd locked away? If these were real recollections, they led to a terrifying possibility.

'I don't think we're looking for somebody who hates you,' she said. 'I think we're looking for the person who kidnapped me.'

# DAY TWO

## THURSDAY – 3 P.M.

Jack splashed cold water over his face and rubbed at it before turning back to Stacey. 'It can't be the same kidnapper. Why would they wait umpteen years to strike again and why target Lyra?'

'Because they didn't get paid the first time around? Because she's my stepdaughter?'

'I don't think so. It's a coincidence they sent one of her shoes. That's all. It isn't an original idea. I understand why you might think this is the same person, but it's unlikely, Stacey. You were kidnapped three decades ago. Are you seriously suggesting the person who abducted you waited thirty years to repeat the act?'

She blinked hard. She was overreacting. If she lost focus, she wouldn't be able to help Lyra. Movement on her phone screen brought much-needed clarity to the situation. 'The bag. It's on the move, along the promenade.'

In a trice, Jack was by her side. 'Cars aren't allowed on there and it's moving too quickly for it to be somebody walking or even running.'

'It could be a bike or an electric scooter. Come on, we might be able to catch up with them.'

She burst out of the door into the brightness, legs and arms pumping madly as she dashed to her car. By the time she'd started the engine, Jack had leapt into the passenger seat. She tossed the phone at him. 'Where's the bag now?'

'Still headed along the promenade. Stacey, we maybe shouldn't do this. If we're seen—'

'There's no other choice. We need to find out who has the bag.' Her tyres squealed as they accelerated onto the main road, past rows of elegant guest houses with vacancies signs visible in windows, over the first set of traffic lights, where she was slowed by a line of traffic held up at a pedestrian crossing.

'Hang on. The bag's stopped moving,' he said.

'Where is it now?'

'Somewhere near or on the jetty.' The lighthouse, part of the café at the end of the jetty, was already visible from where they waited. Behind it stood the white façade of the famous art deco hotel, whose curved frontage overlooked it and the beach. It was still a good mile away. Blood drummed in her ears as they inched forwards, now level with the artwork adorning the blue fencing of the former Frontierland, each picture relevant to Morecambe Bay: the old Polo Tower, seagulls, a replica of the famous Coronation Scot train poster. She turned her face away from a poster of a woman in an old-fashioned swimsuit, diving into a swimming pool. Unable to see over the wall that ran between them and the promenade, she willed the traffic to move quicker.

Jack strained against his seatbelt, head turning to the left as he scoured the tops of heads. 'They might not be where we think. They could have gone into the hotel. Lyra could even have been here, in Morecambe, all the time. Just up the road from home, for fuck's sake!'

They crawled past the large supermarket towards a roundabout. From here, they had a view of the jetty and the surrounding area, including the hotel Jack had mentioned.

'At this stage, we can't be sure of anything. For the moment, focus on what you can see. Look out for anyone riding a bike, scooter or any sort of electric transport,' she said.

'I can't see properly. The wall is obscuring my view. Pull over. I'm getting out. I'll try the jetty and path that runs past the RNLI, you head to the hotel car park and try the gardens next to it.'

She pulled over next to a gap in the wall, grateful for the inclement weather that was keeping the number of visitors unusually low. A group of individuals attired in hiking gear and carrying backpacks strode by, followed by a woman pushing a buggy. The beach was empty save for a couple, who strolled by the water's edge, leaving a line of footprints across the damp sand.

Jack tugged at the door handle then darted away before the door had slammed shut, swerving as he did so to avoid a woman rollerblading towards him.

Stacey snatched at the gear stick, her pulse like a kettledrum banging in her ears. The minutes it took to park felt like hours. Because Jack had her phone, she had no idea where he or the bag might be. At last, she got out, thundered across the tarmac, made for the expanse of grass in front of the hotel before coming to an abrupt halt. On the service road beside the hotel were three boys, no more than eleven or twelve, one astride a bike, a black carryall over his shoulder. She caught sight of a stern-faced Jack striding towards them. He looked like he wanted to thump the living daylights out of the trio. She broke into a trot to catch up with him.

'Jack, I'll speak to them.'

The determined set of his jaw said otherwise. He marched up to the one on the bike.

'Where did you get that bag?'

The boy gave Jack a surly look. 'It's mine.'

'That's not true, *is it*?' His steely tone caused the other boys to lower their gazes.

The boy wasn't as intimidated as his friends. 'It's mine now. Finders keepers.'

'You didn't *find* it. It was under some bushes near the playground. You must have dragged it out. Did you look around to see if it might belong to somebody nearby?'

The boy's jaw jutted. 'No. I found it. On the ground.'

Jack held out his hand. 'I didn't think so. Anyway, it's not yours. Hand it over.'

'No.'

Stacey stepped forward. 'Hi. Listen, this is very important. You did nothing wrong. You thought somebody had thrown the bag away. You're not in any trouble, but we really need to see inside it. Can I take a look at it?'

The boy half handed it to her. 'It's empty.'

'Then you won't mind if we look inside, will you?' said Jack, voice hard. The boy withdrew the bag, clutching it to his chest.

Jack continued, 'We're police officers. A bag exactly like this one has been reported as stolen. I'd like to look inside it. Or should we take you to the station and question you?'

The bravado evaporated. The other boys slunk away, leaving their friend to explain.

'I didn't steal it. It was on the ground beside a picnic table. Like I said.'

Stacey crouched down, unzipped the bag and shook her head. The money had gone. Jack turned to the youngster again. 'We have to return this to its owner. You can't keep it.'

'I don't want the stupid thing, anyway,' he replied. 'Can I go now?'

'Wait a minute. Did you spot anybody else nearby, before you saw the bag?' said Stacey.

'No. There was nobody about. It was just lying there.'

'You sure you saw nobody?' Jack growled.

'Nobody. I wouldn't have taken it if there'd been somebody there.'

He looked slightly tearful, and Stacey wasn't happy at how Jack had spoken to the kid. She rummaged in her pocket, drew out three one-pound coins, held them in her open palm. 'Sorry about the bag. Why don't you buy yourself a drink or burger or something?'

'Ok-ay.' He grabbed the money and began pedalling.

'You didn't need to give him anything.'

'I felt a bit sorry for him. Didn't you notice how threadbare his top was and his trainers look like they're ready for the bin. The bag was probably a good find for him.'

'You should have let him keep it, then.'

'I didn't want him to find the tracking device.'

'For all the good it did us.' He stopped, raised his palms. 'Really, Stace, what the fuck just happened?'

'You're upset? Me too. Why did they move the money from the bag?'

Jack wasn't listening. 'That bag contained every penny I could lay my hands on. We're fucked now. They'll kill her.'

'We'll have to raise the rest of the money,' she said, quietly.

'How? How on earth will we do that? We can't go to your dad.'

'I don't know. Give me a chance to think it through.'

He placed his hands on her shoulders. 'You're right. We'll work something out. There must be a way of getting the remainder of the ransom money.'

She was taken back to their first date, when he'd walked her home and put his hands on her shoulders in the same way before asking if she would consider a second date. Back then, a light current had seemingly transferred from his fingertips to her heart, making it beat rapidly. This time she wanted to break away from his grip.

There was no spark, only desire to shake him off and focus on the business at hand: getting the money and rescuing Lyra. All they'd bought was some time. She bent to pick up the bag, breaking the connection.

'You ought to collect your car. I'll drop you off at Happy Mount Park,' she said.

As they drove, he lolled against the headrest. Stacey stared at the indigo sea, the exact colour of Lyra's eyes. She didn't speak again until they pulled up beside the Porsche.

'For the time being, she's safe. They have the fifty thousand. Like it or not, I'm bringing Ashraf on board.'

'No.'

She was getting sick of his protestations. He knew Ashraf had already helped with the tracking device. Jack was behaving as he had done when they were married: obstructive and controlling. He might have been able to manipulate her back then, but this wasn't about them, it was about Lyra.

'Why the fuck not?' Without letting him reply, she launched a pre-emptive strike. 'The tracker plan didn't work. We haven't been able to trace the kidnapper's phone. We have nothing from CCTV. We can't find her by ourselves! Stop with all this I-can-do-it-alone shit. We need someone who has experience in this sort of thing.'

He began to shake his head. Stacey placed her hand on his knee. 'Jack, please. It's killing me that we're getting nowhere and she's out there somewhere, in heaven knows what state. We must find her and the only way left to us is to bring in somebody with expertise. Who knows how to tackle a situation like this. Anyway, he's already involved. I asked him to look for Mark.'

'You did?'

'Yes.' She squared up to Jack, waiting for him to object.

Instead, he pulled at his nose, snuffled, and replied, 'Okay.'

'Thank you. It gives us a marginally better chance of working out who's masterminding this.'

Jack nodded. 'We should prepare a plan B though. Just in case this bloke can't fare any better than we have so far. I've been thinking.'

'And?'

'We really need to lay our hands on the rest of the ransom. I might have an idea but I'm not sure you'll approve of it.'

She should ask him what he was thinking of, or say she'd persuade Henry to lend or give them the money, yet the words wouldn't come. She couldn't promise what she knew would be impossible.

The air was heavy with silence until she spoke again.

'Don't do anything stupid.'

'I might not have any other choice, Stace.' With that, he opened the door and plodded back to his car.

She watched him drive away, berating herself for not offering again to speak to her father. She was letting him down, allowing him to undoubtedly go some nefarious route involving money-lenders. The only way to prevent him from getting involved in some risky business was to find Lyra. Spurred by concern, she rang Ashraf, who agreed to meet her on the stone jetty.

Back at the coast, she purchased a takeaway coffee and returned to where they'd found the boy on the bike. This time she waited close to a bird sculpture, one of several in the vicinity, her mind turning over events. The delivery of one of Lyra's sneakers was another threat to increase the pressure on Jack, to ensure he came up with the full amount. It was having the desired effect. And poor Lyra! How must she be feeling?

A seagull called out noisily, breaking her reverie. Over the years, Stacey had come to recognise the birds made a variety of calls and were big communicators. This one was attracting the attention of others nearby, creating a persistent *ha-ha-ha-ha* like manic laughter. The gulls were part and parcel of this coastline and although she was wary about eating in their presence, she never worried, like some did, about them attacking.

Remembering she hadn't yet contacted Freya, she tried the John Radcliffe hospital, where she was informed that while there were no phones on hospital wards, a message could be passed onto the patient. She declined the offer.

She sipped her coffee and ambled along the jetty, mulling over what had happened so far. They'd wasted a day on a plan that had gone wrong. It troubled her that the kidnapper hadn't simply taken the bag. Instead, in transferring the contents, they'd increased the possibility of being spotted or exposed. And on top of that, they'd come to Jack's house, soon after he returned from the drop-off, to deliver Lyra's lemon sneaker. Why would they risk being seen? Unless an accomplice had delivered it and the envelope containing Lyra's hair. Could there be two abductors?

She needed somebody to bounce her ideas off, and that person soon appeared – Ashraf.

She lifted her cup. 'Fancy one?'

'Nah. I'm good, thanks. What's going on, Stacey?'

She explained as best she could, while in the foreground black and white oystercatchers with their distinctive bright red beaks patrolled the shoreline, in search of cockles and mussels. Ashraf said nothing until she'd given him every detail, then he leant against the pale blue rails and gave her a tired smile.

'I'm not sure this is a good idea – you, me. I can put you onto my work partner or another guy altogether. They're both trustworthy.'

'But I don't know them. You and I, we have history. You understand what I'm going through. You know how I feel about Lyra. For anyone else, this would just be an investigation.'

'Stacey, when we broke up, when you broke up with me, you . . . I don't need to go over this, do I?'

'I know I hurt you. I just wasn't right for you.'

He rolled his eyes. 'Hurt doesn't begin to cover it. I'd have waited. However long it took, I'd have waited. Anyway, it's pointless going back over it. Let's say I'm in a different place now. I have a family. I can't afford to become . . . sidetracked.'

'You didn't object when I asked for help with the tracker and looking into Jack's business, or when I asked you to find out about Mark's whereabouts.'

'The tracker was a one-off, for old times' sake. I shouldn't have agreed to look into Mark.'

'Jeez, Ashraf, my stepdaughter is being held hostage. The monster who has her is demanding more money than we can get our hands on. I'm scared out of my skull that the kidnapper will carry out their threat to kill her and you are crying off because of what we had?'

'Not because of what we had. Seeing you again. Being with you. It isn't healthy.'

'Ashraf, I have no one else I can turn to. If you ever had any feelings for me, help me now, I beg you.'

He pushed his hands deeper into his pockets, studied her face. She didn't look away, willing him to agree. At last, he dropped his head, exhaled loudly. 'Oh, fuck it. Okay. I'll help.'

Relief flooded her veins. 'Thank you.'

He lifted his head. 'So, this is about Jack?'

'No, it's about Lyra.'

'You and he okay these days?'

'I haven't seen him in a long while. He seems . . . different.'

He nodded. 'You know how I feel about him, don't you? I'll do whatever I can, but not for Jack. I haven't any time for him, not after the way he behaved towards you. I'll do it for you and Lyra.'

'Thank you again. I really need your input. Jack is all over the place and I've made a hash of things so far.'

He folded his arms. 'The tracker was a good idea. Your plan should have worked. It's definitely strange that they removed the money from the bag.'

'I thought so too.'

'Did you actually watch Jack count out the money before placing it in the bag?'

'I saw the brown packages. He told me each contained a thousand pounds. But no. I didn't see the money.'

'Then we can't be sure there was fifty grand in it. Could have been bits of torn-up newspaper.'

'That makes no sense. The kidnapper would kill her if they didn't get paid.'

'Yes. Er, Stacey, what I'm suggesting is Jack might be spinning you a tale. All of this kidnapping story is for your benefit.'

'No! That's too twisted. Why? Why would he do that?'

'To wriggle his way back into your life.'

'That's a fairly dramatic way of going about things.'

'He certainly behaved dramatically in the past.' Ashraf gave a slight shrug to drill home his point. 'It's not me being anti-Jack, even though I am. Just saying you should consider the possibility. You only have his say-so there was money in those packets.'

'I . . . No.'

'And he didn't contact you between arriving at the Eric Morecambe statue and leaving the bag at the drop-off point.'

She shook her head. 'It didn't matter. He knew I was tracking the bag. The kidnapper had eyes on him, warned him off, so he didn't dare make any call. At the time, he was being sent from one place to another, first made to drive and then run to each location within a specified time. He hadn't time or energy to keep me updated.'

'Look, I'm sorry to have to bring it up. I'm a private investigator, Stacey. It's my job to consider every angle. Humour me. He never wanted you to split up. He begged you not to divorce him. He laid it on thick. This could be a desperate attempt to try and win you over: distraught dad who needs your help, you give it to him, fall for him again, then Lyra is found safe . . . boom, happy ending.'

She picked at the cardboard wrapper on her cup. 'Do you know how nuts that sounds?'

'Yes. Won't you at least consider it?'

'No. He knows I'd find out, and would never forgive him for it. He knows how I feel about Lyra.'

The wrapper pulled away in her fingers. She stared at the ribbed cardboard. 'Besides, you haven't seen him. He couldn't be faking his reactions. He's genuinely terrified of Lyra getting hurt. I've seen the video, heard her screams. This is all real, Ashraf. There are many ways to win somebody over, but not this way. Drop the idea. It's ridiculous. Concentrate on helping us get Lyra back.'

'Don't be annoyed with me for suggesting it. It's just you didn't actually see any money.'

'I'm not annoyed. The money was in the packets.'

'Okay, well, all the same, you ought to get the hair in the envelope DNA tested to confirm it's Lyra's.' As she opened her mouth to speak, he showed his palms. 'Listen, I'm not saying it isn't hers. If this was a police investigation, it would have been sent immediately to the lab as standard procedure. Just saying. That's all.'

She pressed forefingers to her temples to dispel the throbbing that was beginning. Involving Ashraf, who despised Jack, might have been a mistake. However, now she'd told him everything, she would have to run with it. 'Of course, you're right. I have it with me. I took it off the table. Seeing it there was too upsetting. Where should I go with it?'

'I can arrange for it to be tested. I know a civilian who could do this fairly quickly.'

She rummaged in her bag before handing the envelope containing Lyra's hair to him. 'Thanks.' She hesitated a moment, wondering if she ought to confess her inner fears to Ashraf. She started with, 'Everything we've uncovered points to Mark Small being behind Lyra's kidnapping.'

'It would seem so.'

Deciding to chance it, she continued, 'All the same, I . . . I'm not sure we shouldn't be looking elsewhere.'

'Where?'

She counted off the items on one hand. 'The video, her hair, then her sneaker. Mark wouldn't know those details. I think there's a possibility that we might be looking for the same person who kidnapped me.'

Ashraf didn't respond. She held her breath as he lowered his gaze. She knew him well enough to know he was digesting the information. He tackled everything in a concise, analytical manner and clearly had doubts about her hunch.

'Stacey, you went through an ordeal so horrific your brain shut it out completely. Sending strands of hair from hostages, or items of their clothing as proof of life is not unusual. It's understandable your mind would make a leap between what is happening to Lyra and what possibly happened to you all those years ago. Honestly, the statistical likelihood of the same kidnapper striking again after all this time is small, and you should concentrate on more likely scenarios than a ghost from the past. Ask yourself: why wait thirty years to take Lyra when she is no longer a major part of your life?

Do you really imagine your kidnapper would have been keeping tabs on you all this time?'

She clung to his words. Ashraf had been the voice of reason when she'd been floundering in her relationship with Jack. He'd been her rock then and again today.

'Thanks. I needed to hear that. I've been so . . . confused. These *memories* have been popping up all day, discombobulating me. Okay, we'll follow up on Mark, who is our most likely suspect.' She pulled up the capture from the CCTV footage of the man beside the dog-friendly beach during the time the girls were there. 'This could be him. What else have you found out about him so far?'

'Only that he drives a 2003 Ford van. As far as I can gather, it didn't leave the boatyard in Upper Heyford, where it's remained for the last few days. However, if we're tossing about theories, then it's feasible he could have used other transport to ensure his van wasn't picked up by any ANPR cameras on the motorway or main roads.'

'I suppose he could have come by train then hired a car . . . or what about Freya's car? If she's in hospital, it's unlikely she'd be using it. He could have borrowed it.'

Two children raced towards them, before chasing each other around and around the large seabird sculpture close to Stacey and Ashraf. It didn't seem that long ago that Lyra had been the same age as those children. Now she was a teenager, experiencing the same horror Stacey had in July 1992.

The reality of what she was dealing with hit home. She had to find Lyra at all costs.

She let out a lengthy sigh. 'Keep digging for information about Mark. One thing struck me. Lyra left Kelly's house on her bike. Wednesday morning, after he got the video, Jack retraced the route she'd have ridden, yet he didn't find it. If the abductor took both Lyra and her bike, they'd need a decent-sized vehicle or a bike carrier. Is there any chance you could get your hands on surveillance footage close to or around her friend Kelly's house and see if there were any potential vehicles in the vicinity Tuesday evening, around the time she was snatched?'

'I have friends who might help.'

She gave him Kelly's address. 'You on board with this, then?'

'I am. Does Jack know about me?'

'Yes, and he wasn't happy about it.'

'Can't say I'm over the moon to be helping him. Does he know about . . . us?'

'I don't think so. By the time we became an item, he and I were separated, barely speaking and headed for the divorce courts. What about your partner?'

'My *wife* knows about you, but she doesn't know about me working for you. I'd rather it stayed that way.'

'You're not wearing a wedding ring.'

'I don't like wearing rings. That's the only reason. Anyway, I'd better get going. How long do you think we have?'

'A couple of days, maybe three. I don't know for certain. Jack hasn't been told when to make the final drop. Ashraf, I'm utterly terrified I'll stuff this up.' She chewed on her bottom lip. By playing amateur detectives, they were endangering a child's life.

He laid a hand on her arm. 'We won't.'

She returned his smile. 'Better get going. I'll keep in touch.'

She crumpled her empty cup and threw it in the bin by the car park. Ashraf had sown a seed of doubt in her mind, regarding the packets of money. She needed to talk to Jack in person. His car wasn't outside his house, so she rang him to discover he'd gone into work for a last-minute client meeting. She agreed to meet at his office afterwards.

Stacey had only visited the offices of Corrigan & Babcock, a twenty-minute walk from where she worked, on a couple of occasions. Jack had been of the opinion that spouses shouldn't turn up at places of work, so during their marriage she'd never dropped by ad hoc, only meeting him outside in the small public park, where they'd often grab a quick lunch when the weather was suitable, or at a restaurant in town. The well-maintained green space was usually only used by those who worked in one of the three-storey, elegant terraced houses, secreted in a pedestrian zone. Each building sported a bright red door. Outside the one she was facing was a brass sign bearing the name of her ex-husband's law firm.

The door opened and a man emerged, briefcase in hand, followed swiftly by Jack. He caught sight of her and beckoned her inside.

'I got an urgent call from a client and had to come in.' He spoke as he led the way through an empty waiting room.

'It's quiet,' she remarked.

'We shut at five.' He held a door open for her and she found herself in his office, the desk empty apart from a large, silver-framed photograph of Lyra.

'Any news?' he asked.

'I need to run a DNA test on the hair in the envelope.'

'What?'

'We can't be certain it's Lyra's.'

His mouth flapped open. 'Of course it's hers. It's the same colour, length. It's hers!'

'It might not be.'

'We don't have time to piss about. By the time we've found out it is hers, she could be dead!'

'We should still check.'

'What about her shoe? That's definitely hers.'

'Again, it might not be. They're a popular brand.'

He rested his hands on the back of a large leather chair and released an angry sigh. 'Stacey, please stop this craziness. There's no time to mess about analysing hair or shoes. The tracker idea failed. We're soon going to be left with no other option than to pay the ransom. We should focus on how we're going to do that instead of trying to hunt down Mark Small, or link this to Freya. Getting that sneaker has shaken things up. It's made me realise we really could lose her.'

She ignored his plea. There was no way of sugar-coating what she wanted to say, so she blurted out, 'Did you actually put fifty thousand pounds into those packages?'

He raised both hands. 'I don't believe this! Why would I *not* hand over the money? Yes, of course there was fifty thousand pounds in the bag. Yes! If there wasn't, wouldn't they have killed her and dumped her and the bag outside the door or rung me or—?'

She rubbed her forehead, which had creased with tension. She was going about this the wrong way, upsetting him further. 'Okay. Stop. I can't think clearly. I'm worried sick too. Do you object to me running a DNA test on the hair?'

'Whoa! Slow down a second. You're grilling me like I'm a police suspect. Where is all this doubt coming from? I thought we were on the same page, working together to rescue Lyra.'

A kidnapping unit would question everyone, including herself, to get a better understanding of what was taking place. They'd have sent the hair and sneaker to the lab by now. They'd have run background checks on Jack and Stacey and all of Lyra's relatives. 'I *am* working to get her back. I just can't make sense of what happened earlier.'

His voice was tight. 'For the record, I put the money in the bag as you suggested. I followed instructions to the letter. I left it exactly where I was supposed to, under the bench nearest the promenade. I have no sodding idea why the person who is behind this didn't take the damn bag, as well as the money.' His slammed a fist against the desk with force. 'Are you accusing me of something, Stace?'

She replied with, 'I want to get the hair tested.'

'Then test it! Test it if it'll get you to see sense and stop thinking I'm the bad guy in all of this. It's idiotic. I came to you for help, remember? I was and I still am, scared witless. I . . . came . . . to . . . you.'

The vein in his temple swelled and throbbed. His lips were a thin scratch in his face. 'I left the fucking money under the bench.'

Their argument was interrupted by a rap on the door. Jack gave her a sharp look and shouted, 'Come in.'

A man in blue overalls shuffled in. He raised heavy brows in apology. 'Sorry to bother you, Mr Corrigan. This was dropped off for you. The courier said it was urgent.' His spade-like hands almost obscured the cardboard box.

'Cheers, Tariq. Leave it there, would you?'

He placed it on the table beside the door, nodded a farewell and left, his work boots softly swishing against the thick carpet as he departed.

As soon as the door was shut once again, Jack hissed, 'How could you even think I'd screw up? This is *my* daughter we're talking about.' He emphasised the point by stabbing his chest with two fingers, a solid *thump-thump-thump*. Each sound distancing them further, reminding her she had no biological attachment to the girl she had once cared for as her own.

He pointed a finger at her and wagged it as he spoke. 'I banked on you, Stacey. This entire money-tracking idea was yours and yet, for some unfathomable reason, you suspect I didn't hand over the money. What do *you* think would now be happening to Lyra if I hadn't delivered that bag, eh?' She wasn't going to back down or apologise. She'd needed to be certain about him.

A vein in his temple pulsed and red spots appeared on his cheeks. 'That's it! I'll deal with this on my own. I don't want you involved any more. Or your savings for that matter. I'll work something out so I can pay the rest of the ransom myself and get my girl back.'

When she didn't move, he marched to the door and held it open. 'Go on. Leave.'

'In any investigation—'

'Out. I can't cope with this on top of everything else. I needed you with me, not against me. I thought . . . I felt . . . We . . . Oh, never mind.' His eyes captured hers again. She understood what he'd been trying to say. They'd made headway, were once more a team and she'd broken the fragile trust they'd begun rebuilding.

She hesitated by the doorway.

'I believe you.'

'Too late, Stacey.' He turned his back on her, picked up the box and returned to his desk. She took her leave, stopping in the waiting room, unwilling to walk away from the place or the situation. She'd screwed up, not Jack. It had been her suggestion to hand over part of the ransom. Now she'd lost his confidence and cooperation. Oblivious to Tariq, in the corner of the room, she kicked at a chair, cursing loudly.

'Everything okay?' he said.

'Fine. Thanks.' She pulled her car keys from her pocket and made for the door.

He headed her off. 'I couldn't help noticing. Mr Corrigan was bawling you out, wasn't he? Don't take it to heart. He gets het up at times. I'm sure he'll explode one day – *whoosh!*'

She cracked a strained smile at his attempt at humour. 'Yes, it's been a tough couple of years. The pandemic has taken a toll on us all.'

'Tell me about it. Both my wife and I lost our jobs. I was lucky Mr Corrigan took me on or we'd have been completely stuffed. I used to be an engineer, now I clean toilets, hoover and dust, and count my lucky stars I have a job at all. Which I had better get back to before I get it in the neck again. Cheerio.'

He picked up his bucket of cleaning materials and disappeared through a door behind reception, leaving her to fumble for car keys and head to the front door.

'Stacey! Stop!'

She spun around. Jack held the cardboard box in his hands. He staggered towards her like a drunk. Her heart jackhammered against her ribcage. She knew even before she looked inside the box. He couldn't speak, hands trembling as he held out the box to her. She lifted the lid and saw what she had already guessed would be inside – a little finger, a pinkie, with a nail neatly painted in yellow.

# DAY TWO

## THURSDAY – 6 P.M.

Jack, with his head in his hands, let out a lengthy moan. Stacey had reacted quickly, determined to get the severed finger into a freezer. A warm, severed limb could be reattached within twelve hours but if it was kept cold, would survive two days or in some cases even longer. The shock of what they'd received soon passed. The bloody finger was a convincing latex fake, authentic in both size and appearance.

She poured brandy from a bottle used to entertain certain of his clients, then pushed the glass towards him.

'Drink it. You're in shock.'

The reception bell rang. Ashraf had arrived. Stacey fetched him into the office.

'Jack, this is Ashraf Khan. He's the private investigator I told you about. He's one of the best.'

'I remember that drugs bust back in 2018. Massive haul, wasn't it? I forget how many millions of that crap you guys managed to pull off the streets, but it was impressive. Nice to meet you, Ashraf. Thanks for coming over. And for helping us out. I don't know what the hell to do next. Fucker scared the absolute shit out of me with that fake finger.'

Ashraf shook Jack's extended hand. 'I'm sorry for what you're going through. Must be a nightmare.'

'No kidding. You got kids?'

'Yeah, one. A girl.'

'Then you'll understand.'

Ashraf nodded.

'What are your thoughts on this latest development?' asked Jack.

'The way I see it, this twisted bastard must have known you were at work, or they'd have had the box couriered to your home address,' he reasoned.

'Then they've been watching my movements. They'll probably know you're here right now.' Jack's voice was flat. He slugged the amber liquid, pulled a face.

Ashraf's face was a mask. 'Nah. I gave the place a thorough once-over beforehand. Nobody's out there. Even if they were staking you out, I could be anybody, a mate dropping by, a client, or even a work colleague.'

Jack shrugged, then asked, 'Well, what do you think our next move should be, Ashraf? We were considering the possibility of this being my other ex-wife and her boyfriend . . . or just her boyfriend.'

Stacey cleared her throat. 'We might have to change tack. That finger. It's . . . made me think we're looking on the wrong lines. For what it's worth, I think this has something to do with me and what happened to me when I was a teenager.'

Ashraf made a soft clicking sound with his tongue. 'The bastard just played a cruel trick. Granted, they maybe know you were married to Jack. They might even know about your disfigurement, but my money's on the fact they simply wanted to scare Jack into paying up. You can pick these things up anywhere online. They're used for pranks or at Halloween. I wouldn't read too much into it.'

Stacey refused to be mollified. 'I disagree. It's starting to look likely: first they cut off her hair, then leave her sneaker on the doorstep and now this—'

Ashraf shook his head. 'We talked about this, Stacey.'

'Before that rubber finger was delivered! I don't want us to screw up because we overlooked or ignored something that was right under our noses. At best, these things are coincidences. At worst, they're sinister clues that shouldn't be cast off without some consideration.'

Ashraf squeezed his nostrils together, a gesture with which she was familiar. It indicated he was considering all possibilities. He pulled his fingers away slowly, leaving white indentations on either side of his squashed nose. 'Okay, but information about your kidnapping will be readily available. It wouldn't require a great deal of detective work to figure out what happened to you while you were being held hostage.' He glanced at her hand to drive home his point.

'The hair. The shoe. The finger,' she repeated.

'Your case was splashed over the newspapers at the time. The abduction of an eminent judge's daughter was big news for a while.'

She shook her head to dislodge the sudden *clickety-click-click* as an imaginary projector whirred into life, throwing pictures upon a screen in her mind . . .

*'Out of the way!' Her father cocoons her in his arms, pulling her towards him to protect her from the cameras. She wants to turn around and race back to the quiet, brightly lit hospital room, where she's been insulated for the last four weeks.*

*A police officer clears away the sea of faces and another one flanks her left side. She is ushered towards their car, where the door is agape. She tumbles inside. Dad slips in next to her. Surrounded by reporters who bang on the window and roof, he remains stony-faced, starts the engine and edges the Jaguar forwards until they begin to fall away.*

*'Animals!' he snarls, accelerating. The people move back further, apart from one photographer, who runs beside the car, camera lifted to the passenger window, and she stares at him, hoping he won't stumble and fall in front of the wheels.*

*'Scumbags.'*

*She sits in silence. Her father has told her they're not going to return home, to the road where she was snatched. They're going to make a fresh start. It will help stop any nightmares and she'll be safe from whomever took her. She is numb.*

*'Dad, will I see my friends again?'*

*He doesn't look at her. 'You saw what happened when we tried to leave the hospital, Stacey. Your life will be hell. We'll be pursued by reporters every time we try to leave the house. Your school friends will be hounded and persuaded to divulge every secret they know about you. Your life will be laid bare, and everyone will talk about what happened to you, stop and stare at you if they see you. You won't be able to forget about what happened, not ever. For your sake, it will be better if we move. The place I've found in Staffordshire is lovely. It's surrounded by fields. You could learn to ride a horse. You'll soon make new friends.'*

*'What about Bella? Couldn't we stop to let her know?'*

*'Bella hasn't once rung to find out how you are. I wouldn't waste your time.'*

*She stares out of the window, at hedgerows racing past in a green blur, and wonders who Bella will take with her to the caravan.*

She blinked the images away. One headline had read, TERROR FINALLY OVER FOR KIDNAPPED TEENAGER. How wrong it had been.

She'd lived in a paralysed fugue for months, scared of every shadow and especially terrified of the dark. Her mind shut down, then no matter how many times the police, her father or the psychiatrist with velvet soft eyes had attempted to coax information from her, she had no recollection of anything from first thing that morning she was taken to finding herself in a hospital bed. Burying the horror had been the only way for her to move forward.

Ashraf's unflustered voice flowed over her as she wrestled with panic that coiled in the pit of her stomach. 'It's still highly plausible that Mark Small is behind this abduction. I asked a fellow PI, who lives in Oxford, to check on him. Even though Mark's phone is transmitting a signal from the area around his houseboat, he isn't on it.'

Jack looked up from his glass. 'Then Mark might be here in Morecambe?'

'What car does Freya drive?' Ashraf asked.

Jack answered, 'A Škoda Superb Estate.'

Ashraf grunted, then said, 'Large enough to accommodate a bicycle.' It was a statement rather than a question.

Jack sat up straight. He began gesticulating as he added to the new theory. 'Yes. He could have borrowed it, driven to Morecambe, and picked up Lyra. She wouldn't suspect a thing if he came up with some reason for collecting her . . . maybe even something to do with Freya. She'd get into the car without question.'

'It makes sense that he'd know Lyra's whereabouts, yet there's something about that rubber finger that doesn't fit the picture. Why would he send you it?' said Stacey.

'To scare me. Make sure I pay the rest of the ransom. It bloody well worked too.'

Ashraf nodded. 'He's right, Stacey. Who knew you were here, Jack?'

Jack traced the rim of the glass before taking another swig. 'Nobody. I hadn't planned on coming into the office until Tariq rang to say there was a client in reception who wanted to see me urgently.'

Ashraf cocked his head. 'And Tariq gave you the box?'

'Yes. A courier dropped it off. Tariq brought it through to me.'

'I doubt it came via a genuine courier service.' Ashraf pulled out a notepad from his pocket. 'Tell me about Tariq.'

'There's not much to tell. About four months ago, the cleaning company I was using went out of business, so I advertised for a cleaner. He applied. He's a grafter. Doesn't complain.'

Stacey took over. 'He told me he was an engineer before he was made redundant. Both he and his wife lost jobs because of the pandemic. Jack, how well do you know him?'

'I don't really. I haven't paid him much attention. He cleans the offices. That's it.'

'You ever given him the brush-off?' Ashraf asked Jack.

'What is this? Are you making out I'm some sort of shithead because I don't talk to the cle—'

Stacey interrupted him, 'Tariq told me you got "het up" at times. Why would he say that?'

Jack shrugged. 'Okay, so I might have been a bit sharpish with him one time. He barged in while I was in a meeting with a . . . client.'

'Tariq works after hours, doesn't he? Was it one of those *extra* clients you've been seeing?' Stacey asked.

Jack had the grace to look sheepish. 'Yes.'

'And that man who was leaving when I arrived—?'

'Yes. Him too. He was one of my private clients.'

'Your client might have—'

Jack stopped her with a shake of his head. 'There's no way he's responsible. He owns huge villas in Spain and the South of France, a jet and is worth somewhere in the region of sixty million. I've been helping him set up trust funds so most of it will go to his grandchildren, not HMRC—'

Ashraf interrupted, 'Hang on a sec. Tariq rang you to tell you the client was there. Am I right?'

'Yes.'

'Then he knows you moonlight?' Ashraf said.

Jack half laughed. 'I doubt he's worked out some of the clients are off the books.'

'He's not a fool. He sees comings and goings, hears voices in the office. Tell me, how do you pay him?'

Jack didn't answer.

'Cash in hand, isn't it?' said Ashraf.

'He's trustworthy. He needs the cash.'

'Which I assume you take out of your office safe to pay him!'

'None of which gives him cause to kidnap my daughter.'

'No, but he might harbour some resentment towards you. He knows about the out-of-hours work you do and probably suspects you keep cash in the safe,' Ashraf replied.

'I pay him what he's due.'

'How much is that? Fifteen? Twenty pounds an hour? Meanwhile, he believes you are raking in money and watches you drive off every day in a top-of-the-range Porsche, while he cleans your office and toilets,' Ashraf added.

Jack's face flushed. 'Are you taking a pop at me?'

'Personally, I don't give a shit how much you earn or what you drive. The fact is Tariq might see things differently.' He made another note, seemingly unperturbed by Jack's outburst. 'Okay, that gives us two potential suspects, Mark and Tariq.'

'No. Three,' said Stacey. 'Whoever abducted me.'

'We can't chase those phantoms, Stacey.' His voice was gentle. He alone knew how much Jack had damaged her self-worth, how rejected she had felt by her father and how frightened she was that one day she would remember what had transpired during her abduction, gaining knowledge that might tip her over the edge.

He turned his attention back to Jack, who was once again nursing his glass.

'Of course, the kidnapper could simply have spotted your car wasn't in its usual parking place outside your house and deduced you were at work, then pretended to be a courier.'

Stacey fiddled with the plume ring on her middle finger. 'You can't question Tariq about the courier without making him suspicious.'

'Don't worry,' said Ashraf, pocketing his notebook. 'Leave this with me.'

She stroked the surface of the ring, an adjustable feather in silver, a symbol of love, guidance and support. 'I have another avenue I want to pursue. Jack, you ought to go home. Do you want a lift?'

'No, thanks. I'll stay here for a while longer. Collect my thoughts. Have another drink. I'll get a taxi when I'm ready. Thanks again, Ashraf.'

'Thank me when we find your daughter.'

Jack gave a solemn nod, got to his feet and opened the door for them. He stopped Stacey as she drew level. 'And thank you. I almost lost it altogether when I looked inside that parcel.'

She gave him a small smile. 'Me too. I'm just so glad it was a horrible prank.'

He drew closer, kissed his fingers and laid them briefly on her forehead. 'I never deserved you.'

She didn't want to hear any more. The touch of his fingertips made her skin crawl. Ashraf had been right about Jack not wanting to grant her a divorce. He'd fought against it for a long time. In Stacey's mind, it hadn't been because he loved her, rather that he didn't like losing.

She nodded dumbly before racing to catch up with Ashraf, who was waiting beside her car. 'I'm worried about leaving Jack alone. I have a feeling he's going to try and get his hands on the full ransom and pay off the kidnapper,' she said.

'If he does, then Lyra will be released, and you'll no longer be riding this emotional roller coaster.' Back in the day, his no-nonsense, say-it-as-it-was approach had apparently riled his fellow officers, yet she found it refreshing. It wasn't that he lacked emotion, merely he saw situations and people for what they were.

'He'd have to go to some seriously dangerous people to raise the amount of cash he needs. He'll never be able to pay it all back and you know what happens to people who renege on deals.'

'And that bothers you why? Do you have feelings for him?'

'No! I don't. He's Lyra's father. I wouldn't want anything nasty to happen to him. For her sake. I was thinking of her. Really.'

Ashraf stared into the distance. 'I don't know. Prejudice aside, there's something about Jack that bugs me. He could have gone about this in a variety of ways, yet he ran straight to you for help. Don't you think it's weird?'

'He's terrified police involvement will get her killed, and for what it's worth I totally get where he's coming from.'

'Exactly my point. You're the only person he could go to who *would* understand and try to help.'

'What are you saying?'

'Just tread carefully. I saw the way he looked at you. He's not over you.'

A man whistled loudly, and she jumped slightly as a panting spaniel shot past them, its feathery tail swishing against her leg to bound after its master. She turned her head, pretending to look at it so Ashraf wouldn't notice the sudden reddening of her cheeks.

'I wouldn't want you to go through all that shit again with him.'

'That's not going to happen.' She gave a small smile.

'Glad to hear it. Catch you later.'

He had the walk of a man brimming with confidence, comfortable with who he was and who didn't take crap from anyone. It was what had first attracted her to him. But Ashraf was spoken for. She'd missed her chance with him. She looked back at the office block almost hidden behind the trees. Jack couldn't possibly imagine she would want to restart their relationship. Yet, his small displays of affection suggested otherwise. She would have to put him straight on the matter, but not until Lyra was home, safe and sound.

She drove under the arches at St George's Quay, where pedestrians walked beside the banks of the River Lune. Her gaze landed on a girl in a bright red top, riding along the towpath on a bicycle, and she yearned for things to return to how they were forty-eight hours earlier, before any of this had happened. She checked the time: almost seven o'clock. She wrestled with an idea that had begun bobbing in her head soon after she'd opened the cardboard box and seen the severed finger. There was someone she had to speak to. The person who had rescued her years ago.

Retired DS Daniella Kennedy, known as Danni, had left the force in 1993 to pursue a career in education, transferring her valuable skills to the classroom. She was one part of the past Stacey hadn't suppressed in the annals of her mind.

Danni had visited her in hospital, kept in contact with the odd phone call and Christmas card, and every year, on the anniversary of her rescue, sent a bunch of gladioli. When Stacey asked why, Danni had explained the flowers, also known as 'sword lilies' because of their blade-like leaves, symbolised hope and strength, and Stacey was to remember how courageous she had been during the ordeal. Stacey didn't fully understand why Danni had extended such kindness until she discovered that only three weeks earlier, her sixteen-year-old sister had lost her life in a car accident. A psychiatrist would explain it as transference, an unconscious redirection of Danni's feelings for her sister being shifted to Stacey, but the way Stacey looked at it was they had been thrown together by fate.

She dialled Danni's number.

'Stacey! This is an unexpected pleasure.'

'I'm sorry, I haven't phoned for a catch-up, even though we're due one. I'm ringing because I need to talk to you about the past . . . about my kidnapping.'

'Why?'

'I need to access some memories and . . . fill in some holes.'

'Surely you'd be better off with a therapist.'

'No time to go through that. And I haven't had great results in the past. You're my friend. You know what happened to me, or at least some of it. I thought you could guide me through what you know. See if it jolted anything. Ideally, I'd have dropped by to visit you and Paul to discuss, but with you living miles away and me needing to act quickly, I thought maybe we could talk over the phone, or FaceTime, if it's convenient. I'm afraid this is urgent.'

'Well, you're in luck. Thanks to the Easter school holidays, we're not in Cornwall. We're visiting the family in Blackpool. And I don't suppose Paul will mind if I slope off for a couple of hours to come and see you. You at home?'

Stacey felt some of the tension in her neck and shoulders release. Danni's voice was like a balm. Seeing her would help focus Stacey. She could maybe help sort out what was important and what wasn't. 'No, but it would be great to see you. How about we meet up at Lancaster service station? It's pretty much the halfway point between us?'

'Hang on a sec.'

She heard muffled voices, and then Danni was back on the line.

'Paul's cool with it. I can be there in about forty minutes.'

'Perfect, I'll meet you outside the Costa Coffee.'

Stacey eased the remaining tension in her neck with small stretches, side to side, each generating a small crunch, before tilting her head back. Above her, invisible hands had painted wide, high stratus clouds, mares' tails, across the skies, turning them milky white. The day was settling into evening and Lyra had been missing for two days. How much suffering would the kidnappers inflict on her before the next twenty-four hours were up? She hoped with every atom of her being that she was wrong in assuming the girl's abduction was linked to her own. She'd managed to survive, but Lyra might not.

The service station was unique, a love-hate structure with an unusual hexagonal tower on the northbound side. Some likened it to a spaceship, others called it a 1960s concrete monstrosity, but Stacey liked the twenty-nine-metre structure because it was designed to resemble an air traffic control tower and anything to do with aviation fascinated her. Originally, Pennine Tower had housed a fine-dining restaurant and a sun terrace; nowadays the top floors were empty, the lifts to them disabled.

Downstairs was relatively quiet, with only a few travellers who'd broken journeys for refreshments. There was plenty of available seating and she commandeered a table directly outside the Costa. Ignoring the foot traffic, she quietened her mind, guiding it back in time to piece together the events leading to her first encounter with Danni. The images broke up and scattered until, without warning, they joined to form a reel . . .


*'Hey, it's fine.'*

*The sobs have started somewhere in her chest and won't stop. They're convulsing, noisy sobs she can't control.*

*'It's shock, Stacey,' the police officer says. 'Just the shock. They'll stop. You need to think of something else. Take my hand. Look at me.'*

*She tries to grab the proffered hand, but it swims out of view, and she loses sight of Danni's face as she sheds more tears. Danni wipes them away with a tissue and Stacey fixes on her sparkling blue eyes, like sunlight on a perfect Caribbean Sea, until gradually the convulsions subside.*

*'That's good, sweetheart. Really good. My name is Danni. I'm going to make sure you're safe until the ambulance gets here. Then we're going to get you to hospital. Your dad has been told you've been found. He'll be at the hospital when you get there. You've been incredibly brave. Keep taking deep breaths. I'm not going anywhere.'*

*She allows herself to be drawn into the deep blue irises, the colour of the sea on the bluest day imaginable, the water mirroring the cobalt of the sky, and she hears seagulls and laughter. She and Bella are on the beach together. The sun is warming her skin and the grainy sand subsides as she runs over it, trying to suck her into it. Bella is holding her hand, tugging her along as they race towards white-topped waves. The air is cool against her hot cheeks. Bella splashes icy-cold water in her face. She squeals and retaliates. When Bella stumbles to land on her backside in the water, they fall about with laughter. They walk further, each pull of the tide lifting them until they are floating, and she lies on her back and allows the waves to support her, so she is floating like a leaf, all the while holding onto Bella's hand. Then the sea becomes rougher. Waves begin to roll in, one after the other, each lifting the girls higher and higher. She grasps Bella's hand even tighter, opens her eyes in panic. There's no sky or sea. She's in an ambulance and it isn't Bella who is holding onto her hand. It's Danni, the police officer who has saved her.*

126

Cue marks, white dots in the top right-hand upper corner of the frame appeared, signalling the end of the reel, and she snapped out of her reverie.

'Well, hello, chief reporter Stacey O'Hara.' The gentle Cornish burr crashed her thoughts, bringing her back to the present. Danni's hair was silver, and light lines crinkled around her eyes, which were the same intense blue that Stacey recalled. She sat down and offered Stacey a broad smile.

'It's great to see you. I've not been stalking you, although I have been keeping abreast of your successes. I'm afraid that's the teacher in me. I always want to know how my protégés are doing. I'm friends with most of my ex-pupils on Facebook. Paul says I'm sad and he can't understand why any student would want to be in touch with their old teacher.'

'I can.' Stacey twisted the plume ring again. It was more than a piece of jewellery. It was a talisman, one she'd bought herself to celebrate her eighteenth birthday, believing as she did then and now that feathers were a sign from the angelic realm. The ring reminded her of Danni, a guardian angel, who even to this day kept an eye on her.

Danni gave a deep sigh. 'I'm not sure how to steer this conversation. We've avoided talking about your abduction for three decades. Are you sure you want to do this?'

'Absolutely. So far, I only seem able to evoke the odd recollection and I'm not even sure if they're real or fake. I hoped if you talked it through with me, it would unlock my memory.'

'Is this wise? Shouldn't you do this little by little, with professional help?'

'I can't go through those channels. It takes too long. I need to know now. I might have repressed something that could help save a life. Another kidnapped girl. Oh, Danni. It's Lyra. Lyra's been abducted.'

Uttering the girl's name brought a lump to her throat that strangled her words. Danni rested a hand on top of hers. 'It's okay. Take your time.'

She was propelled back to her youth, with Danni once again guiding her. She shook her head, swallowed the blockage. 'We don't have any to waste. Not if whoever kidnapped me has also taken Lyra.'

'What makes you think that might be the case?'

Stacey summarised the events of the last two days as quickly as she could.

Danni rested folded hands on the table, the teacher about to address a class. 'The internet has made all sorts of information accessible. It wouldn't take a huge amount of effort for somebody to establish the main details of your kidnapping and emulate them. A copycat, maybe. Your abductor? No!'

'Ashraf said something similar, but I don't see how anyone could find out about details like my hair and shoe being sent to my father. I can't even remember it happening. Nobody talked about it afterwards, so who could know? Dad issued a statement along with a request to respect our privacy in light of all that had happened, what with my mother—' She struggled to continue. Even after all this time, she couldn't talk about her mother's death without faltering. 'He used his influence and position to ensure the media wasn't allowed to feature the story.'

'Yes, I remember. He threatened action if they invaded his or your privacy, and considering the fact the kidnapper was still on the loose, they were effectively gagged. Nevertheless, people still talked. Several articles appeared in the local press. Some of those would be available online. Regardless of how much Henry tried to keep it quiet, there were leaks that the media exploited. Stories like that are gold dust. You know that.'

Stacey understood. However, mindful of the impact the press could have on damaged souls, she'd always trodden carefully, promising never to deliberately exploit another's unhappiness to get a scoop. 'Were you interviewed?'

'I was certainly hounded for information. As it happened, my superiors sensibly requested everyone involved in your rescue and subsequent hunt for your kidnapper was, under no circumstances, to talk. My skipper had a pathological hatred of all journalists. Although I think he'd have liked you,' she added, revealing a glimpse of even, white teeth.

'Who do you think blabbed?'

'School friends. Neighbours. Even somebody who worked at the hospital where you were recovering. Think about this logically. Whoever abducted Lyra knew she was staying with Jack this week, probably even know Freya is in hospital, so they'll certainly know you were once married to Jack, and they'll know something about your history.'

Danni fiddled with her keys, held together by a silver tag engraved with *World's Best Mother*. 'This person is sure Jack is good for the ransom money. They're probably aware he's been moonlighting. In brief, they've done their research. You're far more likely to be dealing with someone who has planned this to make it look like your kidnapping, rather than it being the same person who took you.'

Even though Stacey couldn't fault Danni's logic, fingernails of doubt scraped inside her. 'I hear you, and part of me agrees. We've got good reason to suspect Mark and even Tariq. All the same, I still have a horrible feeling this is something to do with me. Whether it's a copycat kidnapping or Lyra was deliberately taken to get back at *me* for some reason. Maybe I've angered somebody.'

'I seriously doubt that. Surely this is to punish Jack rather than you? To start with, Lyra is *his* daughter. You rarely see her. You and he split up three years ago. Besides, they asked him, not you, for the ransom. No, this has to be about Jack.'

Stacey stared at the keyring. Danni was the most pragmatic and sensible person she knew. In the past, she had listened to her words of wisdom and followed her advice. This time, she couldn't. 'I can't ignore my gut. Not on this. If I could conjure up real memories of my own abduction, I might get an idea of who would want to do this to get back at me after all these years.'

Danni laid the keys down, and levelled her gaze at Stacey. 'It's unlikely any such person would wait thirty years to exact revenge, involving the kidnapping of your stepdaughter, especially as you and Jack are divorced. They would have carried this out while you were still married.'

Stacey didn't respond. She couldn't back down. Danni gave up trying to convince her.

'Okay. If you think talking about what happened to you will help find her, then it's worth a try.'

'Thank you.'

Danni gave a small nod. 'What can you remember?'

'I'm not sure if what I see is fact or fiction. I sometimes imagine I'm watching a film of the events. More frames rather than reels. Snapshots of what might have happened to me. Since Lyra was kidnapped, these visions have begun without me even thinking about them, projected onto my brain. There's one – a wrinkled old man. I'm tied to a chair and he's grinning at me. His expression never changes. When he speaks, his lips don't move. I suspect it's somebody wearing a rubber mask. Before I can work it out, the reel snaps and I lose the image again.'

'Sorry, Stacey. I can't confirm that is an actual memory. There was no mask at the scene when I found you.'

'Then I have no way of knowing if it's true or false. These flashbacks started almost immediately after watching the video of Lyra being held hostage. I really need to establish if they're genuine recollections or fabrications. Maybe you can help make sense of them.'

'They could be phantom memories, brought on by shock.'

'I wondered that too, which is why I needed to speak to you. You know what happened to me.'

'I know *some* of what happened. I can try and fill in the gaps for you.'

A woman in a trench raincoat, carrying a briefcase in one hand and a disposable carryout tray in the other, walked past. Stacey pointed towards the serving counter. 'Fancy a drink?'

'I wouldn't mind a cup of tea.'

'Anything to eat?'

'No, thanks. We had fish and chips earlier. It's a must when you come to Blackpool, isn't it?'

Stacey gave a small smile. 'Definitely. I'll order. It'll give you a chance to think.'

She was queuing when Ashraf rang.

'There's still no sign of Mark. Freya's Škoda isn't on her driveway as usual, and her neighbours haven't seen it for a day or two. I've also found out that since her admission to hospital, she's only had one visitor – her mother. We might be on the right track with her boyfriend; however, I also did some digging on Tariq. His finances are in a mess. He's maxed out on three credit cards and missed the last two payments on his rent. He received a red warning from the letting agency. If he can't pay up, he and his wife will be evicted next month. He's working a second job as a night watchman for a scrap metal company, cash in hand, but my guess is it isn't enough to bail him out of trouble. We should keep an open mind about both of them for the time being, until I can establish their movements over the last couple of days. How are you getting on?'

'I'm with Danni, hoping for some illumination.'

'Illumination? I half suspect you're following up on your theory about this being something to do with your past.'

'Then you'd be half right. Do you think I'm wasting time?'

'You know what I think. This isn't about what happened to you. However, I know you can be strong-willed at times, so you should do whatever you feel is right. I'll follow up on Mark and Tariq.'

The barista signalled for her to approach the counter. 'I have to go. Thanks.'

'No problem. Don't beat yourself up if your chat to Danni is unproductive. We still have two potential suspects.'

Apart from her and Danni, and a table of men downing fizzy drinks and wolfing toasted sandwiches, the café was empty. Music played over the system, an upbeat Dua Lipa number, more suited to a nightclub than a motorway café. Danni looked up with a smile.

'Ah, thanks.' She removed the lid from the cup, added a packet of sugar and stirred it vigorously before replacing the lid. 'While you were ordering, I was debating where to begin. You see, I wasn't part of the investigation into your abduction, at that stage. That was handled by a specialist anti-kidnap unit from Birmingham. In fact, none of us at the station knew anything about it. If it hadn't been for a chance anonymous call, we might never have found you.'

'What was this tip-off?'

'It came through the main desk. Someone had spotted comings and goings at an abandoned newsagent's in Burton-on-Trent. They suspected there might be squatters or junkies living in it. There'd been trouble with trespassers there in the past, so I was dispatched to check it out. I arrived at five o'clock on the dot, patrolled the perimeter and spotted a broken lock on the rear door. I heard a man's raised voice and opened the door. His words were unclear, a barrage of shouts and threats. Then came screams, one after the other, non-stop.'

Danni's words became projected sideways, a line of flickering, unintelligible white letters, announcing the start of a new reel . . .

*His fingernails tap together in an irritating staccato rhythm.*

*'Daddy doesn't give a shit about you, Stacey. The tight-fisted bastard hasn't paid up. He has a fortune, and he isn't willing to part with a penny of it for your safe return. Well, he's had his last chance. The next thing to be delivered to him will be your body.'*

*It can't be true. Her father is all she has. Since her mother . . . She can't think about her mother. It hurts too much. Since then, it's only been her and Dad. This man is wrong. Her father would give everything he owns to get Stacey back. Wouldn't he?*

*He clears his throat in his usual way before lifting an object from the table. The blade glitters as he approaches. Horror freezes her blood. Then from nowhere comes a fresh courage. She isn't going to die without a fight. She screams as loudly as she can to keep him away from her.*

*'Shut the fuck up!'*

*She does the opposite, shaking her head left and right, repeatedly as fast as she can. She continues shrieking at the top of her lungs.*

*'Keep still, you stupid little bitch.'*

*He strikes, catches the top of her ear. She knows there's blood running down the side of her face, yet she continues to move her head, desperately hoping he won't be able to harm her further if he can't focus on a target. Even so, she expects the blade to slice her cheeks, but it doesn't. Her rapid movements seem to be confusing him. He growls at her to stop. She intensifies the shaking and shrieks again and again and again.*

'Stacey, are you sure you want me to continue?'

'Go ahead. It's helping. I had another flashback. This time, I'm sure it was genuine. I remember screaming and shaking my head like crazy to stop him killing me.'

Danni studied her keyring, appeared to steel herself, before speaking. 'You did. I'd never heard screams like them. Maybe I ought to have acted differently. Yelling at the top of my voice that

I was police frightened him off. At the same time, shouting out as I did probably saved your life. I raced through the back room and along a corridor. When I entered the shop itself, there was no sign of anyone other than you, tied to a chair, screaming for all you were worth. Looking back, I believe he was hiding somewhere nearby, knowing I'd be distracted by you. While I was trying to free you, he escaped.' She paused, took a sip of her tea. 'You okay for me to go on?'

Stacey nodded. The flickering began again, that internal film projector casting new images onto her retinas. A primeval instinct told her these weren't fabrications. They'd really happened.

*She's screaming and struggling against her bindings, fighting with every breath and what little energy she has. She feels a hand on her shoulder, giving it a soft squeeze, halting the screams. A gentle voice says,*

*'It's okay. It's over. I'm a police officer. I'm going to get you out of here. Stay still while I try to stop the bleeding. Trust me. I won't hurt you. Don't be frightened.'*

*Unable to distinguish truth from lies and terrified if she opens her eyes that the masked man with the knife will be there, she keeps them shut. Her head is light with shaking it from side to side and the blood loss from the knife wound. She senses she is dying. She gasps a final breath before she heads into an endless black tunnel.*

'I tried to calm you down, let you know I was there to rescue you. You didn't seem to register my words, then, without warning, you passed out. I contacted the station, requested urgent assistance, and while you were unconscious I learned you were most likely a judge's daughter who'd been taken prisoner five days earlier.' Danni picked up her cup, stared at the lid for the longest moment.

A whirring in her head accompanied a fresh reel.

*She wakes. Tenses. She can breathe. She doesn't smell his strong body odour, which he attempts to disguise with pungent spray, or hear his stupid, 'Now you see me!' She doesn't see a wrinkled rubber mask, only blue eyes, the colour of an ocean on a sunny day. Her mouth opens. No words emerge, only a keening noise.*

*The young woman gives a sad smile and reaches for one of Stacey's hands, rubbing it lightly, a kind gesture that evokes a deep, burning gratitude.*

*'Stacey, you're safe now. An ambulance is on its way. We're going to get you sorted. The doctors will fix you up. Everything will be fine.'*

*She wants to believe the woman, but she is fearful the masked man will return, and the torture will begin again. As if reading her mind, the police officer says, 'He won't be back. I won't let him, or anyone else hurt you. I'm staying right beside you.'*

*'Don't leave me.'*

*'I won't.'*

*'Promise.'*

*'I promise.'*

Danni was still talking. 'I don't know how much longer you would have survived if I hadn't turned up when I did. He'd done more than cut off your finger and ear. He'd beaten you, black and blue. You were so . . . damaged. I thought you wouldn't make it.'

The tinny clattering of empty cans being thrown into a bin close to her reverberated in Stacey's ears along with Danni's words, *beaten, damaged, black and blue.* Frames that took her breath away hung suspended on the imagined cinema screen.

*Her cheekbone stinging. Air whooshing from her stomach. Anguish as he grinds a fist into her ribs.*

She squeezed the plume ring for assurance. 'He was going to kill me. He had a knife. And now . . . I recall him hitting me.' A deep frown creased her friend's forehead. 'Don't worry. I can deal with it. I'm okay.' She clenched her hands into fists to stop them shaking as more images rolled in front of her eyes.

'Do you want to tell me exactly what you remember?'

Stacey wasn't sure she did. Speaking about the horrific incidents strengthened the memories. A brief image of Lyra, tied to the chair, forced her to continue. She was doing this for Lyra. To save her. She began, 'The attacks happened out of the blue—'

*The blows rain down on her; she yelps as he strikes her cheek, her shoulder, each punch accompanied by a grunt. She doesn't know where he'll strike next and only when there's a sudden crack and knife-like pains does she understand he has kicked her in the ribs. She gags on the hood and attempts to double over, making herself as small a target as possible. All the while, his breathing is ferocious, like a wild bull. She is sure he will charge again. She begins to lose consciousness and imagines she hears another voice. It might be her own.*

*'Stop! That's enough!' it says.*

Danni's soothing accent transported her back to the café. 'It must have been horrendous. I always felt it was a good thing you could never remember. What you must have gone through, well, it was too much for any person, let alone a teenage girl, to carry around with her. I was worried you would wake up in hospital with your memory restored and it would shatter you. I used to visit to make sure you were still doing well.'

'Even though I was on a cocktail of medication, I remember regaining consciousness periodically. You visited for a few minutes every day, didn't you? At first, I thought it was because it was part of your duties as a police officer, to hang around in case I remembered anything to help you catch my abductor. Then, I came to understand it was more than that.'

Danni's eyes crinkled warmly. 'I wanted to make sure you were recovering.'

'I never told you this before, but I believe, and still do, you are my guardian angel.' She felt for the plume ring on her middle finger, caressed it. It felt odd, opening up to Danni. Although she had seen her many times over the years, the kidnapping had been a taboo subject and they'd talked about the sort of things friends discussed – families, relationships, lives and careers – rather than the past.

Danni shifted in her chair; two pink spots appeared on her cheeks. She rested delicate hands on her forearms. 'I was just an ordinary police officer who took the job too seriously before deciding I wasn't really suited to it. I make a much better educator than copper. And I enjoy it more. I inspire and guide young people rather than caution them or break up their fights or call for assistance when one of them has taken a bad E or been stabbed.' She rubbed her arms like she was wiping away the visions that haunted her. 'Anyway, that's enough about me. Tell me more about these memories you've been having since Lyra was snatched.'

*Footsteps. Heavy tread on the stairs.*

'I think the kidnapper lived above the newsagent's where I was held captive. I have a vague recollection of hearing him come downstairs.'

'You might well have done. There was evidence to suggest somebody had been sleeping above the shop: a sleeping bag, some empty sandwich boxes, drink cans. We tried to gather prints from them but there were none. Clever sod either wiped them or wore gloves.'

*A bottle is raised to her mouth. The smell of rubber gloves like the ones her mother used when she was washing up.*

'Gloves. He wore rubber gloves.' Having established some of the grainy images were real, she wondered if the other flashbacks had been too.

*'Stop it. Stop! She's bleeding. Get away.'*
*Gentle hands administering cream.*

The cue spots appeared all too quickly, and the brief film ended.

'He treated my injuries. He bandaged me.' She held up her impaired hand.

'There were various medical supplies, sterile dressings, antiseptic cream and finger splints. We believed he'd had some basic first aid training.'

*Blackness.* She shuddered at the sudden sensation of insects crawling under her skin, the same feeling she got whenever a room was plunged into blackness. 'There was no light. I couldn't tell what time of day it was.'

'That would have been because your head was covered with a hessian sack, the sort used for storing potatoes. We tried to trace where it had come from but had no joy.'

Her words became muffled as Stacey withdrew into her mind. She was back in the cinema room . . .

*The hood is dragged from her head. The voice is low, sinister.*
*'Now you see me! Eat.'*

*A sandwich is pressed against her lips. She opens her eyes, can't bear to look at his face, so half closes them and concentrates on biting, then chewing. The cheese sandwich is dry so when he proffers a bottle of water, she sucks at it greedily, glad to wash down the stodge.*

*'Enough.'*

*Even though she hasn't finished, the itchy material is once again dragged over her head, returning her to the pitch-black.*

*'And now you don't,' he says with a bored chuckle.*


'It didn't seem like a shop. Even when my head cover was removed in order to eat or drink, I couldn't make out anything to indicate I was being kept prisoner in a newsagent's. No counters, shelves. Nothing.'

'Your back was to the counter and shelving behind it. You were facing a blank wall, the windows and door to your right boarded up. There wasn't any electricity, so there probably wasn't any light.'

*Flickering.*

She worried that her mind might loosen its grip on the memory. She squeezed her eyes, urged it, willed it, centred on the flickering until she could see it clearly on the large screen.

*A faint, flickering light that deepens the wrinkles in the rubber mask. Maybe a torch beam, or a candle. A candle.*

'How long had the newsagent's been empty?' she asked.

'A couple of years. That's the sort of information a copycat could get their hands on. The other, personal details – no. You mustn't allow yourself to believe Lyra is going through the exact same ordeal as you.'

'That sodding latex finger suggests otherwise.'

Danni shot a look at Stacey's hand and the missing digit. 'It wouldn't take a genius to work out you lost yours during the time you were kidnapped. They didn't send an actual finger. That's important. This smacks to me of a copycat.'

She nodded, yet all the while the idea Lyra might be experiencing anything remotely like her own kidnapping ballooned, expanding until it filled her mind with sickening images of what might happen to the girl.

She unconsciously reached for her ear and rubbed it gently. Saving Lyra from a similar horror to hers was crucial. That this was the work of somebody emulating her kidnapper made more sense than the possibility of her own returning thirty years on from the ordeal.

They were mimicking her kidnapping, using whatever information they had. Shit! What else might they know other than basic facts reported at the time? She shivered involuntarily. Her anxiety for Lyra's well-being increased tenfold. The girl couldn't be put through the same torment. Look where it had left Stacey.

If their reasoning was correct, it gave rise to another possibility, a way of finding her. 'Danni, if we're right and the kidnapper is replicating whatever they know about my experience, then there's a chance she's being held hostage in an abandoned shop or similar, somewhere close to or even in Morecambe. After all, I was kept prisoner only six miles from where I lived.' She churned the theory over again before deciding it was worthwhile exploring. 'I should establish if there are any empty shops, warehouses, anywhere deserted or abandoned in or around Morecambe.'

'You need my assistance if you want to pursue that angle. Let me help out.'

'Jack doesn't want any police involvement.'

'I'm not police. I'm a concerned friend.'

There was no denying she could do with Danni's input. She picked at the cuff on her cardboard cup. Danni had turned her brilliant gaze on her.

'The newsagent's was on the corner of a street in a rundown area. A place unlikely to attract any attention from comings and goings, even though, as chance would have it, somebody became suspicious. It's likely a copycat would choose a similar location, maybe one even more remote. I could start looking online for potential sites this evening.'

Stacey considered her options. There was a lot of development going on in Morecambe and plenty of disused premises; further afield it was rural with potential properties spread out. She couldn't do this alone.

'That would be helpful, but what about your family?'

'Don't worry about them.' She edged forward on her seat, her face growing more serious still.

'Something wrong?'

Danni pinched the ridge of her nose. 'Sort of. I'm not sure whether to tell you something else, but since you've begun to piece recollections together, I'd rather it came from me than you have a *moment* and remember.'

'What is it?'

Danni's chest lifted and fell. 'Like I said earlier, you went through a nightmarish time, so it's little wonder your mind blanked it. When I found you, you were bound to a chair. There was also a rope, lying by the chair, and a pole fixed from the shelves to a fitting, above your head. From the wounds on your wrists and subsequent findings from the doctors, we deduced that prior to severing your finger, your captor placed you in a stress position for a prolonged period. Does that jog any memories?'

'No. Or, maybe—' A recall had started to take shape, vanishing as quickly as it had formed before she could anchor it.

'It seemed to us he'd been torturing you – the beatings, the stress position, attacking you with a knife.'

*'Rich little bitch. You need to be taught a lesson.'*

*'Leave her. That's enough, I say.'*

*'Shut up!'*

She unconsciously rubbed her wrists, an action that jump-started a recollection of the tremendous discomfort that had overwhelmed her and obliterated her auditory senses.

*Hands tied above her head.*

It was a stress position, like those used during interrogation. Why had she been treated in such a way? The door to the make-believe cinema edged open. She only had to walk inside to find answers. She allowed herself to enter, stare at the freeze-framed picture on the screen. *The safe!* She'd almost touched on this before while in Jack's office. The still picture vanished, replaced by moving images . . .

*'Where does he keep the key to the safe?'*

*She sobs. 'I don't know.'*

*'Yes, you do. Tell me.'*

*'No. I really don't know. Please, my arms, my shoulders. They hurt so much.'*

*'I'll release them if you tell me what is in the safe.'*

*Tears stream down her face and through the fog of pain, a memory of the silver chain with the incredible blue stone is dislodged . . .*

*Her mother has been gone two weeks and she is in the study with her father who has called her in. The room is normally out of bounds, and although she's been in once or twice when he's been at work, it doesn't hold any appeal for her. The desk is full of files and books, and shelves house dusty volumes of thick law books. The painting of the horse is the only thing of interest in the room. She is surprised when he feels behind it, releasing the picture so it swings in her direction. He removes a key from the bottom of a leather pencil pot and unlocks the metal door which has been revealed. She wonders if her mother ever knew about the safe. A lump fills her throat. It is too painful to think about her frail, beautiful mother who couldn't bear life anymore.*

*He holds out an object. 'This was your mother's. I bought it for her last birthday.'*

*She already knows what is inside the velvet box. She recalls watching her mother twisting her head this way and that in the mirror, allowing the blue diamond to catch the light, her mouth a perfect 'O' as she touches the delicate chain.*

*She can't take the proffered gift. The memory of her mother's death is too painful.*

*'It's yours now.'*

*'I don't want it.'*

*'It's valuable.'*

*She's aware of its value, having overheard her mother gushing about it to a friend. The gem is rare, the colour born from traces of boron present during the stone's formation. Its brilliance is breathtaking. Even so, she doesn't want it, no matter its worth. It belonged to her mother, who was priceless. No necklace or jewel will ever replace her.*

*'I thought you could wear it for special occasions—' He falters, spies the look in Stacey's eyes and grunts quietly. He turns his back to her, puts the box back in the safe and in doing so displaces a brown paper packet that tumbles onto the carpet. Fifty-pound notes spill from it. He drops to his knees immediately, scoops the money back into the packet before returning it to the others that completely fill the lower section of the safe. He locks the door. Neither speak of the safe, the money or the necklace again.*

*Her shoulder muscles silently scream their discomfort. Now she's remembered that strange incident, she has no choice other than to share it with her kidnapper. It might afford her release from her shackles.*

*'The key is in a leather pencil pot. There's lots of money in the safe in packages. And a diamond necklace.'*

*'See, that wasn't too hard, was it?'*

*The tension eases as he lowers her arms to fall into her lap. She sobs with relief.*

'He wanted to know where my father kept the key to his safe and what was inside it. I was so scared, I couldn't remember at first, even after he hit me. That was why he tied my hands above my head. He left me until I thought my arms would fall out of their sockets. Eventually, I remembered.'

'Was that before or after he cut off your finger?'

She closed her eyes for a moment. The discomfort in her shoulders felt so real she rubbed them automatically. 'It happened before.'

Danni shifted again on her seat, her voice dropping. 'What did your dad keep in there?'

Stacey told her.

'So, your captor emptied the safe?'

She shook her head. 'Dad kept the necklace right up until he went into the nursing home. I guess he sold it then to invest the proceeds. I don't know what happened to the cash. I never asked him.'

'Then maybe you should. Stacey, your kidnapper wanted whatever was inside the safe. You were tortured because of it. You ought to find out what happened to the contents. Henry should, at the very least, have discussed it with you.'

'Like you, he didn't want to jolt any memories. He feared the repercussions.'

'Fair enough. I can understand why he wouldn't want that to happen. If you're right and the kidnapper stole a great deal of money from your father's safe, it doesn't explain why he continued to hold you hostage or why he repeatedly hurt you. Even though this has little bearing on Lyra's disappearance, you should question

144

him about it. You need closure, Stacey. Now you've begun to recall what happened, you must uncover all the truth, or this will haunt you forever.'

'It's not worth the upset. Some days, he doesn't even recognise me. I can't drag him back in time. Besides, it won't help get Lyra back.'

'Well, maybe he still keeps money stashed somewhere. If so, you could pay the ransom with it.'

'I doubt it. He prefers his money to be invested on the stock markets, where it earns him income to pay his care home bills. He lets his financial advisors manage his portfolio. I can't even tell you what he's invested in. He's always kept his finances from me.'

Danni opened her mouth, hesitated and then spoke again. 'If you were my daughter, I'd have given you power of attorney before I was in an unfit mental state to sign the relevant forms, not allowed financial advisors to manage my affairs. I would want my family involved, not complete strangers.'

Danni's words stung. Henry had always kept Stacey at arm's length, even when he needed her most, which had upset her more than she was prepared to admit. Danni was staring at the keyring again.

She hesitated before saying, 'Henry told the anti-kidnap and extortion unit that he didn't have the money to pay your ransom. He claimed he was asset-rich but cash-poor and couldn't get his hands on the amount demanded. Yet from what you've just told me, he had a safe stuffed with money and a necklace he could have pawned.'

The revelation thumped Stacey in the solar plexus. She stripped a piece of cardboard from the cup, crushed it in her hand. 'No. That can't be true. The anti-kidnap unit told him not to pay up. It was their fault.'

'I wouldn't lie to you.'

Her voice almost failed her. 'Why?'

'Because he believed the unit would locate the kidnapper and save you. Because he refused to be cowed into submission. Because he was the youngest judge in the country and didn't want to be seen as weak. Only he can answer the question. I think he's a very secretive man, one who owes you an explanation. Tackle him. He might surprise you and maybe offer you the ransom money.'

Stacey plucked at the remaining cardboard, unable to accept what she knew had to be the truth. She almost didn't hear what Danni was saying.

'I can understand Jack not being able to raise half a million. Who of us could lay our hands on that amount at all, let alone at the drop of a hat?'

Henry hadn't wanted to pay up; Jack did. If he had the money, he'd pay up instantly, rather than pursue this crazy angle of trying to locate and save Lyra.

Before Stacey could say anything, Danni spoke again. 'Jack got on very well with Henry, didn't he?'

'Yes. Dad liked him a great deal. What are you suggesting?'

'I suppose it's possible they discussed your kidnapping at some point. Jack could know more about it than you imagine. Which leads the detective in me to wonder if he might even have been influenced by whatever Henry told him. Maybe, just maybe, he believes he can extricate Lyra from this without paying the ransom money.'

Stacey blinked away the real possibility that Jack was emulating her own father's actions. 'He wouldn't be so stupid.'

'You're a brilliant journalist with superb investigative instincts. You've reported on missing children and victims of kidnap. You've had inside knowledge about how police operations are carried out and know some influential people. On top of everything, you've been in Lyra's situation. He could be banking on your first-hand experience and knowledge to get her out without coughing up any money.'

'But I barely made it out alive! If it hadn't been for you . . .' She thumped the remainder of her coffee cup so hard it flattened like plasticine onto the table. 'He wouldn't.'

'How well do you know him? It's been three years since you split up. You don't know how much he's changed during that time. He might be more parsimonious than you think. He didn't display a lot of generosity during your marriage. As I recall, you paid for the household bills, and he spent his money on having a good time – cars, trips out with his friends, top-quality suits . . .' Her eyebrows lifted as she spoke, driving home her point.

It was true. They had both brought in decent salaries but had separate bank accounts. While she'd paid the lion's share of household bills, Jack had always paid for spontaneous takeaways or hotel bills when they went away, although thinking about it, he invariably paid with his company credit card.

'He paid his share,' she replied. 'He wasn't stingy, he paid for meals, drinks . . .' Her words petered out as a cloud flittered across Danni's face. For whatever reason she couldn't explain, she felt she should defend Jack. Maybe it was because she knew how much he loved his daughter. 'You're wrong about this. I've watched him crumble, seen his tears, agony etched on his face. There's no way he'd choose money over Lyra. He truly wants her back.'

Danni steepled her fingers together, tapping them against her lips for a moment before clearing her throat. 'Don't bite my head off at what I'm about to say. I'm trying to look at this with my detective head on. The fact is, if this was a police investigation, we'd have run checks on him by now to rule him out.'

'I know.' She couldn't look Danni in the eye. She understood Jack. Even after a three-year separation, she still had a good idea of what made him tick. For all his faults, nothing would make him happier than for this to end and for Lyra to be returned back home unharmed.

'Stacey, do you still have feelings for him?'

The question froze her brain momentarily. Did she? She thought about how she'd felt recently when he'd touched her, smiled at her. She'd felt nothing other than repulsion.

He might have changed, had therapy or whatever else, yet she would never be able to love him. At best, she would manage friendship, but only because she didn't want to be kicked out of Lyra's life. Jack had the power to stop Lyra from seeing her if he wished, could even forbid her to contact Stacey, and that would break her.

Danni had taken her silence as an answer. 'Sweetheart, you are too blinkered by emotion. You still care about him.'

'No! I don't. I care about Lyra. Hugely. I . . . I love her as my own, Danni. I'm forty-six. I'm done with serious relationships. I shall never have children. She is all I have. She *is* my family.'

Danni reached for her hand again, gave it a gentle squeeze. 'Then the same applies. You are emotionally invested and it's clouding your decisions. I'm merely offering an outsider's perspective. Take a step back from the situation. Imagine you are not personally involved and are reporting on this for the newspaper. Who would you be investigating?'

Stacey groaned softly. 'Mark . . . Tariq . . . and Jack.'

'Exactly. You would look at all of them.'

'I don't know which way to turn. What should I do?'

'Keep an open mind. During an investigation, you must keep searching. You only disregard people once their alibis check out or you find evidence to prove they are not responsible. Sometimes, that means treading on toes.'

A silence fell between them. Stacey considered the advice for the length of time it took to pick up the pieces of cardboard and, cupping them in her hand, raised her face to Danni's. 'I'll talk to

Dad. He might be able to remember discussing my abduction with Jack.'

'That's what a good detective would do. To eliminate suspects, you have to challenge people, ask probing questions and possibly upset them, even if they are those who are closest to you. As soon as I get back to Blackpool, I'll go online to uncover any unoccupied premises in and around Morecambe. I'll check them out tomorrow. Paul will understand.' Danni scooped up her keys, then hugged Stacey. 'Try not to stress too much.'

'You know me. I can keep a cool head in any crisis.'

Stacey headed for a bin and dropped all the pieces of the cup inside it. If she hurried, she'd be able to see her father before he turned in for the night.

# DAY TWO
## THURSDAY – 9 P.M.

The staff at Topfields Residential Care Home permitted Stacey's late evening visit. They invariably made allowances when she came outside of regular visiting times, understanding the demands and irregular work hours her position placed upon her.

Stacey bounced lightly along the thick carpets, a rich checked green, red and cream pattern that would look hideous in a normal house, yet suited this wide corridor with its high ceilings, stylish coving and dangling chandeliers from ornate ceiling roses. The old, grand mansion had belonged to a wealthy landowner who had placed it in a trust fund on the proviso it would be converted into an exclusive care home, offering comfort and grandness to anyone who could afford the fees. A small brass nameplate *Lord Henry O'Hara* was screwed to the solid oak door. The peerage had never impressed her. As with all kids, he was just her dad. A mostly absent one. Henry had always been driven. Having been made the youngest deputy master of a high court at the age of thirty-six, he had strived to greater things, to the detriment of his family.

She tapped lightly and without waiting for an answer, opened the door.

Henry was slack-jawed, a fat pillow propped behind his back, mottled hands hanging over the ends of the padded chair arms. The skin on his once broad face hung in voluminous folds, reaching his jowls. Previously a gladiator of a man, the fierce anger had long since been sucked out of him, leaving a husk of a man in a flesh suit that no longer fitted.

'Hi, Dad.'

His thin lips quivered into a semblance of a smile as she stooped to kiss his whiskery cheek, an act executed more out of habit than affection. She wrinkled her nose at the body odour, which not even the freshly scented cologne she'd brought him on her last visit could mask. The staff had explained it was due to an odour component called 2-Nonenal that increased with age, and it saddened her that Henry, who had been extremely particular about his personal hygiene, was succumbing to the ageing process so rapidly.

She sank into the chair next to his. He'd brought the plump-cushioned armchairs from his house, old favourites that afforded him reminders of the past, along with his Italian writing desk and chest of mahogany drawers and his super king-sized bed. He pointed at the television screen, where people also in chairs or on settees commented on television programmes they were watching. One of them, a young man in a yellow shirt and denim shorts, gasped dramatically, clasping both hands over his mouth.

'Pah!' spat Henry. 'He's overacting.'

He said the same thing whenever he watched this particular reality show, a programme he wouldn't have considered viewing two years ago. Henry had always preferred listening to the radio over watching television.

'I hear you had your favourite for lunch today.'

The statement baffled him. The moment of lucidity seemed to drift off like an untied balloon. He turned dull eyes towards her.

'Did I?'

'Lancashire hotpot.'

It triggered a response, a lifting of unruly, wiry eyebrows. 'Yes. Hotpot. Lovely. Did you make it?'

'No, Dad. I make a terrible hotpot. I'm not very good at cooking. I don't even like cooking. Don't you remember the dreadful Yorkshire puddings I made? They were so rubbery we had to throw them out for the birds and even they wouldn't eat them.'

His eyebrows dropped again as he fought for recollection. Suddenly, he gave a quivering smile. 'Yes. Yes! They were little flat car tyres.'

Sometimes he could recall events way back in time, although not what he'd done that day. Other times he was so lucid, they chatted about events, much as they did before his mind began to wander. Today seemed to be one of those days. She squirmed forwards on the cushion, so she could maintain eye contact and keep up the momentum.

'And that's why I always let Jack do the cooking. He could make a great hotpot.'

The smile broadened. 'I used to enjoy Sunday lunch at your place. Now Jack *knew* how to make Yorkshire puddings – huge fluffy ones that towered.'

Jack had been by far the better chef and loved cooking. Whenever Henry had been due to eat with them, he'd pull out the stops and lay on a slap-up Sunday roast, complete with the amazing puddings and lashings of homemade gravy. Henry, a bon viveur and a wine connoisseur, had been most appreciative of the excellent home cooking. She'd almost forgotten how he and Jack would relax after a meal with a brandy and coffee, putting the world to rights between them, while she cleaned up the kitchen. Though Jack was a terrific cook, he was also an extremely messy one.

'Jack visited me yesterday. He brought me some fudge.'

The abrupt revelation made her heart jump. Had Jack really been to visit? 'Why did Jack come?'

'To see how I was. He brought me some fudge.'

'What did you talk about?'

'Golf.' A frown knotted his eyebrows together. 'We used to play together at Morecambe Golf Club. He still has a handicap of six. I bet I could still beat him though.'

It had been three years since Henry had played.

'Was that it? You talked about golf?'

'He brought me fudge. Is there any left? It'll be in the top drawer of my desk.'

She went through all the drawers. It was with some relief that she told him she couldn't find the sweet treat, deciding he had become muddled. He wasn't as clear-headed as she'd thought. Jack had never visited her father. They'd gone their separate ways before Henry came to Topfields.

'I must have eaten it. Shame. I fancy a piece.'

'I'll bring you some more when I next visit.'

He and Jack had spent a great deal of time at the clubhouse. Back then, she'd been relieved they'd found something in common. Boyfriends before Jack had been wary of the formidable Henry.

'So, you and Jack reminisced about your golfing days?'

He beamed at her. 'Even though I had the higher handicap, I often trounced him.'

'I expect you celebrated those wins.'

He nodded. 'Loser always paid for drinks at the bar afterwards.'

It was the way into discussing the past she needed. 'Dad, while you were celebrating in the clubhouse, did you ever talk about my kidnapping with him?'

He appeared to shrink further into his chair. 'I . . . I don't remember.'

'You remember me being kidnapped though, don't you?'

His eyes took on a faraway stare. 'Yes. I never thought they would harm you. If I had thought you were in so much danger . . .' He turned back towards the television screen again, pointed at the man in the yellow shirt. 'See, he's at it again. Look at his face. Terrible acting!'

She couldn't be sure if his sudden evasiveness was deliberate. He would often use his condition to wriggle out of answering or discussing certain subjects. It was a tactic with which she was familiar, one Henry was very good at pulling off.

'Dad, we must talk about this. I want to ask you about the safe,' she said, softly. 'The one in your office. Why didn't you use the money in it to pay for my release?'

The silence that followed came down like the final curtain at a performance. He wouldn't meet her eyes or respond. If he was play-acting, it was convincing. He genuinely appeared to have drifted into a world of his own. She was thinking of what to ask him next to draw him back out of himself, when he gave a small cough.

'There was nothing of value in it. The money had all been spent by then.'

'And what about Mum's diamond necklace? That was worth a great deal. Surely they'd have taken that in exchange for my freedom.'

'It contained a paste diamond.'

'It was a fake?!'

The skin around his neck concertinaed in and out. 'Coloured glass. Worthless.'

'You told me it was valuable. You wanted me to have it.'

He flicked his hand as if trying to swat an annoying fly. 'I was . . . stupid. I was trying to impress you.'

'Impress? I was a teenager who'd lost her mother. I didn't care about diamond necklaces.'

'You were always so close to your mother. I couldn't replace her. I thought if I gave you the necklace you might love me, like you did her.'

Even though he'd barely acknowledged her existence during her childhood, Stacey *had* loved him. She'd ached for his affection in return, yet Henry had been so wrapped up in his own success and career, he'd neglected his family's emotional requirements. The day Stacey's mother took her own life, he'd forfeited the right to his daughter's love, and she'd stopped caring about him or trying to earn his recognition.

'Bugger off, Bernard!' he shouted for no apparent reason.

Bernard had been one of their neighbours. He and her father had had a falling out years ago, the subject of it never really discussed. Periodically, Henry would shout his name and rant for a while. In his more lucid moments, he'd explained Bernard had spread malicious rumours about her father because he was jealous of Henry's success. 'You are a lying, two-faced home-wrecker, you weasel . . .'

His attention was hooked by a trio on a long sofa, laughing raucously at something they were watching. His jaw began to drop again.

'Dad?'

'I had hotpot for lunch. It was very good. Almost as good as yours.'

'Dad, we were talking about the money in the safe?'

'I don't have a safe.'

This time she was convinced there was no acting. He had retreated into his fog-filled world. 'Where do you keep your money?'

'I . . . A box. Under my bed.'

She got up and knelt by the bed, lifted the quilted valance and discovered a lacquered box in the shadows. The box was inset with mother-of-pearl, a gift from her mother, for his cufflinks and watches. It was unlocked. She worried the lid open, found a leather notebook and counted ten pounds in coins.

'Is this the only place you have hidden money?'

'I think so.'

'There's only ten pounds in there.'

'Ah. Spending money for sweets.'

She replaced the box, then hunted around the room and the en-suite bathroom to no avail. Whatever Henry had done with the packages stuffed with notes from his safe might remain a mystery, but it was certain he had nothing hidden in the room.

'Dad, can you remember exactly what happened to the money in the safe? What did you spend it on?'

He wiped his hands up and down the arms of the chair before issuing a soft reply. 'Gambling. After Julia died, I went wild. Blew it all on poker, women, booze . . . drugs. You see, Stacey, I was hurting too.'

This was news to her. Henry had always kept a close guard on his emotions. He had not shed a single tear before, during and after the funeral, although in the churchyard he'd held Stacey's hand with such force she thought her bones would break. Later that same day, after the mourners had departed from their house and she'd retired to bed, she'd heard Henry's car start up. He hadn't returned until the early hours, an act he then repeated frequently, one that was never discussed. Now the nightly absences made sense.

'Is there any fudge?'

'You've eaten it all. I'm going to bring you some more tomorrow.'

'Are you leaving? Stay. It will soon be lunchtime. You could eat with me.'

'No, Dad. It's late. The staff shouldn't really have let me visit.'

'Okay. I'll see you again soon.'

He gave a brief wave and she pecked him on the cheek again. He snorted. 'That chap on that show is a terrible actor. They could have got somebody better than him.'

'He's not an actor, Dad. He's an ordinary person, watching television.'

'Like me?'

'Yes. Like you.'

'Say hello to Jack for me. Maybe he could come with you next time. I haven't seen him in ages.'

Stacey slipped away and padded down the hallway. She recognised Elsa, one of the nursing staff, as she exited a restroom.

'Hi, Stacey. How was Henry?'

'Good at times. Confused at others. He thought my ex-husband had visited and brought him some fudge yesterday.'

'Oh, he might be right. I saw a sandy-haired man walking down the corridor to Henry's room, around mid-morning.'

'Did you speak to him?'

'Sorry, no. Check with reception. They'll be able to tell you more.'

'Sure. Thanks.'

She made for the desk, which was now unmanned. A large leather-bound visitor's book was open on the desk. She turned the page, checked all the signatures of those who had visited on Wednesday. Jack had not signed in. Maybe he hadn't come at all. Could it have been somebody else, altogether? There must be other men with the same hair colour. Or maybe they hadn't visited Henry. Elsa had only seen them walking down the corridor, not actually entering the room.

The front door shut with a solid clunk. A stone dolphin spraying water from its mouth into a fountain seemed to smile at her, keeping its secrets of comings and goings to itself. There were more questions than answers and a growing suspicion that Jack wasn't being honest about any of this.

She thought that she ought to head home for food and rest. She needed time away from Morecambe, from Jack and Henry, to gather her thoughts and decide how best to go forward.

As she got into her car, the digital display flashed the time. It was almost nine. Lyra had been gone two full days. They needed to up their game if they were to find her. Every minute the girl spent locked away was a minute too long.

Her quaint cottage was set only a little way back from the main road in Hornby. She never tired of the picturesque village nestled in spectacular scenery, with walks alongside the river, and views towards Ingleborough, the second-highest mountain in the Yorkshire Dales and only a half-hour drive away.

The more sedate lifestyle here suited her perfectly. Almost everything she needed was on her doorstep: provisions, a swimming pool, even a castle that opened its doors twice a year in order that locals could enjoy the flower-filled grounds. It was her idyll, a place where she could hide from the rest of the world, secure in the knowledge she was safe here.

The peace afforded by living in this tranquil spot more than compensated for the long hours she spent working. A bonus for Stacey was that nobody here knew or badgered her about her past life. They were friendly, not nosey, and more than willing to accept her into the community without pressing on her the need to socialise.

She unlocked the door, then pushed it open with her foot: bag and keys in one hand, pizza box in the other. She lifted the lid to be greeted by a puff of warmth, carrying aromas of melted cheese and oregano. It wasn't hunger that made her tug immediately at a slice, and bite into it. It was common sense. Hunger brought on fatigue and illness. Moreover, it clouded judgements.

She wiped a smear of sauce from her thumb. On another day she would have relished the spicy topping on the light, crisp dough. Tonight, she was too weary to appreciate anything. The day had been long and torturous, with suspicion falling on Jack and Tariq as well as Mark and Freya. Ultimately, they were no closer to finding Lyra.

She stared at tomato-stained, blood-red fingers. An unbearable melancholy welled inside her. Hot tears burned her eyelids. It wasn't as if Jack was a multi-millionaire or a celebrity, or head of a major corporation. She couldn't shake off the feeling he and Lyra had been targeted for another reason, one that involved her. This had all the hallmarks of a copycat abduction, acted out by somebody who had it in for her too.

She rubbed angrily at the tears. She never cried. Nobody had ever seen her cry, not since the day her mother was buried. Nobody except the man in the rubber mask.

*'Now you see me!'*

She shivered at the recollection, thumped the lid back on the box and headed for the fridge, reaching in for a Moretti beer. She popped the cap, necked it greedily before wiping her mouth on the back of her hand. The simple act reinforced her strength of will. The tears were no longer threatening. Lifting the bottle to her lips for a second time, she made a vow to find Lyra. She may have been exhausted, but she wasn't beaten.

# DAY THREE

## FRIDAY – 4 A.M.

Stacey yawned then stretched, flexing her toes and lifting her hands so far over her head she knocked the coffee table behind her. It was then she remembered she wasn't in bed but had grabbed three hours' sleep on the settee. Her phone alarm rang its merry tune, far too cheerful for the time of day. She turned it off without looking at it. The room was bathed in an orange glow. Stacey never slept without a light on.

She threw off the blanket, then rolled off the sofa, stamping her feet to get the circulation moving again. Brown sheep with white faces wandered the snow-capped fells of Helvellyn on her computer. She lurched towards the screen saver, moving aside the empty beer bottle, to bring back up what she had been looking at before bedding down on the settee.

A copycat kidnapper would only have access to the same online information she had uncovered. The newspaper reports at the time bore scant details about the incident. She'd found photographs of the rundown newsagent's where she'd been held captive, an innocuous, dingy building with faded, ripped posters stuck to boarded windows.

One headline read, TORTURED IN THE DARK! The article was less sensational, explaining in clear, calm terms that missing teenager Stacey O'Hara had been rescued from a five-day ordeal, during which she had suffered serious injuries. Her abductor was believed to still be at large. The public was advised to come forward if they had any information that might help the police with their inquiries.

None of the other numerous articles written about Judge Henry O'Hara were about his private life or his family, other than one, a piece about her mother's funeral. She clicked off it, swallowing the lump in her throat, to read another article about her kidnapping, equally sparse on details. This time it was accompanied by a picture of her pale face staring out of a Range Rover window, snapped the day she'd left hospital and Staffordshire for good.

Her father had pulled a whole bunch of strings to ensure their names weren't plastered across every paper in the country. The girl in this picture was about to start a new life, her mind wiped of the terror she'd experienced, yet still damaged by what had happened.

There was insufficient information online to aid a copycat kidnapping. The only way for such a person to learn about her hair being cut off, her shoe being delivered, and her finger being chopped off was if they'd been involved in, or knew somebody who'd been part of the investigation into Stacey's abduction.

There'd been no way she could have divulged anything herself. Aside from the fact that her mind had blocked it, she only socialised with a handful of people. Right now, she wished she wasn't such a loner. She could do with a support network of close friends.

*Bella! Bella had been her friend. Until the kidnapping.*

She pushed away thoughts of her school friend, focused again on details of the kidnapping. *The safe*. Was it significant that Jack also kept money in a safe or was she, as Ashraf had suggested, seeing connections where none might exist? After all, plenty of people kept money in a safe, and businessmen were known for all kinds of shenanigans to avoid paying tax. She shook her head to free the mental tangle of ideas. By dwelling on the issue of the safe, she might be wasting time, yet the word felt significant, had gravitas.

With these jumbled thoughts came physical associations: the return of the racking pain in her shoulders that still echoed all these years after being tortured. Confusion followed. Could a copycat kidnapper know about the contents of Jack's safe? If so, it was more logical to take Tariq – who knew about the money – into consideration as a suspect.

She rubbed her neck. The nagging ache felt as bad as it did back then, when her arms had been chained.

The imagined sound of a whirring projector sent her mind seesawing back to the past. The girl she saw in the black and white film, a younger version of herself, had been so frightened and compliant, there'd been no need for beatings or torture. The man in the mask could have coaxed the information about her father's safe simply by offering her water in exchange for information. She hadn't been guarding military secrets. His methods had been extreme.

The brief movie reel in her head came to an abrupt end. Somebody had hated her or Henry. Really hated them.

She turned off the computer and picked up the beer bottle. She dropped it into the recycling receptacle in the kitchen, before staring at her back yard. The kitchen lights spread mustard yellow patches across the lawn and lit up the wooden pergola at the far end. Wind chimes hanging from it tinkled in the breeze, their musical notes reaching her ears. Above it, starry pinpricks punctured the black curtain of sky. It would be light in a couple of hours. She preferred the daytime, when she could breathe more easily. The night brought uncertainty along with moments of utter panic. She closed her eyes, allowing her thoughts to arrange themselves.

The hair. The finger. The safe. The holdall. Her father.

It was time to challenge Jack about what she thought he had been holding back.

❖ ❖ ❖

She rang Jack before she reached his house. She didn't care it wasn't yet dawn. If he was as worried about Lyra as he claimed to be, he'd be wide awake.

Morecambe by night was even more beautiful than by day, with streetlights illuminating shop fronts and dwellings the length of the road, throwing their elongated reflections into the water. It reminded her of fairy lights at Christmas.

Jack was waiting at the front door in his night attire, a blue dressing gown covering his pyjamas, the belt tied tightly and double knotted around his narrow waist. He herded her into the kitchen. The coffee machine was burbling. He indicated it blankly. 'I put the coffee on. I take it you want one.'

She decided to blindside him. If her suspicions were wrong, he'd deny it. 'No, Jack. What I really want is to know why the hell you went to visit my father.'

'Oh.'

'Is that all you can say? "Oh."'

'I was going to mention it—'

'When?'

He rubbed the dressing gown sleeve over his forehead and dropped his gaze, like a chastised child. He gave a pitiful sigh. 'When the moment was right. After we got Lyra back. I'm sorry.'

'Well, you can tell me now.'

'Don't make me—'

'Tell me the truth!' She lifted her thumb and forefinger and held them mere centimetres apart. 'I'm this close to calling the police. Explain yourself. Now.'

'I'm sorry. So sorry.' He placed his fist against his mouth, eyes filling.

Stacey clenched her own hands, counted to ten and turned on her heel. She was finished with Jack. She was going to do what she should have done all along. Call in an anti-kidnap squad.

'Don't walk away from Lyra. Me, yes. But not Lyra.'

She hesitated.

'I love my girl with all my heart. Believe me, I only did all of this for Lyra's sake. I should have told you straight up about visiting Henry. To be honest, I didn't think he'd remember my visit, so it didn't matter if you didn't know. Plus, everything's been happening too quickly. There hasn't been a right moment to bring it up or explain.'

'You can explain it right now,' she said. 'And it had better be good.'

'After that video arrived, I fell to pieces. I mean, I completely crumbled. You understand, don't you? You felt the same way after you watched it. You know what I'm talking about.'

He looked at her for confirmation. She gave a small nod.

'I don't know what you felt, but I can't express in language the sensation, or the fear. It was like somebody had scooped out my innards to replace them with a giant bag of ice. I couldn't think for the hissing in my head.'

She was on the same page so far. She'd experienced the icy claws of terror scratching at her insides.

'First there was disbelief, then sheer panic set in. My immediate reaction was to find enough money to pay the ransom. I always got on with your dad and—'

It was going to be as she'd suspected. She didn't need him to finish. He'd tried to squeeze money from her confused and vulnerable father. She turned on him. 'You thought a sick man in a care home would have half a million stashed in his room?'

'No! No, Stacey. Nothing like that.'

'Then what? Because this is sounding like bullshit to me!'

He raised his hands in apology. 'Not his money. I didn't go to him for his life savings. I don't even know how much money he has. I was shooting in the dark. In hindsight, it was madness to even have considered asking him. I thought . . . I thought he must have come across all sorts of lowlifes in his profession and put away all sorts of people for a variety of crimes. I hoped he might be able to direct me. Advise me where to go for quick cash.'

'Are you saying you went to him in the hope he'd give you names or details of criminals who'd be able to help you?'

'Sounds even madder when you say it out loud. I only wanted names of loan sharks. Not drug dealers, although I was in such a turmoil I'd have gone to anybody who could have loaned me the money.'

'Did he give you any contacts?'

He smiled sadly. 'No. He's too far gone, isn't he? He kept asking if I'd brought him any fudge. He didn't make a lot of sense. I'm sorry, Stace. I'm sorry for bothering him, sorry for not visiting him before and sorry for you. It must be tough seeing him in such a state. I only did it for Lyra.'

Her short nails dug so hard into her palms they stung. She rode the discomfort, pressed harder still. 'You're a fucking idiot.'

The room crackled with tension. A puff of air from his heavy sigh whispered across her face.

'I know. It's true that desperate people do stupid things. It was an illogical, crazy idea.'

Her anger evaporated, to be replaced by a sadness. She comprehended his frustration, the fear that drove him to pursue such a ridiculous avenue. After all, she'd tried tracking a bag of money to no avail. 'Have you found a loan shark since?'

He removed a full coffee cup and placed it on a saucer. Treacle-coloured liquid spilled over the edge and dribbled down the side. 'I still haven't had much luck in that department. It's harder than you'd imagine uncovering networks. I've been to some right dives, pubs and other haunts where people like that might hang out. I even tried to find one online. According to the internet, there are loads of them who operate on Snapchat and other social media platforms, yet I can't find a single one!'

There was something about his defeated manner that finally caused her to unclench her throbbing fists and sit down. He was, in his own way, doing whatever he could to ensure the safe return of his daughter.

'Have I fucked up, Stace?'

She shook her head. 'No.'

He dropped onto a stool opposite her, relief and resignation mingled across his features. 'To be honest, I was shocked when I saw Henry. I'd never have visited him if I'd known he was so ill.'

He rested elbows on the breakfast bar and watched her take a sip of the coffee.

'Reason goes out of the window in these situations,' she said.

'Thanks for understanding.' He was on his feet again, the soles of his slippers swishing across the tiled floor. The coffee machine burst to life once more with a series of pops and splutters. 'What do I do now, Stace? What on earth do I do?'

'For now, all you can do is wait. Ashraf's following up on Mark and Tariq.'

'How can you stay so calm?'

'I have to be. It's as simple as that. If I'm not, then we're screwed. It doesn't mean I care less. I have to compartmentalise my emotions and treat this as if I were investigating a story.'

'I always admired that about you – your cool head.'

A text message from Danni interrupted the conversation.

Morning. Couldn't sleep so did some research.

You should try this psychiatrist to unlock your remaining memories.

She is one of the best.

Stay strong.

Danni x

There was a website and phone number for Dr Erin Bell.

She clicked onto the link, studied the testimonials. It was clear why Danni had chosen her. Her reputation as a hypnotherapist was second to none.

'Any news?'

'No. Just Danni checking in.'

'Danni? How is she?'

'Good. She's up here visiting family. She's been looking for places nearby where Lyra might be being held.'

His forehead creased. 'She's ex-police. You know we can't risk the kidnapper finding out about her.'

'She's only checking out disused buildings. Nobody would have any idea about her.'

Jack began to protest, then changed his mind with a shake of his head. 'You've already told her everything, haven't you? There's no point me resisting.'

'It wasn't like that. I needed to talk to somebody. She happened to be in Blackpool. She wanted to help and I was glad of the offer. Checking out abandoned premises isn't a bad idea, and it doesn't carry huge risk. The kidnapper can't be everywhere, watching us all.'

He didn't reply. It was clear from his stance that he was unhappy at her friend's involvement. She pocketed the phone. She'd ring Dr Erin Bell as soon as the office opened and try hypnotherapy if it would help them get Lyra back.

His eyes narrowed slightly. 'Why would you think Lyra might be nearby? She could be anywhere in the country. Is it because you were held hostage close to where you lived?'

She decided to be open with him. 'Yes.'

'You're pursuing the idea your kidnapping and Lyra's are linked?'

'In as much as I think this could be the work of a copycat, yes. Do you think I'm so wrong to consider it?'

The coffee cup was halfway between the saucer and his mouth. A whisper of steam rose, fogging his features momentarily. 'No. One word of warning though: you shouldn't let what happened to you affect your reasoning.'

'I won't. I need to check out every option, even ones that sound highly unlikely.'

He put down the cup and leant forward, eyebrows raised. 'I get it. Just don't get too carried away believing there is a connection when the only one is probably in your mind. You've been there before, Stacey. What about the time you thought you saw your kidnapper?'

She waved away his concerns, keen to drop the subject.

The shaven-headed man had bumped into her in the street. He'd offered no apology as he paced past her, head lowered. As she turned to comment on his behaviour, she caught sight of a tattoo of a bird on the side of his neck, which triggered the certainty that she knew him. She studied his retreating form, then pursued him until he turned into a building.

She'd confided in Jack, telling him that she was sure this man had lived in the same village as her around the time she had been kidnapped. The more she thought about that unusual tattoo – a dove with wings spread wide – the more she became convinced that she knew this man. It transpired, eventually, that she had seen him before, although not in the village where she'd lived. He had been interviewed on television, a documentary about hillwalking in the Yorkshire Dales, and had lived in Lancashire all his life. She couldn't always trust her mind, even when it sent powerful signals to her. For the week she trailed that man, she'd been utterly convinced he'd had something to do with her kidnapping.

She pulled Lyra's notebook from her bag. Although there hadn't been any obvious clues in it when she'd looked earlier, she'd learned a long time ago to check everything thoroughly, then double check. She turned a page and stared at a cartoon dog sitting on its haunches, tongue out. A lead attached to the hand holding it, the dog's owner invisible. Lyra had written one word, *Woofles*, and encircled it with tiny pink hearts. It seemed an odd name for a dog, not the sort of thing Stacey would have expected Lyra to choose.

'You heard of Woofles?'

He shook his head. 'Can't say I have.'

Stacey ran the name through a search engine, which returned a result. Woofles was a dog day-care centre not too far away from where Jack lived.

'Has Lyra mentioned a dog day-care centre?'

'Not to me.'

It planted a seed in her mind. Maybe Lyra knew somebody who worked there. She'd follow it up.

Jack was looking up at her. 'Relevant?'

'I don't know. I should check it out.'

'Want me to do it?'

She put the book back in her bag. 'I'm going out anyway. I'll drop by on my way back.'

'Where are you going?' The neediness had returned in his voice.

'I'm going to take a second look around the area. See if there's any sign of her bike.'

'But I—'

'I know you did. I'm not disbelieving you or hinting you didn't look thoroughly; it's something I need to do for myself, to get a feel of what happened.'

'I'll come with you.' He was on his feet in a flash.

'No. You stay here. I want to do this alone.' She caught the sudden slump in his shoulders. 'It's how I operate. It's not personal. Besides, I need to oxygenate my brain. It's getting clouded.'

He plopped down again, his face elongating; the sudden burst of energy evaporated. 'It's fine. I understand.'

She meant what she had said. A walk would do her good. Jack's words had hit home more than she cared to mention. Maybe she was trying too hard to link the two kidnappings. A more obvious assumption was that Mark had cajoled Lyra into Freya's car. However, she couldn't operate on conjecture. She needed a pointer to set her on the right path.

To that end, she headed along the promenade, stopping at three semi-circular picnic tables with matching wooden benches, all a stone's throw from a children's play area but each private, hidden behind low, trimmed bushes. Jack had been instructed to leave the money hidden in the one nearest to the promenade, easily accessed from the main road, or the promenade. A person hiding in the park, or watching from one of the deserted church windows opposite, or even sitting in a car on the main road could have observed his actions, raced across and lifted the bag. She traversed the empty road, hunted for a way to get into the church and, satisfied it was secure, continued her journey. It still troubled her that money had been transferred from the bag containing the tracker.

Her eyes strained in the dim light as they scanned the area, hunting for places where the kidnapper might have been watching

Jack. The transition came without warning. She was transported to the gloomy cinema, where she stood against the wall and peered into the half-light, not facing the prom with its dark backdrop of the sea, but towards a screen where a film was playing, with her in the starring role.

*She senses his presence. He's been standing in the room for a few minutes. She can't imagine what he is doing other than staring at her.*

*The punch to her head comes out of the blue and dazes her. The ringing in her ears blots out his words until he yells loudly.*

*'Your shitbag father told the police! He told them regardless of my warnings. Right now, they'll be working out how to trick me. They'll put a watch on the money or mark the notes. He's going to need a reminder of what is at stake. What shall we do? Send him your heart in a gift-wrapped box? What . . . shall . . . we . . . do?'*

She released the breath she'd been unconsciously holding. Had Lyra's kidnapper – like hers – guessed there would be a tracker on the bag? No, that was madness. Back then they hadn't used trackers. But they might have marked the notes, or had officers in place at a drop-off, watching for the kidnapper to appear. For all the warnings not to link the two kidnappings, she couldn't ignore the mounting similarities. She strode along the road, towards the dog-friendly beach, each step taking her to where Kelly and Lyra had been playing with the puppy. She reassured herself with reminders that the abductor now had some of the ransom money and would surely be appeased for the time being. It was unproductive to become concerned about what Lyra might be going through based on vague flashbacks and false memories.

Day was breaking, black diffusing to navy blue. Hidden in undergrowth, the breezy chirps from awakening sparrows accompanied her footsteps until she bounded up concrete steps, away from the promenade and onto Broadway, where headlights of oncoming traffic forced her to squint her way along the pavement. Like Jack, she'd taken the most direct route to Kelly's house, one she assumed Lyra would have followed. There were no obvious places where somebody could have dumped a bicycle. Each property sat in its own wide plot. Although she peered behind every railing and paid special attention to a site currently being developed into flats, where a bike could easily be left among the rubble and debris outside, she spotted nothing. She concluded that, having cost over two hundred pounds, if it had been abandoned there was every chance somebody would have, by now, claimed it as their own.

The knowledge that a police unit would have combed this area immediately, and possibly uncovered the bike, gnawed at her. On the other hand, she'd done what she could and there'd been nothing on any CCTV to indicate the whereabouts of Lyra or the mountain bike.

She plodded along Wakefield Avenue, a sought-after area in town, also known as Bare Village, one of the three original villages that had made up Morecambe Bay. One side of the road was lined with semi-detached, Victorian houses, and opposite them, white-washed individual bungalows. Small posters in the windows alerted her to the fact that this was a Neighbourhood Watch area. Kelly's home was at the far end of the road, a freshly painted and renovated property with a two-storey extension and neat front garden. The curtains at the bay windows were drawn tightly. The family would be in Scotland, Kelly fast asleep, with no inkling of what her friend was going through.

Stacey's best friend, Bella, had also been kept in the dark about her abduction, although Stacey had never understood why, afterwards, Bella had not visited her in hospital. At the time, Stacey had been too drugged up and confused to question anything and was terrified the man in the rubber mask would return to take her again. Such was the fear, she readily accepted, without question, her father's suggestion to move away as soon as she was able to leave hospital. When she discovered her friend hadn't even been to the house to ask after her, she dismissed Bella to the past.

She took a last look at Kelly's house. Once Lyra was released, she would see her friend again. This horrible event would bring them closer. Lyra would be able to cry and talk about what happened. She would exorcise her demons. She would not, like Stacey, be whisked away to an isolated house in the middle of nowhere, with surveillance cameras and electric gates, more prison than a home. From the day they moved in, nobody was invited to visit. She was chauffeured to and from a private school by a local taxi firm, too fearful to contact any of her old friends and rake up the past she had buried. She made a silent promise to Lyra that when they found her, she would return to her old life and move forward, surrounded by friends and family who cared about her.

A woman in jogging gear emerged from a house opposite to give Stacey a serious look. Stacey raised a hand in greeting. A moment later, an elderly man came out of a side door of another property, headed for a wheelie bin and dropped a black bag inside it.

'Morning,' he called. 'Can I help you?'

'No, thanks. My daughter was here Tuesday evening, visiting her friend. She lost her bracelet somewhere between here and home. I'm looking for it. No joy though.'

'Which friend did she visit?'

'Kelly Richards. They're away though, so I couldn't ask Kelly to hunt for it.'

The man appeared to relax. It confirmed her suspicions. People here were neighbourhood aware. A young girl being taken against her will would surely have roused somebody's suspicion. Had Lyra been snatched along the main road, the same logic applied. Cars were constantly using the road, even at eight o'clock in the evening. All of which meant the kidnapper would be taking a huge risk if they'd lifted her here, unless, as had been suggested, Lyra went without fuss, because she knew the person.

On a hunch, Stacey took a slightly more circuitous route towards the promenade, one that would take her past Woofles. Lyra had been dog daft for a long while, but ever since she'd heard Kelly was getting a puppy, she'd become more obsessed, up until recently sending Stacey memes and YouTube videos of cute dogs daily. Stacey understood the girl's desire to own a dog. She wanted something that was wholly hers to love, that would love her back. It would fill the gap created by Freya, who was aloof, and Jack, whose over-possessive nature had created a gulf between himself and his daughter. Lyra was at a tricky age, requiring more security, and searching for the unconditional love that a pet would bring. She reasoned the girl might have intended stopping off at the centre to chat or ask about dogs for sale, or just to visit. With nothing else to go on, it was a long shot she was prepared to take.

This street ran parallel to the coast road. Curtains were drawn at every window. Reaching locked gates, her eyes were drawn to the oblong classrooms in front of the main school building that would remain shut until the Easter holidays were over. She didn't know what made her peer through the railings. Maybe it was the fact that this area wasn't overlooked by houses, but lying on the grass, half hidden by undergrowth, was a wheel. Stacey clambered over the railings and parted the tightly knit branches with both hands before staring in disbelief at the turquoise bicycle.

# DAY THREE

## FRIDAY – 7 A.M.

Stacey sat in Jack's kitchen with Jack and Ashraf. Jack had confirmed the bike was identical to Lyra's. What they couldn't agree on was what to do about it. Jack wanted to bring it home. Stacey felt it should be left where she'd found it. Ashraf backed her.

'It's hidden from sight. The school is shut all week. No one will tamper with it. The bike is evidence. The kidnapper might have left fingerprints on it.'

'Can you take prints from it?' asked Jack.

'Even if I could, I haven't got the resources to have them traced. We should leave this for the police. It might help convict whoever has taken Lyra.'

'What if the kidnapper collects it?' said Jack.

Ashraf wouldn't back down. 'If we tamper with evidence, it could land us in the shit. Especially if things go wrong.'

'Wrong? You mean, if this fucker kills Lyra?'

Ashraf cleared his throat.

Jack continued, 'If Lyra is harmed or, heaven forbid, killed, getting into bother over moving her bike will be the least of my bloody concerns!'

'Stop bickering. It isn't helping,' said Stacey. 'We should be using this information to track her down.'

'All we know is she was lifted near the school, probably by somebody who couldn't fit the bike in their car. Which might mean we're no longer looking for somebody driving an estate car or a van. Do we rule out Mark as a suspect?' said Jack.

Ashraf tapped his pencil on the table. 'There could be a number of reasons her bike was left behind. We're not discounting anybody. I'm working on Mark's whereabouts. He's still a suspect.'

Jack gave an imperceptible nod. 'Sorry. I'm a bit worked up. Her bike . . . You understand?'

'Yeah. I'd react the same way. Try and take it easy. It might be better if you let us handle this.'

Stacey studied the map of the area on Jack's laptop. 'What it suggests to me is that Lyra was followed, maybe several times, until the right moment presented itself. I don't think this was a spur-of-the-moment snatch. Her abductor knew her movements.'

Ashraf scratched his ear thoughtfully before saying, 'I don't think they've been tailing her all week, waiting for a golden opportunity to grab her. If they have, then they tumbled lucky, didn't they? The one time she wasn't with you, Stacey or her friend, Kelly, and in an area not overlooked by houses.'

'Surely this has to have been planned. And if so, whoever took Lyra must have known she was staying with me in Morecambe and not with her mum,' said Jack. 'Which keeps Mark in the frame.'

'True, although he can't be the only person to know. Information gets passed around easily among kids these days. Kelly knew and undoubtedly told her friends. You might even have mentioned it too,' said Stacey.

'Only to a couple of people.'

'What about work colleagues?' asked Ashraf.

'Yes. I mentioned to them that I'd be taking time off to spend with her.'

Ashraf waved his pencil. 'Then Tariq might have known too. Tariq and Mark. Both men fit the bill.'

Stacey had been half listening, wrapped in her own thoughts. 'What puzzles me though is how they knew to grab her where they did. There was no way they could have known she'd be headed down that particular road at that time, unless they followed her. Plus, they had to be certain you weren't around to realise she hadn't returned home, Jack.'

Jack winced at the unintended barbed comment.

'The video wasn't sent to you until the following morning. Had you discovered she'd disappeared before it arrived and alerted the police, it would have scuppered the kidnapper's plans. They must have known you wouldn't discover she was missing until you received that video.'

'But . . . that suggests they've been watching my movements too. One person couldn't watch us both. There must be more than one of them,' said Jack.

Stacey shrugged. 'It's possible. Or they tracked you somehow, or maybe Lyra told them you were out.'

Jack put his hands on his head, lifted his face to the ceiling and released a weary sigh. 'Do you want a coffee or something? I need to do something useful.' He got to his feet.

'I'm good, thanks.' She glanced back at the onscreen map. 'Why did Lyra choose Dallam Avenue instead of coming home via the main road? The school is probably the only place where she could have been snatched without arousing suspicion. It's a quiet street. The spot where I found her bike isn't overlooked at all. She might have been lured there.' She rubbed her chin and thought hard.

Jack switched on the kettle. 'You know, it could have been a spur-of-the-moment decision to grab her, after all. Lyra might not have been the intended victim. Once they'd taken her, they found out what they needed to about me and decided to go ahead anyway. You said you wouldn't discount any theory and that's as plausible as any other of the suggestions.'

Stacey kept quiet, unwilling to deflate Jack further when he was clearly trying to assist.

Ashraf, however, was less considerate of Jack's feelings. 'No, mate. Don't fool yourself. Lyra's been the intended target all along. For whatever reason, they think you can settle the ransom demand.'

Stacey zoned out. Lyra had been outside a school that was closed, abducted at a spot where there were no dwellings overlooking it. She hadn't been there by chance. What would make her cycle home down an unlit street? The answer came in a flash. The same reason Stacey had chosen to try that route.

'Let's say this has been planned, for some time. Let's imagine she took that road for a reason – to go to the dog-care centre, Woofles.'

'Surely it would have been shut at that time of night,' said Ashraf.

'Check the opening times.'

He stabbed at his phone, pulled a face. 'Open until eight.'

Stacey felt her way along her theory.

'Okay. What if somebody told her it was open and suggested she go there that evening?'

'Kelly?' said Jack.

'She might have. Although they'd have probably gone together while they were out with the puppy. I was thinking more along the lines that the kidnapper suggested it to her.'

'Somebody here in Morecambe?' Jack's voice was a loud squeak.

'More likely somebody online. They could have chatted to her on social media. It's easy enough to create a fake profile. They might have fed her information about it, even encouraged her to drop by that evening and were lying in wait for her?'

Ashraf grunted. 'I can imagine that happening.'

'It would account for why she was abducted on that road. Jack, check her Facebook account. See if there's any mention of Woofles or any conversations in the private messages about visiting the place.' She moved aside so he could bring up the Facebook page.

'She might have had contact with somebody on a different platform. The same password doesn't work for her other apps or accounts. I already tried them,' he said.

'Ox can break into most social media accounts,' said Ashraf.

Stacey agreed. 'I'll drop in for a visit on my way to Lancaster.'

Ashraf's phone pinged. He read then paraphrased the message. 'I had my partner check out Tariq's movements for the night of the abduction. Tariq was at home when Lyra went missing, playing *Portal 2* online. He didn't leave the sofa between seven and nine.'

'You sure?' asked Stacey.

'One hundred per cent certain. My partner is never wrong about such matters,' he replied, waggling his phone screen at her.

'So that only leaves Mark?'

'Whose whereabouts are still questionable,' said Ashraf. 'In fact, I need to get a shift on. I'm going to Upper Heyford to see a man about a boat.' He pocketed his notebook and made for the door.

Stacey shifted her chair closer to Jack's to better study the photos of Lyra, batting the sadness away as she looked at the joyful images. This wasn't the time to get maudlin. Jack scrolled through the girl's posts, noting the dates, searching to see who had been in recent communication with her.

'It's very sporadic. I don't think she used the site much.'

'I understand a lot of teenagers have vacated Facebook in favour of more fashionable platforms such as Snapchat.'

'Yeah. Lyra's often on Snapchat. But I can't spot anything here about Woofles.'

'Is there a Facebook page for the dog care centre?'

He typed with two fingers, misspelt the name and cursed. He tried again, found the page. Lyra had liked the page.

'See if she's left any comments on it.'

Jack scrolled through photos and videos of woolly-faced cockapoos, tail-wagging Labradors, and fluffy shih tzus in various poses. Lyra had hearted one of a bichon frise, its white fur blown backwards as it hurtled after a ball in the yard, yapping merrily as it chased it around.

'No comments?'

'None.'

A technical team would cross-reference any of the people who liked this page with those who were included in Lyra's list of Facebook friends to establish if one of them was a fake. Although Stacey didn't have a team, she did have Ox. Ox would figure it out.

'Return to her page. Look at her private messages.'

Again, there was little evidence to show Lyra used it. The handful of messages in the column had all been sent some time ago.

'She might have deleted them,' he said.

'If so, she'd have deleted everything, not just the newest ones.'

'Fair point.'

'She's probably using more popular messaging apps. I'll speak to Ox.'

'Ought I to keep searching? I don't know what to look for.'

'Leave it. Try and get some rest. You look done in.'

Ox was not an easy person to find. Unless you were in the know, there would be no way you could trace the hacker's whereabouts. Highly secretive about identity, Ox rarely spoke face to face with anyone. Stacey was an exception.

The Glassworks were originally built as opulent town houses for Lancaster's wealthy merchant class before becoming home to a renowned stained-glass company. Nowadays, they were fully serviced rental apartments, offering long-term lets, which suited the evasive Ox, who liked to keep on the move.

'Take a seat.' Ox glided towards the cream leather sofa, dropping effortlessly onto it and tucking purple leggings under a long T-shirt bearing the image of the evolution of man depicted in Lego.

Ox was non-binary, preferring to be addressed as 'them' or simply 'Ox', a name chosen on account of being born in the Chinese year of the ox. Stacey had only a vague idea of Ox's age, given those under the sign of the ox would have been born in 1997, 1985, 1973 or maybe even 1961. However, there were no age markers on the olive skin or signs of grey in the jet-black hair that flopped over a wide forehead in a long fringe, reminiscent of Noodle from the virtual band Gorillaz. As she observed the hacker reaching out with skinny arms for a vape pen, she decided Ox was morphing into that very character. Stacey knew no details about Ox's private life. As far as work was concerned, Ox was a white-hat hacker who had worked for private institutions and the government. To that end, Ox could well afford to buy an apartment as swanky as this one, yet preferred to shift from location to location, staying within the county, moving house at whim.

If she had been Ox, she would have been reluctant to leave this apartment. Sunlight poured through the window, dropping rays onto the painting of Lancaster Castle on the wall above Ox's head. Puffs of vapour rose to meet the sunbeams and pirouetted in the light. She took the single chair, rested her hands on the wooden arms.

'Is that St John's Church?' she asked, taken aback by the superb view from the window.

Ox grunted. 'The castle can be seen from the kitchen window, if you wish to do some indoor sightseeing.'

The voice was baritone, deep and relaxed, at odds with the scrawny frame and outfit.

'I've no time for the full tour today,' she replied, earning a smile. 'Will you break into Lyra's social media accounts for me?'

Vapour curled around Ox's head. 'Which ones?'

'Snapchat, Instagram, WhatsApp, TikTok. I also need you to cross-check a list of her Facebook friends with those people who have liked a dog day-care page.'

'What do you hope to find?'

'Somebody posing as a friend who cajoled her into visiting the centre two days ago.'

'What's it called?'

'Woofles.'

Ox snorted. 'For real?'

'I'm afraid so.'

'Who conjures up such ridiculous names? Okay, Woofles it is. I can't do it instantly. It takes time. Snapchat is a so-and-so to break.'

'How long?'

'Two to three hours.'

'Call me as soon as you find anything.'

'You bet I will.'

'What do I owe you, for your time?'

'You're trying to find your stepdaughter. I can't take any payment for that. It'd be bad karma. Besides, I still owe you.' Ox blinked through heavily mascaraed lashes. Stacey stood up.

'I appreciate this. You're one of the good ones.'

'Shut up! You're making me blush. Now get out of here so I can crack on.'

Back on the street, she made another call. This time to the psychiatrist Danni had recommended. Explaining it was urgent she saw Dr Erin Bell, she managed to convince the secretary to allow her to come for a quick appointment ahead of the doctor's official list. She punched the address into her satnav. It was time to face more demons from her past.

# DAY THREE

## FRIDAY – 9 A.M.

Dr Erin Bell bustled into reception weighed down by a bundle of Manila files clamped under one arm, a stylish leather bag under the other, and a box of mini doughnuts in both hands. She dumped everything onto her secretary's desk with a breezy, 'Morning! Phew! Didn't think I'd make it up the stairs without dropping the whole lot.' Lifting the box lid, she chose a bun sprinkled with pink sugar. She held it between her fingertips before addressing Stacey.

'You had any breakfast?'

'Er, no.'

'Then grab yourself a doughnut and come in. They're freshly baked and not too calorific. Don't touch the coffee ones though. They're Diane's favourites. She'll sulk all day if you take one.'

Her loose-fitting, beige raincoat swished as she headed for the room bearing her name, where she called over her shoulder, 'Diane, please would you juggle the schedule so we can squeeze a few more minutes for this appointment.'

'Yes, Erin.' The woman proffered the box with a smile. 'Choose whichever you fancy. I actually don't have a preference.'

Stacey reached for the nearest chocolate-coated confectionery with thanks and joined the doctor, who'd removed her raincoat and hung it on a hanger on the back of the door. She smoothed out creases from her oversized cream silk shirt and sighed. 'Looks like I slept in it. I knew I should have worn a jumper instead. This is going to annoy me all day. Take a seat.'

The relaxed chitchat was what Stacey needed to overcome nerves. She guessed it was Erin's usual technique to put patients at ease, especially first-timers. The office was more like somebody's front room, a space with dove grey walls and dominated by a wide green sofa decorated with matching plump green and black striped cushions. A small bookcase stood behind it, adorned with green, white and silver plant pots. Antique books had been placed with their spines facing outwards. An old-fashioned twin-bell alarm clock was strategically placed beside them, so Erin could see the time while maintaining eye contact with her patient.

'Sorry, no plates. Have to improvise,' said Erin, handing Stacey a tissue. Stacey bit into the doughnut, savouring the rich, sweet chocolate that coated her tongue and teeth. She deduced the comfort food, like the surroundings, was intended to loosen her up. Erin finished chewing and licked her thumb. 'Delicious and surprisingly not sticky. There's a washroom next door though, if you need it.'

Stacey shook her head.

'Right. To business. According to the system, I can give you almost half an hour. Diane explained it was urgent that you saw me, so Miss O'Hara, what can I help you with?'

Erin registered no surprise as she sat with her hands in her lap while Stacey ran through the reasons for her being in the doctor's office. When it was her turn to speak, she was frank.

'I can't perform magic. I can't drag these memories out for you. That will be down to you. It will depend on whether I can get you into a deep hypnotic state. We'll require a full-length session, or several, and will have to work together to extract them. They've been locked away for a long time. Although you believe you want to access them, you've trained your mind to refuse entry for a good reason. It might be tougher than you think.'

'I've had therapy before. A long time ago. I practised visualisation techniques. My therapist would use the image of a cinema, have me imagine myself walking through the door to the screening room, where I'd find a seat, then watch myself on the screen.'

'And, given what you've just told me, that didn't work for you?'

'Yes and no. I had visions or imagined memories. I can't be sure what they actually were, only that they messed my head up further, and frightened me so much, I couldn't continue going down that route. Over the last three days, I've been seeing images, black and white, rolling out in my mind. I still don't know if they're real or not, but I'm hopeful you can help me retrieve others that are accurate.'

'Maybe. The fact they are emerging voluntarily could be a good sign?'

'I understand you use your techniques to help treat a number of issues, that you usually assist with altering people's habits and behaviours and that my demands are different. Can you help me?'

'I'm not sure I can. Ordinarily, I'd be reluctant to try hypnotherapy on you until we'd ascertained if the memories were actually returning without intervention.' She crossed her legs, and sat thoughtfully for a moment before continuing. 'If it could help save a child's life, then I'm willing to give it a go. Unfortunately, we require a couple of hours if we're to achieve what you're hoping for, and I must warn you not everybody can be hypnotised.'

'You can't do anything today?'

'When I said "unfortunately", I was referring to my patients whose appointments will need to be rearranged in order to prioritise you. Give me a few minutes to sort everything out.' She popped the rest of her doughnut into her mouth, jumped to her feet and bounced lightly out of the room.

Stacey checked for text messages. There was no word from Ox, Ashraf or Danni. She hoped they didn't call while she was being hypnotised. The hairs on the back of her arm suddenly stood up as if a current of cold air had infiltrated the room and brushed over her flesh. This time she would have to see the therapy through, not shut off when it became too much for her. There could be no backing down. Lyra's life was at stake. She steeled herself for what was to come. She was going to cut and splice the mental reels that made up her memories of the past, even though the thought terrified her.

Stacey felt removed from herself, as if she were watching the person sitting on the sofa with her eyes closed. Her body felt empty, weightless, numb. With the sensation came relief she'd never experienced before. Erin's honeyed voice reached her, asking about the lead-up to the abduction.

*'This place is so boring,' says Bella. They're sitting on a wall outside the block of flats where Bella lives. She reaches into her jeans pocket before pulling out two roll-ups and a disposable lighter. 'I nicked them from Mum,' she says before Stacey can ask. 'She was so out of her skull last night, she'll probably assume she smoked them.'*

*She lights both cigarettes, passes one to Stacey, who sucks on it immediately. Her dad would freak if he knew she'd taken up smoking. The thought causes her to take another, deeper drag.*

*'Looks like we'll be able to go on holiday in Devon as planned. Auntie Vee says we can have her caravan for two weeks if we promise to*

look after it and clean up after ourselves. I can't bloody wait! Two weeks by the sea, away from this shithole.' She looks up earnestly, liquid eyes almost hidden by a fringe of home-bleached hair. 'While we're there, we'll see if there are any vans or places for rent, get jobs and then be free!' She waves arms excitedly.

This is their big plan. Once they have the results of their GCSEs, they're going to find work, along with a place to share. Stacey's father wants her to stay on at school, take A levels and follow in his footsteps of studying law. He can get stuffed.

'So, what do you think?' Bella reaches into her canvas bag and pulls out the sundress she lifted from Primark. She holds it against her skinny body.

'Looks great.'

'Yeah. Those shorts would have looked cool too. You should have nabbed them while you had the chance. Nobody was looking.'

Stacey isn't as accomplished at shoplifting as Bella. She's only ever managed to steal some eyeshadow, which she returned the next day, a fact she isn't going to admit to her friend.

'Listen, why don't we bunk off tomorrow. We're only supposed to go in for some boring end-of-the-year crap about staying on next year and prize giving. We've completed our exams. We've effectively finished school. Meet me at the bus stop at the bottom of your road, at eight thirty. Tell your old man you don't need a lift to school. Make up some shit. We'll catch the bus to Derby instead, find some nice clothes and other bits and pieces for our holiday.'

The idea appeals. She'll ask her father for her allowance early, tell him she needs to buy stuff for her period. He won't question her. She finishes her cigarette and rubs the stub against the wall. She's sick of her life. Her father is always at work. She misses her mum. Life with Bella is a whole lot better. 'Let's do it.'

The muscles in Stacey's stomach twisted at the memory of her teenage self. As she began to surface from the depths of her memory, she wondered if she had really been so angry and hateful? And Bella too? That she hadn't been heading to school when she was snatched was news to her.

Erin's voice drifted over her, encouraging her to release any tension, relax again and return to the past. A kaleidoscope of pictures spun the story of a stroppy girl who dawdled over getting dressed, ignoring her father's pleas to get a move on. A younger version that she didn't recognise, a teenager so self-absorbed she didn't appreciate the patience being paid out by her father, who paced the floor anxious to get to court. She was shocked to see the look on her younger version's face, a mixture of triumph and disdain, when Henry finally yelled that he'd be late for work if he waited any longer for her. The images continued to dance on the make-believe screen, the camera now zooming in on Stacey standing at the top of the staircase, shouting she'd catch a lift with Milly and her mother, who lived on the next street. The front door slammed, leaving the girl performing a triumphant dance.

The scene cut to black. With sudden clarity, Stacey realised Henry hadn't once questioned her about Milly, a girl she barely knew or even talked about. He'd simply taken her at her word. He must have known she was lying. Why had he not challenged her?

She began to struggle for full consciousness and tried leaving the dark room where no film now played, yet as Erin's soothing tones coaxed her back into her seat, she was aware more was to unfold on the screen. Her last conscious thought was that her father hadn't quizzed her about Milly because he had secrets of his own . . .

*Stacey's been sent home from school early. Her head is banging badly. It's only been a week since her mother's funeral, and she still can't focus on anything. It's like she's in a void. People have been kind to her but none of it helps. Unable to contact her father, the school nurse, Mrs Hausmann, has driven her home and dropped her off with instructions to lie down and if she isn't feeling better in a few hours, to make sure her dad takes her to the local surgery.*

*She wants to sleep. For months. Forever. She unlocks the front door, drops her schoolbag on the floor and shuffles up the stairs. On the landing, she hears noise coming from her parents' bedroom. It's a woman's soft voice. She can't explain where the crazy thought has come from, but she is sure it is her mother she hears. Sense is eradicated. Somehow, this has all been a horrible mistake or a nightmare and her mother is alive. Love mingled with hope explodes in her chest. She turns the handle. Opens the door.*

*The murmuring is louder, accompanied by bed rocking and creaking, an aggressive, urgent rhythm. Stacey is frozen by the sight of her father's buttocks and the grey curls of hair that cover his shoulders. There's a horrified squeal. The rocking comes to an abrupt halt. He turns, rolls away from the woman beneath him, grabbing the sheet as he does so to cover himself, too late.*

*'Shit! Shit!' The woman's eyes bulge. She's plump, short-haired. Quite unlike Stacey's mother.*

*Rooted to the spot, Stacey can't drag her gaze from her. A week ago, her mother was in that very bed.*

*'Stacey, get out. Get out* now*!'*

Erin asked her if she was okay. She grunted a reply, her limbs too heavy to move, her lips unable to form words.

'I'm going to take you deeper. Remember, whatever you see can't harm you. I'm with you, Stacey. I won't let anything happen to you. Now, I want you to concentrate on the day you were abducted.'

At ease, with eyes closed and feeling secure with Erin watching over her, Stacey allowed herself to walk between rows of seats in the by now familiar cinema.

Why did she always come here – to this theatre – when she recovered her old memories? Was it the association with her mother? She dropped into a different chair, where she rubbed her hands against the velvet arm rests, concentrated on the day she was meant to meet Bella, and waited for the whirring of the projector.

*Weightless. Being carried. Floating in the dark. She comes to, unable to see. Her face is wrapped in a cloth, an itchy material that makes it difficult to breathe. She's in a seated position, hands behind her back. She attempts to move them, but something cold bites into her flesh. It's the same for her feet. The chair has no cushion, only a hard back that rubs against her shoulder blades. Her head throbs.*

*What's happened? She'd been on her way to the bus stop to meet Bella. There'd been the sound of someone running behind her. A hand. A horrible smell. Nothing. Now she is here.*

*A rattle of a door handle paralyses all thoughts. Footsteps. One. Two. Three. She wriggles on her chair. 'Is somebody there?' she shouts, her words muffled by whatever is over her head. 'Can you help me?'*

*The footsteps draw closer, and somebody clears their throat with a lengthy* Uh-huh, huh-huh. *Is it Bella, playing a daft trick on her? She does crazy things, like the time she locked Milly overnight in the school stationery cupboard. This could be an elaborate joke, an end-of-school prank. However, the voice is nothing like Bella's. It belongs to a man.*

*'Ah, you're awake, are you? Now the fun can begin.'*

*Tugging. The bag or whatever it is covering her head is removed and she gasps at the sight of the old man leering at her.*

*'Boo! Now you see me!'*

*It takes a moment to realise she is looking at a mask. A piece of crumpled, brown paper is lying on the dusty floor, like a dead, dried animal. The masked man raises a video camera to her face.*

*'We're going to make a film, a special premiere for your daddy.'*

*'Get lost. I'm not doing it. You can't make me.'*

*He clears his throat again. 'Really? I expected better from a judge's daughter. I can see I'm going to have to teach you a few lessons.'*

*He puts the camera on the floor and disappears. When he returns, he's holding a pair of kitchen scissors. He snips them right in front of her face, closer and closer until she's sure he will snip off her nose, then he stops. Waves the scissors at her.*

*'What's it to be? Shall I stick these in your eye, cut your ear off or stab you in the chest with them? They're new and very sharp. Look.'*

*Before she can react, he's reached out, grabbed her hair and snipped off a chunk close to her scalp. The golden strands lie limply in his hand.*

*'See how easy that was, Stacey. I could inflict a great deal of damage with these. You wouldn't want that. So, let's make that video for Daddy, shall we?'*

'Stacey, when I finish counting, you will be back in the office, wide awake, relaxed and calm. The memories you've uncovered will remain with you as vivid as when you retrieved them. You'll be able to talk about them without feeling any unease. I'm going to count backwards from ten. When I reach one, open your eyes.'

In her imagined state, Stacey saw her movements in reverse. She rose from the cinema seat, edged past the others towards the aisle illuminated by low-level lighting, then steadily climbed the stairs towards the main door and the daylight behind it.

'I brought you back sooner than I intended. I was worried you were becoming distraught. Don't move too quickly. Let yourself come to naturally. When you're ready, have a sip of water, then we'll talk about what happened.'

'Did I say anything?'

'Nonsensical outbursts. Undoubtedly at times you were recalling distressing moments. How do you feel?'

'Okay. I was in a cinema auditorium. It was a similar experience to the one I had when I had therapy as a teenager, only this time was different. I wasn't so scared. Why the cinema?'

'Each person has a different experience. It's natural your mind would plump for a familiar path. The groundwork to how to find those memories was laid back then. I see no reason for you not to tread the same route if you're comfortable with it.'

'It isn't working as I hoped. I didn't really discover what I wanted to.'

'That's because your mind has chosen to cherry-pick. Some memories might still be too raw for you to access. You've made a start, created a pathway, cleared some of the undergrowth away and, to extend the gardening metaphor, will be able to reach those memories still buried in the undergrowth. Don't give up yet.'

Stacey shuffled into position. Her body felt surprisingly light and free of tension. The cup of water was within her grasp, and she sipped it. 'The day of my abduction, I didn't go to school. There were presentations about further education, other stuff too, to do with speech day. Instead, I was planning on spending the day at the shops, with my best friend, Bella.'

Erin nodded encouragingly.

'Bella was a wild card who always challenged the system. She wasn't always my friend. At first, we ignored each other. We were chalk and cheese. She thought I was some rich bitch, a goody two shoes, somebody to be ignored. I had her down as a hard nut, a loner with a massive chip on her shoulder. One day, we were teamed up on a school project. Turned out we made a good combination.

Our effort was voted the best in class and to celebrate we went into town. Within a short time, we became friends. We became even closer after my mum died. I was going through a bad patch at the time. I was trying to ditch my prissy image. I fed off her rebellious nature, wanted to be more like her. Looking back, it was probably normal teenager behaviour, only I had more resentment inside me than most. Not as much as Bella though. She hated almost everyone, especially her mum. Anyway, if I hadn't arranged to meet her at the bus stop that morning, my father would have dropped me off at school and the kidnapping might never have taken place.'

'Do you suspect Bella had something to do with it?'

'Maybe.' She didn't want to contemplate the thought.

'Did you discover anything else while you were under hypnosis?'

'Yes. Although nothing that will help me find Lyra.'

'I wouldn't be so sure about that. Unlocking the past can benefit the present. Tell me what you saw.'

Stacey shrugged loosely. 'I found my father in bed with a woman only a week after my mother died. It isn't relevant.'

'As I said, it was probably an obstacle that needed removing for you to journey further. In fact, you might discover that, now you've unblocked some sticky memories, others will surface voluntarily throughout the day.'

'I really hope so.' She blinked back a vision of the man in the mask. 'I also remembered the beginning of my captivity. My kidnapper threatened to cut me with scissors if I didn't make a ransom video. I never saw that video; however, the one of Lyra was also filmed in a dimly lit location, like a basement, abandoned warehouse or garage.'

'Then you have a clue.'

Stacey nodded. 'That's true. I'm worried about her, Erin. The screaming in the video . . . She was terrified.'

Erin blinked slowly. 'I completely understand. I wouldn't ordinarily suggest this, but given the gravity of the situation, would you like another session today, to see where it leads you?'

'Please.'

'Right, I'll free up a second appointment for you.'

'Thank you.' Stacey got to her feet. She felt more relaxed than she had in a long time.

'Shall I pencil you in for five o'clock?'

'Yes, unless I have to be elsewhere.'

'Of course. If that's the case, give Diane a ring to let us know.'

The session had taken one hour and ten minutes, less time than expected. As it transpired, it meant Stacey was outside the building when Danni rang.

'I've got quite a list of disused places similar to the newsagent's, where somebody could hold a hostage. Do you want to investigate a couple with me?' Danni asked.

'Definitely. Where first?'

'Woodbank Street. There are several premises, and little foot traffic. I thought we could see if any of them look like they've recently been broken into.'

Stacey agreed it was worth checking out and it gave her the opportunity to talk to Danni again. The recent memories had given her food for thought about her own kidnapping. Maybe Danni could help enlighten her further.

# DAY THREE

## FRIDAY – 11 A.M.

An air of urban decay clung to the exposed brickwork of Charlene's hair salon. The painted exterior was a mixture of colours, layer after layer peeling from the last as if the building were undressing and exposing its past life. Beneath the bullet grey, the dirty red and the dingy cream was a base coat of bright yellow along with a hint of blue signwriting, the letter *B* followed by *E*. It wasn't the worst property along the street. Filthy shutters covered several frontages, some graffitied, others rusted by weather and time. For Sale signs were outside several of them, in place for so long the estate agents' names were illegible.

She spotted Danni's car, halfway down the street, manoeuvring into a space in front of a dental laboratory, its windows covered by blinds. The soles of her boots slid against the greasy surface of damp cobbles; a mixture of red interspersed with grey to create a swirling, modern pattern completely at odds with the rotting premises that bordered the pavement. The upgrade to the pavement, along with permanent bollards, ensuring visitors only used the parking bays, would have been expensive. It was a vain effort to entice people back into a rundown street – a project yet to come good. Since the pandemic, people had adopted new shopping habits, favoured fewer outings to the high streets. This one had suffered more than most.

Not all the properties were in dire need of renovation. Several shops appeared to be open for trade, although for how much longer, Stacey couldn't guess. She and Danni were the only people in the street.

They drew level outside a defunct tanning salon, where a poster of a once-bronzed bikini-clad woman filled the window, her suntan now the colour of straw.

The wind caught Danni's hair, whipping it across her face until she yanked a baseball cap from her jacket pocket and rammed it onto her head. 'Did you fix up an appointment with Dr Bell?' she asked.

'I did. She was really nice, moved her schedule so she could fit me in first thing this morning.'

'And?'

'I remembered a few things and now something's bugging me, but we'll talk about it later. Let's look at these places first.'

'We can probably walk and talk. There are twelve unoccupied properties along this street, almost all at the far end. I thought we'd do a walk past then check out their back yards.'

'Sounds like a plan.'

They retraced Stacey's steps, pausing by the hair salon.

'This one,' said Danni.

'I already looked through the windows. There's a mountain of old letters and bills on the floor and a lot of dust. It doesn't look like anybody's walked over those floors in a few years. We'll scout around the back, all the same.'

They stopped by each rundown establishment: a boarded charity shop, a shuttered pet shop, claiming to be the number one in the area for small animals and birds, where somebody had spray-canned a menacing Mr Tickle on the glass. Stacey stood beside the blanked-out windows and listened for noises inside. Hearing nothing, she moved on.

'Come on, tell me what's bothering you,' said Danni.

'Did any of the police officers on the case talk to my friends about my abduction? I imagine somebody would have followed it up and spoken to everyone who knew me, to try and establish who might have kidnapped me.'

'Yes. As the person who found you, I was seconded to that investigation. We spoke to your school friends, teachers, even neighbours. It was ongoing for a few weeks, but we couldn't find anything to indicate who'd been behind it. It was suggested it was either somebody who'd been convicted by your father and subsequently been released after serving their sentence, or who was related to somebody convicted by him. He didn't want us to pursue that angle; in fact, he spoke to the superintendent and requested the investigation be dropped. He felt it would cause you too much anxiety and stress.'

'Did anyone speak to my friend, Bella Hawkins?'

'As it happens, I did.'

'What did she tell you?'

'That she had no idea who might have snatched you.'

'Here's the thing that's pecking at me. Bella was my best friend at the time, and I was supposed to be meeting her to go to Derby the morning I was abducted. Now, did she raise the alarm?'

'No. Nobody raised any alarm. Your father was the only person who was aware you'd been snatched, and he contacted the anti-kidnap unit.'

'See, that makes no sense. Bella knew I was meeting her. She ought to have come looking for me or tried to contact me. Yet she didn't. She didn't even come to visit me in hospital afterwards. Now that I've remembered it was her idea to bunk off school and meet at the bus stop, it seems suspicious.'

Stacey turned her head and stopped walking.

Danni continued, 'One of the reasons I remember Bella after all this time is because she was very fiery. She didn't take kindly to being questioned. As for why she didn't visit you, I think you'll find she left the area. She told me she was going on holiday to her aunt's caravan, and she had no intention of coming back.'

It still didn't feel right to Stacey. Bella wouldn't have upped and left without seeing her.

They'd reached the end of the road.

'This way,' said Danni, turning first into a gloomy alley, then along a narrow road. 'This leads to the shops' rear entrances.'

Stacey came to a sudden halt as she realised where she was. The Trinity Methodist Church that stood opposite where Jack had left the bag of money was only a short block away.

Woodbank Street was wide enough for bicycles and pedestrians, even a mobility scooter, but not cars. Each property was hidden behind walls or fencing and locked gates. Yards were tiny. Two-storey extensions spilled out into mossy stone walls, the whole street a deformed architectural mess of timber, bricks and plaster, stuck together like a badly constructed model made from children's plastic bricks. Danni scooted to the second gate, belonging to the pet shop. It was hanging limply by one hinge. They scraped it open between them, clambering over a pile of rubble to reach the back door. There were no signs of an attempted break-in.

They moved silently towards the next, the gate firmly fastened. Danni managed to climb over the broken wall beside it and peer in through murky windows. Stacey made for the third, at the back of a charity shop. This gate wasn't secured. The yard contained wheelie bins that spewed rubbish and a discarded plastic chair. Among the weeds poking out from dirty, cracked concrete lay several beer cans and cigarette ends. She tiptoed to a small, single-paned window beside a boarded door. Spying smears on the glass, she pushed it gently. It swung open, revealing a broken latch. She ducked below the frame. Hugging the wall, she listened intently for any sounds within. A scratching inside caused her to plan her next move.

She was too large to fit through the gap. Danni, however, was petite, the height and size of a sporty teenager. She returned to where Danni was waiting.

'I think I heard something inside,' she whispered. 'I don't think I'll be able to squeeze through the window to check it out though.'

'I'll go.'

'No. Too risky.'

'I'll be careful.' Danni was off before she could stop her. She too listened by the window before giving a thumbs-up. She'd also heard a noise coming from inside. She hauled herself through the window with the ease of a practised gymnast, and no sooner had she vanished than Stacey's phone lit up with a text from Ox.

Fake friend – Trudy Bonham

Identity created six months ago

Lyra friended her three months ago

Messaging between them was deleted recently

Can't recover messages 😵

Her hunch had paid off. Trudy had most likely lured Lyra to the road where she was abducted. However, Mark remained a suspect. She shoved the phone back in her pocket and edged forwards. Could they have stumbled on the kidnapper's lair so easily? It felt too good to be true. There was a shout followed by a crash.

'Danni!'

'It's okay. It's empty. Apart from a freakin' ginormous rat.' Her face reappeared at the window. 'Somebody's been in here. There are used needles. Lyra's not here.'

'Do you want a helping hand out of there?'

'I'm fine. I knew all those Downward Dogs and Eye of the Needle poses would pay off one day.' Stacey held the window open as wide as possible while Danni squirmed through. She landed lightly and dusted off her jeans. 'That rat was huge. Gave me a right start.'

'Sorry about that. Ox texted while you were in there. Lyra was in contact with somebody calling themselves Trudy Bonham. Fake identity, of course.'

'There's too much of that on social media. Can you find out who the person is?'

'I think it is too great a test of even Ox's skills.'

'You never know. Shall we try the next place on the list?'

They had no luck at any of the empty buildings. Danni remained upbeat. There were, she declared, plenty of others to have a go at. They were driving, in separate vehicles, to an industrial estate when Ashraf rang.

'Can you FaceTime?'

'I need to pull over. Wait a sec,' said Stacey.

She parked on a side street, turned off the engine, then contacted Ashraf again. This time she could see his face and behind him a narrowboat with its distinctive palette of red, black and green. She could make out the word *Plus*. This was Mark's narrowboat.

'I've been inside. Nobody's on board. His mobile is on the bedside table. The other houseboat residents haven't seen Mark for a couple of days. According to one of them, he empties the boat's waste tank once a week, regular as clockwork. That involves moving the boat to a pump out, which takes a couple of hours. He leaves every Wednesday, around lunchtime, to make the trip. I thought I might hang around on the off-chance he shows up.'

'If he isn't there by two, come back.' She didn't comment on how he gained access to the boat. There were some things better left unsaid.

'His phone is password protected.'

That came as no surprise. 'If he's left it there to provide himself with an alibi, then it's unlikely there'll be anything incriminating on it. I expect he's using a burner phone. Any giveaways inside to suggest he might be the kidnapper?'

'I'll show you.'

The picture lurched, granting her snapshots of grass waving in the breeze, clouds, water, then the wooden floorboards of the deck. The camera bounced again. A door opened, revealing steep wooden steps that led into a galley kitchen. She caught flashes of an empty sink, overhead cupboards, a small hob. The dark-brown wood made the room seem old, austere even. Only the bright crockery, painted in primary colours, which adorned the limited workspace, cheered the place. Pans, pots, crockery were neatly arranged, washing-up cloths folded by the sink. Her own kitchen looked far untidier. The picture changed, the kitchen replaced by a dinette-cum-sitting room, containing nothing more than a foldaway table and a faded banquette. Ashraf turned the camera onto himself.

'It doesn't smack of wealth in here. Everything is past its best and needs replacing. I wouldn't be surprised if the boat doesn't need urgent repair work, either. The seat cushions definitely need chucking away. There's a horrible fusty, sour smell in here. There's not much to see so far; however, let me show you the bedroom.' He vanished. The camera swept over wooden ceilings then a porthole, covered with faded, floral curtains. The picture bobbed up and down, past a washroom, no bigger than an aeroplane toilet cubicle, to focus on the room in question. A double bed covered with black satin sheets filled the entire space. A square of red, sheer fabric hung over a bedside lamp, another at the porthole, and a large scarlet satin cushion sat in the centre of the unmade bed.

'And the pièce de resistance,' said Ashraf, tilting the screen.

'You're kidding! A mirror on the ceiling?'

'Very 1970s brothel, isn't it?'

'I wouldn't know.'

'Let's just say it's how I'd imagine one to be. There's nothing to suggest he's been planning a kidnap. There's no computer or iPad. The DVDs on display are mainly action films.'

'Any photos of Freya and Lyra?'

'None. No sign that either of them have been here or that he's in a relationship with Freya. Everything on board points to a single man living here.'

'Where is all the storage space? He must store his clothes somewhere.'

'It must be in the corridor. I haven't found it yet. Ah, this looks promising. Got to move this folding chair out of the way first.' The picture on the screen turned upside down. 'Here you go.'

The small space was rammed with folded clothes.

A splash of yellow caught her eye. 'Ashraf, what's that in the corner of the cupboard?'

'Looks like a backpack.' He yanked it out.

Stacey craned her neck. 'Are those . . . sunflowers?'

He gave a long, drawn-out 'Ye-es,' before unzipping the bag, tipping it upside down, and giving it a shake. Nothing dropped out.

'Lyra was carrying a similar backpack. If Mark turns up at midday to move that boat, I want to know about it.'

Stacey met up with Danni again, this time just outside Morecambe. Stubbs Farm Business Park was situated at the far end of a lane, invisible from the road.

They approached it from behind, using the network of hand-built stone walls that segregated the fields. The ground was uneven and the gradient steep, causing Stacey to tread carefully.

'I wish I'd brought Paul's binoculars,' said Danni.

'We'd have still had to climb up to the farm.'

Danni bounded ahead before crouching and cupping her hands in front of her eyes. 'A vehicle has pulled up, in front of the units.'

Stacey followed the direction of her outstretched arm, spotted movement in front of the units. 'Looks like a delivery van. Let's check it out.'

They climbed further until they had a clear view of the business park. The old farmhouse that dominated the plot still retained its original features, slate roof and sandstone rubble brickwork, while former farm outbuildings that stood in the yard below it had been converted into flat-roofed workshop and office units, each seemingly fitted with metal shutters.

Opposite them was a huge, half-timbered barn. Doors to the entrances were shuttered. To Stacey it looked impenetrable until she spotted steps on one side of the building that led to a door – a fire escape. The van had no markings on it; the driver was still at the wheel.

'It's odd nobody's got out yet.'

'Maybe they already have and the driver's waiting for them.'

They hunkered down, out of sight. Within moments, the figure behind the wheel got out. Stacey's pulse pounded in her ears. Could this be the person they were looking for? Could it be Mark, coming to check on Lyra? Danni was clearly thinking along the same lines. She reached for Stacey's hand, squeezed it tightly. Time paused. With no further movement, and no sign of the driver, who had disappeared behind the van, Stacey was considering moving even closer when the driver, now wearing a high-vis jacket, came into view. He began circling the yard. Bean-thin and tall, he wasn't Mark.

Danni said, 'What's he doing? Checking nobody is around or watching him?'

The man's movements were unhurried. Stacey would have expected some level of furtiveness. 'Maybe.'

He walked back to the van. The side door opened with a loud *swoosh*, swallowing his torso as he leant inside. When he re-emerged, it was with a tripod and what appeared to be a telescope.

Stacey groaned. 'That's a theodolite for determining location and distance of a point. He's a surveyor. He's undoubtedly going to be here for a while. We'll have to come back later to check out the site.'

The steep descent was difficult to navigate, both women leaning backwards to fight the pull of gravity, with ponderous steps. The rush of adrenalin Stacey had experienced while waiting for the van driver to appear had evaporated, leaving her heavy-boned and slightly despondent. They hadn't even been able to check out the buildings for signs of Lyra.

'We didn't finish discussing your friend, Bella,' said Danni.

'There's not much else to add.'

'Well, something's been nagging at me since you mentioned you were supposed to meet her the morning you were snatched. When I interviewed her, I wasn't under any impression you were best friends. She didn't show any excess of concern. Yet, from what you said, she should have. More importantly, she should have mentioned she'd been going to meet you. I can't fathom why she would have kept that secret. You said she was a tough nut. A loner. Was she involved with any rough types?'

'She hung out with some local kids who had a reputation for getting into trouble.'

'I was thinking somebody more hardcore. Someone who might have kidnapped you.'

Stacey had no difficulty in dragging up memories of Bella. They weren't locked away, merely filed in a different part of her mind . . .


*Stacey's alone in the form classroom. She doesn't feel very sociable, partly due to Bella, who didn't turn up to the canteen at lunchtime, leaving Stacey hunting for somewhere else to sit. She'd got lumbered with Patricia Knowles, who was a tedious bore and had the worst case of acne she'd ever encountered. She'd bummed Patricia off, leaving half of her macaroni cheese so she wouldn't have to put up with the girl any longer, and now she feels like a shit. Before Bella, she and Patricia got along quite well.*

*She flicks through the set text,* Lord of the Flies, *and wonders if everybody in her form was dropped on a desert island who of them would survive. Bella for one.*

*She continues reading, engrossed in a passage where the boys turn on one of the weaker members, when a voice shouts, 'Oi, swot!'*

*Bella is meandering through the doorway.*

*'Get lost. I had nothing better to do,' she mutters to her friend. Then, catching sight of Bella's red-rimmed eyes, she asks, 'What's the matter?'*

*'Nothing.'*

*'Yes, there is. You've been crying.'*

*Bella squares her thin shoulders. Her flat laugh is forced. Stacey puts the book away in her schoolbag and says, 'Come on. Tell me.'*

*'There's nothing wrong, alright?'*

*She sits down in a huff, folds her arms, and the sleeves on her blouse ride up to reveal a series of marks on her forearms.*

*'What are those?'*

*Bella pushes her away. 'Fuck off!'*

*'Are those burns?'*

*'Leave it. Trust me, you don't want to get involved.'*

*Stacey spins from her chair and sits on Bella's desk to face her. 'Of course, I do. What on earth has happened?'*

*Bella looks away, stares out of the window, feigning indifference, arms still folded.*

*'Bella.'*

*'It's nothing.'*

*'It's an armful of nothing. Tell me now or I'll tell a teacher.'*

*'You wouldn't,' she scoffs.*

*Stacey gets to her feet, straightens her pleated blue skirt and flounces towards the door.*

*Bella says, 'I owe some money to somebody, and they wanted paying today. Trouble is, I don't have the dosh.'*

*Stacey turns back. The bluff has worked.*

*'Who do you owe?'*

*'Somebody who wanted me to sell some gear, alright?'*

*'Drugs?'*

*'What are you? Fucking Miss Marple? Course drugs. It's only coke. I just don't happen to have sold all of it and they expected to get paid today. These burns are to "keep me focused".'*

*'Is that why you disappeared at lunchtime? To see these people?'*

*'Like I said. Best if you keep your nose out. We wouldn't want the judge's daughter mixing with crims.'*

*Bella always swears or uses sarcasm when she's trying to put on a brave face. Stacey can tell she's pretty shaken up about what has happened.*

*'You can't let them do this to you, Bella. Tell somebody.'*

*Bella snorts. 'Like who? The Old Bill? I'll be fine. I just need to shift this stuff and pay them off.'*

*'What you're doing is illegal.'*

*'Bloody hell, you really are sharp today, aren't you? I know it's illegal. I'm not like you. I haven't got a rich daddy and I'm not likely to be scouted for a modelling agency, so I have to make money when and how I can. In case you hadn't noticed, I live in a shitty council flat with my mum, who is usually so wrecked she doesn't know what day of the week it is. It's not easy getting hands on money to pay the rent, let alone anything else, not like you with your en-suite bathroom in your mansion. Not everyone has the same breaks, so don't preach to me.'*

*'I'm not preaching. I'm only concerned these people will hurt you again, maybe do something worse.'*

*'I'll get the sodding money, so get off my back, alright?'*

*She's up in a flash and storming out of the classroom again, pushing past other kids who are coming in for afternoon registration. Stacey decides to leave it. Bella lives in a different world to her. She'll be capable of handling anything she comes up against.*

They'd almost reached the road and the slope had flattened out. Stacey felt for her car keys.

'Bella was brought up in a rough area. Her dad bailed on them when she was six. Her mum hit the bottle soon after. I don't think I ever saw her sober. Bella pretty much fended for herself. It's a wonder she wasn't taken into care. But yes, she took risks, hung out with the wrong sorts. She did a bit of dealing and transporting for people, carrying packages for them: drugs, firearms, money. Whenever I asked her about it, she'd tell me to butt out. With hindsight, I'd say it was obvious she was being exploited by one of the local gangs.'

Danni looked around, as if somebody might be watching, her shoulders loose. 'Then there's every chance she got involved with some rough types who put her up to duping you. You said she used to call you a "rich bitch" until she got to know you. There were probably others who lived in the same part of town as her, who felt the same way about you and assumed Henry would pay to get you home safely.'

Stacey watched a black and white cow approach, tail swishing: a relaxed, loose gait, almost a swagger. Bella had walked like that – like she could take on the world. It halted by the five-bar gate and waited, as if expecting them to converse with it. 'I think deep down I suspected something when she didn't contact me. I simply didn't want to admit it.'

Danni crossed over to the animal and stroked it. 'It would explain the unnecessary violence towards you while you were chained up. Whoever it was, was a nasty piece of work.'

'That makes sense.'

'It would also explain how he knew there was a safe in your father's office. I trust Bella visited your house?'

'A few times. She was always good at sneaking about. I suppose if someone instructed her to search the house for valuables, there's a good chance she'd have stumbled on the safe.'

Danni patted the cow for the final time. 'Furthermore, if Bella set you up so that a gang or gang member kidnapped you, it's doubtful they'd have also taken Lyra.'

The cow ambled back to the herd. Stacey wondered if Bella had ever made it to the coast and if so, what had become of her. Although there'd been many opportunities to search for her friend, Stacey had chosen not to. The reason, she'd always known, was buried deep in her subconscious – Bella was a bad apple.

'True. Much as I don't want to accept Bella was involved, it would explain a great deal. It also means whoever it was wouldn't have taken Lyra. Besides, there's the unexplained backpack in Mark's boat. Everything points to him. I have to shake off this awful feeling the two kidnappings are linked. Thank you. You've helped me get things straight in my head.'

'You're welcome, although unless you can find and speak to Bella, it will only remain a theory.'

'I can probably live with that.'

# DAY THREE

## FRIDAY – 3 P.M.

Stacey took Danni for a coffee at a homely café, in a terraced row of Victorian houses, now businesses with apartments above, overlooking Morecambe promenade. The bell tinkled merrily as Stacey shoved open the front door and stepped into a long room, filled with the smell of cooked bacon. She stopped beside the counter. Danni's mouth opened at the sight ahead. The entire far wall was a colourful mural consisting of vintage saucy postcards.

'Wow!'

'Good, aren't they? The chap who painted them is also a musician, a member of a band that sometimes plays live music here. He did that one too.' She pointed at the fabulous painted art deco scene, of a band playing behind arches. In front of each pillar stood a larger figure: to the right, a moustached waiter holding a tray of drinks aloft, and to the left, a purple-uniformed waitress, wearing an immaculate white pinafore, carrying an arched holder of ice cream cornets. Above the scene it read *Ruby's Ice Cream Bar*.

'It's very 1930s,' said Danni. 'I love it. The ice cream in that cabinet looks tempting too.'

A friendly-faced woman appeared from the far end. 'Hi. Sorry to have kept you. I was prepping for tomorrow.'

'That's okay. I was debating whether or not to have an ice cream,' said Danni. 'However, these look delicious,' she added, pointing out the muffins behind a glass cabinet on the counter.

'They were baked this morning.'

'I'll take one, please, and a flat white. Stacey?'

'Same for me.'

'I'll bring them over. Where are you going to sit?' asked the woman.

'At the back,' said Stacey.

They headed up steps to the higher seating area and tucked themselves into the far corner. Danni spied a black and white photograph of the place.

'It looks like it used to be a milk bar. You can imagine the counters against the walls.'

'Yes, it's the only purpose-built café in town. Like many of the places here, it's had an interesting past. I think the kitchens were originally upstairs.'

'I love these historic places.'

'Me too. This one is Lyra's favourite café. They have *the* best ice cream.'

She paused. Talking about Lyra wouldn't help. She had to remain distant. The discovery of the backpack on Mark's boat had thrown her for a while. Now her mind had untangled itself. The coffees and cakes arrived. Danni bit into hers with gusto and made appreciative noises.

Stacey fiddled with her phone, debating whether to ring Ashraf. If Mark was sticking to his routine, he ought to have turned up to the boat by now. She punched out a text message and pressed the Send button. Within seconds, Ashraf was FaceTiming her again.

'Mark still hasn't been seen. Which goes to further substantiate our suspicions that he is behind this.' Ashraf's face was close to the screen, the car headrest surrounding his head like a cream halo.

'I've been thinking,' said Stacey, resting her elbows on the table to better see the screen propped up against the purple coffee mug. 'Something doesn't fit.'

'Go on.'

'The backpack for one. Why would he empty it and dump it on the boat? Why not leave it full? Why not dump it *and* the contents at the same time?' A word floated to the surface of her mind. *Trophy.* She ignored it and continued. 'If he drove Lyra all the way to Oxfordshire to keep her hostage there, wouldn't he have left the backpack with her?'

'They could have become separated. He left Lyra someplace before realising he still had her backpack in the car, so dropped it off at the boat,' said Ashraf.

'Empty?'

'Hmm. Maybe not.'

'Besides, none of the houseboat owners have seen him the last few days. It doesn't sound as if he's returned to the boat since Lyra went missing.'

'Stacey, it's a backpack with sunflowers on it, pretty much identical to the one Lyra was carrying when she disappeared. It's stuffed in a cupboard on *his* boat. I doubt he bought it for himself. It's all suspicious behaviour. The bag, him going walkabout at the same time Lyra disappears, Freya's car not on her driveway. Not to mention the fact his mobile is still on board *Tranquillity Plus*. These are all undeniable facts. If this was a police investigation, Mark would be a credible person of interest and we'd want to question him.'

A gentle tinkling made Stacey look up. 'Hang on a sec, Ashraf. We might have to take this conversation outside.' A couple in their thirties had come in, eyes drawn to the postcard mural. She waited to see if they'd come closer and was relieved when they ordered takeaway drinks. A blender burst into noisy life.

Stacey continued, 'It's okay. We can carry on. They are facts, yet I don't buy into the whole travelling up and down the motorway idea. It's a seven-hour round trip. There'd be too much toing and froing.' She moved her hands in a wave motion as she spoke. 'He goes to Morecambe to snatch Lyra. He returns to Oxfordshire to hide her. He heads back to Morecambe to orchestrate the pickup. And he has to travel back down the motorway to make sure she is okay. She needs food and water at the very least.' *Lyra's dead. He's kept the backpack as a trophy.*

Danni joined the conversation with a murmured, 'Don't discount the possibility somebody else is keeping an eye on her. Mark might not be working alone.'

The ominous voices in Stacey's head disagreed. *She's already dead.* 'What about her bike?' she said.

Steam hissed and metal clattered against metal as the café owner knocked out old coffee grains from the machine and replaced them with fresh to brew coffee.

Stacey continued, trying not to raise her voice too much against the background noise. 'Mark only had to tell Lyra that Freya had sent him to pick her up, make up some bullshit about them needing to go to the hospital, or tell her another equally convincing lie, and she would have got into the car with him. There's plenty of room in the back of a Škoda Estate for her bicycle too, which begs the question why did he dump it under a bush in the school grounds?'

Ashraf was quick to retort. 'I get that you're unsure about Mark. I could come up with any number of counterarguments: that his accomplice snatched Lyra, not him; Lyra didn't believe him, so he forced her into the vehicle, and he didn't have time to load the bike as well; and so on.

'What we shouldn't ignore are the facts. That was how we always operated in the police, Stacey. We followed the evidence.

Not this shilly-shallying *what if* speculative nonsense. Mark has disappeared. He left his mobile behind. There's a backpack exactly like the one Lyra was carrying in a cupboard on his boat.'

His reasoning refocused her. 'Okay. Okay. I just don't think we should put all our eggs in one basket.'

'No. I know what you're *really* thinking: that this is somehow linked to what happened to you. I understand why, but that is what is holding you back. I worry you're too involved to see clearly.'

She shook her head. 'No. Danni and I have spoken about that. If I'm honest, my concern is that if Mark really is behind this, he might not want to keep Lyra alive. After all, she can identify him.'

Beside her, Danni's teeth worried her bottom lip.

'She's his girlfriend's daughter. That would require a whole new level of malevolence,' said Ashraf.

Concern lodged itself in Stacey's mind. *Trophy. He kept her backpack as a trophy.* She forced it away. 'We don't know enough about him. His relationship could have been part of an elaborate plan. Get involved with the mother, gain the girl's trust, set up to kidnap her when she wasn't on her home turf where suspicion might fall on him, get a ransom from the dad and head off to start a new life. He hasn't been to visit Freya in hospital. Isn't that strange in itself?'

'You're speculating again.'

The hissing in the background ceased. Stacey's insides churned. She wrestled with her decision then decided it was the right call to make.

'I'll ring the police. This is too much for us to handle.'

'You'll be going against Jack's wishes,' said Danni.

'I don't care. This might no longer be a kidnapping.'

'Okay. It's your shout,' said Ashraf. 'Wait up. There's somebody pulling in. Shit! It's a Škoda Superb Estate.'

'Is Mark at the wheel? Ashraf!' He'd disconnected. Danni's face was blank. Stacey picked up her coffee, sipped without tasting. She could do nothing other than wait for him to get back in contact. A mother and daughter came into the café, the girl about six or seven, dressed in a fairy outfit, a bodice with dainty rosebud and ribbon detail, the skirt, several layers of soft pale-pink net. As she stood on tiptoe to better see the ice cream flavours in the cabinet, she adjusted the tiara headband with matching pink detail and Stacey blinked away an image of Lyra at around the same age, standing between her and Jack, steaming the glass cabinet with her breaths as she took in the vast selection.

'Stacey!'

'Sorry. I was thinking.'

'If . . . If Mark has done the unthinkable, you must accept you could never have saved her. You mustn't allow guilt to eat you up over this. You believed you were handling a kidnapping. Your priority was to find and save her. None of us bargained on this being anything else.'

'You've always been very kind to me,' said Stacey. 'Of all the people who might have come out that day to follow up on the anonymous tip-off, I'm so glad it was you.'

She willed the mobile to ring again. Ashraf had to know she was desperate for news.

'Are you going to eat that?' Danni nodded at the muffin.

'Do you want it?'

'No. I want you to eat it. You're all skin and bones.'

'My mum used to say that. Even though we both know it isn't true. I've plenty of padding.' She gave Danni a warm smile. It was nice to know there was somebody watching out for her. She broke it in half, popped the soft sponge into her mouth.

Her gaze drew to the little fairy again, who'd chosen a mixture of strawberry and vanilla ice cream and was now licking around the cone to prevent dribbles running down her hand. Her mother stroked her silken head. Stacey had never allowed herself to get so close to Lyra. Like all her relationships, with men, her father, friends, she'd held back. The kidnapping had changed her on many levels. She hadn't ever stroked Lyra's hair like that. She hadn't possessed a mother's love for her child. Why would she? Her own mother had chosen death over her. Stacey doubted she could love anyone. Which made it even more difficult to explain the painful sensation in her chest when she thought Lyra might be dead.

Her phone buzzed. 'Ashraf, have you spoken to Mark?'

'Mark didn't show. His girlfriend came instead.'

'Freya?'

'No. Another woman. Judging by the necklace she was wearing, her name's Holly. I assume he's seeing her behind Freya's back. I didn't ask her straight out, said I was an old friend of Mark's who dropped by when I couldn't get him on his phone.'

'Why do you think she's his other woman?' She couldn't ignore the sinking disappointment that accompanied the idea that Mark was cheating on Freya. Was he treating her as shittily as Jack had done?

'Clues like she was here to take the boat to the pump out on his behalf and collect his phone, which he accidentally left behind when he spent the night at her house – the same night Lyra went missing.'

The idea that Mark was playing away while Freya was undergoing major surgery left a bad taste in her mouth; however, if the man had an alibi, he couldn't be responsible for kidnapping Lyra. 'Why didn't he collect the phone himself?'

'There was no time to go back to the boat to fetch it. He had to drive to Banbury first thing the following morning. He's got some temporary work in a boatyard there, helping to clean out hired narrowboats. I rang the place up immediately. The owners confirmed he's been there the last two days.'

'And why was Holly driving Freya's car? I take it, it was Freya's car, not her own?'

'Yeah. Turns out she's Freya's best mate. She borrowed the Škoda because her car is in for a service.'

Stacey let out a sigh. Poor Freya! 'What about the backpack?'

'Ah, that's another reason she came here. It belongs to one of her two daughters. She used it to carry some stuff to "brighten up the bedroom" and forgot to take the bag back home.'

Stacey thought of the red gossamer-thin material draped over the lamps and the round satin cushion. It added up. The relief she had experienced thinking Lyra hadn't been killed by the man was short-lived. If Mark hadn't snatched Lyra, that left the possibility of a copycat or a more chilling alternative – Stacey's original abductor was back.

Danni looked up from her phone, forehead wrinkling as she spoke. 'I've got a text from Paul. There's been some trouble back home. The police have contacted him about an apparent break-in at our house. He wants us to pack up and return to Cornwall immediately. He's worried any burglars might come back and try again. I'll have to go with him. We only have the one car, you see. Unless . . . I rented a vehicle.'

Stacey knew Paul wasn't in the best of health. Fifteen years older than Danni, he was almost seventy. In 2021, he'd suffered a heart attack that had weakened him considerably. Worry about a break-in was the sort of thing likely to bring on another. Danni needed to be with him. 'No, that's crazy. You ought to go back with him.'

Danni looked from her phone's screen to Stacey and back again. 'But I haven't finished checking out those properties.'

'Go. I can investigate them.'

Ashraf spoke up. 'I could maybe step in, after I get back.'

'It's okay. I'll involve Jack. He can help me.'

'Okay, I'll make tracks,' said Ashraf. 'We'll speak again after I get home.'

The screen went blank. 'Are there many places left to look?' she asked Danni.

'Quite a few. I should stay. You need me.'

'No, Danni. Paul needs you to go with him. Jack and I will check them out. Let's face it, there's no guarantee Lyra is in any of them. We're chasing around because of a hunch. It could prove to be a complete waste of time.'

Danni eventually nodded. 'Okay. I'll email you a full list of the properties as soon as I can.' She lifted the plate containing the half-eaten cake and pushed it in Stacey's direction. 'And for goodness' sake, eat!'

Stacey remained in the café. People came and went. Children with teetering ice creams, couples with cups of coffee and toasted sandwiches. The world was still turning, people doing ordinary things, following routines, and everything was normal, quite unlike the chaotic state of her mind.

They'd discounted the only two people they'd believed to have taken Lyra. Although there was every chance the culprit was somebody with a grudge against Jack, she came back to the elephant in the room – the similarities between this abduction and hers. Ashraf had warned her not to. Jack and Danni had offered similar advice, yet she couldn't leave it.

Her thought process led her back to Bella, who might have set her up. But could Bella be behind Lyra's kidnapping? She chewed over the possibility that her friend had never really liked her, had always borne a grudge against her for having what Bella didn't – a comfortable existence. What if Bella had read about her success as a news reporter and was once again trying to destabilise Stacey's life? Because this theory required further exploration, she rang Ox.

'My, my. I'm popular all of a sudden.'

'I'll make it up to you.'

'I'm sure you will. What is it this time, O'Hara?'

'I'd like you to find somebody from my past. The name is Bella Hawkins. That is, if she hasn't changed it.'

'You do like to challenge my capabilities. What else can you give me?'

She relayed Bella's old address in Burton-on-Trent, along with as many details as possible, including the last thing she'd known about her friend. That she'd gone to Devon to stay in her aunt Vee's caravan and hadn't planned on returning to Staffordshire.

'Leave it with me. I take it you haven't found your stepdaughter yet?'

'You'll be one of the first to find out when we do.'

'Good to hear that.'

She swept the phone into her bag, mind made up. Regardless of what others thought, she was going to pursue this avenue. Erin might be able to help her access more memories of Bella. Before her next appointment, she'd ask Jack to check out the properties on Danni's list. They only had two days to locate Lyra before the kidnapper would want the balance of the ransom. It wasn't a long time, but it might be long enough.

Jack hadn't left the house and although he'd showered and shaved, he still looked as wrecked as when she'd left him.

'Any news?' he asked as soon as she crossed the threshold. She brought him up to speed.

Jack pulled a face. 'Mark is in the clear, then?'

'It seems so.'

'Then what next?'

'We keep looking. I still believe the kidnapper is holding her nearby.'

'On what basis?'

'On instinct. Danni thought so too. It's worth checking out premises she's identified.'

'Stacey, anybody could have abducted her. She could be in somebody's loft, cellar or garden shed. She could be bloody miles away.'

'She's nearby! I know she is.' She fought back angry tears. 'Okay, Ashraf and I will do it without your help. I'm going to check out these places, regardless of what you say. I don't know what else to do. This is all I have for the moment.'

'Hey, hush. It's okay.' He put his arms around her, drew her towards him.

The soothing only served to upset her more. She looked up, preparing to speak again. In that moment, his face drew closer, his lips brushing hers. It was mercifully brief, and he broke away before she pushed him off her. He gave her a predatory smile, which froze her to the spot.

Her sluggish mind couldn't react. What the hell had just happened? She fought for clarity in time to hear him say, 'I suppose, if you have a gut feeling about this, we should run with it. Even if it takes up valuable time. I'll check out the list with you. If you're sure this is the right way to go.'

Stacey snapped out of her confusion. Why Jack had kissed her became irrelevant. Instead, her heart weighed heavy at his words. He clearly remained unconvinced that searching empty properties was a good idea, and was merely going through the motions to appease her. The prospect of finding Lyra hidden in an abandoned shop suddenly seemed so unlikely, she almost relinquished the idea until she looked at him again. His face had taken on a familiar expression of disappointment. It was a look he used to adopt when he wasn't satisfied with her performance. When she'd worn what he'd considered to be the wrong dress. When the meal wasn't to his taste. When he wanted her to feel bad about herself.

It wouldn't wash this time, however. She wouldn't be swayed by his sighs or facial expressions. She thought instead of Erin, who felt the key to the present lay in Stacey's past. Of Ox, willing to track down Bella. And Danni, who'd spent all night searching for places to recce. They hadn't thought her ideas foolish. They'd supported her. She shouldn't ignore any hunches. Hers were invariably good. Moreover, they had often resulted in her best news articles.

'I'm sure,' she said, checking her phone for emails. 'In fact, the list from Danni has arrived.'

'Okay. Forward it to my email. I'll start on it straight away.'

'No heroics, Jack. Look for obvious signs of break-in or vehicles parked outside but do not, I mean this, do not go inside if you find anything. You ring me immediately. Clear?'

'Clear. I want her back safe and sound. No heroics. Where are my car keys?'

'Try the fruit bowl in the kitchen,' she said. She checked the time. It was quarter past four. There was only another forty-five minutes to wait until her appointment. She crossed her fingers Erin would unlock more memories.

The kitchen door was ajar. Propped up on the table, holding a mug bearing her name between its paws, was Lyra's toy dog, Fred. A wave of sadness threatened to drown her. For all his faults, Jack still adored his daughter.

He reappeared, keys in hand.

'I think she'll be happy to see the welcome party,' she said, nodding towards the dog.

'You don't think it's stupid? I wanted her to feel . . . loved.'

She understood and it was touching that he'd carried out such an act. 'Not stupid at all.'

She made for the door, all the while praying her instinct would prove right. Pausing before she left, she said, 'Can I ask you a favour?'

'Ask away.'

'Will you come with me to see my father tonight? I want to ask him a few questions about the past. If he sees us together, it might jolt his memory, take him back in time.'

A fleeting frown creased his brow. 'Ask about the past? Sure. What time?'

'Seven thirty. I'll meet you at the nursing home.'

'I'll see you there.'

With a little time to kill before her appointment with Erin, she meandered back along the promenade, where she sat on a bench to watch the seagulls. She hadn't always loved the coast. Bella had been obsessed with living beside the sea. In retrospect, it was probably because the freedom of all this vast expanse of ocean represented the opposite of the world she knew. She craved freedom and the coast offered her that.

*'You ever been to the seaside, Stacey?'*

*'I went to Majorca on holiday once.'*

*Bella pulls a face. 'Majorca,' she repeats in a fake, posh voice.*

*'It's not fancy there, Bella. It's just an island with a coastline. There weren't even any decent beaches where we stayed, just rocks.'*

'Majorca!' Bella snorts. She hitches up her school skirt to better expose her skinny thighs before leaning closer to the mirror above the sink to slick on mascara.

'You know Miss Henshaw will force you to remove that as soon as she sets eyes on you, don't you?'

Bella ignores her comment, continues swiping the wand over already lengthy lashes.

'Bella!'

'I'm not fucking deaf. She won't see me because I'm bunking off. Meeting somebody.'

'This another one of your jobs?'

'Might be.'

'You need to be careful. It's one thing doing it outside school hours and another when you're supposed to be in double English.'

'That's where you come in. You tell her I had terrible stomach cramps and had to go home. She'll believe you.'

'I'm no good at lying!'

Her face suddenly screws up and she doubles over, clutching her stomach. 'Ow . . . Ow . . . Ow! Stacey!'

'What's happened? Are you okay?'

Bella collapses forward onto the sink and Stacey drops her schoolbag, rushes to her side.

'Bella, it's okay. I'll find a teacher. We'll sort you out.'

Bella turns her face and grins widely. 'Gotcha!'

'You bitch! I thought you were dying or something.'

She stands up, adjusts her skirt again and says, 'At least you won't have to lie now. I was in the toilets screaming in agony.'

Stacey kicks Bella's bag, but her friend only laughs. 'Gotcha. Good and proper.'

'I'm not doing it.'

Bella's face becomes serious. 'Oh, come on. I was only messing. I'm sorry if I scared you. Listen, I really need you to do this for me. This one *is a good earner. I need the money, Stace. I'm saving up to move away. I want to live by the sea. I want to get up every day and see absolutely nothing but water, miles and miles of blue water. If I don't carry out these deliveries, I won't get paid and then I'll be stuck here forever. Please. Please cover for me.'*

A gull circled overhead, hopeful of finding food.

'Got nothing for you, mate,' Stacey said.

As if it understood, it circled one last time and flew off.

The tide was out, leaving miles of sandy beach. In the distance, the water appeared to be striped amethyst green and amber. Two figures walked along the shoreline. She'd often walked along it with Jack and Lyra. Three people, not two. She had to get Lyra home.

She wondered if Bella really made it to the coast and if maybe she was also sitting on a bench somewhere reflecting on her past life. Somehow, she doubted it.

# DAY THREE

## FRIDAY – 5 P.M.

Erin poured a glass of water and placed it on the table. 'You know what to expect this time. Is there anything you want to ask me before we start the session?'

'Only that I'd like to go as deep as possible. Even if I become distressed, I want you to leave me in a hypnotic state.'

Her face grew solemn. 'I can't do that. It could be harmful.'

'It's my decision. It's imperative I recall as much as possible. I'm running out of time and hope.' Stacey held Erin's gaze until she acquiesced.

'On the condition that if I truly believe you are stressing more than I think you can cope with, I bring you out.'

'Agreed.'

They wasted no time, Erin coaxing Stacey back into a relaxed state, away from the anxieties she'd been facing, until she was once again in the cinema theatre, watching the screen flicker into life.

*She's been in her bedroom, trying to block out the shouting going on downstairs. The arguments have been getting worse, but this is the worst.*

*Her mother is on her hands and knees with a dustpan and brush, sweeping away the debris, a china cup, a casualty of the heated argument. Instead of the tears she expected, she sees only defiance.*

*'You okay, Mum?'*

*'I'm perfectly fine, cherub. Are you?'*

*'The shouting—'*

*'Is over. Your father has gone out to cool down.'*

*She taps the dustpan, and the porcelain pieces slide obediently to the end, and she takes it outside for disposal in the two-handled black waste bin that stands by the back door. When she returns, she replaces the set in the cupboard by the sink and washes her hands.*

*'How would you feel about moving away from here?' she asks, patting her hands dry on a tea towel covered with pictures of teapots. Stacey focuses on the one that looks like the pot in her illustrated copy of* Alice in Wonderland.

*'Are we moving?'*

*Her mother hangs up the tea towel then straightens her shoulders. 'It might be nice to start a new adventure in a new place.'*

*'What about my friends? I don't want to leave them behind.'*

*Her face changes as if she's suddenly going to cease being her mother and shift shape into some alien creature. Before it happens, she regains control of her features, and smiles.*

*'No, we're not moving, cherub. It was only hypothetical.'*


The reel broke, leaving Stacey staring at a blank screen. The door to the cinema opened and light filtered through. She began to stand, hands resting on the wide arms of the velvet-covered chair, ready to leave, until Erin's voice reached her.

'You're back in the newsagent's, Stacey. The man in the rubber mask is with you. He can't hurt you. I'm with you. You can't be harmed. Study him closely. Pay attention to your surroundings and know you are completely safe.'

Stacey felt her muscles slacken and the projector behind her started up with a rattle, casting black and white images of a girl tied to a chair before her eyes.

*Her mouth is so dry her tongue has almost stuck to its roof. He's there with her. Periodically he clears his throat as if he's going to speak but nothing is said. She hears the sound of somebody flicking their nails together.*

*'Do you want something to drink, Stacey?'*

*Her response is no more than a croak.*

*The hood is removed. The only light comes from a candle. No, not a candle. It's a lantern or a hurricane lamp like the one her parents sometimes use in the garden. That's why the light is flickering and casting long shadows against peeling wallpaper, like demons dancing. His face pops up in front of her and makes her jump. He chuckles at her dismay and pushes the open bottle against her lips, and she glugs the refreshing liquid, like a newborn lamb feeding from a teat, until without warning, he pulls it away, leaving a trail of water dribbling down her chin. Now she smells him, the mixture of sweat, anger and musk, in spite of the peppery spray he's used to disguise the smell, causing her nose to wrinkle. He stands and begins to pace, flicking his thumb against his middle finger repeatedly.*

*'This would be over if your father hadn't been such an arse, Stacey.'*

*'Can I have another drink, please?'*

*'What nice manners you have. Only to be expected from somebody in a privileged position. "Please. Thank you. May I get down from the table, please, Mama." Oh, sorry. You can't say that, can you because she died, didn't she? Took her own life. Did you ever ask him why, Stacey?'*

*She hates the way he repeats her name almost at the end of every sentence. She hates him for a lot of reasons, but now she hates him even more.*

*'Ooh, look at you, baring your teeth. I think we touched a nerve there, didn't we? I'll leave you to think about that then, shall I? I'd like to be a fly on the wall in your house when you do confront him.'*

'No!' She heard the cry and was sure it had come from her. She'd leapt to her feet, while the film was still running, her hands gripping the chair backs as she stumbled towards the aisle and exit.

'Two. One.'

Her breath was coming in gasps as if she'd been running. Her face felt sticky and this time she didn't feel relaxed in the slightest.

'Stacey?'

Erin's voice was pure concern.

'Stacey? Speak to me.'

Stacey winced at the brightness. 'I'm alright.'

'Thank goodness. You gave me a scare. You started hyperventilating. I had to bring you back. I'm sorry if it stopped you from finding out anything.'

'No, it's okay. I learned something new. It's another piece of the puzzle. What time is it?'

'Almost seven. Do you want me to try and put you back under?'

Stacey's heart was still racing from the scenes that had played out. Despite the fact that she wanted to learn more, going back under hypnosis would cause her to run late. She could ring Jack and the care home to arrange a later visit. Erin gave her an encouraging smile. The last vision still felt real to Stacey, like a nightmare she couldn't shake off. Why had Mum taken her own life? The urge to talk to her father outweighed her desire to continue the session. She needed to clear this matter up. It was, as Erin might put it, a blockage that needed removing. She rubbed her forehead. 'Erm. Thank you, but I ought to shoot off. I have to see my father. Could you see me tomorrow morning, instead?'

'If you can manage an early start, say half past six, it wouldn't interfere with my appointments, and I could do a full session with you.'

'I'll be here at half six, on the dot.'

Jack was true to his word and waiting for her in the car park at Topfields Residential Care Home. He thrust his hands in his jacket pockets and ambled towards her.

'I've had no joy. There are still another twenty properties to look at. I'll pick it up again, after we've visited your dad.' He gestured towards the well-kept lawns and the fountain. 'This is swanky, isn't it? I can see why Henry chose this place.'

'Thanks for coming. I thought we could say a quick hello together, then you could make up some excuse and leave us alone for half an hour.'

'I can do that. Erm, about earlier. When I kissed you. I couldn't help myself.'

She didn't want to upset him. Not when they were about to see her father. She didn't want to have to deal with two potentially volatile men. 'It's fine. I . . . I didn't mind.'

He gave her a smile. 'I didn't think you did.'

They climbed the stone steps and passed into the hall. The curved desk was befitting of a top hotel foyer and the receptionist manning it was smartly attired in a white blouse and blue suit. During visiting hours, Topfields ensured both residents and visitors felt well treated.

'Good evening, Miss O'Hara.' She tapped at her screen and brought up the daily report. It was normal to give relatives an update of what their loved ones had been up to and how they were coping with their illnesses. A doctor's report could be requested at any time, while the nurses and carers were on call 24/7. Stacey couldn't have wished for better treatment for her father.

'This reads well. Henry is in a positive mood today. He even asked for a newspaper so he could do the crossword. He ate all his breakfast and had poached salmon and beans for lunch followed by a fruit salad. He's had a light supper of scrambled eggs on wholemeal toast and spent the afternoon in the day room.' She beamed at Stacey.

It was unusual for Henry to leave his room or eat much food. This was positive news, and a good sign for what she had in mind.

'Thank you, Rachel. This is Jack. He's coming in with me for a few minutes. Would it be alright if he pops out for half an hour and waits in the canteen?'

'Certainly. Would you like me to arrange something to eat and drink while you wait, sir?'

'I wouldn't mind a coffee, please.'

'I'll sort that for you when you come back out.'

They walked down the corridor towards Henry's room.

'It's exactly like a five-star hotel. I'm coming here when I'm old and feeble.'

'Better get your name down now. The waiting list is humungous.'

'The residents are so well looked after they probably never pass away.'

The humour was welcome. She returned his smile.

Henry was propped up in his chair, a copy of *The Times* folded at the crossword page. His face broke into a crooked smile when he saw them both enter.

'Well, well, well. What a lovely surprise. Jack! I haven't seen you in a long time.'

'Hello, Henry. I brought you a little something.' Jack pressed the small package into Henry's hand.

He ripped at the paper like a child opening a present. 'My favourite! Fudge. How did you know I liked it?'

'A little bird told me.'

'That bird would have been me.' Stacey pecked her father on the cheek before sitting on the settee. She patted a plump cushion as invitation for Jack to join her. His leg brushed against hers as he dropped down beside her. Henry seemed pleased to see them together. He'd always approved of their marriage.

Henry cleared his throat. 'You still swinging the clubs, Jack?'

'Not as often as I used to.'

Henry began to chuckle. 'Me neither.' He slapped his hand weakly against his thigh.

After a few more minutes of chitchat, and deciding he was in good enough health to participate in a more serious conversation, she squeezed Jack's hand.

Jack took his cue. 'I have to pop out to make a phone call. Do you mind, Henry?'

'Not at all. I was a lawyer too, once upon a time.'

Jack slipped away and Henry reached for the fudge, pulled off a piece and sucked it.

'Now I've got you alone, can I ask you about something?' said Stacey.

He nodded, jaw moving.

'It's about you and Mum.' She blinked away the vision of her mother on her knees, cleaning up the broken cup. No tears on that occasion, but plenty on others. 'Did you and her ever talk about splitting up?'

His cheeks seemed to implode as he sucked more intensely on the fudge.

*'It might be nice to start a new adventure in a new place.'*

'You see, I've been getting weird flashbacks, some to do with my kidnapping and others that don't seem related at all. I believe she planned on leaving you. She wanted us both to go.'

He swallowed at last and said quietly, 'I know she did.'

'Why? Were you having an affair behind her back?'

'Julia was having an affair.'

'Mum was seeing somebody else?'

He averted his gaze.

'I don't mean to be heartless. I need to know the details. I'm not raking up the past to punish you, Dad.'

For a moment, she thought he'd retreated again, lost in his mind. She feared she'd been too blunt, pushed him too hard. After all, his memory was fragile. Like her, he'd shut down a lot of the past because it hurt too much to think about it.

'Dad?'

'Julia was in love with Bernard. She wanted to take you and leave. Go with *him*!'

The only person she knew called Bernard had lived next door to them. It was also a name Henry had shouted out on occasion after his apparent senility had settled in. 'Bernard? Our neighbour?'

He nodded again.

Suddenly things fell into place: coming home to find Bernard at the kitchen table; her mother saying, 'Bernard fixed the blocked sink', or, 'Bernard popped around with some fresh strawberries from his allotment'. She remembered watching them talking over the garden fence, the looks that passed between them. She'd never liked Bernard. She was sure he didn't like her much, either. Maybe back then, he was worried she had understood what was going on and would reveal all to her father. Of course, this was the real reason he and her father had fallen out. It was nothing to do with Bernard spreading rumours. Bernard hadn't been jealous of her father. It had been the other way around. It explained his angry outbursts – his 'Bugger Bernard' moments. Moreover, her father had lied to her for years.

When she looked again, his face had transformed back into the formidable Henry of old. His fist was clenched. 'I wasn't going to let him take either of you anywhere. I dealt with him.'

The revelation stopped her in her tracks.

'What on earth did you do to him?'

'Me? I didn't do anything. I hired a professional to give him a pasting.'

She recalled seeing Bernard hobbling up his path on crutches, his lip and eye swollen. Sometime soon afterwards, his house had gone up for sale and Bernard left the area.

'He told everyone he'd fallen off a ladder,' she said.

'There was no ladder. And if he hadn't moved away when he did, he would have been carried out of his house in a wooden box. Nobody was going to take *my* girls away from me.'

A picture in her head became clear . . .

*Stacey is sitting at her bedroom window, from where she can see her mother hammering on Bernard's door.*

*'Bernard, please! Open the door,' she cries.*

*Earlier this morning, Mrs White told them Bernard had left to stay with his sister in Newport and wasn't returning. He was putting his house up for sale.*

*This is the fifth time her mother has banged on his door since then. Stacey can't understand why she's so upset. Bernard was creepy, always hanging about the place, supposedly doing jobs but spending more time talking to her mother than working.*

*Her mum runs back to the house. The back door slams and Stacey descends the stairs to comfort her.*

*'Mum?'*

*Sooty mascara has stained circles around her mother's bloodshot eyes.*

*'Mum!'*

*Her mother remains tight-lipped, sobs convulsing her shoulders.*

*'He was only a neighbour. Don't get so upset about it.'*

*'Go away. Leave me . . . alone.'*

Henry snapped off another piece of fudge. His eyes flashed, revealing more of the man he had once been.

'What became of Bernard?'

'I neither know nor care. I told him to remove himself from my doorstep and if he ever came to my home again, I'd shoot him myself!'

'I thought Bernard upped and left shortly after coming out of hospital. When did you last see him?'

The glimmer of fierceness evaporated. Henry transmuted into an old, frail man. 'It was the day after your mother's funeral. He came to the house that evening in a rage. Said it was my fault she took her life.'

Stacey was speechless. If a bitter, hurt and angry Bernard truly blamed her father for her mother's death, it was reason enough for the man to kidnap her.

She was about to speak again, then noticed her father's sudden pallor. The questioning had exhausted him. She guiltily acknowledged that she'd taken advantage of his better health only to send him backwards. Moreover, she'd been pushing too hard. She changed the subject.

'Rachel told me you spent the afternoon in the day room. What did you do there?'

'My crossword.'

Apart from golf, Henry's other interest had been crosswords. He rarely left one incomplete, even if it took him several weeks to finish it. She'd often found unfinished puzzles on the arms of chairs and was quite good at working out the clues herself.

'How are you getting on with it?'

His face brightened again. 'Good. Good. Almost done.'

'Do you want me to give you a hand with it?'

'I'd like that.' She took the paper from his blue-veined hands and read through the first few clues and answers. 'What do you mean you're almost done? You've completed it yourself. You don't need my help at all. Well done.'

He smiled with pleasure, a child being praised. She stood up and pecked him on the cheek again. She wouldn't probe any further into the past, not during this visit. She owed him some father-and-daughter time. She rested the newspaper on the table next to her. The puzzle may have appeared to be finished; however, Henry had filled in nothing more than gobbledygook. The word 'fudge' had been repeated over and over, with additional letters thrown in to fill in the squares.

By the time Jack returned, Henry was becoming quite confused.

'I remember you. You used to cook the best Sunday lunch,' he said, pointing at Jack.

'I handled all the cooking. Stacey did the cleaning up.'

'Quid pro . . . Quid pro.' His eyelids fluttered as he searched for the word.

'That's right, Henry. Quid pro quo.'

'Are you a chef?'

'No, Henry. A lawyer.'

'Ah. I'm a lawyer too.'

'No. You were a judge, Dad.'

Henry rubbed the backs of his hands, fatigue lengthening his features and draining his face of colour again. 'Yorkshire puddings. Ha! Remember those?'

'I do. Flat and rubbery. Listen, I think we'd better leave you to rest. It's been lovely chatting to you,' said Stacey.

'Yes.'

'I'll be back again soon.' She dropped a kiss on his head. Jack shook his hand.

As they left, she heard him mutter, 'Fudge. Judge. Fudge. Judge.'

# DAY THREE

## FRIDAY – 9 P.M.

Immediately after leaving the residential care home, Stacey and Jack had resumed looking at abandoned spaces. Although nightfall had begun to hinder their search, Jack, desperate to visit as many places as possible, had insisted on heading to an abandoned barn, on the outskirts of town.

'Are you sure you're okay with this?' he whispered, his lips close to her ear.

'I think so.'

His fingers reached for hers. The connection gave her comfort and courage to pad through the huge building, by his side. The beam from Stacey's torch landed on rope, coiled like thick-bodied pythons lying in wait beside hessian sacks. Nerves ricocheted around her body as she trod lightly over them. Jack hung onto her hand as they crept quietly over dry stalks of hay, towards a wooden ladder, propped against the mezzanine.

The broken padlock on the ground outside, along with the flattened water bottle, had given rise to suspicions somebody was inside. Handing him the torch, she checked the ladder was secure. The bottom rung had snapped away, jagged splinters protruding from one side.

'I'll go,' Jack hissed.

For a fleeting moment, she thought of Danni and how she'd looked after Stacey when she found her. If Lyra was there, she wanted to be the one to discover her.

'No. Train the light so I can see.'

She placed a foot onto the second rung to test it for her weight. It bent but held fast. Repeating the process, one rung at a time, she made it to the loft. Here old hay bales lay forgotten, some intact, others ripped apart, contents scattered across the floorboards. The smell was strong, of rot and something acrid, a smell she'd come across when she'd uncovered evidence of vermin under a cupboard – mouse or rat urine.

Light from the torch infiltrated the broken floorboards, allowing her to make out shapes. Her eye was drawn to something in the far corner, a bundle of rags. Stealing herself for an attack, she withdrew a second Maglite from her back pocket before aiming it at the shape, an occupied sleeping bag, with a half-empty water bottle beside it. She edged forwards, little by little. 'Identify yourself.'

There was no movement. She kicked it, gently, felt the bag yield under her boot, and crouched down. It was full of stale clothes, a stash belonging to a homeless person who, judging by the dust on the water bottle, hadn't been here in a while.

'Nobody here,' she called to Jack. 'I'm coming back down.'

The skies had darkened further and here, in the countryside, there was no light pollution to take away the brilliance of the stars. The crescent moon cast sufficient light for them to navigate the track back to their vehicles. It was, however, reckless to keep searching.

'It's not safe to continue roaming about disused properties at this time of night. We should call it a day. Start again tomorrow.'

'You're right. Is there anything else we can do in the meantime?'

'Get some food and rest.' She unlocked her car. 'Thanks for playing along earlier with Dad.'

'Did he tell you anything useful?'

'Yes. I think so. You can never tell with him if what he is saying is accurate or fabricated, a product of a befuddled mind. Apparently, Mum was having an affair with our next-door neighbour and so serious about him, she intended leaving my dad.'

'She didn't leave him though, did she?'

'No. Not in that sense, at least.' Stacey suddenly didn't want to share any more thoughts with Jack. This was personal information about her parents' marriage, one that appeared to have had cracks and problems, much like her own to Jack. 'Night. I'll be in touch again tomorrow.' She opened her car door and hopped inside before he could invite her home or make another move on her. She didn't want to complicate things for the time being. He was vulnerable, terrified for his daughter's life and grateful for her support. When this was over, he might think differently about her, and if he didn't, well, she'd have to burst his bubble.

Back home, she untied her boots and kicked them off. It had been another long, fruitless day. With Mark and Tariq no longer in the frame, they were no closer to finding Lyra.

She trudged into the kitchen, pulled a plastic container of chilli from the fridge and tossed it into the microwave, set the timer and rubbed the back of her neck. Her body ached with fatigue, yet while Lyra was still missing, she could ill afford to rest. Her father had thrown a spanner in the works. If Bernard had been responsible for abducting her, it made no sense for him to come back into her life years later to snatch Lyra. His anger had been directed towards Henry, who he blamed for her mother's suicide, not towards Jack. Unless . . . Unless his hatred for her father spilled over to include her? She was, after all, her father's daughter. And Bernard might have suspected her of blowing the whistle on their affair. Unfortunately, it still begged the question of why he would wait so long to try again, and why target Lyra this time?

The combination of fatigue and confusion caused her head to pound. She was relieved when the phone rang.

Ashraf sounded as jaded as she felt. 'I might have something. After I returned from Upper Heyford, I got in touch with somebody who knows somebody who knows somebody at Companies House. Jack's return was filed but it was sent back at his accountant's behest. It appears there were discrepancies on it, not down to Jack. He blamed one of his employees. That's all I know. I suggest you talk to Jack about it because if it all blew up, there might be a disgruntled, sacked employee who wants payback.'

Jack had told her he could think of nobody who might bear him any resentment. This contradicted him. He'd lied again. The gap in which she could only hear Ashraf's quiet breathing told her there was something else on his mind.

'There's more, isn't there?'

'Yes. Financially, his practice isn't in great shape. You know, there is an outside chance he's orchestrating this?'

The microwave pinged and she threw open the door while still speaking. 'I doubt it. We were together long enough for me to know when he's lying. He was never good at concealing his emotions in front of me. It shows all over his face. He is worried sick about Lyra. Although it is weird he's not being more transparent.'

'It was just a thought. I don't want to force the issue. If I'm wrong, then I'll live with that. I'd rather be wrong than deliberately ignore something I'm uncomfortable about. Jack bothers me.'

'Noted.'

'Good. I'll talk to you again tomorrow.' He ended the call. Stacey wrestled with the plastic lid and yanked it off, stabbing her fork into the bean mix and throwing it into her mouth. What was it with Jack? He'd lied about visiting her father, the extra work he took on outside hours and now his company's finances. There was no shame in admitting his business was struggling. More importantly, by saying nothing about the accountancy error, he might have unwittingly protected a potential suspect. It could have been dealt with quickly, yet now it was an obstacle between them, making her doubt him again. She was unable to appreciate her food, grinding it hastily and swallowing without tasting it. She'd only eaten three forkfuls before there was urgent hammering on the front door.

Jack was on the doorstep. Before she could even begin to tear him off a strip, he spoke. 'I'm sorry. I didn't know what else to do.'

She was about to send him away when she noticed he was wearing slippers and had left the driver's door wide open in his haste to reach her.

'You might want to close that first. Then come in.' She plodded back to the kitchen. Whatever this was, it wasn't going to be good. Jack brought the cool night air into the kitchen with him.

'I've had another text. A warning this time.' He held out his mobile.

The picture was a sheet of paper held against the lens, each word cut from a magazine or newspaper.

You told

You know the consequences

'What the fuck does it mean? Will they kill her?' His voice was nigh on hysterical.

She fought sudden nausea, making every effort to appear non-plussed. 'They've probably spotted us together. Don't panic. They've no idea of what we're trying to do. We were married. It's logical I'd visit you.' It sounded weak to her own ears. Everything hinged on what exactly the abductor knew and when they'd been spied together. If she'd been seen emerging from Jack's house, they could claim she'd only been passing by. If they'd been observed going into the nursing home together, that too could be explained. However, if they'd been spotted together casing out empty buildings, it was another matter. And if either phone was tapped . . .

'What about Ashraf? He's an ex-cop. So's your mate, Danni! The kidnappers might think I involved the police.'

Her mouth went dry.

'No. They're bluffing. This is designed to frighten you,' she said as calmly as possible. 'Like the rubber finger.'

'You don't know that. Not for sure.' His voice grew louder. 'I said all along, no police. I trusted you. You brought in these people and now this!' He waved the screen in front of her face.

Guilt assailed her. She snatched up the container of chilli and scraped the congealing gloop into the dustbin, letting the lid fall noisily. Her mind buzzed. To know about her involvement with Danni and Ashraf, the kidnapper would have had to follow her. She'd been ultra-cautious from the start, checking her surroundings, any people nearby, searching for faces she'd already seen. Maybe she hadn't been cautious enough. Likewise, before Ashraf had entered Jack's house, he'd scouted the area to establish nobody was watching. Had he done a thorough job? She recognised the warning signs that Jack was on the edge: his rigid stance, the vein pulsing in his right temple. Whoever had snatched Lyra was taunting him. It was part of the game to them. This message was intended to add pressure, to ensure he didn't step out of line. That decided, she tossed the plastic tub into the sink and faced him.

'We're at the kidnapper's mercy. If they contact you, Jack, you'll need to box clever, persuade them we're still friends and make up something about how I often pop over to visit. I can't think what else to do.'

'Then how do I explain Ashraf, or Danni?'

'You've not been seen with Danni. If they know about her, it's because they've spotted her and me together, in which case you tell them she was in the area, visiting her family, and caught up with me. Which is the truth. As for Ashraf, he and I have worked together before. Explain I asked for his help on an article I'm writing about corruption in Morecambe council offices. If they want to know why he was at your house, tell them he stopped off to give me the heads-up on some information.'

Jack's shoulders dropped and his hands relaxed. 'You think they'll believe me?'

'Why wouldn't they? They warned you not to involve the police. You're trying to keep up normal appearances. It would look more suspicious if you cut off everybody you know and hid away.'

'I'm not so sure. Stace, it's getting messy. Don't you think we should we let Ashraf go?'

'Absolutely not. I'll make sure Ashraf stays away from you, your house, office. I'll only contact him by phone. I'll get a burner in case mine's been tapped.'

'Wouldn't it be better if we didn't involve him at all?'

'We need his expertise. More so now that Danni is no longer able to help. It's either him or we go to the police.'

'No police.'

'Then we keep Ashraf onside.'

'I don't see what he can do. We're looking at empty properties. He's not doing anything to help, unless he's on to something you haven't told me about,' said Jack.

That Jack wanted rid of the ex-police officer only served to fuel her concerns. Did he want Ashraf out of the way because of what Ashraf had already discovered?

'He's working different angles. He has experience from his time on the force, along with contacts, and he will do everything in his power to get Lyra back.'

Jack finally mumbled his assent.

'While we're on the subject of different angles, you assured me there was nobody you could think of who might bear you a grudge, yet a few minutes ago Ashraf told me about somebody you thought was fiddling the accounts. Did it not cross your mind to tell me about this?'

'He did?' He touched his forehead as if recalling something important. A ghost of an apologetic smile flickered across his face. 'No, it didn't cross my mind to bring it up, Stace. You wanted to know if I could think of anybody who hated me enough to abduct Lyra. Alistair isn't that person. He wouldn't say boo to a goose.'

'Did you sack him?'

'Yes, I let him go, but he isn't the sort to be vindictive.'

'You can never guess what some people are capable of. Many well-known serial killers looked harmless. How many times have you watched the news about a murder in a close community and whenever neighbours and friends are interviewed afterwards, they always express surprise? "He seemed such a nice person" is a phrase that crops up frequently. Tell me more about Alistair. Why did you fire him?'

'It's . . . complicated.'

'Then you'd better sit down.' She threw open a door to the sitting room, choosing one of two chairs either side of a fireplace with a period marble surround, purchased from a reclaim yard. On it were two photographs: the first of a sandy beach overlooking a vast blue ocean, the other of a puffin standing on a rock, one foot mid-air, and a large fish in its coloured beak. It looked as if it was about to perform a celebratory dance. Both pictures had been taken long before she met Jack, during a year's sabbatical when she'd travelled over several continents and lived the life Bella would have loved.

Jack had assumed a position she was by now familiar with, head in hands.

'What excuse are you going to come up with this time?' she asked.

'No excuse. I never meant for it to happen. The truth is my accountant picked up on some anomalies in the business accounts the very day they were submitted. She managed to recall them before they went through the official channels at Companies House. The irony is, she thought she was doing me a favour, ensuring I didn't send in false accounts. You don't need to know the specifics. The books had been cooked, as they say, not by Alistair, but by me. I'd fiddled some invoices. I'd changed totals and issued replacement invoices that totalled lesser amounts, then pocketed the difference.'

'And in so doing, committed fraud.'

'Yes. This sorry tale only gets worse, Stace. Alistair became my scapegoat. Once the accountant alerted me to the situation, I couldn't think how to extricate myself. Alistair had assisted with spreadsheets and the like over the year, so in order to take the heat off me, I accused him. I redid the spreadsheet, reinstating the original invoice totals, and claimed the errors were Alistair's doing. I wriggled off the hook this time, although I'm sure my accountants will have put a black mark against my name. I've no doubt any future accounts will be heavily scrutinised from hereon in. I've since resubmitted the correct totals to the accountants and obviously will pay the tax due. Which means, technically, I haven't committed any crime.' His words came out slowly as if they were being dragged reluctantly from his mouth, a confession that laid his soul bare. 'Although, I fired Alistair to keep up pretences.'

Stacey swallowed the bad taste in her mouth. Jack had fallen a long way in the last few years. Maybe he always had been a bit of a bad egg. His handsome face and winning ways disguised the rot inside.

'How did Alistair take the news?'

'Meekly, as I expected he would. He denied it, of course. I told him how sorry I was to let him go, but that I had to take a stand and he had been the only person other than me who used the computer system.'

'He simply walked away?'

'Yes.'

'Didn't you expect more resistance, even anger and a threat of an unfair dismissal claim?'

'No.'

'He can't be that mild-mannered?'

'He is.'

'No, Jack. I don't believe that would be the case. You falsely accused an innocent man of fiddling your accounts, then kicked him out, even though you knew him to be innocent.'

'Alistair's dying.'

'What?'

'He has terminal cancer. He told me four months ago when I reprimanded him on his frequent absences and lack of commitment to the firm. He begged me to keep him on, to help keep his mind off his illness. I let him stay, even though he wasn't pulling his weight. That's how I got away with claiming the invoices had been misfiled – I explained Alistair was seriously ill, and the medication he'd been taking had affected his judgement and work. I know how horrible that sounds, but I was down a hole – a massive, fucking crater.'

This was a new low for her. She got to her feet and stomped into the kitchen. Jack Corrigan was a heartless dickhead. She kicked out at the plastic pedal bin, knocking it against the wall. She should walk away from him now. Except she couldn't. Because she wasn't doing this for Jack. It was for Lyra. She scooped up the bin's contents that had spilled onto the floor, wiped away the chilli sauce stuck to the tiles and recomposed herself. Jack was still in the sitting room when she returned. He looked at her from under damp lashes.

'I understand. I can tell by your face. You don't need to say anything. I've well and truly fucked up this time. I'm on my own, aren't I?'

'Give me Alistair's contact details. I want to see him myself.'

'It isn't him. He hasn't taken Lyra.'

'Give . . . me . . . his details,' she hissed, irritably. 'Then piss off. I don't want to see you again until I've calmed down.'

'And Lyra?'

'Just give me the bloody details, alright!'

He told her what she needed to know, then got to his feet without a further glance in her direction.

She didn't unclench her fists until after she'd heard his car engine fade into the distance.

# DAY FOUR

## SATURDAY – 7 A.M.

Stacey had been sitting in the fictional cinema for a while now, Erin's voice encouraging her to search for the clues in the film reels of her past that might help make sense of what was happening today, yet this time the visions didn't appear. Although her muscles were relaxed, the revelation of the night before was holding her back. That Jack could treat a dying man with such cruelty troubled her deeply.

In her time with Jack recently, she'd seen both sides to his personality: charming and repulsive. When they'd been married, he'd been manipulative, narcissistic and able to run rings around her, causing her to lose self-worth. Discovering he could extend this to others, especially to someone so ill, left her cold. Had it not been for Lyra, she would walk away from Jack and happily not see him again.

Erin continued to talk. Stacey did her best to ignore thoughts of her ex, instead concentrating on the lulling tone. Erin hadn't given up. Nor should Stacey. If she didn't relinquish the angst, she would not be able to help Lyra. Lyra was what mattered. She pictured the girl, waiting for Stacey to rescue her. Gradually, the image began to shift until the face Stacey saw was no longer Lyra's but her own.

'Forget current events, focus only on your younger self, when you were a schoolgirl. Allow yourself to drift back to your life at that time, before the kidnapping, to when your mother and you were close.'

At last, the make-believe projector spluttered into life . . .

*'Listen, cherub. I know you're worried about leaving behind your friends but imagine what it would be like to live by the seaside. We could get a cottage in one of those quaint villages in Cornwall, go to the beach every weekend, go swimming, you could take up sailing or surfing. It's hugely popular with surfers. You'll find all the kids go there, especially during the school holidays.'*

*It's been two days since the broken-cup incident and Mum hasn't been herself. She's antsy, jumping every time there's a knock on the door, and there's a chill whenever her father comes in. They are on speaking terms, yet the tension between them is unbearable. Stacey can't stand being in the same room as the pair of them.*

*'Will Dad take up a job in Cornwall?'*

*'He'd stay here for the time being. It'd be you and me to start with.'*

*Mum, who's been chopping carrots for a casserole, busies herself again. 'What do you think?' she asks as she pulls potatoes from a sack in the pantry. Stacey isn't stupid. She knows what her mother is really trying to say.*

*The doorbell rings. Her mum looks up, potatoes in hand.*

*'I'll get it,' says Stacey. It'll give her the chance to avoid answering her mother.*

*Their other neighbour, Mrs White, the street gossip, is at the door. Her face looks like it needs ironing. 'Hello, Stacey, love. Is your mother in?'*

*Stacey calls her, then heads upstairs, where she sits on the top step to hear what Mrs White has to say that is so important.*

*'Have you heard? Bernard Naseby's been rushed to hospital. People are saying he was attacked.'*

Stacey stretched her fingers, sensation returning to her extremities. She was coming out of the trance-like state.

'Relax, Stacey. You are comfortable in the past. You have questions you need answering. Keep searching in the depths until you find something. Breathe in deeply and now . . . exhale . . . And inhale . . .'

Erin's voice was silky smooth, the equivalent of a mother singing a lullaby. Gradually it became more distant, masked by the droning of a vintage projector that drew Stacey's attention back to the screen on which a drama was unfolding, one that proved her mind was very much still in the past.

*Her finger, or the space where her finger once was, is throbbing like a hundred minuscule needles are stabbing her flesh.*

*The hood is back on, and she wishes she was dead. She tries to draw on memories to help her through the agony, but she's empty. The loss of her finger was punishment: not hers, her father's. Prior to it happening, she recalls hearing hushed whispers between two people, words that had floated over to her without meaning . . .*

*'The safe's empty.'*

*'It can't be. There should be stacks of cash and jewellery.'*

*'There's nothing of value in it. We should give up. Let her go.'*

'That sneaky git has hidden the money somewhere else. He's not getting away with this. Not after the way he's treated you . . . me . . . He owes us! He fucking well owes us. I'm going to make him pay up. All he needs is the right incentive.'

'No! Put that down!'

'He needs to wake up. Realise we aren't pissing about . . . that we mean business.'

'You can't harm her. I won't let you.'

'Go ahead. Try and stop me. I'm not taking orders from you anymore. I'm done with listening to you. You have no idea how to handle this.'

'Listen to me, please. This has got out of hand. I've got another idea—'

'I said I'm done! Shut the fuck up!'

There's a clap or a slap or something she can't make out. She strains to hear more but can only detect faint whimpering.


Under the itching hood, Stacey doesn't understand what is happening. By now, she should be at home. Pain makes her cry out. She wants to rub her hand, stop the agony.

'Shh! Let me fix it.'

The voice sounds different, whispered and low. This is somebody else, or the masked man is playing games with her.

Her hands are untied and warm, soft hands envelope hers. The dressing covering her hand and finger stump is removed. There's a hiss as ice-cold spray is applied to her wound, followed by a stinging sensation before it is bound up again.

'It's clean. I've sprayed antiseptic on it. I'll get you more painkillers.'

The person disappears and Stacey is left confused. Although the voice was hushed it sounded female.

It took a while to register she had left the dark room and was once more in Erin's office. Erin pushed the glass of water towards her. 'You feel up to talking about what happened?' she asked.

'I . . . I don't know. I'm not sure what to make of it.'

She wrapped hands around the cool glass. Two voices? Had she really heard a man and a woman's voice? Or had anxiety over Jack's employee, Alistair, infiltrated the trance-like state, corrupting what she thought she'd heard? She might have transposed her need to comfort him into the scenario she'd watched on the screen in her head. Or, maybe, suspicions about him abducting Lyra had influenced how the scene played out. Whatever it was, the urge to visit Alistair had become a sudden priority, eclipsing her visit to Erin.

'I have . . . stuff on my mind. I'm not sure if it affected what I think I saw.'

'I won't say that's impossible. Tell me what you saw and why you think it might not be true.'

Stacey began to explain, then shook her head.

'I'm sorry. I really need to visit somebody. Until I do, I can't think straight. If my mind isn't playing any tricks, then I might have learned that I was kidnapped by two people, one of them female. I don't trust my mind, Erin. It's let me down in the past.'

'We've been having strong results with these therapy sessions. I wouldn't be too quick to dismiss whatever you saw.'

'Do you mind if we talk about it another time? I really should be going.'

'That's absolutely fine.' She gave a smile. 'Whenever you're ready.'

◆ ◆ ◆

Drained from the therapy session, it required great effort to get behind the wheel and make the one-hour journey to Alistair's house. The constant bombardment of rapid recollections was becoming too much for her and it took the entire drive for her to anchor herself in the present.

A beige-coloured Great Dane, with a black muzzle, rested huge paws on the window ledge and looked at Stacey with a questioning stare. She rang the doorbell and although she expected to hear barking, there was none. A man with a balding pate and sunken cheeks answered, the dog by his side.

'Alistair Hampton?'

'That's me.'

'I'm Stacey O'Hara. I used to be married to Jack Corrigan.'

'I know who you are. What do you want?'

'A chat.' One look at the man and she knew he was unlikely to have arranged for Lyra to be abducted. She would handle this differently to how she had planned.

He studied her face before giving a nod and moving to one side. 'Come in. Don't mind the dog. She looks formidable but Cindy's actually docile.'

Stacey rubbed the animal's head as she crossed the threshold into a sitting room. A television was on low volume. The bedding on the sofa suggested the man didn't move far. He pushed a blanket to one side and sat down, leaving the armchair free for Stacey. Cindy curled up by her master's feet.

'Do you live alone, Mr Hampton?'

'Apart from Cindy here. Lost my wife two years ago. Now it's only me and the dog.'

The scent from the lavender air freshener on the sideboard wasn't sufficient to disguise the fusty scent that seemed to emanate from the chair. Her gaze swept the room. Paperwork had been arranged in tidy piles on a dining table, obliterating its surface. Open cardboard boxes stood on the carpet, filled with silver trophy cups and porcelain ornaments all higgledy-piggledy, as if somebody had merely tipped out the contents of a cabinet into each container. She stared at a brass cyclist on a small plinth, an award for a cycling event. It was difficult to place the man in front of her as some sort of athlete. What was evident was that the room was being stripped bare as Alistair prepared for his inevitable fate. His voice was gentle.

'I guess you're here because Jack couldn't face me.'

'In a way. Late last night, he told me what happened. I wanted to find out how you were, hear your version of events, and see if I couldn't make life a little easier for you.'

He rubbed at whiskers on his chin. 'I have everything I need. So, Jack confessed, did he? I didn't expect him to.'

'Only to me. He resubmitted the accounts, with correct details.'

The dog shifted position, laid its big head on his master's leather slippers.

'Has he got the guts to come and see me himself?'

'I know he feels huge remorse. I can't make him visit you. I can only hope he will.'

'And so he should. I thought he had more about him. You know, after my wife died, he couldn't have been kinder. He was patient and understanding, even when I wouldn't turn up because I was having a really bad day, or when I lost concentration. He encouraged me to get back out into the world, made sure I went out with colleagues after work, invited me to play golf with him. He'd even pop around here, now and again, to make sure I was okay. I appreciated his kindness. I needed it more than I realised at the time. I was desperately lonely and what he did for me back then meant more to me than he'll ever know. Tell him what upset me most was that he didn't confide in me, explain the situation. If he had, I'd have volunteered to take the blame, you know? It hurt me that he simply pointed the finger, without any warning, discussion, or consideration of my feelings. That he didn't even have the decency to talk to me about it, well, that really hurt.'

'I'm sure it did.'

'I've always thought highly of Jack. I regret it had to come to this though.'

Stacey was surprised by the depths of this man's loyalty. Jack had clearly misjudged how far Alistair would have gone to help his employer.

'Mr Hampton, is there anything I can get for you, do some shopping, organise some home help?'

'You don't need to do that. You shouldn't be feeling guilty.'

'No, Jack should, and he is.'

'Has he told you I haven't got long left to live?'

'Yes.'

'I'd have probably had to give up working soon anyhow. I'm planning on going to my brother's place in Bolton. He and his wife are going to look after me, you know, in my final days. I'm putting my affairs in order.' He swept a hand towards the table. 'It's sobering. It makes you place higher value on things like family, friendships and kindness.'

'Don't you feel any anger about what happened? Jack threw you out. He cast aspersions on your character?' Her words were the final test and he passed it.

'I have no time left to waste on negative emotions. What's done is done. Jack's been good to me over the time I've worked for him. This was . . . unfortunate.'

'Did you know the firm was in a bad way?'

'I had a fair idea it was in trouble; after all, I helped put the invoice information onto spreadsheets. Truth be told, I'd also worked out Jack was fiddling the accounts. There's been a fall-off in business for a long while. Plus, Jack's been unable to take on any new blood to help grow the practice. I don't condone what he did. All the same, I understand why he did it. I would like him to drop by though. I wouldn't want to pack up and leave without putting this behind us or without saying goodbye for the final time.'

She reached for his hand, held it in her own. It was as light and fragile as a dry leaf. 'I'll talk to him. He'll come.'

◆　◆　◆

She picked up Danni's voicemail as she drove from Alistair's house. While there'd been no further break-in attempts on their house in Cornwall, her husband, Paul, was still nervous about burglars returning and didn't want to leave the house. Danni, however, was considering driving back up to Morecambe alone, to continue helping them search for Lyra. Stacey rang her straight back.

'Have you found her yet?' Danni asked as soon as she answered.

'Not yet. We're still looking into empty properties.'

'I ought to return.'

'It'll take a good seven hours with no rest stops to get here, then what? I'm not sure myself which way to turn. We might have to go the route of paying the ransom.'

'How?'

'I'll pull out whatever savings I can. I'll try and get a loan from the bank, against my inheritance. I'll pawn the few bits and pieces I own.'

'Oh, Stacey.'

'For the moment, Ashraf and I are still shaking trees and waiting for something to fall.'

'I have a little money set aside for a rainy day.'

'No, Danni. That's not an option. Listen, something came to light during my last session with Erin. I can't be positive, but I think I was kidnapped by two people – a man and a woman.'

'Could the woman have been Bella?'

'Maybe. Ox is on the hunt for her. I should go. I need to talk to Jack on a separate matter. I'll speak to you again very soon.'

She stood on the pavement, unable to move. What route should she take next? Unless she continued to pursue her gut feeling that her own kidnapper was responsible for abducting Lyra, there were precious few other options. She was sorely tempted to ring Ox, yet knew it was futile. Ox would be in touch as soon as there was any information about her friend. Instead, she rang Jack, asking to meet him at his office. The least he could do was visit his faithful employee.

There was a sign at Jack's reception, informing clients to ring the buzzer. She was about to find her way to his office when he came into the empty waiting room.

'You have to visit Alistair. He's leaving soon and you need to put things right between you.'

He nodded. 'I know. I'm such a fuck-up. I've been fighting to keep this place going and really, I should have let it go and gone to work for another firm. At the end of the day, what does it really matter? For five years, it's ruled my life, forcing me to make some truly terrible decisions. I should have unshackled myself from it as soon as I saw the warning signs. I knew during the early stages of the pandemic it was going to be a problem and still I allowed it to happen. If I hadn't let my pride get in the way, Lyra might be at home now. Now, because of my pig-headedness, I might have lost my most precious . . . the thing . . . the person I value most.'

Had he been going to say possession? His most precious possession? It wouldn't have surprised Stacey if he had. That was how he viewed people – her, Lyra, and probably even Alistair. They belonged to him. That was the real reason he hadn't wanted Stacey to leave him, why he'd fought tooth and nail to stop her divorcing him. It wasn't that he was deeply in love with her, rather he didn't want anyone else to *have* her.

'We all have choices in life and we don't always make the right ones. Running this practice was a big deal for you,' she said.

'And if they kill Lyra, it will all have been absolutely pointless.'

At that moment, his phone rang. 'Unregistered caller. It's probably the kidnapper.'

'Tell them we've begun dating again. That's why they saw us together. Tell them straight away. You'd better tell them I'm here now, in case they're watching us.'

He held the phone to his ear. 'I haven't told the police. I swear.'

'What about the reporter?'

'She's my ex. We've recently started seeing one another again. It's nothing more than that. She's here now.'

The voice fell silent.

'Then it's unfortunate.'

'What is? What have you done? Please don't hurt her.'

'You have twenty-four hours until I ring for the final payment. Don't disappoint me.'

'No! I have to know she's alive. I won't do this until I speak to Lyra.'

'That won't be possible.'

'Then I'm not paying you!'

The line fell silent again.

'Daddy!'

'Lyra! Lyra baby. I love you.'

'Don't let him hurt me anymore.'

'Oh, baby—'

'Twenty-four hours.'

'Lyra!'

His hands trembled as he stared at the blank screen. Stacey placed an arm on his shoulder.

'She's alive. She's still alive,' she repeated. Her words didn't penetrate his angst.

'But she's hurt and what do they mean by "It's unfortunate"?'

Stacey got straight on the phone to Ox. 'Did you get anything that time?'

'I couldn't triangulate an exact location. I got one ping from a mast in Heysham.'

'Then they are in the area?'

'For sure.'

She relayed the information, words gushing over her lips. There was no time to waste. 'We have to redouble our efforts to check out empty buildings. I'll coordinate with Ashraf. Lyra is somewhere in or near Morecambe. We *can* find her.'

The pep talk seemed to bring Jack out of his reverie. 'Where shall I start looking?'

'Let me speak to Ashraf and put a plan in place.'

'I'll get my keys.' He set off in the direction of his office.

She tried Ashraf without success. The call went directly to the messaging service. She headed to Jack's office to let him know and found him in front of his desk, back to her, stock still. A package was in the centre of his desk with a typed piece of A4 propped against it bearing Stacey's name.

His voice trembled. 'Stacey, somebody has put that there while we've been in reception.'

'Go outside.'

He didn't move.

She kept her voice level but firm. 'I'll deal with this. Go outside!'

He backed away, one step at a time.

The rectangular cardboard box was unsealed and so she lifted the flaps to reveal a smaller container, the length of a pencil case. The lid was closed with a magnetic clasp, which she undid. Even though the plastic bag was smeared with blood she could make out what was inside. A small finger. This time it wasn't made of rubber.

# DAY FOUR

## SATURDAY – 12 P.M.

Stacey had raced back to Jack's house and shoved the box, containing Lyra's finger, in the freezer. One way or the other, they'd get her back, at which juncture they'd ensure she was rushed to hospital to have the appendage reattached.

Jack's lips were pressed together, elbows on the table. All the blood seemed to have drained from his face.

'I'm taking no more chances. I need the rest of the ransom money.'

'I'll go to the bank, get a loan.'

'There's not enough time for that. I need a moneylender and quickly. There must be somebody I can go to for a loan of this magnitude. Surely you have an idea where such people hang out. You have contacts all over the region. You've investigated cases where people have taken out loans and not repaid them.'

'I can't let you do that.'

He turned on her. 'Why the hell not?'

'I'm worried about what would happen to you if you can't pay it ba—'

'Worried? For crying out loud! That's Lyra's finger in the freezer! You think I care about what might happen to me? She's my daughter!'

'But—'

'No! I've beaten myself up over this, spent sleepless hours wondering what on earth I'd done for this to happen. But now, I'm not sure this was my fault. The note on the box was addressed to you. Lyra could have been abducted because of some vendetta against *you*, not me.'

'They must have seen us together. They said on the phone "it was unfortunate". You were told not to contact the police. Maybe they see my involvement as some sort of betrayal on your part. It could be another warning for us to toe the line.' Her heart bashed against her ribcage as she spoke. She prayed she was right, that Lyra's kidnapping was not her fault.

The vein in his head pulsed. 'Maybe. However, so far we've come up with diddly-squat. We can't locate Lyra and now that animal has amputated her finger. The warnings are working. I want a backup plan! When that scumbag rings me tomorrow, I'm going to have the ransom ready to hand over. So, tell me where I need to go to find the sort of people who will provide the money with no questions asked. Unless you can think of an alternative way to get our hands on that sort of money.'

She licked dry lips. Her thoughts were scattered like driftwood on a beach. Was this her fault? Up until now, everyone had assured her she was crazy to assume her kidnapper would enact revenge on Jack. Nobody had thought he might still want to punish Stacey. Her abductor had been cruel, to the very last minute when he'd almost killed her. She'd escaped. Had he waited all these years for payback? This time, it would be Lyra who might die.

'Well?' His eyes fired darts of anger at her.

Should she ask her father for the money? No. There were too many hurdles to surmount: he might not be in a fit state of mind to comprehend her request; those who handled his affairs might object; it would take far too long to organise. 'I'm not sure if my information would be up to date.'

'Don't stall me. Give me a name. Better still, give me two.'

There was no option other than to acquiesce. 'I need a pen.'

He got up without a word, rummaged in a drawer and handed one over, along with an old envelope. She scribbled down potential names and locations on the back of it. 'I've got Ox working on something important and Erin is going to see me again later.'

He snatched the paper from her. 'I can't wait any longer. If you want to carry on hunting for her, then go ahead. I'm going to do what I should have done at the beginning. I was wrong to tackle it this way. I shouldn't have dragged you into this mess.'

'I'm not giving up. Give me a few hours. That's all I ask. Until six tonight. That'll still leave you time to get the money.'

He turned away, ran his hand over his neck and sighed. 'Until six. No longer.'

The gnawing was back in her stomach. All she had were vague memories and a name, Bernard Naseby. With Ox already occupied trying to track down Bella, she opted for visiting Bernard and left Jack to arrange a rendezvous with Ashraf.

As she approached her car, she spotted an envelope under one of the windscreen wipers addressed to her. With shaking hands, she ripped it open and let out a cry as she read the four words composed of cut-out letters from a newspaper. She'd been right all along. This had always been about her, not Jack.

The note read:

Stacey liked the compactness of Lancaster, a relatively small city compared to neighbouring Manchester and Liverpool. Facilities were all within relatively easy walking distance and there was sufficient vibe to make it an interesting place, with arts and music regarded highly in the region. With its rich history, it justified the tourist-friendly strapline, 'Small City Big Story'.

This was her patch. Jack wouldn't find anyone to loan him money here. The names she'd given him were of go-betweens, people who would be able to fix up a meeting with somebody from out of town. If he went down that route, it would open another can of worms and although Lyra might be returned, he would have to watch his back if he couldn't fulfil his side of the bargain and pay back what he owed. She couldn't let that happen to him. She also couldn't dwell on the fact that she was to blame for the kidnapping, for Lyra losing her finger and for all the distress she'd caused. She'd do whatever she could to find the girl before six o'clock, then she'd go to her father, coax the money from him or get the bank loan she'd discussed to pay back the moneylenders.

As soon as she'd read the note, she'd rung Ashraf, told him of her fears for Lyra. He'd agreed to meet her immediately. Leaving the Kia in a municipal car park, she paced along the pavements towards Williamson Park, in her opinion the fifty-four-acre jewel in Lancaster's crown. It was her go-to place when she needed to get out of the office for some quiet-thinking time. Here she would ordinarily stroll around the park or woodlands or simply sit and take in the spectacular view, again over the coast towards the Lake District. It was difficult to imagine these magnificent gardens had once been a disused quarry and had it not been for the benevolence of a local benefactor, might have been transformed into something far less appealing. Today, however, she had no time to enjoy the beauty or feel any calming benefit. Her heart raced as she took in the significance of the note. Her abductor was back!

She sat at one of the tables outside the pavilion café, foot tapping impatiently until she spotted Ashraf striding towards her.

He pulled out the chair. 'Show me.'

She pushed the note towards him. He clicked his tongue. 'What next?'

The lack of preamble suited her. She told him about her old neighbour.

'How old would Bernard Naseby be by now?'

She made an approximate calculation. 'In his sixties.'

'Have you asked yourself why he would wait all these years just to do the same thing again?'

'I have and the answer is I don't know. Any more than I can work out why Bella would. I can only follow my hunch that whoever held me hostage has Lyra. The box containing her finger was addressed to me. Nobody other than me would understand that message you've just read. Bernard is the only person I can think of who had sufficient grievance against my father to abduct me.'

Ashraf rested his elbows on the table, chin on top of clasped hands, forcing his lips into a downward frown. He clearly wasn't on the same page. 'Why would he take Lyra?'

'He clearly hated me back then. Enough to torture me, beat me up, amputate my finger and now it seems he's doing the same to Lyra. Could you not at least follow it up for me?'

His nostrils opened widely, and with a sigh he sat back. 'Okay. I'll see what I can do. I'll probably have to call in some favours from the old team. It would be helpful if I had more than a name. We don't have the luxury of time.'

'I've done some digging and the neighbour who lived on the other side of our house, Mrs Rosalind White, still lives there. She was the local busybody. She might know more than me. Maybe one of your old unit could find contact details for her.' Ashraf had been a valued and popular member of the squad. He'd relied on a bunch of comrades who still had his back, even to this day. He would know somebody on the technical side who would assist.

'Okay.' She could tell Ashraf was only going through the motions. He shifted in his seat, about to get up, but leant forward instead. 'I know you're doing your best to catch this person. It might, however, be better to help Jack get the money instead.'

'If by six o'clock, we're still floundering, I shall. Promise. I want her back too.'

He patted her hand. 'And whatever you may think, this isn't your fault.'

'I realise that. My father's wholly to blame.'

On the way back to her car, she passed the butterfly house, another place they'd brought Lyra, who'd loved the fragile creatures, their delicate wings, and had been thrilled when one had settled on her. The picture of her radiant face as she extended her palm to Stacey to show her the tiny blue butterfly stayed with her all the way back to the car, as did the lump in her throat.

Erin was on a lunchbreak, but agreed to see Stacey anyway. Stacey sat on the sofa and told her the latest news. Erin damped her lips on a paper serviette. The salad was laid out to resemble a multi-coloured flower: cucumber rounds balanced on rocket leaves were the outer petals, then layers of tomato, carrot and yellow peppers as petals, and beetroot at its centre.

'I should advise you that another session this soon after the last is not likely to be productive.'

'I'm desperate.'

Erin reached for the plastic lid and pushed it back onto the tub of salad. 'Then we shall have to see what we can do, won't we?'

It took over half an hour for Stacey to become less tense and to lose herself in the past. The images were blurry, and the faces distorted, but the soundtrack was clear.

*'Bloody hell, Stacey. You're in a terrible state. I had no idea you'd look like this.'*

*It's Bella's voice. She can't see her face because the hood is still covering her head. The painkillers are making her woozy, woozy, and she drifts into a quiet slumber.*

*She registers a slight squeeze on her good hand and for a second almost comes to. Bella is still speaking, but her voice is distant and muffled, as if she's at the bottom of a well.*

*'Jeez, Stacey, I'm really sorry.'*

*She wants to ask why she's sorry. Bella didn't cut off her finger. She's her friend and they're going on holiday soon to the sea.*

*'I should've . . . police . . . sorry . . . got to leave town.'*

*She wants to ask Bella why she's in the kidnapper's lair. She fights for consciousness, the drugs making her efforts impossible. When she finally opens her eyes, she discovers she isn't in the dimly lit room. She is in a hospital bed.*

Stacey was gasping for air. Erin was by her side. 'I take it that was a nasty one?' she said.

Stacey shook off her confusion. 'Not really. Bella came to visit me when I was in hospital.'

'Then that's good. You were beginning to have doubts about her being part of this.'

'She apologised for not going to the police, and for the fact that she was going to leave town. She probably knew who was behind my kidnapping.'

'Can you not contact her?'

'Somebody is trying to locate her, but I'm not holding out much hope.'

'You don't think she's behind Lyra's kidnapping, do you?'

Stacey was baffled. She'd had no contact with Bella for almost thirty years. She knew nothing of Stacey's life or had any reason to abduct Lyra. There was no vendetta.

'I can't be sure. Maybe. Maybe not. But if she isn't, then she might hold the key to it. What time is it?'

Erin looked over Stacey's shoulder at the alarm clock. 'Ten past two.'

'I have to make tracks. I need to find Bella.'

She grabbed her jacket hanging on the back of the door and thanked Erin again.

'I'm sorry about making you miss your lunch.'

'No matter. I can have it later. Good luck.'

There was a voicemail from Ashraf. While she'd been under hypnosis, he had discovered Bernard had moved to Prestwich, midway between Bury and Manchester, and only an hour's drive away. His voice was loud as he spoke over the sound of beating rain against his windscreen.

'I'm headed there now. I know there's a chance he won't be at home, especially if he is responsible for snatching Lyra. Can't leave anything to chance though.'

The message had been left forty minutes earlier. As she walked, she thought about Bella again. That Bella had visited her to apologise, then left without a trace only supported the theory she'd helped set up the abduction. She hoped she was wrong, that Bernard had been responsible. Somehow that felt more justifiable.

Her father was in the day room, staring across the bay. He was wearing a silk maroon cravat with his shirt and cardigan. A pair of tartan slippers protruded from the blanket on his lap.

'Hello, you look very smart.'

'Have to keep up appearances, my dear.' He continued staring and she thought how old he looked in the daylight. Steely whiskers that had resisted the blade curled from hollows in his cheeks, like miniscule corkscrews. Old-age spots, like errant brown paint marks, were splodged over his face and the back of his hands. She hadn't properly looked at him in a long time. To her, he was always the formidable, bullish giant who, if she was honest, slightly frightened her.

The other residents in the bright conservatory were occupied with jigsaws or were playing cards or reading. Her father, however, was simply sitting.

'Do you remember what we were talking about yesterday?'

'Was it yesterday?'

'I came with Jack.'

'Ah, yes.'

She didn't know if he remembered the visit or not. Often, he would agree with her simply to give the impression he wasn't confused.

'You told me about Bernard Naseby and how you had him attacked because he wanted to take Mum and me away.'

He didn't respond.

'Where did Bernard go?'

His eyelids fluttered. 'Far away.'

'He came back though, didn't he? To challenge you over Mum's death.'

'Julia took her own life.'

He seemed to shrink before her. She knew what was going on in his head. Some things couldn't be forgotten . . .

*Stacey runs upstairs to change out of her school uniform to find her father is leaning against their bedroom door. His tie is half undone and his face the colour of her white socks.*

*'Go next door, Stacey. Stay with Mrs White until I come and get you.'*

*'Why?'*

*'I'll explain . . . Later. Go.'*

*'But—'*

*'Go!'*

*She does as bidden. When her father wants her to do something, she asks no questions. She's halfway down the stairs when there's a sound like a soft explosion. She turns back, hand on the banister. Her father has slid down the door and is now on his haunches, head against the door, sobbing.*

Henry let out a strangled yelp.

'I know, Dad. I know.'

He lifted his chin, the light catching unshed tears. 'She took her life because she was unhappy. She said I kept her a prisoner.'

'No, Dad. She could have left you if she'd really wanted to.'

'Not after what I did to Bernard. She loved him. Deeply. More than she'd ever loved me. She was so frightened I'd have him killed the second time round, she stayed with me and eventually became so unhappy, she chose to end it rather than continue living with me.'

He'd never spoken about her mother's death. Judge Henry O'Hara had continued as normal, working all hours, presiding over important trials, maintaining his all-important image. His lips trembled, then he spoke again.

'She left a note.'

This was the first Stacey had ever heard of it. That her father was managing to remain lucid for such a long period was equally puzzling. Ordinarily, his grip on time and reality slipped quickly. But unburdening himself like this was anchoring him to the present, at least for the moment.

'In it, she told me I had to try and love you enough for both of us. And I did. I just wasn't very good at showing it. I still have the note. I read it every day. I keep it to remind me of what I did to her, to you both. I forget, you see. I might forget all sorts of important things, but never why she took her own life. The staff here all know to make sure I read that note every day. I won't ever forget your mother.'

'I had no idea.'

'I'm not someone who is demonstrative when it comes to emotion. And to that end, I'm afraid you have inherited that from me. It doesn't mean we are incapable of feelings, merely we can't express them like others.'

'You don't have to punish yourself like this.'

'I deserve it. Julia was right. I was keeping her a prisoner. And worse, I was a hypocrite.'

'What do you mean?'

He fell silent. Outside, brown-overalled gardeners were cutting the lawns with red sit-on mowers, doing speedy laps and leaving behind neat paths of clipped grass. The blanket began to slip, so she stood up to adjust it for him. He wrapped cool fingers around her hand and tugged gently on it.

'In those days, my morals were more . . . fluid. I intended no harm. On an emotional level, it meant nothing. I was vain and arrogant and flattered.'

'It's alright. I remember the incident, when I walked in on you in bed, with another woman, just after Mum died.'

He tightened his grip and pulled again. 'You don't understand. I met Nicola years ago, while I was practising law and we had a brief fling. We were both married and decided to end it for the sake of our respective partners. A few years later, her husband died and we started seeing each other, only once or twice a month. She knew I would never leave your mother. Then, my secretary left and Nicola took over. It was . . . difficult to end the affair. When I discovered Julia was seeing Bernard, I became jealous. Insanely so. Especially when my own dalliance was a meaningless fling that had gone on far too long. I ended it there and then, the very day I found out about Julia and Bernard. Julia, however, refused to stop seeing Bernard. She said she was in love. It wounded me that she could be so happy with another man. I couldn't stand the thought of them together. I forced her to stop seeing Bernard.'

'And what about Nicola?'

'She wouldn't take no for an answer. She was . . . persuasive.'

'You carried on seeing Nicola, after forcing Mum to give up Bernard?'

'Yes.'

'Did Mum know?'

The answer was a slow whispered 'Yes.' He released her, his hand flopping back on the arm of the chair. The confession had taken it out of him. His eyes began to glaze. 'I have to read the note to remember. When I forget to read it, or can't make sense of it, you must remind me. Promise me you will remind me. And you must read it to me. Promise.'

'I promise.'

'I'm so sorry about Nicola,' he said.

A familiar, vacant stare returned to his eyes. He was retreating once more. 'Julia, I'm so sorry, my love. Nicola meant nothing to me. I tried to end the affair . . . so many times. Really, I did. I wanted us to be one happy family again. You meant the world to me. I never abandoned you, not ever, not when I was with her, not ever. She was poisonous. Cunning. She blackmailed me. There were threats. I called her bluff, but I feared she would tell you eventually and you would leave. It was . . . easier to keep her onside. Julia, forgive me!'

'It's Stacey, Dad. Mum isn't here.'

He looked about, mouth open, eyes rheumy. 'Julia?'

'No, Dad. I'm Stacey.'

'Stacey? Julia wants to take you away with her. With *him*. Don't leave me, my precious girl.'

'I'm not going anywhere.'

He became increasingly agitated, hands rubbing the arms of the chair. 'Don't believe her . . . when she tells you about Owen. He's a nasty individual. He had a look about him. I never took to him from the first time I saw him. I can smell trouble when I see it and he was trouble. I never took to him. I wanted nothing to do with Owen.'

'Owen? Mum was seeing Bernard. Who's Owen?'

The hand rubbing became even more frantic. 'No . . . I don't mean Owen. I'm . . . mixed up. I mean Bernard. That man's an utter bastard. You must warn Julia about him. Tell her not to leave with Bernard. Tell her.'

'Dad, listen to me. That was in the past. That all happened years ago. You're in a nursing home now. Mum isn't here.'

'No?'

'No, Dad. She died.'

'Nicola died?'

'No, Dad. Mum died. You were with Nicola for a while afterwards. I saw her with you. In our house. After Mum died.'

He removed his hands from the arms of the chair and began to wring them slowly together. 'No, I broke it off with her once and for all then. She wanted marriage, the works. I couldn't go through with that. I never liked her enough to make her my spouse, entitle her to half my estate. That was all she really wanted. She was like a limpet. I couldn't shake her off. I had to get her out of my life. She was becoming too much, too demanding. I had no choice. You must understand, I had to be cruel to get her out of my life.'

Her scalp began to tingle, as it always did when she felt she was onto something. 'Cruel?'

'I was horrible. Vile. The way I behaved was appalling. But there was no other way to rid myself of her.' He looked away.

'Dad, do you remember when you broke up with Nicola?'

'I'm so sorry, Julia. It was my fault Stacey was abducted.' His lip trembled. Tears tracked the creases in his sunken cheeks.

No matter how much she wanted to, Stacey couldn't continue. 'Don't get upset, Dad. Let's get you a cup of tea.'

'Don't leave me, Julia. I'll change. I promise.'

She patted his hand and made for the door. This was more than either of them could bear.

Outside the care home, her phone rang again.

'I've found Bella!' Ox sounded jubilant.

'Great! Where is she?'

'First, let me tell you she wasn't easy to track down. She switched names by deed poll. She's been living in Lytham St Annes all this time. In August 1996, she purchased a flat there, then twenty years ago took on a guest house in the same town.'

The dual seaside towns of Lytham and St Annes were generally regarded as upmarket, boasting smart cafés and stylish independent shops. Visitors didn't come to this part of the coast simply for the extensive sandy beaches, but to visit the Victorian pier, spend time on manicured lawns in pretty parks, or play golf on one of the four 'royal' golf courses. Residents lived along wide tree-lined avenues in genteel late-Victorian, Edwardian and 1920s villas. That Bella, a girl from a rough council estate, had ended up there was a surprise.

'How the hell did she afford to buy a property?'

'Housing was a lot more affordable in the 1990s. She paid thirty thousand pounds for a one-bedroomed flat. Same place has tripled in value since then.'

'She didn't have thirty pounds, let alone that amount.'

'Well, according to the documents in front of me, she paid full price for it. She didn't even take out a mortgage on it.'

'Then either she was given the money or somebody else paid for the flat and put it in her name. Where's her guest house?'

'Same street as St Annes Library. The place is called Seaside Hideaway.'

'And her new name?'

'April Moss.'

# DAY FOUR

## SATURDAY – 4 P.M.

While Lytham, with its historic windmill, was a smaller, more residential town fronting the estuary of the River Ribble, St Annes-on-Sea was on the Fylde coast. Although she was astonished Bella had ended up here, Stacey also understood the appeal it held for the girl who had wanted to go kitesurfing, swim every day in the sea, and spend hours on a perfect sandy beach.

The library was baroque, a grade II-listed building built of red brick and buff terracotta, with an impressive octagonal domed tower. The houses along the road were grand in both size and structure. She couldn't place the cursing, angry Bella with bleached hair and black roots and don't-give-a-damn attitude here in this slice of suburban paradise. Stacey imagined that the owner of this property with its curved bay, stone-surround windows and meticulously trimmed box hedging would be the antithesis of the rebel she had known. The lawn resembled a well-kept bowling green. A hanging basket, brimming with healthy spring blooms, was suspended from a hook next to the porch entrance. Stacey straightened her shoulders, followed the red-brick paving and rang the doorbell.

The woman who answered was dressed in a scarlet shift dress, her bare shoulders and arms toned from regular workouts.

Shoulder-length, liquorice-black hair fell neatly to frame her weathered face. The smile she had worn as she opened the door froze, exposing tiny cracks where her red lipstick had bled. She lifted a pair of glasses and put them on, her opal eyes ginormous behind the lenses.

'Stacey? Oh my gosh! Is that you?'

Although the wind was fresh, Bella seemed content enough without a jacket or cardigan as she wandered beside Stacey along the promenade. 'I always fancied one of those for myself,' she said, as they passed the brightly coloured beach huts. 'They never seem to come up for sale though. I'm not surprised. Who'd want to sell one if they owned it?'

Stacey caught sight of a couple inside one of the huts, him in a jumper at the table typing into a laptop, her in a deckchair, glass of wine in one hand, book in the other. A garland of flags hung along the wall and a large sign: *HOME*.

'Why are you here, Stacey?'

The question had been avoided until now. Bella hadn't invited Stacey inside, saying she had guests staying there and they ought to take a walk instead. They'd made light conversation, discussed how much St Annes had changed over the years, and touched on their choices of careers.

'You visited me while I was in hospital. You stayed beside my bed, and you talked to me.'

Bella kept walking. 'Oh! I thought you were out for the count. The nurses told me you'd been sedated, that you didn't know what was going on.'

'I didn't remember a thing about that time until recently. Something happened to make me visit a hypnotherapist. She's helped me access a lot of memories.'

278

Bella dropped her head and maintained her steady pace, before drawing to a halt and facing the sea. 'We were going to move to the coast together. Do you remember that?'

'The caravan in Devon. Hunting for more permanent accommodation while we were there. Going swimming every day, living life, escaping the ones we hated so much. Yes, I remember.'

Bella gave a sharp laugh. A flock of screeching gulls swept by, twisting and diving into the gloomy waters. 'Even after all these years, I still love it here. I can barely remember how imprisoned I felt back then. I've had decades being free, coming here whenever the mood takes me to look out across the waters. And every time I wander down here and stare out, I think of you, Stacey. Every . . . single . . . time.'

The battle-grey sea hurled foamy waves against the shore. Bella spoke again.

'I should have come forward sooner. If I had, you wouldn't have gone through . . . I can't imagine what hell. Seeing you in that hospital bed, your face bruised and bandaged . . . I . . . I knew I would never forgive myself.'

A sharp blast of air rattled a beach hut door, making it creak like a wooden boat on high seas. An arm extended from inside and pulled it to. Gooseflesh pimpled Bella's arms, which hung loosely by her sides.

'I saw exactly what happened. I was at the bus stop and spotted you coming my way. I hid behind the bush so I could jump out and scare you. Then I heard you scream. I peered out in time to see you being stuffed into a car. Before I knew it, the car was off down the lane. I was going to ring the police.' She paused to fix her hair up with an elastic band, drawing it into a ponytail.

'In the end I got scared. You know what I was like back then. I was up to my neck in shit . . . Delivering *packages*. I got this stupid idea if I told the cops what I'd seen, they'd ask all sorts of questions about why I hadn't been at school and eventually find out what I got up to. I didn't report it because I figured your dad would. When there was nothing on the news, I went to your house to tell him what I'd seen. He was nice to me, asked me to describe the vehicle and the person who abducted you. Then it got weird. Really weird. He said I wasn't to speak to anybody else about what had happened. He assured me that everything would be alright. You would come home.'

She suddenly rubbed her shoulders. 'Bit cold, isn't it? Come on, let's keep moving.'

Stacey said nothing.

They continued past the beach huts, where Bella slipped off her shoes and carried them down to the beach. Stacey followed, keeping her own boots on. The sand sucked at her soles as she struggled to keep up with light-footed Bella.

'Three days later, he came to our flat,' said Bella. 'Everything was okay. You'd been rescued, but he didn't want me to visit you. In fact, he didn't want me to see you ever again. Apparently, you were too traumatised. He was going to take you away from Burton-on-Trent to help your recovery. It wasn't to be a short trip, either. More a permanent move from the area. I asked if, when you got out of hospital, you could at least come on holiday with me. Told him about the caravan. He said there'd be no way you could, not after what had happened, and that I should go without you. He made me promise not to tell a soul I'd spoken to him about what I'd seen. He wanted to compensate me for keeping my silence and for losing you as a friend. He offered me forty thousand pounds to put my mum into rehab. Stacey, the money was my ticket to freedom. There was enough money to get help for Mum and to give me a chance to escape my life. If I'd stayed, stuck it out in Burton-on-Trent, running drugs or whatever was in the packages for local hoodlums, I'd have eventually been beaten up, or ended up in jail, or on drugs myself. I couldn't refuse. I took it.'

She faced Stacey. 'In spite of what I promised him, I visited you in hospital. I sneaked in when he wasn't around. I'll never forget how you looked or how bad I felt about the part I played in allowing that to happen. One phone call to the police sooner might have saved you all that trauma. I'm truly sorry. I hope you understand.'

'I never held any malice towards you, only anguish because I couldn't understand why you walked out on me. Now I do.'

'And you what, forgive me?'

'Of course I do. None of this was your fault. If anybody was to blame, it was my father. He lied about you to me, said you hadn't rung or visited, that you'd gone to the caravan and didn't intend coming back.'

'I guess he wanted you to have a fresh start. He was helping you sever old ties.'

'I don't think that was the reason.' There was little doubt her father had kept them apart to ensure Stacey would never uncover the truth. 'So, you saw the kidnapper's car?'

'Yes. It drove past as I was crouching in the bushes. I snuck a look at it through the branches.'

'What exactly did you tell my father?'

'The car was a silver VW Beetle and the woman who drove it had red hair.'

Something shifted in Stacey's head . . .

*Stacey's been sent home from school early. Her head is banging badly. It's hurting so much she barely registers the silver VW Beetle parked on the road outside the house. It's only been a week since her mother's funeral, and she still can't focus on anything. It's like she's in a void. People have been kind to her but none of it helps. Unable to contact her father, the*

281

*school nurse, Mrs Hausmann, has driven her home and dropped her off with instructions to lie down and if she isn't feeling better in a few hours to make sure her dad takes her to the local surgery.*

*The noises from the bedroom. Her father. Naked.*

*He turns, rolls away from the woman beneath him, grabbing the sheet as he does so to cover himself, too late.*

*'Shit! Shit!' The woman's eyes bulge. She's plump, with short, bright-red hair. Nothing like her mother.*

*Rooted to the spot, Stacey can't drag her gaze from her. A week ago, her mother was in that very bed.*

*'Stacey, get out. Get out now.'*

It came together in an explosive flash that almost overbalanced her.

'Stacey? Is everything okay?'

Stacey recovered her footing. Of course. It all made sense. Her father's affair with his red-headed secretary, Nicola, a woman who wouldn't take no for an answer. 'I think I know why he wanted you to get out of my life.'

'Then are you going to explain it to me?'

'Yes. Soon. I have to go, Bella.'

'Will I see you again?'

'Would you like to?'

'Yes. Very much.'

'Then I'll come back.'

'Take my phone number.'

Stacey hastily tapped the details into her phone and looked up. For a split second, she saw old Bella, the girl who wanted to live by the sea, full of angst and frustration, then the face changed back to the new Bella, older, but content with life. Stacey was glad she'd seized her opportunity to transform her life and future. 'I'll ring. Promise. Now, I really have to go.'

She battled her way over the beach to the promenade. When she turned back, Bella was waving. She returned the gesture, then ran for her car to speak to Ox.

'Nicola. That's all I have. No surname. That's right. She was my father's secretary. I'm not sure when she started working for him, but she left in 1992.'

Ox grunted. She could hear the faint tapping as fingers flew over the keyboard. She tightened her grip on the steering wheel, eager to get going. The clicking continued. A woman pushing a buggy headed towards her. She stopped before reaching Stacey's car, where she stooped to pick up a fallen fluffy toy. She wiggled it backwards and forwards in front of the child, the smile on her face spreading as white-stockinged legs kicked up and down in excitement, before returning it to the baby, and continuing her journey. By the time she'd passed Stacey's Kia, Ox had found the information she needed.

'Surname is Martin. Her address is 29 Deepside Gardens, Liverpool. South of the city centre.'

She stabbed the information into the satnav. 'Ox, have you found out the exact date she left my father's employment?'

'One sec. Here we go. Wednesday 1 July 1992.'

Nicola had been fired two days before Stacey was abducted.

'The records show that she was dismissed for breach of contract.'

There were only two obvious reasons Nicola wouldn't have tried to challenge her dismissal. The first: she had been madly in love with Henry, holding out hope he would take her back. The second, and more likely: Henry had bullied or threatened her somehow, much as he had Stacey's mother. He would have found some way of ensuring she left her job without fuss and kept quiet about their affair. After all, he'd hired a professional to injure Bernard and had driven her mother to suicide. Mental cruelty and threats would explain why Nicola had kidnapped Henry's daughter.

'I'd need a car registration or part reg to identify the VW Beetle you mentioned. On top of which, I doubt she'd still own the vehicle,' said Ox.

'What you've given me is helpful enough for now. Thanks.'

'Any time. Scrub that. I don't mean it. Not *any time*. Despite what some peeps might think, I actually have a life outside of the web.'

She sped away. Nicola Martin, the woman who had been spurned by her father, who had lost not only her lover, but her job, her security and no doubt some self-respect. Henry had always been formidable. It didn't take a great leap of imagination to guess how he might have spoken to Nicola, employing years of experience of legal jargon to confound her, together with absolute confidence and his trademark icy streak. Heaven knew what other tricks her father had pulled to get rid of his secretary and lover. He might even have threatened her with a similar fate to Bernard's, an accident from which she might never have recovered. Whatever tactics he'd employed, and whatever was said, had upset her enormously.

It made sense to Stacey that Nicola was responsible for kidnapping Lyra. It seemed plausible that, having failed to secure a ransom the first time around, the woman was trying again. Maybe she knew Henry had recently had a stroke and assumed Stacey had power of attorney, that Stacey would pay the ransom. She ignored her inner voice that questioned the fact that Nicola would surely have tried before now or why she'd sent the demand to Jack. Instead, she persisted in following her instinct. The more she thought about it, the more logical it became. Nicola knew every detail of Stacey's kidnapping. It explained the hair, the sneaker, the finger and the note. There Stacey's reasoning fell apart. Nicola hadn't chopped off her finger. Nicola hadn't been the man in the rubber mask. Had she involved the same accomplice again? Stacey fervently hoped that wasn't the case. With her heart pounding, she floored the accelerator. Nicola wouldn't get away with this abduction, either.

◆ ◆ ◆

The grey, rendered terraced house wasn't in bad order. The front lawn, more weed than grass, had at least been recently mown. The street was one of many, secreted in a labyrinth of twisting roads, that Stacey wouldn't have discovered easily without the assistance of her navigational aid. The property was an end terrace. High panelled fencing separated it from a neighbouring garden, against which Nicola had placed three wheelie bins: purple, grey and green, in a tidy line. The drive, like the property, was tired and in need of more attention than a pressure wash. Slabs, where old moss had rested for long periods of time before being removed, were stained darkly. The low brick wall with steel railings that fronted the house needed replacing, and when Stacey opened the loose gate, it dragged along the ground, emitting a harsh shriek that caused the downstairs curtains to twitch before quickly swinging back into place.

She rang the doorbell, knowing she had been spotted. The door opened silently and a man with an open face answered. He balled a large, freckled hand loosely and held it to his throat, clearing it before speaking.

'Yes?'

'I'd like to speak to Nicola Martin, please,' she asked.

His features distorted momentarily, invisible threads tugging at eyebrows and lips simultaneously, as if in sudden pain. 'I'm afraid that's impossible. My mother passed away two weeks ago.'

'I'm very sorry to hear that. Please accept my condolences.'

He gave a little cough, an *uh-huh-huh*. 'It was expected. She'd been ill for a few months, but thank you anyway. Can I help at all?'

Having been certain Nicola was behind, or in some way involved in, Lyra's abduction, this news floored her. 'No. I don't think you can.' She made to leave, yet couldn't. She had no clue where to go next. The man hadn't moved, either. He cleared his throat again.

'How did you know my mother?'

'I didn't. My father knew her.'

The man stared blankly, and Stacey explained. 'She worked for him. Many years ago.'

'Oh, right.' His brows danced again. 'My mother was one of those people who believed work is work and home is home. She never discussed what she did.'

'She was my father's secretary.'

'Oh, right. Yes.' He flicked his middle fingernail against his thumbnail as he spoke. 'She did a lot of temping.'

She was unsure where to take the conversation; after all, she couldn't blurt out the truth. Whether it was her reluctance to leave his doorstep, or something else she gave away unconsciously, he suddenly cocked his head.

'There's more to this visit, isn't there? You wouldn't simply drop by to see her because she used to work for your father. Why are you really here?'

'It's not important.'

He cleared his throat yet again. 'I think there's more. My guess is you believe they knew each other on a more personal level.'

She ought to move and leave this man to his mourning and yet his silence drew out a response. 'You're right. They were in a relationship for a long while.'

He opened his palms. 'Listen, my father died when I was five. Mum never got married again. She brought me up single-handedly. I'm aware there were men in her life. If you're here to drag up dirt from back then, you're too late.'

'No, no dirt. Just wanted to be sure of my facts.'

He clicked his fingernails again and asked, 'Did your father send you? Did he want to see her, or have you come out of curiosity?'

'My father doesn't know I'm here. He's in a nursing home. His memory—'

She couldn't work out why she was revealing such details to a stranger. She shook herself free of his understanding gaze.

'Anyhow, I'm sorry to have disturbed you.'

He clicked his nails again, a nervous habit. 'No. It's fine. In a way, it's sort of nice to be able to find out something about her. Although she was my mum, she wasn't one for sharing information, not even with me. I've been sifting through her personal possessions, trying to make sense of the story behind them, piecing her life together, as it were, so I can learn what she was really like. It's nice to be able to talk about her, even if the subject matter is a little uncomfortable.' He tried for a smile only for his lips to quiver slightly.

'I don't want to distress you.'

'You haven't. Not at all.'

'I'd better go. I'm sorry for your loss.'

As she turned, she caught a strong whiff of body spray, a masculine, peppery scent that stayed trapped in her nostrils until she reached her car and was behind the wheel. The fact that she'd behaved the way she had was perplexing. She'd conducted hundreds of interviews for the newspaper and had never felt so awkward while speaking to somebody. It wasn't simply down to Nicola being dead. She closed her eyes, inhaled the scent of pine from the dangling air freshener, and it hit her. She knew this man. Erin had been right when she'd said unblocking various parts of her brain would help it to unlock memories of its own accord. This one unfolded as if it had never been hidden, triggered by her auditory senses . . .

*Prowling. Slow footsteps. Behind her. In front of her. The odd guttural noises he makes, as if clearing his throat. He does it again, a quick* uh-uh, *then clicks his fingernails. He does that a lot. Especially before he becomes violent and hits her or just before he took off her finger. She's learned that it's a precursor to anger.*

*'How are we going to make Henry see sense?'*

*She can barely make out the hissed words and she tenses, waiting for him to strike. The blow doesn't come. Instead, there's another voice, quieter, and the clicking and pacing both stop. She strains hard to listen.*

*'This was . . .* not *the plan. You weren't to harm her.'*

*'He should have paid up, like you said he would!'*

*'This isn't her fault.'*

*'Then what do you suggest we do now? Let her go? Not now we've almost got him on the hook. He'll pay soon. He knows we mean business.'*

*'I wish I hadn't let you talk me into this.'*

*'You were the one who was so angry you wanted payback. You came up with the idea.'*

*'I didn't expect it to pan out like this. And you? What the hell has happened to you? How could you treat her so cruelly? It was a good thing I came back when I did, or heaven knows what else you might have inflicted on the poor girl! I had no idea you could be such a monster.'*

*'If I am, I got it from my parents.' He spits the final word.*

*There's more whispering she can't hear, then, 'I've checked her wound and it's clean, but make sure she takes these tablets. She's suffering with the pain.'*

*Stacey doesn't hear any footsteps depart, only another* uh-uh *and another long gap until the hood is pulled off her head.*

*He gives a cold bark of a laugh. 'Now you see me!'*

*A peppery smell, from a body spray, aftershave or similar, assaults her senses. As he presses the water bottle against her lip, the strong scent infiltrates her mouth, adhering to the back of her throat.*

She drove off, anxious to get out of his line of sight. The body spray, the nail-clicking, the soft guttural clearing of the throat. *He* was the man in the mask. He'd have only been about twenty at the time. Young, angry, resentful. His mother had roped him in and then lost control of him. The soft hands hadn't belonged to him. They'd been hers. She'd been the one to tend to Stacey's wounds. Nicola had kept her fed. This man had been the torturer, and had she not been rescued in time, he'd have been her executioner. Now she understood why the pieces hadn't fitted. Nicola's anger had been directed at Henry, not at Stacey. Nicola wouldn't have allowed another girl to suffer the same way Stacey had. She wouldn't have allowed Lyra to come to grief.

What sort of person was her father? He had known all along that his ex-mistress had taken, tortured and maimed his daughter. He had put a contract out on Bernard, yet done nothing about Nicola or her son. He'd paid no ransom. Furthermore, he'd allowed Stacey's kidnappers to go unpunished. Having failed to get what they wanted the first time around, Nicola's son was trying a second time. Was he doing it purely for the money or because he wanted to hurt her some more?

With shaking hands, she rang Ashraf.

'I know who's abducted Lyra. It's Nicola Martin's son.'

'I take it you have no name for him?'

'None. Or an address. His mother died two weeks ago. He's currently at her house. I can't tell whether that's because he's sorting out her estate as he claimed, or because it's closer to Morecambe than where he normally lives.'

'And what's your reasoning? Why has he abducted Lyra?' asked Ashraf in his usual no-nonsense voice.

'He and his mother kidnapped me. He was the man in the rubber mask.'

'How sure are you? I don't want us to go down a wrong path.'

She thought about his scent, his peculiar habits, memories of both crystal clear in her mind. 'One hundred per cent.'

She'd taken the precaution of parking the non-distinctive Kia out of sight down an adjacent street. Even if the man had watched her walk away, he couldn't have known where she was parked, what vehicle she was driving, or even if she'd come alone.

She grabbed hold of the steering wheel and fought down the urge to scream in frustration. As she did so, memories unleashed from her encounter with Nicola's son rained on her, giving her focus so she could finally piece together the sequence of events surrounding her own kidnapping. The fortifications encircling memories of the kidnapping exploded into ruins, releasing every detail as if it had only happened the week before. The fear she had always expected to accompany the revelations didn't come. Instead, she viewed them dispassionately, as if watching a film in which actors played out the sequence of events.

*There's no sign of Bella at the bus stop. She's beginning to wonder if her friend has cried off, when a car comes into view and slows. She pays it scant attention, nor does she fully register the quick footsteps behind her, a peppery scent that suddenly envelops her as a hand is clamped over her nose and mouth. Although she struggles, she can't escape her captor, who lifts her with ease, strides towards the car and flings her into the boot. Her head smacks against a hard surface or object and immediately stars appear, and the world begins to turn black. And as she is sucked into the darkness, she tries to hang onto relevant details, the large hand covered in freckles, the car . . . then no more.*

Nicola's son had snatched her, yet Bella had only spotted red-headed Nicola. He must have been waiting and watching for Stacey to leave home, then contacted his mother, who was waiting nearby. Stacey had heard urgent footsteps before he'd clamped his hand over her mouth and nose. He'd been behind her. This was the only logical scenario. How else would Nicola have known to drive past at that exact moment? They'd been patiently waiting for such an opportunity.

Everything slotted into place: the bedding in the newsagent's flat, where Nicola had left her son to keep a watchful eye on Stacey, while she orchestrated the delivery of a package of shorn hair and demanded the ransom. When no ransom had been forthcoming, her son had become angry. Nicola had appeased him with assurances that Henry had a safe that surely contained valuables he could sell or pawn to raise the money. She'd left again. In a fit of sudden rage, he'd taken it upon himself to torture Stacey and beat her until she told him what was inside the safe.

It was at that point her logic became unstuck because there'd have been no way Nicola could have found out that the safe was empty unless she'd accessed it. With the relationship between her and Henry soured, she wouldn't have been welcomed at the house, especially with Stacey missing at the time. She drummed her fingers against the wheel. She was convinced she wasn't wrong; however, this missing piece suggested she might be.

The ringtone broke her thought process.

'His name is Owen Martin. Unmarried. Lives at the same address as his mother. He was convicted of assault in 1999 and served a community sentence. Same thing in 2002 but served eight months in jail, and again in 2005 when he served a further ten months. He was working as a local nightclub bouncer until the pandemic started and has been unemployed ever since. We should report him to the police,' said Ashraf.

Owen! Her father had mentioned the name: *'Don't believe her . . . when she tells you about Owen.'* At the time, she'd believed him to be confused and to have muddled Bernard with another person's name. Had he known of the man's involvement in her kidnapping all along? There was no time to dwell on the matter. 'No! We must find Lyra. If the police take him in for questioning, that's more time lost. And what if he won't divulge where she is?'

'Yeah. Poor kid. You're right. What do you propose?'

'I'm waiting here until he leaves. Then I'll follow him. Last time he rang, Jack wouldn't agree to his demands until he could speak to Lyra. He might think the same thing will happen when he rings to issue instructions for the final drop. He won't want to take a risk that Jack won't pay up, meaning he needs to be with Lyra when he next calls.'

'That's logical. Did Owen seem spooked by you?'

'No . . . But he'll have worked out my identity, which might make him doubly cautious. He put on a good act, behaving as if he had no idea who I was. He'd have pulled it off too if I hadn't had an epiphany.'

'Then my guess is he'll make a run for it. He'll suspect you've worked out who's taken Lyra. I'll get over there as soon as possible. Where are you?'

'Parked on the street that connects with the one he lives on.'

'Have you got a clear view of the road, should he leave in that direction?'

'I have.'

'Then hang fire until I reach you.'

As he spoke, a green Honda Accord drove by, Owen at the wheel.

'Too late. He's on the move.' She terminated the call, switched on her engine and eased forward, ensuring a safe distance from his car. She had a good idea he was heading to Morecambe. There was no need to draw attention to herself by sitting on his tail.

# DAY FOUR

## SATURDAY – 6 P.M.

Thanks to roadworks, the traffic slowed to a crawl. Soon she found herself only eight car lengths from Owen's Honda in the outside lane, which was moving more slowly than the vehicles in her lane. For a while, she drew ever closer, only for his car to pull ahead as his lane sped up. She rang Ashraf.

'I'm on the M6 northbound.'

'Okay, I'll make my way towards Morecambe. There's every chance he's keeping Lyra hidden somewhere in that area.'

'I'm pinning all my hopes on that fact. Where are you?'

'A65. I'll be a while.'

'Traffic's dense here, so we might be too.'

'Keep me updated.'

She tried hard to quell the anxiety swooshing in her stomach. Catching a fleeting glimpse of the back of Owen's head, she sank lower in her seat, hoping he hadn't spotted her in his rear-view mirror. She drew level with the service station where she had met Danni only two days earlier. It felt like weeks ago to her. Those same two days would feel like months to Lyra. Her insides somersaulted at the thought of the wounded child.

This time, there would be no Nicola to bathe the girl's wound or insist she received regular painkillers. There was nobody to control Owen when his mood flipped. She'd witnessed his volatility first-hand. Many of her injuries had been inflicted through malice. Owen had got off on hurting her; each beating had brought out the worst in him, feeding the vitriol that bubbled inside him. With Nicola gone, he would be capable of unimaginable atrocities. The idea he might play out his fantasies on Lyra was unbearable.

Gaps appeared in the traffic as vehicles picked up speed. She accelerated, ensuring the Honda remained in sight. She quelled a rising nausea with reassurances that Owen was on his way to ensure Lyra was alright.

Another thought, like a metal ball on a Newton's cradle, collided into the first, expelling it from her mind. Lyra might already be dead. Owen had fifty thousand pounds. He might have decided it wasn't worth hanging out for the remainder of the ransom. He could be headed somewhere else altogether, nowhere near where he had held Lyra prisoner. She gripped the wheel even tighter, until her knuckles ached. The ideas kept clattering backwards and forwards until the noise was almost too much for Stacey.

She wiped damp palms against her jeans. If she'd got this wrong, Owen would sail by the turn-off for Morecambe. Everything depended on having made the right call. Fields flew past, blurs of green spotted with browns and whites as cows grazed beside the motorway. Her heart rattled against her ribcage. So much depended on this. She would never, ever forgive herself if Lyra did not come home.

An HGV overtook her, only to return immediately to the nearside lane, blocking the visual she had on Owen's vehicle. The exit to Morecambe was fast approaching. It would be imprudent to overtake the lorry, only to cut it up. At best, it would annoy the driver. At worst, that person might blast their horn, drawing attention to her vehicle. She had to keep trusting her instincts. She flicked the indicator to join the slip road, where she was relieved to discover the Honda at the traffic lights, seven cars ahead of her.

'Ashraf, I'm coming off the M6. He's in the lane for Morecambe.'

'I'm . . . minutes . . . Keep—'

'Ashraf!'

The signal had given out.

Cars slipped slowly through the junction, held up behind a huge, slow-moving HGV. However, before she could follow suit, the traffic lights turned amber and the car in front of hers stopped.

'Shit!' She watched the Honda drive away and smacked her steering wheel with the palm of her hands. She tried ringing Ashraf again, only for her call to go directly to voicemail. Just when she was about to scream with frustration, the lights changed to green, and she was on the move again. She overtook the car, joined the dual carriageway and floored the accelerator.

She willed the Honda to reappear. As she passed the slow-moving lorry that had held them up at the traffic lights, she spied Owen's car approaching a roundabout, right indicator flashing. She had caught up with it in time. Even though he wasn't headed into Morecambe, he had to be headed somewhere nearby, to check on Lyra. *Or kill her.*

She maintained a prudent distance from the Honda, following it along a twisting lane. She'd come this way with Danni when they'd been hunting for disused premises. Had they been this close to finding Lyra? What had they missed? Her phone rang.

'Ashraf! Thank goodness.'

'Where are you?'

She told him, adding, 'This road is familiar. Danni and I came along it the other day to check out a farm here. At least, we intended checking it out, but a surveyor turned up. I don't know if Danni went back. It was around that time she had to leave, and Jack took over the list. It might have slipped through our net.'

'I'm about twenty minutes from there.'

The road climbed, gaps in the hedgerows affording her glimpses of Owen's vehicle as it slowed to take sharp bends.

She spied the roof of Owen's car as it turned off the main road onto a track. 'He's stopped at Stubbs Farm Business Park. I'm going to park up and head up on foot, so he doesn't see my vehicle.'

'Stacey, that's too dangerous. Wait for—' Once more the signal cut out. She pulled over and bounded from the car without a thought for her own safety, making for the same gap in the hedgerow she and Danni had used. Ashraf knew her location and would soon arrive; however, that might be too late for Lyra. Driven by the need to reach the girl, she made for the stile and bounded over it, then ran up the hill, mind solely on reaching Lyra. This spurt of energy took her halfway before the gradient began to beat her. All the same, she ignored the fire in her leg muscles, kept Lyra's face in mind and powered upwards with gasps and splutters until the tops of the outside buildings were visible and the end of the long, converted barn came into sight.

Several deep inhalations later, she set off again, each step taking her closer to Lyra's assistance. She'd forgotten how steep the incline was. She fought for oxygen, bent over to catch her breath and, when she lifted her head, noticed light bouncing off a green vehicle in the yard. The sight of Owen's car parked directly in front of the half-timbered barn injected a fresh boost of adrenalin, enabling her to scramble over the fence and sprint past the smaller units towards the large building.

He had to be inside the barn. The outside fire escape seemed to be the only possible entry point. The steps to the door were constructed of bricks, their treads so narrow only the balls of her feet could balance on them. She mounted them slowly, one at a time, hand on the guard rail to prevent her from tumbling to the tarmac. The staircase rose sharply and her thighs, already fatigued from the steep hill, screamed at her until she reached the door. She issued a silent prayer that Lyra was still alive and inside this building before pressing gently on the handle. It gave under the pressure and swung open.

She stepped onto plush pile, where she blinked to adjust her vision. Evening sunlight streamed through the numerous skylights, rebounding off glass walls of inner offices. Trapped among the rays, millions of dust particles danced and spun. She edged around the office furniture and past doors bearing washroom signs. There were three further workstations before she reached another door. It opened onto a stairwell. From below came unidentifiable sounds.

She tiptoed to the ground floor: a reception area, where a muffled cry propelled her down an unlit corridor. She felt her way along, pausing beside each door, pressing her ear to the wood, listening for life behind it. Darkness wound itself around her, rendering her immobile until another low cry unfroze her. She inched towards it, fingers trailing over the cool walls and another doorframe. There her feet became leaden again.

Whimpers from within the room next to her shot shards of ice through her ribs. A piercing scream galvanised her into action. She rested her hand on the door handle. A voice in her head kept her glued in position, reminding her that Owen could be armed and close enough to Lyra to kill her before Stacey could intervene. She endeavoured to make out noises that might help her ascertain their positions. Her inner voices counselled her again, warning her not to be hasty. Ashraf was on his way. She didn't know the layout of the room and might run straight into an obstacle. It was thanks to this intense cogitation that her senses let her down. She was unaware of the movement behind her, or the person who struck her with such force her face smashed against the door. Her assailant pushed hard on both shoulders, forcing her into the room.

There was an explosion of stars in her head. The ensuing intense throbbing obliterated all logical thought. Propelled back in time, she believed she was reeling from one of Owen's blows. She couldn't breathe. The hood was too tight. Panic set in. She sucked and coughed, spitting out phlegm and something else. She felt for her face, ran fingers over sticky liquid. Her nose was bleeding. There was no hood. She opened her mouth to inhale, calmed a little. She wasn't suffocating.

'Get up.'

The voice brought her round further. The room was dimly lit by a small lamp. Shadows, like demons, danced on the wall.

No. She wasn't in the newsagent's. She wasn't being held captive. Lyra was.

The pain subsided marginally. Wincing, she blinked in the gloom, a sense of familiarity enveloping her. She made out a chair and table in the middle of the room. Owen stood beside them, a sly grin on his face. The rubber mask dangling from one of his hands looked like it was melting, its features stretched beyond recognition, yet she knew instantly what it was – an old man's mask.

He pressed a button on a mobile lying face up on the table. The room filled with whimpers, followed by a scream that chilled her. She recognised the sound. She'd heard it before.

Before she could gather her thoughts, she was shoved hard again. This time she fell forwards, smacking her forehead against the table as she did so. She crumpled. Hands dragged her to the chair. She had no fight in her, limbs unable to respond to her fuddled mind. Lyra wasn't here. Where was she?

Owen's face swam into view. Behind it another – Jack's.

She scrabbled for sense and found none.

Jack tutted. 'You are disappointingly predictable, Stacey. As soon as Owen rang to say you'd turned up at his house, I knew you'd lie in wait and follow him. I suggested he make it easy for you. He let you keep him in sight and when he lost you at the traffic lights, he slowed down so you could catch him up.'

She tried to move her lips. He lifted a finger to his mouth.

'Shh! Don't try to speak.'

Her head throbbed.

'Where's Lyra?'

'I told you to be quiet. Lyra isn't here. She's staying with her grandmother. I drove her there myself on Tuesday evening, after she returned from visiting Kelly.'

'Does she know?'

'Know? Know about all of this? Of course she doesn't! Oh, I suppose you're wondering why she hasn't rung you. Or why she hasn't been on social media. Especially as she's never off that blasted phone. She was so mad keen to have a dog, I made a deal with her. I promised if she turned off her phone, stayed off social media and didn't contact anybody for a whole week, I'd buy her the bloody puppy. I made it easier for her by dropping her at her grandmother's. The old bat doesn't have a computer or even a smartphone. Lyra will be bored rigid for a few days, but at least she'll get her own way. Can't say I'm overjoyed, but a promise is a promise, and I couldn't have carried this off if she hadn't kept out of the way. The hard part was getting her to agree to keep the challenge a secret until it was over. She wasn't supposed to tell anyone: not Freya, not Kelly and especially not you.'

Stacey could do nothing other than sit slack-jawed while Jack cocked his head this way and that, bemused by her utter confusion. Owen sat on the corner of the desk, mask in hand. Jack spoke to him.

'Worked like a charm, eh? I promised you'd get your reward and here she is.'

Owen grunted. 'True to your word.'

'I . . . don't understand.' Stacey squeezed her eyelids together tightly. The pain ricocheted around her head, setting all her nerves on fire and making her gasp. When the agony finally abated and she opened her eyes, Jack was crouched in front of her.

'No. You don't. That was the plan. Lyra was never kidnapped.'

'Her hair . . . Her finger . . . Her bike.' Her words sounded mumbled to her ears, like she was drunk.

'The hair is off the internet. You can buy wigs of human hair. I cut off what I needed from it. The finger, well, again, you'll be surprised what hard-up people will part with for five thousand pounds on the dark web. As for the bike. I planted it. In fact, I set the whole thing up to make it appear as if Lyra had been snatched on her way to the dog day care.'

'You?'

He appeared to take a small bow. 'Yes, I planned it for months. I was Trudy Bonham, her friend on Facebook and Snapchat. I told her about Woofles. I wanted to make sure she didn't return home along the promenade, where there are CCTV cameras, so it was *Trudy's* suggestion she drop by Woofles to enquire if they knew any good dog breeders who had puppies for sale. I dropped off her bike some time later, to make it seem as if she'd been snatched next to the school, when in fact, by then, she was safely with her grandmother.'

Stacey tried to move, discovered her hands and feet were tied down. He watched her antics as she struggled against her bounds. 'I wouldn't if I were you. They're cable ties and if you fidget too much, they'll probably end up cutting right through your wrists.'

'The video? That was Lyra in it.'

'Wrong. It was another set-up. I convinced a wannabe actress I was a television scout, hunting for actors for bit parts in a new series of the television drama filmed in Morecambe – *The Bay*. That was her audition piece. She was damn convincing, wasn't she? I'd have mistaken her for Lyra myself if I hadn't known otherwise. It took ages to find her. You must agree, she was well worth the wait. It's amazing how easily people can be duped. You included. That poor girl didn't get the part, of course. Never mind. She can chalk it up to experience. Anyway, you want to know why I went to all this trouble, don't you? Of course you do. You want to know why I set it all up.' He glanced at Owen again. The man remained silent.

'Money. I'm surprised you didn't get that part of it. I needed the money. I've run up significant debts over the last four years. You don't need to know all the details, but you were partly to blame. After you left me, I was in a bad place. I lost my way. Let's just say I spent more than I ought to have on recreational substances and other distractions. The law firm was already struggling and then Covid screwed things up further, so what with my expenses and so on, I found myself down a financial hole.

'You almost caught me out. Wednesday morning, I visited Henry to convince him to loan me the ransom money. I hadn't anticipated his memory being so poor he wouldn't recognise me or have a clue what I was talking about. He didn't even remember I had a daughter! Then I figured he'd have had the sense to give you power of attorney and I'd be able to convince *you* to pay the ransom money. After all, you never forgave Henry for not paying yours.

'I'll admit, finding out you couldn't access his accounts was something of a stumbling block, leaving me little option other than to convince you to cajole the money from him. And that's when things started to go wrong. You didn't want to ask him, did you? I thought at one point you might. I even played along and pretended I didn't want you to, knowing you would be less likely to suspect my motives if I didn't seem keen. You backtracked after that, never mentioned again going to Henry. Instead, you came up with the ridiculous idea of asking for a bank loan. Then, even when you firmly believed Lyra's life was in danger, you chose instead to hunt down her kidnapper rather than try and get the ransom money together. Jeez, you were so damn blinkered. Why didn't you choose the obvious route and ask Henry? You always were too stubborn. You didn't care about anyone but yourself. Shit, you were even prepared to let me broker a deal with loan sharks rather than speak to him about it.

'How could you? Oh, Stacey. I really thought you cared more about Lyra. You really should have gone straight to Henry, forced him to hand over the money, rather than keep playing detective. Do you want to know what I think? I think you actually didn't care what the outcome might have been. You were as unwilling as he was to touch his fortune, even to save Lyra. For all your bullshit about how much she means to you, you're the same as Henry. You have the same ice-cold heart.'

She hit back, determined to make him hurt too. 'That's not true. I love Lyra. She and I share something you never can with her – a friendship, a closeness. I'd have paid off any loan you took out, but of course, she was never in danger! You know, I never really trusted you, Jack? I always suspected you were up to something.'

Her words found their mark. His features contorted briefly, as if he'd been slapped in the face. His eyes narrowed as he stabbed her shoulder with his forefinger.

'Bitch! You can't love anyone. You haven't a clue what love is. I gave you love. I adored you. What did you give me in return? You flirted with every man that sniffed around your skirts.'

'No! I didn't.'

'Oh, you did. And you cheated on me. You slept with that shitweasel, Ashraf.' His lips twisted into a gruesome grin. 'Oh, look at the mock surprise. I knew about your disgusting tryst, you filthy whore! How did you bed him, eh? Did you convince him to be your knight in shining armour? "Oh, Ashraf, my husband doesn't treat me right. Boo hoo! Please look after me." I bet you did!'

The horrible, girly voice, the look of contempt on her ex-husband's face, sickened her. Who was this man? Despite the arrows piercing her skull, she was beginning to get a handle on what was happening. She had to keep him talking. Ashraf was on his way.

'You're wrong. So wrong about that.'

He gave a loose shrug. For the first time, she noticed how soulless his eyes had become; the pupils were pinpricks within a marble grey iris. 'No, I'm not. You shouldn't have crossed me, Stacey. You shouldn't have run to that slimy toad. You shouldn't have involved him in this – my business, either. I was willing to give you another chance. I'd have tried again to make things work between us, but no, you asked Ashraf to help find Lyra. You not only brought your lover into my private life, but you also refused to do the one thing that could have made all the difference to us . . . go to Henry for the money. It was the most obvious solution! So whatever happens, it's your fault. Your payback. You have nobody to blame but yourself. What's about to happen is because *you* didn't care enough to raise the money for me. This is your fault. Your payback. And Henry's.'

'This isn't Dad's fault. Why do you want to hurt him?'

His face changed again. He stood up and threw Owen a smirk. 'I told you she would never guess. All these years, she's been unable to remember a thing about the abduction, and even though she's been delving into the past over the last few days, she still hasn't got a fucking clue.' In the murk, he looked demonic. She wondered if Ashraf had found his way here yet. Was he running up the hill at this very moment?

Jack crouched in front of her again, eyes burrowing into hers, puffs of stale breath blowing in her face as he spoke. 'Henry has been paying for my silence. At least, up until his stroke. Then, the motherfucker couldn't remember a thing about our deal. It seems convenient memory loss runs in your family.'

Still she couldn't fathom what he was talking about. What deal? In the end, the blank look she must have been displaying irritated him enough for him to stand up and kick at the table leg.

'For fuck's sake! Come on. Keep up! You're the reporter here. It's quite simple. He and I had a financial arrangement. He paid me regularly. Helped me out when I needed a cash injection. And in return, I kept his secrets. Boy that man has some whoppers!'

'And how do you know about them?'

'Alcohol. Admittedly, once he became loose-tongued, I kept plying him with whisky until I knew the whole story. It happened a few years ago, after one of our golf sessions. He began by talking about his failing marriage and affair, then your mother's suicide, and finally, of course, your kidnapping. Wow! What a screw-up that was, wasn't it, Owen?'

'Too right it was.'

Owen had been so quiet that Stacey had forgotten he was in the room.

Jack carried on, 'Afterwards, Henry begged me to keep quiet about it, which I did. But the more distant you became, the more I decided you both owed me something. I forced him to buy my silence. Not for an exorbitant amount. It was nothing compared to the ransom he ought to have handed over to get you released. Fifty thousand pounds here, a law practice there.' He laughed at her. 'Don't look so shocked. Yes, Henry purchased Corrigan & Babcock, although the firm was placed solely in my name. He paid old Babcock off on my say-so.'

He rested his hands on the table. Owen sat patiently, eyes trained on Stacey the entire time.

'Like I said, Henry is a devious old sod. He's not as far gone in the head as I first thought when I visited him on Wednesday to ask him for money to save Lyra. He knew damn fine who I was. His memory loss is surprisingly selective. He pretended not to recognise me, much like he pretended not to recall our arrangement. Like he pretended he hadn't seen me for ages when I accompanied you to the care home on Friday. I sussed him though. Him and his "fudge, judge" routine. He might have you and the staff at the care home fooled, but not me. You can't kid a kidder. I went back to Topfields earlier today. Let's just say this time I persuaded him to part with all the money, which is now sitting in my bank account.'

There was a buzzing in Stacey's head. The sound of a hive of angry bees. Somewhere behind the noise, Jack was telling her an incredible story about kidnapping his own daughter and blackmailing her father. One that beggared belief.

'Did you hurt him?'

'What do you take me for? I don't do violence. You know that. I simply told him I'd met up with Owen, that I knew the whole truth about him, and was going to spill the beans to you. He thinks this time he's paid me off for good. Gullible old fool.'

'I suppose Owen filled in the blanks about my kidnapping, so I'd get really worried about Lyra. Why is he here now?' she asked, her mind calculating where Ashraf might be. He was taking his time. She wasn't sure how much longer she could keep Jack talking. He ignored her question, preferring to crow about how clever he had been.

'As usual, you were the one who made things difficult. You simply wouldn't listen to me. You had to do it your way, didn't you? You brought in Ashraf and then Danni, even after I explained why I didn't want any outside involvement. That tested my patience, Stacey. That pissed me off big time. If only you'd listened to me, none of this would be happening.'

'I was helping.'

'No, you were interfering, screwing up my plans! It was bad enough you brought in Ashraf, but Danni! You caused me a lot of extra effort, Stacey. Good thing I was one step ahead of you. I fixed it so Danni had to return to Cornwall, and you had to ask *me* to check out potential places where a kidnapper might hide Lyra. Which meant I found this barn – the perfect place to hold somebody hostage. Of course, Danni didn't really have to go home. There was no emergency. I rang her local police station, explained I'd witnessed suspicious activity outside their house and thought a break-in was in progress. I knew the police would contact her, and once she got back, it'd be unlikely she would be able to return to assist you.'

Where the hell was Ashraf? She shifted on the chair, causing the ties to bite into her flesh. Her ex-husband seemed so full of himself, puffed up and . . . utterly heartless.

'Why is Owen here?' asked Stacey for the second time.

Jack barked a low laugh. 'You are his *reward* for helping me to set it all up: the phone calls, the deliveries, the messages, were all thanks to him.' He swept his arm towards the table, where Stacey now spotted a toolbox. Jack's voice maintained a steady monologue. 'You have a lot of catching up to do. He's also going to benefit from some of Henry's fortune. Only fitting really, given Henry flatly refused to accept him as his own. What a monster, eh?'

'I don't—'

'Understand. Yeah, we get it. You're painfully slow today, Stacey. That knock on the head has really affected you. Henry and Nicola *and* . . . Owen. A happy fa-mi-ly! Daddy's girl. Daddy's boy.' He pointed to each of them in turn.

Her belly cramped. It couldn't be. Of course, Henry had hinted at something like this, hadn't he? He had mentioned Nicola blackmailing him. When he'd believed Stacey to be her mother, he'd said,

*'Don't believe her . . . when she tells you about Owen.'* He'd told her he didn't like the man, had never taken to him, all the while referring to Owen and not Bernard as she'd thought. He'd then backtracked, fooled her with his pretence, so she believed he'd muddled names due to his condition. Except, it hadn't been a mistake. Henry had almost blurted the truth – Owen was her half-brother!

Owen cleared his throat with a soft *uh-huh* before speaking.

'Henry's a lousy father, Stacey. He wouldn't pay for your release. He wouldn't accept he was my dad. He flatly refused a paternity test, claiming that legally, because my mother had named her deceased husband as my father, he didn't have to take one. He wouldn't believe her. He threatened to have me roughed up if she persisted in what he called "her lies". He may as well have ripped out her heart and stamped on it. She was so scared he would carry out his threats to harm me, she didn't even tell me, not until the day he fired her and kicked her out of his life for good. That's when I came up with the plan to kidnap you, my little *half-sister*. I masterminded it, not my mother. He owed us.'

She couldn't bring herself to look at the man in the corner. They might be related, yet he hated her. She looked up. Jack was talking again.

'You're up to speed now. And yet there's still one vital question you haven't asked me about Henry. Come on, Stacey. What should you have asked me earlier? Or are you frightened of the answer?'

She blinked away fireworks in her head. 'I . . . don't . . . understand.'

He slammed both hands on the table. 'Not that again! Yes. You do. You do understand. Come on. Ask me!'

'What . . . ?'

He looked at her keenly. 'Go on. You're almost there. What did . . . Henry . . . erm . . . come on! What did Henry tell . . . ?'

*The secret.* 'What did he tell you that was such a big secret, he paid you to stay silent?'

'See! I knew you'd get there eventually.'

'Was it that Owen was his son?'

He returned to her chair, crouched down so his face was level with her, malevolence glittering in his eyes. 'Better than that. Henry *found out* Nicola had abducted you. He visited her, told her he wasn't going to pay the ransom, but promised, if she released you, he wouldn't tell the police about her involvement. He already knew Owen was going through a difficult patch, had a drug addiction and had been playing up. But when Nicola warned him about Owen's violent temper, explained that she'd lost control of him and only paying the ransom would save your life, Henry didn't take her seriously. He told her to get lost. He wasn't giving her a penny. He knew what Owen was like, and he left you with him. It was a good thing Danni stumbled across you when she did, because Owen would certainly have killed you.'

Owen grunted. 'I was so angry with him – and I was off my head on drugs at the time – I probably would have.'

'I can understand you felt rejected—'

'Rejected!' Owen almost exploded with anger. 'You can't begin to know what it feels like to be told the man you thought was your father, wasn't. Worse still, that the man who'd been screwing your mother for years, was. He pretty much ignored me whenever he visited. He could barely bring himself to look at me, let alone speak to me, and all the while he *knew* I was his son. He looked down on us, on where we lived, who we were, yet still couldn't keep his hands off my mother. He never stayed overnight, never actually got to know me, never tried to be part of our family. Mum said it was because the area was too rough for him and, as a judge, he couldn't be seen around those parts very often. It might have been too rough for him, but he obviously thought it was fine for his son to be brought up there. Meanwhile, you were cosy in some fuck-off palace in an upmarket village, away from gangs, drugs and the other shit that went on where we lived.' He paused to wipe a sleeve across his nose. Stacey wondered if he was still taking drugs, maybe even high now.

*Come on, Ashraf,* she urged in her head.

Owen hadn't finished.

'Henry must have known I was depressed and using. Mum would have told him, even if he hadn't worked it out himself; all the same, he didn't lift a finger to help us move out. Instead, he left me to flounder. So, *rejected* doesn't begin to cover it. For years, I watched my mother give herself to a total wanker who she believed would eventually leave his family for us. Then . . . Then I discovered *he* was my real father. She kept it from me all that time. He made her keep it from me! That piece of shit ruined my mum's life. He didn't deserve her. He doesn't deserve anybody.'

'You said you were on drugs?'

'Yeah. Kids like me back then: we didn't get the breaks that you did. Life was pretty hard, being brought up by a single parent on a rough estate. I had to learn to survive. The drugs were part of that culture, so don't even begin to judge me.'

'I'm not. I'm trying to—'

He pointed a finger at her, angry words spitting from his lips. 'For all that he didn't want to be part of my life, he couldn't leave me alone afterwards. He promised Mum he'd say nothing about the kidnapping, then do you know what he did? He put out a contract on me. A fucking contract! If I so much as mentioned his name, I was going to be dead meat. To keep me in check, he sent regular reminders to keep my mouth shut – tough bastards to rough me up. A couple of times the police got involved. Somehow, on both occasions, the truth got twisted and I was the one charged with assault. I spent over a year in total behind bars thanks to dear old Dad. A fine upholder of the justice system he turned out to be.

He's as bad as most of the criminals I met inside. The difference is, he keeps his hands clean by paying others to do his dirty work.'

This fresh knowledge regarding her father's callousness speared her even more than the ache in her head. Owen had reason to detest her father. Why he was involved with Jack in this set-up was still a mystery.

'You and Jack. How long have you known each other?'

Jack answered. 'Only a few months. It was thanks to Henry and that drunken night. Henry stupidly told me Nicola's name. After I got into my recent financial difficulties, I decided to hire a private investigator to track her down. Had some vague idea of using her to blackmail him into giving me more money. Unfortunately, by then, Nicola was too ill to worry about the past or seek further revenge. Not so for Owen, who I met by her bedside. As you can guess, he still has unresolved issues.'

Jack rested a steely gaze on her, before dropping his voice to a conspiratorial whisper.

'As nice as this chat has been, I'm going to hand you over to your brother. He has a lot more he wants to share with you.'

She was running out of time. Mindful that Ashraf might be moments away, she had to keep him talking. She tried another tack. 'No. Wait. When you kissed me, there was definitely something between us. It was more than just a kiss. You still have feelings for me. You can't really want this to happen.'

He tutted again. 'I was play-acting, Stacey. After we split up, I hit an all-time low. I'd never wanted anybody as badly as I wanted you back then. I was broken at the time. *You* were the reason I lost my way, turned to drugs and alcohol. You're to blame for the debt choking me. I kissed you to see if you could feel enough about me to fight for me, for Lyra. You failed the test.'

'But I did care about you.'

'Tsk. Words, Stacey. Just words. You should have shown me your passion through actions. Like I did.'

'He'll kill me, Jack. If ever you loved me, please let me go.'

He got to his feet, brushed creases from his trousers. 'Don't be so dramatic. He just wants to set you straight about Henry. He assured me he'll let you go. And, for the record, I loved you more than you deserved.' He was gone in an instant.

Stacey was struck dumb. Jack had abandoned her to this maniac. Owen opened the toolbox, began removing implements, one by one. Why hadn't Ashraf arrived yet? Had something delayed him? Was he even coming?

Keeping Jack talking hadn't been difficult. He had wanted to establish his superiority over her, crush her spirit. Owen, however, had already spoken his piece and, judging by the cold look now on his face, preferred actions. Time was rapidly running out. She had to face up to the fact that she might not get out of this unhurt or even alive. Her instinct was to engage him in conversation; after all, he had grievances too.

'What are you doing? Jack said you wouldn't hurt me.'

He grinned, slipped on the mask and moved towards her.

'Now you see me!'

A shiver raced through her. He cleared his throat again.

'This is like old times, eh, Stacey? You have no idea how often I've thought about you and how it might have ended. If it hadn't been for Mum, you wouldn't have escaped from the shop. I'd have killed you on day one. Henry stole everything from my mother. Her dignity, self-pride, her worth. I think, at the time, she even loved him more than she did me and to see her crushed like that was the pits. You might think we got away with kidnapping you, but it was never over for us. He made sure of that. He had us both watching over our shoulders for the rest of our lives. He stole my mum from me, so I think it's time for another trade-off. You seem to be the only person he cares about, so I'll take you from him. I lied to Jack. I have no intention of letting you walk out of here alive.'

'He's got dementia. He won't know.'

'But I shall.'

'The safe,' she blurted, trying to buy time, keep him from harming her. 'How did you discover it was empty?'

'Mum used your key to get in. She hadn't expected it to play out as it did. Henry hadn't paid the ransom and I, well, I had a lousy temper and a short fuse, as you found out. I'll admit the drugs didn't help, either. I was getting pretty pissed off at being fucked about by then. Mum hoped to bring back some money and then we could let you go. Might have worked if the safe hadn't been empty, although I can't be certain I'd have let you go. You know, Stacey, Mum didn't want you to suffer at all. She hoped we'd have you for a day, then give you back. She actually cared about you, which is damn ironic given Henry didn't give a shit about me. Enough talking! I'm sure you don't really care what I have to say, any more than Henry does.'

He waved a pair of bolt cutters. Her stomach lurched. 'Remember these? I thought we'd start with them and work our way up my collection. I have saws, knives, hammers. All manner of toys—'

The door burst open with a resounding clatter, silencing him. It had to be Ashraf.

Relief washed through Stacey's veins as he crashed inside, entering the room at lightning speed. Owen turned in time to catch a high kick to his jaw that sent him crashing against the table. The toolbox clattered to the floor. He lunged at Ashraf, bolt cutters swinging.

Stacey yelled, 'Look out!'

Ashraf deflected the attack with a swift movement, following it with another kick, this time in the groin. As Owen doubled over, Ashraf kneed him hard in the face. Blood spurted in a bright red arc against the wall. Owen folded to the floor, hands pressed either side of his nose.

'You okay?' said Ashraf as he dropped to his haunches to dig through the toolbox.

'Yes. Thank goodness you arrived when you—' She was too slow to shout a warning as Owen leapt to his feet, grabbed Ashraf's neck and tried to smash his head against the wall. Ashraf bucked and grappled, eventually seizing Owen's fingers and bending them back further and further until there was a sharp crack and he screeched. Ashraf took advantage of the moment to donkey kick Owen, sending the man crashing to the floor, where Ashraf jumped on him.

There were loud grunts and groans, but Stacey had now lost sight of both men. She had no idea how long Ashraf could keep up his attack. She remained silent, trying to identify legs and feet as both men kicked, punched and writhed, the air full of heat and sweat. She tried to move position, without any luck. Jack had ensured she was tightly bound. The entwined shapes on the floor gradually disentangled. One lay motionless while the other got to his feet. She held her breath.

'Hey,' said Ashraf.

'Thank goodness! I couldn't see you.'

'Hang on. I need to tie this tosser up. I spotted some cable ties somewhere.'

His giant shadow moved against the wall. This time, she wasn't terrified. The shivering that had begun somewhere deep inside stopped.

Ashraf reappeared, a Stanley knife in his hand, and sawed through Stacey's restraints.

'Are you sure that you're okay?' he asked.

'My head hurts.'

'It's bleeding and you have a bump the size of an ostrich's egg, but I think you'll be fine. Tough girl, eh?' He gave her a smile. 'We'll get you checked over. Police are on their way.'

'What about Jack?'

'Don't worry. I jumped him outside. He's not going anywhere. Come on, let's get you out of here.' He put an arm under hers, lifted her gently from the chair. The room began to spin.

'Whoa! Hang on in there. We're going to walk outside to get you some fresh air.'

Stacey couldn't work out if she was under hypnosis. Her feet dragged against the carpet, or was it sand? Steady hands guided her. Was it Danni? She couldn't remember. She was out of the darkness now, going up, up, up. Was she in Erin's office, waiting to break through the waters? Above her, the sky was orange. She was headed to the beach with Bella for an evening swim. They'd run and jump in the waves and laugh. The last voice she heard before she passed out was Ashraf's.

'It's over Stacey. I've got you.'

# DAY FOUR

## SATURDAY – 11 P.M.

Stacey hunched over her kitchen table, cupping a large glass of brandy. 'I still can't believe you reached me in the nick of time.'

'Regular superhero, aren't I?'

She couldn't raise a smile. Her heart was a heavy stone in her chest. She'd missed all the signs, ignored the warnings from Danni and Ashraf. Moreover, she'd allowed herself to be taken in by Jack, even developed feelings for him again. 'You are. I'm sorry. I should have trusted you. You had your suspicions about Jack from the outset and I was . . . blinkered. I've been utterly stupid.'

'No. Don't do this to yourself, Stacey. He was credible. To be honest, the only reason I was so down on him was because I've never liked the guy. The way he treated you when you were married pissed me off big time. My assumptions were largely based on prejudice. I wanted him to be responsible, but not for it to have panned out the way it did.'

The alcohol had numbed the ferocious throbbing in her head. Ashraf sipped his own drink, then continued.

'I'm so relieved that I disliked him enough to plant a tracker on his car. Once you told me you were at Stubbs Farm and saw he was headed towards the same location, I had a really bad feeling. Then I received that timely call about the DNA test on the hair . . .'

*Ashraf's heart is racing. He's twenty minutes away from Stubbs Farm and racing down the dual carriageway to reach her. Her lowlife ex's car is almost at the same destination.*

*There's something about smooth-talking, well-groomed Jack the lawyer that goads him. The way he treats Stacey as if nothing untoward happened during their marriage. He is oblivious to all the mental anguish he caused her. Moreover, he seems to have wrapped her back around his finger with his distraught-dad act. Or is it an act? If anyone took his precious daughter, Ashraf would want to kill them. The difference is, he would have gone directly to the police, not played detective like Jack.*

*Stacey may understand why Jack doesn't want to involve the authorities; Ashraf doesn't get it. Lyra would stand a better chance of being rescued with an anti-kidnap team on board. Stacey, well, she has a different viewpoint. She almost died during her ordeal.*

*This whole business hasn't sat right with Ashraf from the start. At first, he wrestled with the idea he might be jealous that Jack was back in Stacey's life. After their divorce, he'd plucked up courage to make a move on Stacey. They'd become such close friends; he'd developed strong feelings for her. All the same, he'd given her the space she deserved. She'd not been ready for another relationship, especially after the way she'd been treated. Eventually, patience had paid off and every day they were together, Ashraf had fallen deeper for her. Trouble was, Stacey was damaged. The greater the feelings she began to have for Ashraf, the more she pulled away. In the end, they'd parted. Ashraf, unable to break down the wall she had erected, moved on. Now he had a family and Stacey would always be special to him. Very special.*

*It wasn't jealousy that made him suspect Jack was hiding something, more a hunch, a copper's gut feeling that had seen him through his career in the police force and as a private investigator.*

*His phone rang. 'Yes!'*

*It wasn't Stacey. His friend Tom, a forensic specialist, said, 'Hi, Ashraf. How's it going?'*

*'Good, thanks, mate. You got some news for me?'*

*'Yes. The hair sample you sent me is just back from the lab.'*

*'I'm all ears.'*

*'The DNA doesn't match the sample you sent me.'*

*The hair didn't belong to Lyra!*

*'That's great. Thanks a bunch for pushing that through for me.'*

*'You're welcome. Don't tell my boss. You owe me a pint.'*

*'Defo. We'll catch up very soon.'*

*If the hair wasn't Lyra's, had Owen been playing a trick on them, as he had with the fake finger? If so, he was even more twisted than they'd thought. Ashraf floored the accelerator. His gut screamed that the son of a bitch was up to no good, and Stacey could be in danger. He sped round the roundabout and up the lane. Stacey's Kia was squeezed in beside a hedge. She'd gone on foot to the premises. He took the turning to Stubbs Farm and, spying Jack's Porsche behind a line of flat-roofed offices, manoeuvred his own car behind an outbuilding, out of view. His instinct told him Stacey hadn't rung Jack to tell him she was here. Her ex was involved or had even masterminded this whole thing.*

*He killed the engine and leapt out, a large spanner that resided in his door pocket in his hands. He crept towards the Porsche. As he did so, he spied Owen's car outside a large, converted barn. As he toyed with the idea of trying the barn, a fire door upstairs opened and Jack emerged. Ashraf slid out of sight, flattened himself against the wall of the office block. Jack's cheerful whistling became louder. The second he appeared, Ashraf revealed himself. Jack drew to a sharp halt.*

*He quickly recovered his composure, gave a friendly smile. 'Hey. You surprised me. What are you doing here?'*

*'Where's Stacey?'*

*Jack turned to his left and right. 'Stacey? Can't see her car. Why would she be here? I've been meeting a client who's interested in buying this place. Needed some legal advice about purchasing it. Ah, hang on, my lace needs tightening.' As he spoke, he stooped and reached for a length of wood. Before he'd tightened his grip on it, Ashraf had swung the spanner hidden behind his back, smashing Jack's shoulder and causing him to drop to the ground. Ashraf straddled him.*

*'I'll ask you again. Where is she?'*

*'You're . . . too . . . late.'*

*'Fuck you!' Ashraf punched him in the throat. It felt good. He reached for the handcuffs taken from his glove box and fastened Jack's hands to a drainpipe. Then he was off, as fast as he could run, up the staircase and through the door Jack had exited.*

'What do you think will happen to him?'

'Jack or Owen?'

She almost couldn't bear his name to pass her lips. 'Jack.'

He shrugged. 'I hope whatever they charge him with, it results in a prison sentence, preferably a long one.'

Jack may not have harmed his own daughter, but he had attacked and injured Stacey, blackmailed Henry, stolen from his bank account and, furthermore, was accessory to abducting her. Had things turned out differently, he'd have been accessory to murder. She shivered at the thought he might get off any charges. Ashraf read her mind.

'Don't worry. He won't get off scot-free from this.'

She got to her feet and stared at the moonlit sky. She thanked the universe for allowing her to walk away from death a second time. Now it seemed incredible that she'd been completely taken in by Jack's lies. She'd fallen under his spell yet again. She'd never once suspected that he, like her father, would be a jealous, possessive husband, unwilling to let his wife leave without repercussions. Mind-boggling though it was, she couldn't deny Jack was just like Henry in many ways.

The truth was frightening; she hadn't known her husband at all. In fact, she hadn't known either of the two most important men in her life, both of whom had been willing to let her die.

Ashraf's low voice broke her thoughts. 'I'm so glad I reached you in time.' He caressed her cheek softly.

A spark warmed her heart. Not all the men in her life had been lousy. Ashraf had looked out for her. His hand travelled to her neck to rest there. She lost herself in his eyes, filled with emotion, and before she could stop herself was pressing her lips against his. The embrace became more urgent, the hunger for him greater. His hands were on her back, her body melting into his. They were made for each other. She should have believed in him, in them, sooner. The memory of a child's voice tugged at her. *Dada*. She drew back, saw again the hurt on his face.

'Your daughter. Zara. I . . . I can't.'

He held her gaze, lowered his hands.

'I can't let you break her heart. This sort of behaviour has repercussions. We can't—'

'It's fine. I understand. You're right. I have . . . responsibilities.'

She trailed her fingers over his hands, caressing them for the final time. 'I'm sorry.'

He pulled away. 'Me too.' He cleared his throat. 'For the record, I won't be billing you for my time.'

He made a face, indicating how daft it probably sounded, which in turn made her smile.

'You should. It was business.'

'No. Forget it. You hired me to help save Lyra and she didn't need saving. You did. Just promise me you'll stay out of trouble, Stacey. I won't always be able to turn up on my white horse.'

A smile tugged at her lips. 'Promise.'

'You all sorted now?'

'I think so.'

'You have my number if ever you need a PI or if you need to talk about . . . this. They'll both get what's coming to them. I'll make sure the police have everything they need. I'm to give a full statement about what I witnessed in the room. Owen won't get away. Not a second time.'

'Thanks, Ashraf . . . for everything.'

He gave a small salute. 'Any time.'

She couldn't bring herself to think about Owen. Like her father, she preferred to ignore the possibility they shared any DNA. Tomorrow, she would visit her father. She'd read her mother's last note to him. Some things should never be allowed to be forgotten.

# TWO WEEKS LATER

The woman held Stacey's hand in hers. 'I'm truly sorry for your loss.'

'Thank you. And thank you both for coming. I appreciate it.'

Ashraf's wife, petite, brown-haired, with sparkling eyes, gave her a gentle smile. Stacey returned it, then excused herself in order to circulate with the other guests. Ashraf was standing by the kitchen door, talking to one of the *Lancaster Echo* journalists, a bottle of red wine in one hand, white in the other. She moved towards him.

'I expect you need a top-up?' he asked.

'You know me too well.' She held out her glass. Red wine splashed into it, tiny foamy bubbles bouncing against the sides of the cut crystal.

'That was a nice service for Henry. Your speech was very touching,' he said.

'Cheers. It's a pity a few more people didn't come to see him off.'

'Yes. There'd better be loads at mine. I want a massive affair, music, booze, laughter, dancing.'

'Even though you'll miss out?'

'That's not important, the fact I'll *know* you are all partying on my behalf will be good enough.' He glanced about. 'The guest list seems to be more weighted towards those who have come to support you rather than say goodbye to Henry, although I'm not surprised Lyra and Freya aren't here.'

'Me neither. It's been a tough couple of weeks for them, with everything that's happened. In fairness, they didn't really know Henry. Lyra only met him on a few occasions. It's not like he was a proper grandfather to her, and Freya still has to take it easy for a month.'

She glanced around the small gathering. Judge Henry O'Hara had been a formidable man with a fearsome reputation who had put a legion of criminals behind bars and yet only three of his old friends, two ex-colleagues and two staff members from the care home had turned up to say goodbye to him.

Recent events had given Stacey a lot of food for thought. Although her career was important to her, she wasn't going to fall into the same trap as he had, where work had become more important than life or those who shared it with him.

'Thanks again,' she said. 'I'm glad you're here.'

'Couldn't let you deal with this alone. That's what friends are for.'

'Hear, hear!' Bella had appeared from nowhere. 'Stacey, have you got any lager? Kenzo's more a grain than grape sort of guy.' She nodded in the direction of a distinguished man with a neat grey beard, a professor at Lancaster University, who she'd recently begun dating.

'I'll sort it,' said Ashraf and headed back towards the kitchen.

'How are you *really* feeling?' Bella asked as soon as Ashraf had gone. 'I mean about your dad and . . . stuff.'

'I'm fine. I'm actually relieved it was another stroke that took him in the end. It was dreadful watching his mental health decline. And it saved me from ever having to have *that* conversation.'

'The one about why he didn't pay the ransom?'

'Yes. It's best I don't know. He had reasons he believed to be right at the time.'

'Have you forgiven him?'

'I don't think I can. I can live with it though. It doesn't give me nightmares or trouble me. I know he loved me, in his own way. He simply made some bad calls.'

'I guess so.' Bella didn't sound convinced.

Stacey changed the subject. 'You still up for it, tomorrow?'

'Paddleboarding with my bestie school friend? You bet. I'll be there at eight on the dot, in my new wetsuit.'

'Good.'

Bella cocked her head; her teardrop earrings sparkled in the light. 'You know he was wrong?'

'Who was?'

'Jack, when he told you you'd inherited your father's cold heart.'

'You reckon?'

'I know so. You would have done anything to get Lyra back. You even offered to hand over your savings to help free her. And you didn't have to give your father a proper send-off today. You've done him proud, all this quality wine and top-notch buffet. I'm not sure I'd have been so magnanimous.'

Stacey caught a glimpse of Ashraf, putting an arm around his wife as he chatted to Danni. She gave a small shrug.

'The past is the past.'

'To the future, then.' Bella raised her own glass and tapped it against Stacey's. Stacey sipped the Chateau d'Issan 2015 Margaux, allowed the silken liquid to caress her taste buds and searched for the rich flavours of plum and cherries, along with the hint of truffle and cinnamon, before relishing the velvety tannins. The wine had cost almost seventy pounds a bottle, but to Stacey it was worth it. Henry would have hated her spending so much for other people to enjoy. He'd have declared it a travesty, even though he'd have thought nothing of buying a bottle double that price for his personal enjoyment.

She permitted herself a small smile. How he would have detested this send-off.

*Her father's cheeks are tear-stained, dirty rivulets against grey skin. She isn't going to leave until she has spelled out every last detail and made it clear how she feels about him.*

*'After my friend Bella told you she'd witnessed a red-haired woman, driving a VW Beetle car, kidnap me, you knew Nicola was responsible and what did you do about it? Did you rush to her and ask where I was? Did you tell the police so I could be rescued, and Nicola put away? No. You went to her home to tell her no matter what she did to me, you wouldn't pay her any money.'*

*'I . . . I—'*

*'Don't deny it!'*

*He nods, wringing his hands as he tries to explain but Stacey won't let him get a word in.*

*'You did that even though they sent you my severed finger! What sort of father are you!'*

*'Nicola, I don't believe you. You're a whore, a liar and a deceitful bitch, but even you wouldn't hurt my daughter.'*

*'I'm not Nicola! Stop pretending you can't remember. Jack told me you can. You are putting a lot of this on.'*

*He shook his head, tried to cower from her rage. 'Let Stacey go free. Let her go and I'll say nothing. You get to walk away. I know you'll release her. Be sensible.'*

*'You didn't know! That's the point. You should have been scared for my life and done whatever Nicola wanted to get me home. You should have paid her. You knew Owen took drugs. You knew what he might be capable of!'*

*He blinks, tugs at his shirt collar. 'You don't understand. Nicola only ever wanted my money. She wouldn't have hurt you. If I had thought for one minute that she would have harmed you, I'd have paid the ransom in full.'*

*'She did harm me. Or rather* your *crazy son did! They kept me prisoner for five days. I was beaten, tortured, had my hair and finger and part of my ear cut off!'*

*He winces as if she is stabbing him with every word. She continues, voice shrill, wanting him to remember, wanting him to suffer. He tries to appease her.*

*'I really didn't know. At the time. I didn't think—'*

*'Don't bullshit me! Did you honestly believe they were looking after me and would send me home with a pat on the head and an apology?' Her voice rises to almost shrieking point, and she fights to regain control. 'You were simply too mean to pay. Admit it!'*

*He is silenced. His lips tremble and tears roll down his cheeks. 'Yes. Yes, I was. I didn't want the money-grabbing whore to have what was rightfully mine. She meant nothing to me. And Owen? Well, he was a total disgrace. I wanted nothing to do with him. No son of mine would have turned out like that. He'd have wasted every penny. People like him never make anything of their lives.'*

*For the first time ever, he has told her what he really thinks. She swallows the bile that has suddenly pooled in her mouth.*

*'I'm . . . sorry. So sorry. I made mistakes.' He tugs again at his shirt collar.*

*'Mistakes! These were more than mistakes. You have made some truly terrible judgement calls. First with Mum and then me.'*

*He hangs his head and wet splodges fall onto his beige trousers, patterning them with tiny drops. 'But . . . I . . . Where . . . ? Julia . . . Sorry . . . Fudge . . .'*

*Even after his words have turned to confused mumblings, she doesn't desist. Now she strides around the room, waving her mother's suicide note, reading the words out loud, over and over, until his shoulders judder with shame. Still dissatisfied he has not suffered enough, she*

325

*is about to launch into another tirade, when he clutches his chest. His head rolls back and his mouth flaps.*

*Stacey doesn't go to his aid, nor does she ring for assistance. She watches him fight for his existence. She watches the light in his eyes extinguish. She waits until there is no further movement before folding the letter back up and replacing it in the tin.*

# ACKNOWLEDGEMENTS

I would like to start by thanking you, my reader, for purchasing *Behind Closed Doors*. I hope you have enjoyed reading this stand-alone thriller as much as I enjoyed working on it.

There are many people who have helped bring this book to publication, all of whom deserve a mention. I'd like, however, to bring to your attention a family-run café in Morecambe. The café is not named in the book, nor are the owners, Theresa and Cara, so it is only fitting I thank them here. If ever you are in Morecambe Bay, look up Ruby's, where you will be able to admire the murals Stacey and Danni discuss while enjoying great home-cooked food . . . and those delicious muffins that are mentioned!

Thank you Amy Tannenbaum, my dynamic and efficient agent who offered sound guidance on the manuscript before submission and helped me pitch the book, which is a task I always dread!

Sincere thanks to my terrific developmental editor, Russel Mclean, whose cultural knowledge continues to astound and educate me and whose hilarious asides cause me to snigger throughout the edit.

To my superb editor, Victoria Haslam, and everyone at Thomas & Mercer who has been involved in producing this book. Hugest of thanks to you all. I'm so lucky to work with such a dynamic team.

As always, sincere thanks to my other half, Mr Grumpy, who accompanied me on all the research trips and encouraged me to write this standalone novel, then sensibly stayed out of my way for several weeks while I worked on it.

To all the bloggers who take part in the book tours, share their reviews, shout out about our books on social media and give endless support to writers like me, for no reward. You are priceless! I speak for many when I say thank you enormously for all your efforts.

Finally, a shout out to Lancashire, a region I have totally fallen in love with. I shall definitely be setting more of my books here.

# ABOUT THE AUTHOR

Carol Wyer is a *USA Today* bestselling author and winner of the People's Book Prize Award. Her crime novels have sold over one million copies and have been translated into nine languages.

A move from humour to the 'dark side' in 2017, with the introduction of popular DI Robyn Carter in *Little Girl Lost*, proved that Carol had found her true niche.

February 2021 saw the release of the first in the much-anticipated new series featuring DI Kate Young. *An Eye for an Eye* was chosen as a Kindle First Reads and became the #1 bestselling book on Amazon UK and Amazon Australia.

Carol has had articles published in national magazines such as *Woman's Weekly*, and has been featured in *Take a Break*, *Choice*,

*Yours* and *Woman's Own* and in *HuffPost*. She's also been interviewed on numerous radio shows, and on Sky and *BBC Breakfast* television.

She currently lives on a windy hill in rural Staffordshire with her husband, Mr Grumpy . . . who is very, very grumpy.

To learn more, go to www.carolwyer.co.uk, subscribe to her YouTube channel, or follow her on Twitter: @carolewyer.

Printed in Great Britain
by Amazon

17094985R00194